MIND SWEEPER

A Mike Stone adventure

JIM RAWLINS

What compels a man who has everything
he could ever want, to willingly sacrifice it
all to desperately seek for more.

Contents

1

September 21st, 1991,   Hamburg, Germany.

Kyela Kuznetsov, with the help of her brother Mikhail, admitted herself into the Marien General Hospital in Hamburg, Germany. It was an older hospital that showed signs of use and maintenance. While paint and plaster were damaged in some areas, the floor was spotless and exposed to a high wax gloss, and as they walked down the hallways to her room, they had the impression of it being sanitary and safe.

She was in her ninth month of pregnancy, and today was the day her doctor said she would most likely give birth. Her brother was with her to offer assistance and support through the birth. Mikhail had never witnessed a birth before, and he was filled with a mixture of excitement and nervous anticipation. Kyela often found herself coaching him at times. Mikhail was three years younger than Kyela. He was skinny, which gave him the appearance of being tall. He read books and studied articles on the birthing process, and most of the information he read explained what normally takes place; however, most included the problems that could arise during birth as well. What if this happened, and what if that happened, and so on? Kyela laughed at him and told him he was a wreck. Mikhail looked at her with his wire-rimmed glasses, not understanding what was so humorous. He went back to his nervous bantering and research with a smile of satisfaction; he loved his sister deeply. Mikhail was Kyela's baby brother, and they were very close; even as children, he would do anything for his sister. When they were kids, Kyela would play teacher with him as the student and help him with his schoolwork. Everyone marveled over Mikhail's grades in school, but Kyela would never take away his accomplishments by telling others that she helped him; in fact, she added to the praise. Mikhail was the one who talked her into and initiated Kyela's extraction from Moscow. Mikhail has good friends who have good friends. The extraction went like clockwork, except they were unable to find Kyela's son, who was not there at the time they had to leave. His friends helped him prepare; it took over a month to complete all the passport documents and name changes well in advance.

Mikhail never liked Kyela's partner; they were not married yet, and Mikhail thought Andrei Volkov was a terrible person and was mean to Kyela and their son. Once, he hit Kyela across her face, and he went after their son because he wouldn't stop crying, with such rage that he broke the child's arm. Kyela had to take their son to the hospital, which was against Andrei's will, and when she got back, he hit her so hard she ended up with black eyes. Mikhail could not understand what she saw in this man and why she stayed around so long. He finally talked her into leaving Andrei and was so happy for her. Maybe she stayed because of the children, or possibly because she lived in a palace that was beyond her wildest dreams, but with the new baby coming along, she realized it was time. After a while, they would have to go back for their son, a challenging thought, to say the least, with the other looming thoughts of him finding and coming after them now that Kyela was gone. With her leaving and having the birth outside of his control would really anger him, and hopefully, the efforts in name changes and leaving Russia itself would delay him enough so that they could safely leave Germany and seek refuge elsewhere. Mikhail pulled out a pistol from his bag and put it under her mattress while making sure it was fully loaded and ready to shoot. Kyela was a bit surprised he would have brought this gun into her hospital room during the time she was giving birth to her baby. She remembered what kind of man Andrei was and what he may have done since she left to give birth to the baby out of Moscow. She gently nodded, with the thought that Andrei may very well send one of his henchmen. She cringed at the thought of what he may do. Her thoughts went off to her son and prayed that he was safe and that no harm had come to him. She missed Lev, she wished he could be here to watch his baby being born.

Kyela was a strikingly beautiful young lady with long blonde hair. She attracted all the boys in school and won the two beauty contests she entered as a teenager. Her father was very proud of her, not just because she was attractive, but because of her inner beauty. He admired her for what she was willing to do for others. He would watch her work with her brother on his schoolwork and help others in the community. Her father was also aware of the dark elements that were encroaching on the community that she also attracted. Her mother and father dedicated their lives to convincing her to see the way towards a safe and rewarding life. These elements would keep creeping closer to her, trying to influence and forcing her to go astray.

When Kyela was sixteen, a gang from Moscow set up a brothel in their community. They engaged in drug sales and initiated the establishment of a prostitution network within the locality. They had become successful in luring and recruiting attractive young girls from the area into their business. The outcome was ugly for the girls, as well as the families affected. The police were aware of the activities of the gang but kept saying they could not do anything about it. The people in the communities understood this was due to the gangs paying off the police to leave them alone. Given the substantial amount offered to them, this was a typical occurrence in Moscow.

Kyela's father was well respected in the community; he was the person everyone would go to for help and was always there for them. He received a call one evening that one of their friends saw Kyela being abducted and thrown into a van, and it drove off. Kyela's father convened the community at the town hall, where the townspeople voiced their concerns and emphasized the urgent need to rescue Kyela and others while also calling for decisive action to halt the activities of the gang. Some thought the police should be notified, and others yelled out that the police were of no use. They came to understand they needed to act themselves. They eventually developed a plan they all agreed to that would get rid of them once and for all. There were over a hundred and forty community members at the meeting. They all vowed there would be no gang members left standing after they were done. They vowed at the meeting that no one would ever speak a word of their actions tonight. They all left to meet downtown by the brothel with every rifle, shotgun, and pistol they could gather. Five community group members went inside, posing as customers with concealed pistols, and the other hundred and thirty rushed in the front and back doors. As the gang was not expecting to be attacked, they were caught off guard. The towns people attacked the brothel from both inside and outside the building, and the plan was orchestrated perfectly. Kyela was found high on an unknown drug, and she had to be carried out. They removed all the girls from the building out on the street. When no one was left in the building other than the bodies of the gang members, they lit the building on fire and left. Kyela's parents nursed her back to health as the drugs wore off.

A week later, while Kyela and Mikhail were in town shopping for their parents, four thugs came into their house, killing Kyela's mother and father. It was a horrible sight for Kyela and Mikhail to come home, too. These thugs went on to kill three other families in the community who were instrumental in organizing the raid on the brothel. It was assumed they were part of the gang that the community killed and set fire to. Kyela and Mikhail felt a deep sense of helplessness; they were devastated. Kyela and her brother lived in the house for about a year after the incident but couldn't live there anymore; there were too many memories and continuous flashbacks of what they saw when they returned to the house on that day from shopping.

Kyela and her brother moved to an apartment closer to the city of Moscow and worked in a grocery store. She and her brother were happy there; they were able to forget and move on to a new life. Kyela was very selective with whom she talked to; she really liked one of the workers at the store, and she was a good friend to Kyela and her brother. Natasha Gusev talked to Kyela about a party on the weekend that she was going to and asked Kyela if she would like to go. There would be several businesspeople and a great way to make some new contacts there; if she wanted to go, Natasha said she could get her an invitation. Kyela immediately said no but thanked her anyway. She later told her brother about it, and he talked her into going.

"You need to go out and have some fun, Kyela," Mikhail said.

Kyela thought about it for a while and decided after a while to go after all. She put on the most appropriate dress she had available after consulting Natasha, but Kyela could have worn anything in her closet and attended the party looking beautiful.

> "You look gorgeous, Kyela!" Natasha exclaimed, then added, "No, really, you look stunning!"

> Kyela was being modest, even though she felt fantastic. "Thank you, Natasha, and you look beautiful yourself; those are very classy earrings, beautiful."

The two girls mingled amongst the guests when out from the crowd came a young man who was very confident and very forward. He introduced himself, and over the following months, Kyela and Andrei became very close and later became pregnant with their first child, a boy. She moved in with Andrei at his home, which they called the palace. Their relationship grew, but there was never a discussion about marriage. This concerned Kyela, but she swept it aside; after all, she was living in a beautiful home. She watched fondly as Andrei and their son played together; they were very close, and it made her smile.

One evening, she went to visit Natasha, and they had a great time laughing and talking about some of the daily things that had taken place. Natasha's brother, Lev, came to see Natasha and was introduced to Kyela. She thought he was handsome with a charismatic swagger that made Kyela and Natasha laugh out loud. He said he was a carpenter making furniture in the city. He stayed for a while, then left to go home for dinner. The following week, Lev called her to invite her for a lunch picnic in the park by the pond, which was very popular with the local people. She hesitated long enough to remember how much fun she had at Natasha's when he arrived and answered him that she would love to go. They saw each other several times after that; however, about two months later, he stopped calling.

Shortly after, Andrei took Kyela on a Caribbean holiday on a yacht for two weeks, exploring all the Islands and beaches. They took their son Vlad and watched him enjoy the water, build sandcastles on the beach, and chase little crabs when they came close to him. They brought along a nanny to watch over him and give them both some privacy throughout the trip. It was a magical holiday; it brought them both closer.

Shortly after, she was pregnant with their second child; things seemed to change a bit; he started having mood swings and was not the same man that she was with in the Caribbean. He was becoming too busy at work and found he was coming home late at night twice with blood on his suit jacket and shirt, a lot of blood, and she confirmed both times that it was not his blood.

> She asked him several times what kind of business he had late at night and was brushed off with a "none of your concern!"

When the physical abuse started up with him, it didn't take much convincing from Mikhail for her to move on and leave for Germany.

2

The contractions were intensifying, and she sensed it wouldn't last much longer. She alerted the medical staff, and they examined her, deciding to take her into the delivery room right away. Mikhail was starving and went out for a quick sandwich to returning to the ongoing birth. He lost what little self-control he had over his fears and fainted at Kyela's first scream of pain. Mikhail regained consciousness just after he hit the floor. The medical staff went to him to offer medical assistance, but he was directing them to look after his sister. He got his feet under him again and pretended to be that rock that Kyela needed.

In between the surges of pain that she was experiencing, she looked up at Mikhail, "You, OK?"

He replied nervously—barely getting out a "What, me? Oh yea, I'm fine. How are you?"

At that exact time, the baby started on its way, and Kyela gave an enormous push and screamed at the top of her lungs. Mikhail could feel himself fading again and was looking for a softer place on the floor to land.

The doctor told her, "One more good push, and she will be all the way out!"

Kyela pushed as hard as she had the strength to and gave another scream. This time, Mikhail seemed to be able to endure the tension he was feeling, gripping her hand tightly. The medical staff worked quickly to get the baby breathing as they cleaned the mouth and checked it's breathing and airway, and determined it was functioning normally. It was over, and both Kyela and Mikhail breathed in a deep sigh of relief. The medical staff wrapped the baby up, and the nurse handed the baby to Kyela.

"You have a beautiful baby girl," she remarked.

Kyela smiled and said, "Oh, she is beautiful, Mikhail."

Kyela couldn't stop looking at the baby. After, she looked at her brother and asked, "Do

you want to hold your niece?"

Mikhail barely got out a few words, "No, that's fine, I'll work my way into that."

Over the next two days, Kyela and Mikhail would spend their time exploring this new human who came into their life. She was perfect, her little toes and hands, her little smile, or what they thought was a smile anyways. They couldn't get enough time with her before she would nod off for another sleep.

Mikhail was organizing the next leg of their journey away from Kyela's partner's clutches and on to their new life. This stage would be the easiest; they had already gotten a fake passport for the baby, and all other documents were in order. The only thing left was to get a clean bill of health from the doctor, and a discharge from the hospital, and the three of them were gone. Tomorrow, the doctors would be conducting the final blood tests to make sure she was a normal, healthy baby.

The medical staff were too busy to notice a man and a woman closely watching the room that Kyela and Mikhail were occupying.

In the morning, the nurses came by to take the baby to a testing room, where they took the blood samples.

Mikhail asked, "Why does she need to be taken somewhere? Why not just take the blood samples here?"

The nurse explained, " some parents see the process of removing blood from their baby, and they get very agitated, and we don't need that, do we."

Mikhail considered that for a moment and agreed. As the nurse wheeled the cart out of the room, a man and woman watching with keen eyes were un-noticed. They followed the nurse along the hallway and into the testing room; they were observant that no one was watching. At the same time, another nurse brought another baby into the room, and as the man and woman entered, they startled the two nurses.

The older nurse said to the couple, in a commanding voice, "you can't be in here!"

As the man pulled his pistol out, the other nurse pushed the carts away to safeguard the babies. The two carts moved around each other, coming to a final stop at a desk on the other side of the room.

Their captors told them, "You could cooperate with us or die right here!"

The older nurse asked, "what are you doing here?"

The man explained to them, "it is none of their concern unless you try something stupid!"

They tied up the two nurses, quickly placed tape over their mouths, and turned to the baby carts. Pausing for a while, they realized that during the commotion, they lost track of which cart had Kyela's baby. They decided to take them both; they had to deliver his baby, or Andrei would shoot them both, at least, that's what Andrei said. He also said he wanted Kyela killed, and that was another point of business they had to complete before leaving the hospital. The woman took both babies and gave the man her gun to cover her as she left in case security or someone were to come after them. They left the examination room, and as they walked past the nurses station, the nurses behind the desk were too busy to notice. The woman turned left along the hall to the stairway. The man knew where Kyla's room was and walked directly to it. And as he entered, he saw her look up at him and shoot her in the shoulder. Mikhail happened to be in the washroom at the time and heard the shot. He flew out of the bathroom and hit the intruder with all he had at hand, which was a toilet plunger. This was just enough of a distraction for Kyela to grab the pistol from under the mattress and place a shot dead center in his chest. As the bullet left the barrel of her gun, her assassin squeezed off a fatal shot. Seeing this, Mikhail dropped to his knees, holding his sister. Mikhail was crying in disbelief, unaware that Kyela's baby had also been abducted and taken from the hospital.

At that moment, Mikhail's life felt very hollow, and after spending six grueling hours being interrogated by German police, he was exhausted. He told his story the same way five or six times, each time, and each time telling the truth. They kept hounding him about where his sister got the gun. Each time, he told them that he did not know, it was a question they should be asking his sister, which agitated them each time he told them. He had to write out a statement and sign it and was asked about why they took the other baby, which Mikhail knew nothing about. They asked him who would do this to his sister, and he had no problem telling them it was Andrei, her partner in Moscow. He told them about the extraction from him in Moscow, and he sent these people to retrieve the baby. Then they accused him of kidnapping, and he explained that the baby had not yet been born, so how could this be kidnapping? It went on and on until, finally, they had no more questions or accusations and released him without charges.

An executive jet was waiting for Alina and the two babies at the airstrip outside Hamburg. When they arrived, they boarded immediately, and the jet taxied along the runway and on its way to Moscow. Upon the arrival of the jet in Moscow, a stretch limousine was waiting. Alina, along with the two babies, got in it, and it left for Andrei's palace. She could see that Andrei was in a good mood, and she was grateful for that.

> *Andrei was sitting in the back sipping on his favorite Remy Marten, "Alina, you did well, but why two babies?"*

She explained the situation they were faced with at the time and had to bring them both, not knowing which was your baby."

"That's fine. You will have a DNA test done on them both, and we will just get rid of the other one; I see Pavel did not make it. Did you kill Kyela, or did he?" Again, she explained, *" Pavel went into Kyela's room to look after her, but after three shots, he did not come out, and I had to keep going!"*

"My contacts tell me she was killed; you did a very good job, I will not forget," Andrei said, smiling.

3

Mikhail was lost; he had no one left in the world. He went back to his hotel room and cried himself to sleep. When he woke up, he prayed that it was all part of a dream but realized soon enough that it wasn't. He went to a restaurant and tried to get a piece of toast down, but two bites were all he could eat, and he sipped on his coffee. He had things to arrange now but had no idea where to start. He decided to go back to his hotel room and have a shower, which has helped him get things in order in the past. He paid for his toast and coffee and went back to the hotel, and the long walk helped him get straightened out. He thought of his mother and father and how he wished he had them for strength and courage right now. It hit him as he turned the block before the hotel entrance. He would take her back to Ruza and lay Kyela's body to rest. He would go back to his hometown, in the community, where he still had friends and people who supported his family. This is what he needs right now—to have support, to be with friends, and to be with Kyela. He burst out once again in tears as he thought of his sister, and he would never see her again. His face then became very serious and very determined, maybe for the first time in his life, and he thought that he would also be close to Andrei. He was the madman who had her assassinated and whispered gently to himself, " I will see you again, and you will pay for what you have done!"

The DNA testing confirmed that neither baby was the offspring of Andrei. Alina was shocked; she could not grasp what had happened. They identified the baby from Kyela's room and followed it as the nurse rolled the cart with the baby to the testing room. Besides the second baby that came in, there were no others. She asked the medical staff to retest; they must have made a mistake. The forensic specialist told her there was no mistake made and there was no need to retest.

Fear surged through her body as the adrenaline kicked in, realizing what Andrei would say or do. He would definatly kill her on the spot. She saw him do it before to others. After some time spent considering the few options she had, she decided to pick one herself and go with that. She went through her decision again in her head and thought to herself that Andrei would never find out.

Ivan Petrik was a middle-aged man who worked for Andrei for five years and would do anything he asked. Ivan came from a large family; however, he and his wife were unable to have children. He was told to get rid of the other baby, but Ivan was having problems carrying that request out. Ivan spent time thinking that the assassination of people was considered a typical day on the job. But killing a baby and dealing with the remains seemed to him as being in a whole different league that he did not wish to participate in. His boss, Andrei, wanted him to get rid of it, and that's what he must do. He noticed since Kyela left, Andrei had been very irritable, even for him, and appeared to be getting worse each day. There was no telling what he would do to himself or his family if he did not follow through. He thought of adopting it himself since he and his wife had not been successful in having their own. He brought the baby to his wife, Anya, to look after it until he got this figured out. His wife, in her mid-thirties, adored the child, and Ivan was starting to get concerned as she was getting too close emotionally with the baby.

Ivan proceeded to research opportunities in North America and in the UK. There was a family in Utah, in the States, that was searching to adopt a child, and he contacted them by mail. They replied with a couriered letter two days later with interest. The letter identified they were willing to pay up to $50,000 US cash and expenses. The only problem was they had to have the baby brought to Salt Lake City, Utah, and they wanted it healthy. Ivan talked to his wife, and they agreed that she would take the baby.

The money was much needed and could set them both up in good financial shape. They could also get away from Andrei and live a normal life. The passports would need to accompany them, and she would work on this under her maiden name to avoid suspicion.

Anya was a slender woman with shoulder-length curly hair; she had natural mother instincts. As a child growing up, she looked after her two sisters and brother while her mother worked in a clothing store.

The trip took twenty-two hours, and she was on the final leg of the trip from Denver. She tried sleeping, but somehow, the plane would hit turbulence, or the baby would fuss and wake her up. She landed at the Salt Lake International Airport with the baby; she was exhausted from traveling. Her return flight was in two days to avoid suspicion of immigration entering the US.

As Anya and the baby entered the arrivals area, she noticed a man and a woman watching everyone coming through the doors. As Anya came closer, they watched with what seemed great anticipation. When they saw her carrying the baby, they immediately came over and introduced themselves, making sure that she was the person with their baby. Anya's first impression was that they were a sweet, loving couple who would look after and love the child forever. They were around forty years old, well-dressed, and warm when interacting with the baby. As she handed the baby over to the lady, Anya started to get emotional, and Mrs. Riley saw the tear that ran down her cheek and felt sorry for her. Anya's English was not great, but they communicated enough for the Riley's to understand that she wanted to get some sleep and offered to take her to their house to get some rest. She agreed, and they picked up her baggage from the carousel, leaving the airport in their family car. With the baby well looked after, Anya was finally able to relax and fell into a deep sleep, relaxed, without the responsibilities of the baby or turbulence from the plane. She had a dream about having a beautiful home in Russia and having family over for holidays and laughter and kids playing, but not her kids.

When they arrived at Riley's home, she woke and decided to start a family of her own; Ivan found this baby, and surely he could find others for their family. The Riley's brought both the baby and Anya into their home and showed her around the house, making her feel at home.

Anya thought, "What a beautiful home," the house was spotless, and she took her time to study the pictures hung on the walls and displayed on shelves. The kitchen was a dream to her as she noticed how nicely it was laid out and how easy it was to work in. She could see the baby growing up to be a good cook and mother for her own children.

After she had a shower, Anya came downstairs as the Riley's were making supper, " I should give baby a bath now."

Mrs. Riley said to Anya, "I had already bathed her when you were in the shower. Relax, Anya, you have worked hard to bring her over to us, and we are grateful. After dinner, Anya was convinced the baby was well looked after and went to her bedroom to sleep. She thought the Riley's paid a great deal of money for this baby; maybe after finding babies for their family, Ivan could find and sell other babies for the same money or more. She will talk to Ivan once she goes home. This could make them rich and live a good life and have a nice home like Riley's.

4

35 years later

Joseph McGee worked his way through the early morning crowds going to work. He carried his lunch in a bag in one hand and stopped at a Bistro for his favorite coffee, carrying it in the other hand. He thanked those who opened doors for him and scowled at those who didn't. He had just arrived in his casual office attire, placing his lunch in the fridge to keep it cool. He was a brilliant computer software engineer who worked for Standard Computer Programs in New York.

His father showed him the value of a dollar and supported him on newspaper routes, his grass-cutting business, and bottle returns.

When Joseph was seventeen years old, he developed a program using algorithms to forecast the stock market directions. He took his total savings at the time, of twenty-five hundred dollars, and turned it into two hundred and fifty thousand dollars by his twentieth birthday. At thirty-two, he was financially independent. He didn't have to work for a living. Joseph earned his master's degree from Yale and was hired before graduation by Standard. Four years ago, he completed an artificial intelligence program for a client, and today, he is often questioned why he is still working, and each year, it becomes more difficult for him to answer that question honestly. He met his wife, Rachel, at a ski hill in Colorado; it was love at first sight, and this was the most romantic time the two spent together. Joseph and Rachel were married on the ski hill. It was a small wedding with only a few closest friends on both sides and family. Life happened, At thirty-eight, Rachel was doing most of the asking about when he would retire or at least semi-retire; they had the money, and she had other ideas about how they should be spending their time. She missed skiing; for example, she was a very good skier, participating in the 2002 Winter Olympics in Salt Lake City. She was unsuccessful in winning a medal, but just competing at that level was a life experience. It was very hard for her to go from that level of life excitement to watching her husband spend hours staring at a computer screen day after day.

Rachel and Joseph were born two years apart, making them thirty eight and forty respectively. Rachel dreamed of having a large family on an acreage with trees big enough to hang a swing on, and she also wanted her tennis court. Tennis was Rachel's second love of sport; she wanted her own court that she and her friends could play on whenever they wanted and for as long as they wanted. So far, Joseph has not provided either, and this was the start of many of their domestic disputes.

Standard considered Joseph a genius and assigned him the most challenging projects for their most important clients, such as governments, corporations and universities with specialized requirements. Currently, Joseph was tasked with developing a program that deciphered brainwaves into a readable format. The information from the data could be analyzed for medical diagnosis and treatment for neurological patients. The program had endless potential for future applications, and Joeseph was anxious about further developing it to see where it evolved. He considered that exciting. This was Joseph's baby. He brought this from conception a year and a half ago to a working application today. He was very proud of what he considered his accomplishment. He rarely shared credit for the recognition he received for these accomplishments with his fellow workers. This alone bred dissension amongst the group, and despite him being able to teach at a higher level, most wanted out of his department.

Growing up, He only had his twin sister, who was the opposite of him, which led to several disputes between them. She was the social one who had people around her or calling her and surpassed him in social and leadership skills. He was constantly in competition with her since she developed an MLM business netting her almost two million a year this business while she raised four children. He recognized her successes and because of this, he was jealous, always trying to do one better than her.

His assistant, Sharon Riley, worked with Joseph for the past two years, primarily to enter the bulk programming entries. Sharon was very smart and took on a much bigger role than what Joseph thought she could do. It was his design and input that made the program run, and from time to time, he made her aware of that. Joseph felt it necessary to put her in her place from time to time in response to ideas she brought forward. Both Joseph and Sharon understood how technically advanced this program was, and he believed he could get a great deal of money for it on the international market. Was this right? No, he signed a contract with his company that anything he developed was the property of the company, but on the international market, who would find out? Joseph had a Russian interested, but he needed to do some research on them, and he would just have to be selective. Joseph did not think about the choices that one has to have to be selective. So far, it was only the Russians and a few queries by an Asian firm, with no commitment or follow-up intentions. Joseph went for a walk and sat down on a park bench and realized he only had one potential client. He expected several potential clients vying for the program, but at the present, it was the Russians or nothing.

He went home early, and his wife, Rachel, could tell there was something going on inside that head of his.

"You want to tell me what's going on with you?"

"Oh, the same old thing at work, you know," Joseph answered.

"Okay, but when you are ready to include me in your life, let me know!"

Rachel was very good at getting Joseph out of his "frump," and he knew it, but this was huge, even for her to handle. He made the decision to tell her everything. He told her about the program that could do this and that and put it up for sale on the international market. He told her about the Russians who wanted to buy it and that there were more coming.

Rachel listened to the words he was saying and watched his body language, and the two were not lining up. She told him.

> "So, this is really about this competition you are having between you and your sister, isn't it? As you were talking, I never heard any reference about me or kids having any part of <u>your</u> plan."

Joseph started to argue with Rachel about what he meant, but she cut him off.

> She turned abruptly toward him, saying, "Fine, do what you want. If it's not about the kids and me, then I don't care what you do." At that, she stormed out of the room.

Joseph wondered what had happened to him and his family's values. He thought of when Rachel told him she wanted to marry him and when she told him when she was pregnant. What happened to him? At that point, he knew she was right. He would complete this transaction with the Russians and then retire, he would have enough money and he could take the family on holidays and spend quality time with Rachel and the kids. Yes! he thought, immediately after this sale. He left with a smile on his face; he was a happy man.

5

Sharon Riley was a successful single female in her thirties, with a smaller stature but not petite. Her brown hair was just above shoulder length, and she wore glasses that made her somehow look academic. She enjoyed playing tennis, but more for exercise or a hobby. She joined a tennis club to meet and socialize with people her age. Her parents put her through university and supported her in her desire to be a computer programmer.

When Sharon was twelve years old, her parents explained that she was adopted, but this never bothered her at the time; she was happy and loved the Riley's just the same as though they were her paternal parents. When she turned eighteen, things started changing how she reevaluated her outlook on various matters. She still loved the Riley's, but she wanted to know more. She was determined to uncover the identity of her biological parents and the circumstances surrounding her adoption. She embarked on an extensive research journey, diligently pursuing various leads, only to find herself in a frustrating dead end. Using the limited German that she learned in university, she continued her research and found an incomplete birth certificate for the same day as her birthday and a connection to a hospital in Hamburg, Germany. Even though her parents told her that she was of Russian descent, maybe they were misinformed, and she was German; she had to know.

At the age of twenty, she traveled to Hamburg and visited the hospital in hopes of finding her birthplace and her parents. At the hospital, she talked to the staff of two shifts, explaining who she was and the circumstances of her visit. No one knew of anything thirty years ago, and despite their eagerness to help her, they were busy and gave her limited time. One of the nurses at the hospital told her about a retired nurse who worked in the maternity ward around that time. The nursing staff at the hospital were reluctant to give her contact information; however, after pleading with the nurse, Sharon finally got the phone number from her and called Helena.

Sharon filled her in on why she was calling, and as she was talking, the retired nurse was a bit wary and surprised. She told Sharon she couldn't possibly remember a specific baby that was born there thirty years ago but recalled an abduction that happened around that time. She said she couldn't remember much more than that since she was working the night shift and the incident took place during the afternoon; she also felt that the odds of her being that same baby were very slim. Sharon thanked Helena for her time and wished her well in her retirement.

Sharon found the Newspaper Archives and spent some time viewing old newspapers around her birthdate. When she was about to give up, she read an article explaining the whole situation, which took place three days after she was born, giving the names of the parents of the baby who was kidnapped from the hospital. With considerable effort, Sharon was able to contact them and asked to see them, not telling them the circumstances. She met with them, explaining why she wanted to visit them, and neither the husband nor the wife believed that she could be their kidnapped baby, and they asked her to leave them alone. She could see an old emotion rise in their demeanor, so dark and deep that she had no intentions of challenging them; she could tell that this was a very deep wound they were recalling.

> She explained, "There is a way to prove it, one way or another, and that would be to have a DNA test done."

> "Why would we believe a test result that you orchestrated?" they said.

> Sharon didn't think about their side, and she answered them, "I agree. What about if you collect all the samples and select the laboratory, and I will pay for it? I understand

how uncomfortable this must make you feel after all these years, but you must understand my side of the situation as well; I want to find my paternal parents as much as you would like to find your daughter."

They both thought about it for a while and agreed. They swabbed her mouth as well as theirs and cut a piece of her hair as well as their own, putting each sample in individual baggies; they wanted to make sure the samples were well representing each of the donors. Sharon helped them find laboratories that perform DNA testing and left the selection up to them. After they were finished, she thanked them, and she left.

Two days later, the phone rang for the first time since she left for Germany; it was the longest thirty-eight hours of her life.

She answered the phone, "Hello?"

A male voice answered, "The results came back confirming you are not our daughter; I knew this would happen; you opened all the torment that we experienced when our daughter was first abducted, and now, we must go through it again. We never want to hear or see you again!"

He completely broke down and hung up the phone; this was not how she wanted this to go. But if she was not the other baby, then she must have been the one the abductors were after in the first place. She thought her past was very strange, and she needed answers, which required a completely different strategy.

Sharon returned to Salt Lake City and worked two jobs in order to save enough money to get a good education and attend a good university. That education did not come easy. She sacrificed going to parties and socialized only with a few students who were as focused as she was on getting an acceptable average. She completed the five years to obtain her engineering degree in computer programming with an eighty-six percent average. Her average was just two percent lower than the minimum requirement of the major companies that Sharon wanted to work for.

Over the next three years, she worked for two separate companies, which did not look favorable on her resume and did not attract many employers; however, Sharon managed to get on with Standard Computer programming three years after Joseph did. She was insecure about herself and her value to the company; Joseph was a tough act to follow. She continued her education during after-hours classes at a nearby university and got a degree in computer science. She wanted a project that she could put her signature spin on it to call it her project, and she was getting tired of being placed under Joseph's control and hearing about how great Joseph was. Her personal life had gone downhill as relationships had come, but all went after a short period of time. She was looking for that special person, but there was no one that stepped up to the plate. She even had a six-week fling with Joseph, knowing full well he was married, despite her feeling disgusted with herself. She was having an affair with a married man, and she knew it, but she felt even worse when he broke it off; he no longer wanted her, and it hurt.

She was financially in good shape, saving as much as she could, but she just hated the job she spent so much time on and the many years in university to get a degree, and this was not the dream she had when it all started. Sharon started searching for new opportunities within the company. Maybe she needed a new job, or maybe she just needed to prove herself. It was the latter that would lead her to the drama that would enter her life that she was truly looking for but wished she hadn't.

6

Sergei Petrov was the computer technician for Andrei Volkov. Ever since Andrei started studying Trotsky, he wanted Sergei to design a computer program. He wanted to enhance the skills and abilities of his men dramatically. Sergei worked tirelessly on the program but needed a secondary program to run simultaneously with what he already developed. He made several attempts but failed. He was on the internet and found a program that sounded as though it was what he was looking for. He explained to Andrei that this program would save him years, and Andrei set the wheels in motion to find out more about it and purchase it.

It was a cold evening for spring, even in New York, and the bitter wind made it feel colder. Even though his winter coat, Anton shivered occasionally in his last attempt to ward off the bitterness. Anton Ivanov was medium height with a stocky build that was emphasized with his heavy winter coat. He remembered his childhood in Russia, sliding down the snowy hills and having fun with his friends. In temperatures like this, he never concerned himself with the cold; maybe he was getting soft from the American way of life.

On the park bench, he sat thinking about his homeland, and today, he missed it very much. Anton Ivanov was born in Albania to peasant farmers who barely had enough money to feed their family. Anton grew up knowing that he would never accept poverty, no matter what the cost; he just knew he would be in money sometime. At the age of twelve, he began to learn the skills of a seasoned thief and was very good at picking pockets, especially in crowds. He loved the excitement of getting away with his crime. At fourteen, he became a good soccer player and was once selected for the national team. His father took ill, and he was the only son in a family of five; his mother needed help on the farm. His sisters were all hard workers, but they were younger than him and physically unable to complete many of the farm chores that needed to be done. They worked in the warehouses in the area to bring in the much-needed money to live and help pay for bills. Anton left his soccer career to help his mother on the farm and pitch in some money to keep the boat afloat. At the age of eighteen, Anton established himself as a dealer, selling drugs primarily to high school kids and their friends. But he was smart; he had his client base and did not stray from them. If someone new came along, he would tell them to find someone else to buy for them.

When Anton was twenty years old, his mother died of pneumonia, and all the family left the farm to go their separate routes and live their separate lives. Anton packed up what he had and moved to Moscow to work for the only friend he knew there. Vlad introduced him to prostitution and human trafficking; when he shot his first man, he sometimes reflected on his first, thinking there have been so many since. It never bothered him to take a man's life, and he understood there would be a time when someone would kill him. Anton thought about someone killing him, but at least he wouldn't die poor.

Anton Ivanov and Vlad were good friends, and they both worked for Andrei Volkov, the "Boss." It took Andrei two years of watching Anton demonstrate, time and time again, proof of his loyalty to Andrei. Then, finally, one day, Andrei demonstrated his trust in Anton by giving him a district in Moscow to look after. He took Anton for a ride in his stretch limo in the country.

> Andrei explained to him, "You are taking the place of a man who decided to skim some money off the top of my business and put it in his pocket; he did this for his personal gain. I pay my people good money to look after my business, and that's what I expect them to do; any questions?"

> Anton calmly answered, "No."

Since then, Anton met or exceeded Andrei's expectations.

Andrei wanted Vlad to take on a much bigger role in the business and assigned Anton to Vlad, knowing they were friends and to enable Vlad to succeed with the additional responsibilities.

Anton was tired of waiting as he sat on the bench in Times Square; the phone finally wrang, and the scruffy-faced man answered in a rough Russian accent,

"Yea, who is this?"

The voice at the other end is also Russian, "It's Vlad; I have something for you. The boss said there is an engineer in New York who has developed a special computer program that he is interested in. He said it can read a person's mind, crazy!"

There was no reply from Anton, and Vlad continued, "Boss wants us to contact this guy and get the program. I will text you his contact info. He also has some computer guy that knows how to set things up right on our computer system once you get it."

Anton thought for a moment and said, "What do I do with them once the program is installed?"

Vlad answered, "The engineer will be a liability. The boss wants everything neat and tidy when we are done."

Then Anton questioned, "Why doesn't he get a Polygraph? They are available, you know?"

Vlad replied, "We want information. We want more than just finding out if someone is telling the truth about a question asked, understand?"

The man answered in broken English, "I get program."

Anton called his crew together to meet later and go over the particulars of this next job. He looked at his phone as it sounded a tone; it was the information from Vlad to contact the engineer; now he had everything in place that he needed. Anton was a very detailed person; everything had to be set up and ready to go. He liked working with Vlad. He was direct and to the point but gave Anton room in the conversation to ask questions or give input. He was quite satisfied reporting to Vlad; he hated talking with Andrei. With Andrei, you did what he told you, and you didn't get a second chance. If you didn't accomplish the goal as he outlined, you might as well find another country to live in and hope he never finds you.

Vlad was relaxing in his home located on the outskirts of Moscow and had been working for Andrei Volkov, the "BOSS" for as long as he could remember. During that time, he worked very closely with Andrei and witnessed him acting on several issues that had to be "looked after," which made Vlad's skin crawl and, with that, gained his respect. He was truly a man to fear. He was rich, heavily tied to upper political members within the Russian government, and feared no one. He was a very powerful man.

As for himself, Vlad Lived in a prestigious home with a beautiful view of the Bockpacehckne lake, which he and his wife Anna had a great deal of enjoyment looking at over their morning coffee. He met Anna five years ago, and despite her being several years younger, they had a very strong relationship. He met Anna in Romania at a Café on the street. As she walked past his table to leave the Café, the coat she was carrying knocked over the wineglass and spilled the entire glass of wine on him. She felt bad and tried to wipe what she could, but she was limited to what she could do using a napkin and a glass of water. The waiter came over, but all he could offer was an apology. She asked him what she could do to make it up to him, and suggested she pay for his clothes to be washed, but he suggested she have dinner with him that night, and she accepted.

They were married ten months later and had their honeymoon in Hawaii, where she had not been. Originally French, her family moved to Brussels and later to Romania. She had done a lot of modeling but was breaking into the fashion design industry, which was her true passion, and had several designs on the international market. The possibility of not having children was the toughest issue they had to deal with as a married couple since both wanted a family of their own to raise but had not been successful. Her parents kept talking about grandchildren, which didn't help.

His responsibilities within his boss's organization were getting much larger as well since Andrei was trying to establish his organization to run on its own, allowing Andrei to spend time traveling and doing what he wished. There were a lot of people who did not make the cut to Andrei's needs, and depending on the person, the cut often meant death. Vlad understood what Andrei wanted and, so far, has been looking after the responsibilities that were given to him.

The problem they were having was getting information from potential informants. They didn't know if they were telling the truth, withholding information, or if they were telling the truth and had no idea what they were being asked. It was becoming a problem, though; of the 11 suspected of withholding evidence, six had succumbed to injuries during the interrogation, with no gain of information sought after. Of course, there is the other side of the coin that is always unknown, and that was, maybe they truly don't know, that's where this program would really shine. He had known Anton Ivanov for the past 18 years, and he gets things done the way he was asked, even though he is rough around the edges. He paused for a moment to reflect on how well he was doing. He thought of his sister, how he had not seen her in years, and that soon they would be reunited, and this made him excited.

"Soon," he whispered to himself, "Soon."

With that, he walked over to the 18th-century bureau and poured himself a healthy glass of Cognac. He often missed his mother; his father told him that she left them when he was very young. He could never understand why she would leave him; he loved her so much, and he always enjoyed her singing to him at night to have him go to sleep.

The phone rang, "It's Anton; the meeting has been set-up."

Vlad replied, "Very good! Do you have enough men?"

Anton answered, "Yes, I have my regular crew of eight."

Vlad smiled as he sipped on the strong-tasting elixir. He did not know his smile and his feeling of excitement at this time would be short-lived.

7

Sharon Riley was having breakfast in her apartment. She had just sat down when the phone rang.

She picked it up, "Hello."

The elderly female voice responded, "Hello dear, it's Helena. Did I catch you at a good time for a little chat?"

Surprised, Sharon answered, "Yes, how are you, Helena?"

"Oh, I'm fine. I have been doing some digging around for you in the hospital archives and found some information I thought would be of interest to you."

She cleared her throat and then proceeded, "After Kyela passed, the body was sent to Ruza, in Russia, it's a community just West of Moscow. Her brother made all the arrangements."

She paused for a moment as she reread the notes she was reading, "Her brother's name was Mikhail Kuznetsov." She told her, "The body was sent to Ruza, just West of Moscow. I also found out from Alana, another retired nurse who happened to be on duty that same day!"

She continued, "She does not wish to be contacted but suggests if you need more information. You need to speak to Mikhail. Apparently, he and his sister were very close, and he was devastated by the incident; he may not want to talk to you because of that."

"That information was very important to me. How was Mikhail's last name spelled?"

"KUZNETSOV," she replied.

Sharon asked Helene, "Was Alana sure that Mikhail lived in Ruza at that time?"

Helene answered, "She didn't say, but you could assume so."

Sharon was grateful, "I cannot thank you enough, Helena."

Helena added, "Also, when I talked to Alana, she told me to warn you that these people that abducted the babies are very dangerous. It was rumored that Kyela's husband orchestrated her murder. Just rumors, though, from what Mikhail was heard saying to the police. This was the main reason she did not want you to contact her. She wishes you well, though."

Sharon was writing all this information down on a notepad. She considered every word the nurse said to her.

"Thank you again," Sharon added.

Deep inside, Sharon had a burning need to understand her abduction from the hospital. With the new information, she discovered that she was not the other baby in the abduction. Her curiosity intensified with the need to know. She discussed it with her parents, and they understood; they both thought this day may come.

Sharon scheduled some time off work and bought a plane ticket, leaving for Moscow in six months. Sharon was excited about the trip, not that Moscow was high on her priority list of holiday retreats, but to find Mikhail and find out the why to her abduction and why her potential mother was murdered. All her questions seem to be able to be answered by this Mikhail. She didn't even know if he was alive, but the only way she would ever get these burning questions answered was to take a risk. The worst thing that could happen would be that she got to see Moscow. The problem she faced was she did not know how to speak Russian, and this would become a huge barrier; she had six months to learn as much as possible.

This was the closest Sharon had come to discovering her paternal mother's family, even though she knew she was not alive, but maybe she had an uncle who was close to her mother who could tell her all about her mother and clear up things that she had questions about. She got on the internet and researched everything about Ruza, a town she had never heard of before today. She also tried to research Mikhail Kuznetsov but found little information of value for her.

She decided if she must learn Russian in a short time frame, that she might as well start today. After finishing her breakfast, she found a site online and got started, hopefully, in time, it would make sense to her, but after day one, she found herself battling the language instead of learning it. Sharon realized she was not going to learn fast enough and decided to immerse herself in the language. She joined a Russian cultural group that was intended as a support group for Russian immigrants coming to the United States. They were reluctant to allow her to join until she told them her story, and feeling sad for a young lady who discovered her family in Russia, they brought her in, supporting her with her desire to speak Russian with her uncle. It worked out well for the support group as well since they ended up with someone who was willing to help teach the new immigrants English. Being with this group not only helped her speak Russian but also helped her understand the language to articulate a conversation and the Russian culture.

She became friends with many of the people she met at the support group, especially a young man about her age who said he came from Ruza, and he talked to her about the town and its beauty and places to see if she ever went there. Aleksandr was tall and skinny with curly blond hair that always looked uncombed. He would make funny faces as he talked, sometimes as he explained something that made Sharon laugh. They got along well, and Sharon spent a great deal of time talking with him as she learned pronunciation and proper sentence structure. He was a good friend and helped her learn the language to the point where she could not only speak it perfectly, but also read and write it as well.

One day, Aleksandr introduced Sharon to three of his friends. At first, they seemed fine, but shortly after meeting them, they started talking about her making big money and wanted her to take a pill that would make her feel good. She refused to take the pill, and then they started pushing her to have a drink with them, and she refused that as well. She was becoming scared since she was the only female with four young men who, by this time, had her surrounded. She looked at Aleksandr and told him she wanted nothing to do with this, and she wanted them all to allow her to leave. Aleksandr looked at her and told her to consider it payment for lessons he gave her to speak Russian. She happened to notice a police officer within earshot from where the boys had heard surrounded and then started screaming as loud as she could. Once she had the officer's attention, she started fighting them off to leave. As the police officer came over to see what was going on, the boys left on the run, and she told the officer what took place. Because Sharon knew Aleksandr, they arrested him and started looking for the others. She never went back to the Russian support group again, but at least she learned how to speak their language.

8

Joseph McGee spoke with Anton Ivanov about the program, and the price as well and the follow-up services he will provide to make sure everyone understands how to use it. Anton told him they would meet at three O'clock pm in the Catskills area at the co-ordinance he texted. They will download the program onto their computer with our computer technician. He may have questions, but from that point on, there will no longer be any follow-up or discussion needed. Joseph challenged him, explaining that to get the most from the program, there are functions within the program that need to be opened and operated.

Anton told him in a commanding voice, "Then include the manual."

It's not so much what he said, instead more like how he said it, but Joseph was getting wary and became nervous about doing business with the stranger on the phone.

Joseph explained, "I have decided not to sell you the program. You need to source elsewhere for a program to suit your needs."

Anton answered, "That is not an option; you know nothing of me. Let me tell you what I know about you. You and your wife Rachel live at 1367 Harrington Way; your sister lives at twenty-three Oliver Street. Your nephew is a very talented baseball player who has practice with his team at Carlyle baseball park at five thirty this afternoon. I could go on if you like."

Joseph was shocked; he had no idea what kind of people he was dealing with. Now he really wanted out of this transaction but was unable to. He had to continue with the transaction. Anton went on to explain to Joseph that any further reluctance to give them the program would result in personnel risk, and he would not wish that on anyone. Joseph explained if they were to go through with the transaction, it would still cost them three million dollars that we previously agreed on. Anton agreed.

Sharon Riley was in the computer lab working on a data input helmet for the program and overheard Joseph McGee talking to someone on the phone about specifics of the program that were considered confidential. What caught her attention was the person on the other end was telling Joseph what he would be doing rather than asking him. It almost sounded like blackmail, and Joseph was charging him three million dollars for it.

> Sharon approached Joseph, "I was just over by the data impulse helmets and overheard you. Are you selling the program to someone?"

> Surprised that Sharon was in the lab, Joseph stammered a bit, "I'm taking a much-deserved bonus for developing this program. No one else could have done it!"

> Sharon stood up to him, "I spent just as much time as you did, and you are not the only one to take the credit!"

> Joseph started laughing, "You? You only entered the bulk data in the program, and I had to tell you what to enter. What a joke."

> Sharon was starting to get mad, "You think you are so good; you think you are the king of the programming world, don't you? Well, I could have designed that program as well!"

> Joseph started laughing hard, "Ha! That's the funniest thing I've ever heard. Are you really putting yourself in the same category as me? Sharon, you are pitiful!"

Sharon started to feel very insecure. She was being beaten down and put down, and her head started to hang low. She felt that she was less than him, worthless as a programmer, a failure.

Joseph observed this and came at her again, harder to finish her off. He wanted her to quit and never come back to bother him. How dare she challenge him and try to stand in his way to get what he deserves?

> He looked at the frail head as it hung down and told her, "You are the worst, most incompetent programmer that I know in the industry. You should be begging me to keep you from losing your job. You are absolutely pitiful!"

Joseph was trying to crush her emotionally, take away the last bit of confidence she had holding her head back up. He wanted her to quit and never bother him again in his pursuit to sell the program, but it did not work. Her alter ego kicked in, and as she raised her head, her facial expression more closely resembled someone to fear than someone to crush. Sharon stared directly at Joseph, making perfect eye contact without blinking and without expression.

> Sharon explains to him with a very strong and demanding voice, "Okay, Joseph, here is the deal. I will take one million dollars of your three-million-dollar fee, and I will be involved, and I will take a key role in the transaction between you and our clients."

Joseph felt as though she had just put him in his place. How dare she demand anything from him.

> Joseph said, "You don't understa....."

Before he had the opportunity to finish, Sharon cut him off. "No, it's you that doesn't understand. I will report you to the company's ethics hotline, and you will be fired on the spot. I will spread what you are doing through social media so fast and so hard that you will never get another job in the industry, no matter how good you think you are. And finally, I will go to your wife and inform her that you and I were having an affair, and you will lose your marriage. Got it!"

Joseph definatly got it; she continued to tell him what he would do, and all Joseph could do was agree with her.

Sharon and Joseph took a few minutes to grab a refreshment and cool down before they continued, removing the emotions of what each other just said, and calmly resumed talking about their plan. Joseph had a few reservations.

"I am a bit concerned that they want to meet at a very remote area. We have no backup plan in case these guys decide to just shoot us and walk away without paying us."

Sharon agreed, "Do you know of a reputable security company that could help us? It would be ideal if we could have them in place prior to the meeting."

Joseph considered for a moment, "Yes, I do know someone, and they owe me a favor."

Joseph gets on his cell phone and tries to make a call, but they were out of cell range. He would call on the way back and bring them in. Sharon had a good idea: if the security employees were in place well before anyone showed up, they could be in strategic locations to provide the best coverage for them.

The next day, Sharon rode out with Joseph to the arranged meeting place on the South side of MacGyver Pond. She was exhausted with only two hours of sleep, dozing on and off during the ride out. Sharon and Joseph drove out early and the security members slept in their vehicles to place themselves in the bushes well in advance of the meeting. When Joseph and Sharon got there, the Russians were already there. Anton boldly asked who Sharon was and why she was there. Joseph introduced himself and explained she was here to provide additional assistance once the program was downloaded and working. She can assist them in running the program and troubleshoot if necessary. Anton yells that he did not ask for her and tells one of the Russians to get his computer ready. He told them that he has his own computer tech that will look after the downloading and will figure out how to operate it. Having Sharon there really aggravated Anton, but Anton's main responsibility now was to get the program on their system computer and acknowledge that the program worked. He placed the computer on the tailgate of the truck, and Sharon brought over the program operating disk. Their tech, Sergei Petrov, placed a downloading flash drive into one USB port and the flash drive that Sharon had in the other port. Once downloading and installation were completed, the tech removed both flash drives, placed them on the tailgate beside the computer, and booted up the program to make sure it was working. As Sharon reached to retrieve her program flash drive, she picked up the Russian system flash drive at the same time without anyone noticing and placed them both in her pocket. After the Russian tech was satisfied the program was downloaded and operating correctly, he nodded to Anton.

> Joseph McGee said, "Now that you have the program and have determined it works, there is a matter of the three million dollars payment."
>
> Anton grabbed his pistol from the holster with his right hand and pointed it at Joseph McGee's forehead, yelling, "Why do we need to pay you at all when I can shoot the both of you right now?"

Just after Anton made his intentions well known, shots rang out from the bushes nearby, hitting Anton in the left shoulder and another Russian square in the chest, killing him. Both Joseph and Sharon ran away as fast as possible, avoiding a frenzy of additional shooting and crossfire. Anton gets up off the ground, holding his left shoulder, yelling at his team to kill them. The Russian computer technician yells out that Sharon has stolen the system drive. Anton yells at his team to kill her, and the Russians focus their attention to start shooting at her. A shot hit her, grazing her right hip, and she fell down an embankment on top of an old tree stump sticking upwards, breaking several ribs. Joseph ran along the clearing to seek better protection behind a mound of dirt and was shot in the leg, which put him down on the ground; shortly after, a second round was shot by the Russian team in the chest, and Joseph did not get up. Additional shots from the bushes swing Anton's team's attention back to the security members, and one of the shooters was killed, while the other two turn and escape.

Sharon was fighting for her life; she saw Joseph go down but not get up, and she was terrified for her life, and tried to distance herself as far away from the Russians as possible. In the process, as she ran as fast as she could down a hill, she lost her balance and tumbling on he injured side. The pain was the most intense she had ever felt. She thought she would most likely break some ribs. With every breath she took, another wave of intense pain would overtake her body. Eventually, Sharon comes upon an area heavily treed with thick underbrush by the pond and hides up in a thicket to rest. She was in severe pain and did everything she could do to find a comfortable position to ease the pain and her desire to yell out and moan as she moved. The Russians ran after her once the shooting stopped from the Russian assailants to search for Sharon but were unable to find her. At one point, they came within ten feet of her but were unable to see her. They are left in confusion about what took place. They determine they need to take Anton for medical attention and one other of the Russian colleagues. Anton argued a bit with his crew but eventually agreed to go to have his shoulder looked at. They will find and kill Sharon another time, but he first wants to check out a road that leads to a cabin. She might be there.

9

Becky and her mother, Jen Fulton, arrived at the cabin and backed the SUV close to the front porch to make the unloading easier. It was a beautiful day in the Catskills overlooking the North end of the pond,

> "I think Dad comes later just so he doesn't have to unpack the car!" Becky jested as her mother was coming out for another box.
>
> Becky's mother, Jen, laughed, "We will get Allen to load the car when we are packing to come home while we drink lemonade on the porch!"

The cabin was older, built to appear as though it was a real log cabin, but it was a typical wood-framed building with interior walls finished with wood paneling and some plaster in the bedrooms. The windows were old single-pane wooden windows that stood through many families visiting the cabin on holidays and looking through them at the view of the pond. The cabin was nestled amongst trees, offering protection from the winds of storms that frequent the area.

Both mother and daughter laughed at the thought of Allen's face as they sat on the porch while he worked.

> Becky said, "Naw, we couldn't do that to Dad."

The mother and daughter were very close, almost like two best friends on a girl's day away. They continued their conversation on the porch as they were sucking up the rays. Once they finished their lemonade, they both went for a walk on a familiar path along the pond. They talked about whatever came to mind. They talked about when Jen was Becky's age. Becky had questions about her

Grandparents, whom she never met. Jen enjoyed reminiscing as she told Becky in detail what they were like and some funny stories about them. Jen told stories about things she did that were humorous, and they laughed as they walked along the path.

The red-winged blackbirds were singing their song as they chased each other in the bullrushes along the shore of the pond. The two stopped for a moment to watch the dragonflies dart this way and that, catching mosquitoes in midair as they flew by.

As they walked to the Southern end of the pond, they heard shots from firearms and some yelling. The two considered it must be someone target practicing, and they went back to telling their stories. As they approached a heavily forested area, they heard a faint moaning and a female voice calling for help. They both crept into the thicket to investigate the source of the voice and as Jen got closer, they found Sharon holding her left side and wincing with pain.

> "Oh my, are you alright? What happened? We can help you?" Jen said in shock.
>
> Sharon answered, "Get down and hide and don't say anything. Be quiet!"

Shortly after, two Russian gunmen, including one they called Anton with his gun drawn, came down the path looking for Sharon. The three of them came closer, walking within 20 feet of them. Jen notices that the one man they called Anton was giving orders and was holding his left shoulder, with his shirt covered in blood. They stood talking to each other for a while as they screened the area, which seemed to the girls as hours. They eventually moved on, returning to their vehicles. The girls waited to hear their vehicles drive off before standing up to leave their hiding spot. As they walk, Jen finds out more about Sharon's situation. Sharon summarized what took place once she and Joseph got there but held back the complete story; she did not want to tell a stranger all about the program and the proposition to the Russians. As they come into sight of the cabin, they see the Russians going through the cabin and their SUV. They retreated into a densely treed area and assessed the situation. Then Jen tried calling her husband, Allen, to fill him in, but with the poor cell range, she was unable to. She then tried texting him and was grateful the text got through to him and filled him in on their situation. He said he was calling local authorities, and an ambulance, as his FBI agents would be attending. However, it would take some time for the three of them to stay well out of sight and stay silent.

Jen returned to Becky and Sharon and summarized her conversation with Allen.

"Your husband is with the FBI?" Sheron asked.

Jen nodded, "Yes, he is the director. He will be coming out immediately."

Sheron relaxed, knowing this crisis she got herself into was over and reputable help was on the way, but she knew it was far from over. Jen and Becky tended to Sharon's wounds the best they could but were unable to stop all the bleeding from the gunshot wound since it was deep. They covered the wound with some ripped cloth from their clothes, tied it tight, and applied pressure to the area. Her side was something they could not do anything about; her side was bleeding internally, and they saw the extent of the injury from the excessive bruising on her side. They laid her down flat to attempt to make her comfortable. It appeared it might be a while before they could move her, and just waited it out until someone came to help.

The Russians were going through both cabin and car and throwing items and papers all over the ground. It wasn't windy, but a gust would come up occasionally, and they could see the papers take flight. The Russians either found what they were looking for, or they gave up, and Jen could see them get in their cars and start to leave. Becky wanted to go to the cabin to get the First Aid kit, but her mother told her to stay put.

They could hear footsteps coming down the path from where they first saw Sharon, and Jen whispered to both girls to shut up and stay still. The man did not look hurt and watched him walk along the path past them and continued towards the cabin. He was of average build with blonde hair and, wearing a hoody and a baseball cap, packing a rifle. He didn't seem to be looking for anyone as he walked right past the cabin. Sharon and Becky did not recognize his face, but Jen said that what she could see of his face, she recognized him from somewhere, but she couldn't put a name to it.

Allen called his agents and sent them straight out to the cabin immediately as he had Jon follow him as he passed Jon's office.

"What's going on, Allen?"

Allen answered him just after he called dispatch to send an ambulance as well, "No idea, but we are needed. There's been a shooting, people are hurt, and I guess some are dead. Jen and Becky are involved somehow. That's all I know right now."

10

The local police were contacted by the FBI to assist in a potential abduction in progress, and Sheriff Borhan called his people to respond. The Sheriff knew the area well and led the convoy of four patrol cars to the area. At the left turn off onto the gravel road leading to the cabin, there was a sedan parked on the right side of the road with two passengers along with a driver. It looked out of place considering the area and terrain and caught the sheriff's well-trained eye, and he got on the radio.

"Someone wants to get the license plate number off that car?" He yelled.

Lieutenant Gurman replied, "On it, sheriff!"

Lieutenant Gurman was driving the last patrol car in the police convoy, and as the first three cars made the turn and drove ahead, Lt. Gurman parked just behind the sedan and got out. He then took out his notepad and wrote down the license number, and as he put the pad back in his shirt pocket, the two passengers in the sedan got out of the car with semi-auto rifles and started shooting at him. Lt. Gurman ran to the front of the car to take cover from the shooting and called for backup. The three cars that drove ahead turned around on the narrow road and started back to where the Lieutenant was. The road had loose gravel with slick mud at the edges, and despite the rush and sense of urgency, their traveled speed had to be reduced significantly in order to navigate along the road safely.

As they got closer to where the lieutenant was held down with gunfire, Sheriff Borhan turned left along an old logging road. He drove about another mile, then turned left again along a narrow path that led him up the hill along several switchbacks to the top of the hill. He got out of his car, walked just over the crest of the hill, and placed himself directly above the gunfire. He heard the shooting and could see his people were in a poor position since they came in from one side. He was concerned and could see the gunmen trying to reposition themselves to surround Lt. Gurman. The Sheriff loaded a shell into his rifle and inspected the scene through the scope, resting the gun on an old stump. As one of the gunmen was getting too close to Gurman, he placed his finger on the trigger and, with experience and a career of acquired skill, squeezed the trigger, placing a fatal shot in the center of the gunman's chest. As another gunman resituated himself to be protected from the sheriff on the hill, Lt. Gurman shot him. Sheriff Borhan could see the last gunman was working his way toward the driver's side of the Sedan and tried to shoot the tires flat twice, but he was unable to make a clean shot and missed both times. Lt. Gurman was trying to figure out why the Sheriff was after the tires on the sedan, but he had a clean shot and decided to shoot out the two rear tires.

With no rear tires on the sedan, the last remaining gunman threw down his weapon and put his hands up in defeat. The lieutenant was closest, so he put the handcuffs on him and patted him down to find another gun and one knife. The lieutenant led him over to the patrol car and pushed him in.

They heard two other cars coming along the gravel road quickly from the cabin, and the police turned their attention towards these cars. They stopped, and three gunmen got out with military rifles, spraying rounds after rounds at the police. Sheriff Borhan heard the gunfire but was unable to see much from where he was on the hill, so he drove back to get behind the attackers hopefully.

When Sheriff Borhan got to the main gravel road, he was in perfect position and got out of his car using it for cover and resting his rifle on the engine cover as he shot. His first shot wounded one gunman, and the second shot killed another. Before he could get the third round away, the one Russian who had a previous injury and a blood-soaked shirt started yelling in Russian, and they jumped in their vehicles and drove through the blocked road. As the first car drove up to the parked police car, the gunman's car sped up and knocked the police car off the road and into the ditch, allowing the second car to drive through. As they bashed their way through, the police fired at them, wounding the driver in the front car and blowing out the second car's radiator. The police heard them stop, and all got into one car and drove off. The two patrol cars and the Sheriff's car were the only ones operable, and they took off after the gunmen. Lieutenant Gurman was in the lead police car catching up with the gunman's car and noticed they threw something out the window directly behind them. It wasn't until Lieutenant Gurman drove over the top of it that he recognized it was a grenade. The explosion took place in the rear left corner of the car as it drove over, turned the car over on its top, and skidded down the road about 50 yards before it stopped. Since the fuel tank was located at the rear of the car, it caught on fire immediately upon the explosion, engulfing the whole car in flames and killing Lt. Gurman and the Russian prisoner in the back seat.

Sheriff Borhan parked at a safe distance. He felt sick to his stomach, he jumped out of the car and ran over to the burning wreck. One of the officers grabbed his fire extinguisher in a feeble attempt to put out the blaze. He was putting himself in harm's way, and Sheriff Borhan warned him off. Nothing could be done. He got back in his car and contacted the FBI agents coming in from New York to ask them about setting up a roadblock to stop them. He took off down the gravel road and chased these guys. That's all he can do now for the lieutenant.

Anton and the remaining Russian gunmen were driving as fast as they could for two reasons: to escape and to find medical aid for Anton. His injured shoulder was getting worse, and with all the activity, he was slipping in and out of consciousness. Then, as they turned a corner in the road, an ambulance was headed their way. The driver pulled over in front of it, and the gunmen got out.

"We need you to fix this man up!" One of the gunmen shouted to the medic.

"I'll need to look at the injury first," explained the medic.

"You look as we drive back." Commanded the gunman as he pointed his gun at the medic.

One of the Russians situated their car in front of a cliff by the road, got out, and let it roll over the edge, crashing all the way to the bottom, leaving it barely noticeable from the road. They all got into the ambulance and drove out. As they passed the FBI barricade, their emergency lights were on, and the agents thought nothing of letting them through.

11

Allen Fulton was traveling in his Suburban at full speed, lights flashing, with Jon Marion in his vehicle close behind him. Two other agents and the SWAT team were close behind them. The ambulance he called for Sharon came local and was ahead. Allen was concerned about the well-being of both his wife and daughter. It was the first time anything like this had ever happened to his family. He had dealt with others whose families were involved in abductions and worse, but this was happening to his family. Allen was the FBI director, looking after the New York district, and brought Jon along to act as lead on the case. Since Allen's family was involved in the abduction, Allen was potentially too close to the abduction to make effective and important calls in the field Allen made that decision. Jon had been with the FBI for fifteen years. Jon started with the FBI when he was fresh out of university with a degree in criminal law. He quickly rose to lead and worked alongside him before Allen was promoted to Director. Using their earbuds to communicate,

> "So where are we setting up the barricade? I'm not that familiar with this area." Jon asks.
>
> Allen replied, "About sixteen miles up the road, there is only one road they could turn off. I would like to set up on the other side of that. But of course, there is the danger of them passing us before we get there, and then it's a high-speed chase with the chance of losing them. Let's set up here, Jon."

When they arrived at their location, they stopped their vehicles, got out to throw out a spike belt, and radioed the two units behind them to take over their barricade. Once the agents drove up to them,

Allen and Jon quickly took off towards the intersecting gravel road.

When they reached the intersection, Jon thought about it for a while, "where does the road go?"

"The road starts in good condition but progressively worsens for about 15 miles. There is no exit. It ends at an old gravel pit. Occasionally, workers go in to fire up the rock crusher and haul some gravel for road maintenance." Allen replied.

Jon adds, "We could also move up the barricade once we get there."

Allen agrees, "Great thinking, Jon, get them on the radio and get them to grab the belt and move up. The road is just around the corner."

Once Allen and Jon set up at the road going to the gravel pit, they radioed the other two agents to move the barricade up to their location. By the time they arrived, the SWAT team had caught up to the group, and they had a strongly fortified barricade that could not be breached.

Allen said to Jon," Let's try contacting the Sheriff and find out where he is. It shouldn't be much longer."

Just then, the ambulance was driving up with lights on and travelling at a fast speed.

Jon yelled at the team, "Let the ambulance through!"

Approximately fifteen minutes later, they see both the Sheriff's cars coming around the corner, and everyone is shocked to see him before the gunmen. Allen knew the Sheriff and went over to him. Allen was on good terms with the Sheriff, but under the circumstances, he left off the pleasantries and got right into the conversation.

He looked directly at Boreham, "where the hell are they?"

The Sheriff answered, "I have no idea. I was behind them."

Jon spouted up, "Are you sure they traveled this way from the cabin road?"

"Absolutely, no question, and you are saying they didn't come this way?"

One of the other agents said, "Except for the ambulance."

"What ambulance?" the Sheriff blurted," you mean the one that was going to the cabin for that injured female. It didn't get there?"

Allen said in frustration, "So, they were in the ambulance. Did you see their car?"

The Sheriff answered, "No, I did not. Better get another ambulance on the way."

"Jon, you can look after this. I'm going to the cabin where my wife and daughter are and check things out there. You will have another ambulance sent out?"

Jon replied, "On it."

Along the trip to the cabin, Allen could not believe the destruction at the attack site prior to arriving at the cabin. When he got there, his stomach sank as he saw the doors open on their family car, with personal items strewn all over the ground around it. The front door to the cabin was opened, and as he ventured in, with his pistol in hand, he searched the carnage of personal items all over the floor. He started calling Jen and Becky's names, with no answer. He tried calling them on their cell, but there was insufficient range for the call to go through, and he texted as a last attempt. He was thankful the text went through, but more thankful when he got a response back, ensuring him they were fine and well hidden, but they said that Sharon was not doing as well as they were. He ran down the trail along the pond, finding them safe and giving everyone a big hug. Allen assessed Sharon's condition, and while the ambulance may be a while, he decided she was well enough, picked up

Sharon, and carried her back to the cabin to wait for the second ambulance to arrive. He explained to them what he could, based on what he knew, but so many pieces didn't make sense and didn't fit. Emotions were surging through Allen. As scared as he was of what could have happened to his family, he was a lot madder that someone had done this and put his family in harm's way. He told himself that his team would find the people responsible, and they will be held accountable.

Jen cut into Mike's thoughts, "Did you see a fella in a hoody and a baseball cap with a rifle walking along the road when you came in?" She proceeded to fill him in.

12

The crime scene investigators from the FBI were on the scene with their cameras, site sketches, and mannequins, diligently and with detail, developing a re-enactment from all evidence of the three incident sites. Since there were three sites and because of the police fatalities, the team placed a greater emphasis on their jobs. For Jon, since he was the lead FBI investigator, he not only had the statements from Sharon, Becky, and Jen to deal with, but all the officers within the Sheriff's department and the other FBI agents and SWAT team that came later, plus all the pictures, and to hunt down the ambulance attendants and get their statements. Jon was busy, and Allen organized additional agents to assist Jon in creating a war room. Splitting them into three groups: 1-Statements and facts found in the field, 2-crime lab findings, autopsy and crime scene data and trends, and the last one 3- information from external sources and departments.

Jon worked on several of these multi-incident situations before and was well-versed in how to get things underway quickly. There was always someone, a politician, a wealthy contributor or someone with influence. There were always those who felt important, by letting the FBI know they were being watched, and the timeliness to solve the crime, it was important to complete the preliminary report within 24 hours. Allen worked with Jon to get all the statements and information he needed to complete and submit the preliminary incident report to the Sheriff's department to discuss any errors or omissions before submitting the report to the FBI head office. Since the FBI will be reviewing the Sheriff's Department statements and report, it was critical to have his report written with the exact same time and order of events as the Sheriff's report. In the event of a discrepancy, an informal investigation would be conducted to determine the correction before the report is submitted. They had a lot of work to do as quickly as they could.

This was far from an open-and-shut case; Sharon's statement had several holes in it, and they had no idea what part the medics played. Jon and Allen had a lot of questions for both. They needed to clear up with further investigation. Since she was injured, Sharon's well-being was a priority, and getting her the required medical attention at the hospital was a priority over questioning at this time. Answers to their many questions would have to be conducted at the hospital later.

> Jon got on the radio, "Reynolds, Smith, find out who was involved in attending the ambulance that came out here and have the lab go through it. I want to have their backgrounds checked and bring them in. I have questions for them."

> The agents replied, "Right away, Jon."

Once the scene was secured and the medics transported Sharon to the hospital, the local authorities and FBI, with the presence of Allen Fulton, questioned and took statements from Becky and Jen. They went through the events in detail, answering questions as they were asked. Jen went through the items that they brought into the cabin, and Jen and Becky could not see anything missing.

> "What were they looking for?" Becky asked.

> Her dad answered her, "There is no telling what exactly they wanted or expected to find, but they do have your name and address from the insurance and registration of the car documents. We will have to put you up in a safe house until all this blows over."

> Jen blurts out, "Shit."

Allen helped Jon with some of the scene management and directed two female agents to change clothes with Jen and Becky. He asks

Jen for the keys to their SUV and explains they will be staging Jen and Becky's drive and return to their home.

"I want armed agents in my home dressed as Jen and Becky for the next week, if necessary, to give them the indication that my family came home and is Living in the address they have found." He looked at Jon, "We need agents to follow Sharon and the ambulance into the hospital and get some questions answered here!"

"Jackson, Hawn, follow that ambulance in, and let's get answers to some questions. Why was she here? What were they doing here? What part did Standard have in this mess? You know the drill. Also, let's set up security on her, make sure these guys, whoever they are, don't try to kill her again!"

Everyone followed the director's and the leads' orders, packed the stuff that Jen and Becky unloaded into the cabin, and placed it back in their SUV. Jen and Becky exchanged clothes with equal-sized FBI agents and left in the same car as Jen and Becky came in. Jen and Becky were transported to the safe house in Allen's Suburban, and the agents drove Jen's SUV straight to their home and unloaded the items from the SUV back into their house.

Agents Beson and Renolds were sweating from packing the boxes in the house and took a break halfway through the chore. Renold's holster for her pistol had loosened, and she was adjusting when they heard a knock on the door.

Benson decided to acknowledge since they could have easily been seen outside, "Can I help you?"

"It's just Catherine. Thought you could use some help."

Benson answered, "Thanks, Catherine, we got it."

"OK, Jen, but if you need help, just give me a call."

Benson answered, "Thanks again, Catherine."

Both agents standing in for Jen and Becky had been made. They weren't sure who this Catherine was, but she definitely would have recognized a different voice. They called Jon to report it. Jon was quite surprised the conversation went on like it did as well, regardless of the fact he and his wife Catherine were best friends with Allen and Jen.

The agents filling in for Jen and Becky were completely unaware they were being watched as they unloaded the SUV by the Russians two blocks away.

13

The forensic team processed the scene and removed the bodies of four Russians, one American, the Sheriff's men, and Joseph McGee. Lee Magnuson came out to supervise and offer his unique experience as his team gathered and documented evidence for the investigation. Lee was fifty-seven years old, and though he was the oldest, he had the utmost leadership respect from his team. Everyone knew that before anything was moved or removed from its resting place when found, Lee had to see it first. This is where Lee spent his time training his team, and they were sponges as he told them the specifics of what to watch for. Often, Lee would go on talking about past cases where what he was teaching was relevant, further explaining the learning experience, but not in this case. There was too much evidence to go over and not enough time. Lee brought out special shell casing containers he purchased many years ago to properly document and keep empty shell casings in, avoiding cross-contamination between casings and saving fingerprint integrity. They found eighty-seven shell casings from the rifles and sidearms used in the shootout. All were placed and labeled with specifics of caliber, location, and proximity to the fallen victims.

> Lee examined one of the casings and explained to his newest team member, "See the primer in this casing. There is a lot that can be learned from it. The firing pin appears to have hit the primer twice since it shows a slight secondary dimpling specific to that gun. This indicates poor head spacing between the rifle's bolt face and the shell casing primer when it was shot. This may not be important in the investigation into this case. However, it may be a huge contributing factor. I remember a case where…

Remind me later to tell you about it. Unfortunately, we don't have time right now."

The team took blood samples found in the vehicles and on weapons at each site, and there were samples taken of blood that was found on the victims, identifying if there was cross-contamination. Lee examined the sketches his team submitted of spatter found, ensuring quality and thoroughness. Castings of tire marks and shoe imprints were taken, and of course, the one hundred and thirty-four pictures taken of the various sites identifying evidence and its location to dead bodies and other evidence collected.

As Lee examined the castings taken of footprints, he looked at one in particular, "Take me to where this casting was taken."

Lee knelt to examine the prints closer and told the technician, "You only have the right foot casting. If you look closely at it, you will find the tread pattern damaged, with a slice out of the shoe's sole. Here is the left print. There is no damage to it. Knowing this, a suspect could be positively identified, and he could be set free without it! Details, details, details. Cast the left foot."

As each sample and piece of evidence was bagged, tagged, and photographed, they were placed in boxes labeled with the specific site. They were then loaded into one of the Suburbans, and once Lee was satisfied everything was in order, they were delivered to the lab for processing. The forensic team worked tirelessly with great detail, focusing on procedure and the experience each one brought from crime scenes processed before.

At the laboratory, the autopsies were completed, and all relevant information was distributed to key individuals investigating the series of crimes committed. The crime scene investigators entered all the information in their computer program to show a re-enactment of what took place at each site. To enable the crime scene investigators to get a clear picture of what took place, Lee had his team set up Mannequins at each site and, in the Sheriff's presence, go through each detail of the crimes step by step. Several questions were asked and answered, and the input of the involved Sheriff's people was also added to the exercise.

Jon told the group, "We need Sharon Riley's interview to clarify the whys to this. I'll find out what Jackson and Hawn have found out. Thanks all for your hard work to this point and this re-enactment. You have all helped considerably."

Jon left the site to go to the hospital to talk to Sharon. After the re-enactment and summary of the events, he had some questions he would like to ask himself.

He arrived at the hospital and went straight to Sharon's room. Jackson and Hawn were nowhere to be found, and Sharon had been stabbed several times, looking lifeless. He opened the door and went into the hallway.

"Get some medical attention in here, NOW!" Jon yelled. "She's been stabbed!"

The nurses and a doctor came rushing in. They knew Jon and realized he would not act this way unless there was a good reason. After assessing her, they immediately wheeled her to an operating room to try and stop the internal bleeding from the knife wounds. Once they left with Sharon, he went inside the room to protect any evidence there may be. Jon did not understand where Jackson and Hawn were. He looked to his right and saw the bathroom door and ran over, opening the door to find Jackson and Hawn on the floor in a pool of blood, with their handguns and ear wicks missing. He ran out into the hallway again to call the nurse in to tend to his fallen agents, but it was too late. They were both gone. He got on his phone and called a familiar number,

"Lee, I need you and some of your team down at St. Mary's Hospital. We have two of my agents dead and the eyewitness severely stabbed. I don't know if she is going to make it."

"My God, Jon, what the hell have you gotten into on this case?"

Jon replied to Lee, trying to rush him, "I have no idea, Lee, but we are about to find out."

After talking to Lee, Jon contacted Allen to summarize the recent incident and update him on the case.

"You need to stay with your family, Allen, on a full-time basis. I believe they will be targeted next!"

14

Jon answered his phone as he was driving from one site to the next, "hello."

His wife Catherine started, "Hi, it's just me. I was just calling to find out about Allen's family. Are they alright? Is Jen and Becky safe now?"

It wasn't unusual for his wife to ask such a question about Allen's family. They were the closest thing to a family they had.

Jon answered, "Yes, all three are safe and sound, and we have agents watching over them."

"All three?"

Jon realized he said something he shouldn't have, "Everyone is fine, dear."

Catherine asked, "Were they hurt or injured at all?

Jon replied," No, they seem fine. They were checked out by the medic."

Catherine added, "Jon, I was doing some baking here at home, and I thought I would take some cake and cookies for them at their house. Would that be fine? I gave you a call because I did not want to be arrested and thrown in handcuffs just for giving them some cookies to an old friend."

Jon answered her, "No, dear, that would not be a good idea. We are on high security with those two right now."

Jon's wife was quite tenacious, pushing him, "OK, then I will take it over to their house and give it to one of your agents to take in for me."

Jon abruptly cut her off and said, "No!" he paused. "Were you over at Allen and Jen's place earlier today?"

"Yes, to help pack their boxes in, but Jen sounds quite different. Is she okay?"

She continued, and he hung up on her for the first time in their marriage. When they were married, he explained to her that their personal life stayed at home and their professional life stayed at work. He made it very clear that he is not able to reveal some information about his investigations away from work, including her, even for reasons she most likely would never understand.

She called back, "That was not very nice to hang up on me. If they are not at their place, then where are they?"

Jon was surprised that his wife wouldn't let this go, " I never said they weren't at their place, you did."

This time, she hung up on him. He called his senior agent at Allen and Jen's house and explained that his wife Catherine was at the door trying to get in and talk to Jen. "No one gets through."

He dialed a number he had on speed dial. Ruby answered, "Hi, mister Jon. How can I help you today?"

"I'm great, Ruby. I have a personal request, just between you and me. I would like calls in and out as well as texts on a cell number. Can you help me?"

"I sure can, mister Jon. Do you want me to send the record to your FBI email or your personal email?"

Jon answered, "My personal email, please, and thank you."

As soon as Jon ended his call with Ruby, his cell phone started ringing.

"Hello, Reynolds, what's going on?"

"I found the ambulance by its tracking device. It ended up in an abandoned warehouse yard in an industrial park, and both medics in the back dead. We need the lab boys out here. There is a bunch of bandages and other items with blood."

"Dam! Okay, I will get in contact with Lee again. Thanks, guys, good work!"

"There's more, Jon, we found a packsack on the passenger side of the cab. It had four smoke bombs and three hand grenades, US military origin."

Jon was set back, "Wow, who are these guys? Send me a pin on your phone so we know where it is. Okay, keep me in touch with anything new!"

After notifying Lee and sending him the pin locater of the ambulance, Jon sat in his Suburban for a few minutes to digest everything and got out a fresh new notepad and started writing everything that had taken place, including the most specific detail, including a chronological time log. He thought about his wife's call, considering if it was relevant, but he remembered his training years ago in how everything was relevant until evidence proved it wasn't. He was summarizing their call in the notepad when his cell rang again. It was Sheriff Boreham.

"Yes, Sheriff, how can I help you?

The Sheriff responded," Jon, my boys found the gunmen's sedan. They pushed it over the bank so I wouldn't see it when I drove by, smart. I figured your people would be busy, so I had our technicians look at it. We got a bunch of fingerprints, and they found a grenade secured to the passenger door down real low with tape and a wire hooked to the pin attached to the driver's door. Thank God my officer saw the wire across the seats before opening the door. I'll send you the fingerprints and associated names we found by email, and I will bring the grenade into your bomb squad tomorrow."

"Thanks, Sheriff. I appreciate your cooperation on this case. By the way, whose ordinance is the grenade?"

"US military issue Jon!"

Jon finished writing the last few events into his notepad and called Allen to summarize what had taken place since they last talked. He received a text from the doctor treating Sharon's wounds. He stopped Allen for a moment and read the text indicating that Sharon was on the road to recovery. He told Allen,

> "Fantastic news, finally we are getting this nightmare turned around. I want you to tell everyone that for the time being, the records must identify that Sharon passed away and that she did not make it through her operation. Hopefully, we can keep her safe for a while longer. I can't figure out how they know so much about what we are doing; have your phone checked for tapping devices."

With what Allen just said, he remembered the missing ear wicks on his two dead agents,

> "Allen, I just remembered something that you should know. When I found Jackson and Hawn in the bathroom at the hospital, their ear wicks were missing."

> Allen was in shock, "now they will know where Jen and Becky are!"

After talking with Allen, he called the hospital to talk with Dr. McCann, the doctor looking after Sharon.

> The nurse answered, "Hi Jon, sorry you are out of luck. He just left for the evening. Can I help you?"

Jon was battling whether he should trust her or not, but under the circumstances, he had no choice but to involve her.

> Jon started, "You know that I am with the FBI, don't you?

> The nurse, not sure where this was heading, replied, "Yes."

> "Okay, I need you to do something that is very important. I need the records to indicate that she did not make it

through the operation and you to make it well known that Sharon passed away."

Surprised, the nurse looked at him, "I can't do that!"

Jon took the time to explain the situation," There are people out there who want Sharon killed. If they believe she is alive, they will come back there, and your life and the lives of those who work there and the lives of the other patients will be in jeopardy. Did you understand that?"

The nurse was very quiet and said, "Then we need to take her to another room. Is there going to be someone to guard over her?"

Jon answered, "Yes."

"Okay, then tell them she is in room 238."

"Thank you!"

There was not a "you are welcome" coming from her. He called two other agents and had them watch over Sharon for the night.

15

Anton was resting in his living room, going over the events of the disaster in the Catskills. He was considering his next move. It had to be successful. When he calls Vlad next, he must have those two women in his capture. As for the other one called Sharon, she is dead, and that was fine.

They were able to get the earwicks the FBI used, and with them, they were able to locate the safe house. Anton had four of his best men watching the house and ready to move in. They counted six FBI on the outside and estimated two inside with the two women. Anton consulted his lead man and came up with a plan to hit them hard at the decoy house first to create a distraction, while Anton's team hit the safe house shortly after to get the two women out and leave before the SWAT team knew anything about it. It was a good plan; they will do it tonight. Vlad told him they wanted to fly the two women to Moscow in Andrei's jet to use them to experiment with the new program he developed from Joseph McGee's. But right now, he needed to get some sleep. It would be a long night for him.

The Russians watching the safe house saw the Pizza being delivered. The delivery boy took the Pizza inside and then, shortly after, left the house for his delivery van. About one hour later, a police car came to the house, and both officers walked into the house. After about twenty minutes, they left in their patrol car. The two Russians didn't think much of it except they both really wanted a piece of that Pizza right now. They continued to monitor the activity around the house.

Allen had no intention of leaving his wife and daughter in a house where these Russians could find them. He had an agent of his dress as a pizza delivery boy and had his wife leave the house dressed as the pizza delivery boy and drive four blocks away from the safe house to meet with him. Then, he did the same thing with his daughter and the two police officers. He took them about an hour out of town to a Motel to stay the night. After bringing in additional weapons and ammunition, he went to sleep with a pistol under his pillow. It was a long night.

The Russians stormed Allen's home, but The FBI was ready for them with the SWAT team readily available, only four blocks away with six heavily armed agents inside and the SWAT team arriving quickly and cutting them from a retreat. Of the six Russians taking part in the intended abduction, three were killed, and three were arrested. They were handcuffed and placed in the back of the police vehicle and on their way to lock up.

Around the time the Russians left in the patrol cars, the other team of Russians attacked the safe house. This was a different attack by the Russians. There were more of them, and they circled the house after they broke through the agents who were positioned outside the house. One of the Russians climbed up on the roof and placed tear gas bombs down the plumbing vents and the chimney, which totally filled the inside of the safe house with gas. When the SWAT team arrived on the scene, the Russians were just about to breach the house. The SWAT leader had his team cover the house's front and rear entrances. As the SWAT members approached the rear of the house, the Russians threw two grenades at them, killing two and injuring one other. The tear gas inside was too intense for the agents located inside the house, and they started coming out, desperately searching for fresh air. As they came out, the Russians picked them off, one at a time, killing two and injuring one. The SWAT snipers, now in place, were firing on the Russians, and once the snipers started changing the direction of the battlefield, the Russians were finished with five of the nine surrendering.

Both the SWAT leaders contacted Jon, giving him a summary of the events from each scene. Jon looked at his watch, and despite it being late, he decided to call Allen to update him on the attempted abduction from both houses, the casualties and injuries on both sides, and the arrests made.

Allen came out of a deep sleep and checked the time as he answered the phone. It was 11:25 pm, "Hello Jon, what's up?

Jon, trying to put words to a detailed summary, said, "We had two attacks by the Russians, one at your house and one at the safe house. You made a good call getting them out of there. I won't ask you where you are, but I have another safe house for your family. It will have agents already there."

Allen thought for a while and said, "Okay, thanks, so what are we going to have in place that we did have before that will prevent another attack?"

Jon thought that was a very good question, "I'm going to have two snipers in position twenty-four seven. They effectively turned things around for us with the attack on the safe house."

"Since they used tear gas on the latest attack, I want gas masks inside the house."

Jon wrote this down on his notepad, "when do you think you guys will be there?"

"Not sure, Jon, might not go with the safe house."

Jon paused, " you don't have many options, Allen."

Allen wasn't happy when Jon told him that he had no options. He carefully orchestrates everything he does, so he always has options.

As Allen calmed down, he said to Jon, "As bad as things may seem, I always have an ace up my sleeve."

Jon was thinking it must be a big ace because these guys mean business. He would not want his family to go through what Jen and Becky are going through. Jon thought he was the boss, and it was his family to protect any way he felt appropriate. He wondered if this was one of those situations where he should have Allen take some time off and take over the case himself. If he chose to do this, Jon would lose all integrity with Allen, and his career would look a lot different. He decided to leave this in Allen's experienced hands.

16

Allen was preparing himself to go back to sleep. Tomorrow is a new day. As he rolled over in the bed, he reached over to turn out the light. He noticed something about his pen lying on the night table that he never noticed before. Maybe it was the way the light shone on it or the angle. An untrained eye would easily overlook it, but Allen has taught tracking and bugging devices classes. He sat up on the bed and dismantled his pen, inspecting each piece with detail. Finally, within the clicking mechanism, the tracker, with a small wire to the microscopic component, he saw when the pen lay there on the nightstand. He was being tracked, and they knew exactly where he and his family were.

Allen jumped out of bed and woke his wife and daughter; they had lots of questions, but he told them there was no time. They grabbed their bags and scurried off to Allen's suburban, and they took off without checking out.

"What's going on, Allen?" Jen asked.

"I found a tracking device in my pen; they know where we are," Allen replied.

Jen asked her husband, "Allen, who are these guys? What do they want from us?"

Allen answered and talked to Jen and Becky, " They probably think you were both potential eyewitnesses to that gunfight at the pond."

Becky asked, "What do they want with us if they catch us?

Allen heard the question, but he would not answer her. He saw so much darkness with the gangsters and the organized crimes in his career; he tried so hard to keep it away from his daughter, but here she was.

They drove towards town in hopes if they needed help, it would arrive faster than if they went away from town. He thought he should contact Jon.

"Jon, after our conversation this evening, I discovered a tracking device in my pen. They know where we are, and we are in a bit of a situation."

Frustrated with it all, Jon asks, "Where are you? I assume you ditched the pen."

"Yes, I threw it in the box of a pickup truck in the Motel parking lot. I'm hoping for a break, and they didn't see me leave!"

At that time, a sedan pulls out to pass Allen on the road and swings sideways to a stop in front of them. Allen drove the suburban into the shallow ditch and back on the road, avoiding the sedan.

"No such luck, Jon. They are on me, and we are being chased!"

"Send me a pin, and I'll be on my way with the team!"

Allen gave his phone to Jen to send Jon a locating pin to their exact location. The car chasing him caught up and tried to get by them again. Allen lets them get passed them and turns the wheel hard, forcing the front of the Suburban into the rear of the sedan, forcing it to slide sideways down the road and finally flip over several times. Allen drove by the wreck and, as he came around a corner, met two cars side by side with their headlights on high beams coming down the road. This time, Allen could not enter the ditch, hitting one and careening off the road upside down. Allen was unconscious. Becky was trying to get out of her seat belt when a man came over and cut her belt off. He grabbed her by the scruff of the neck, pulled her out of the Suburban, and gave her to one of the others to tie up and put in the car. He then went back for Jen, who was conscious but beaten up badly from the accident, and pulled her out, kicking and screaming, until Anton came over and hit her in the face with his fist.

"Tie her up and throw her in the car with the other one."

He walked over to the driver's side of the car and gently put his finger on Allen's neck, feeling for a pulse.

"He's still alive, burn the car!"

Two of Anton's men scurried around, grabbed a container of gas from their trunk, and started splashing gas over the suburban and on Allen. As Allen slipped in and out of consciousness, he felt the horror of his family being torn from him. As the gas was poured on him, he knew what was coming but was unable to get clear of the steering wheel as it pressed firmly against his legs, pinning them against the seat, as he hung upside down in the cab of the Suburban. He watched the car with his wife and daughter leave to wherever, and thankful they did not have to see him burn to death, they were about to light the gasoline on fire when he saw the red and blue lights. He heard two shots, then a few more in succession, and the Russians took refuge in their car and left.

Sheriff Boreham happened to be driving from an accident and came around the corner to witness one car taking off while three men were splashing gas on Allen's Suburban. The Sheriff hit the switch for the flashing lights and siren on his car, and before the Russians could light it on fire, they left. Since the Sheriff recognized the suburban as an FBI unit, the Sheriff stopped to find Allen, and he was starting to regain consciousness. The Sheriff pulled Allen safely away from the car and called it in, requesting an ambulance. Soon after Jon came by,

"My God, what happened?"

Allen looked up at Jon and said, "They have my family. Those bastards have my family!"

The Sheriff looked at Allen, "If only I was just a bit sooner, I could have stopped this!"

Allen looked at the Sheriff, "Sheriff, you saved my life. If you got into a gunfight with all these guys, we both would have been killed!"

The ambulance arrived, and the medics checked Allen out, bandaging facial wounds. He road back home "wherever that might be tonight," and Jon helped him check in to one of the hotels close to the office.

"Go get yourself some sleep, Allen. You've been through a lot today."

Allen looked at Jon, "Really? I mean, put yourself in my shoes. Do you really expect me to sleep? I'm going to find them and shoot every one of them."

Jon looked at Allen, "What can we do at this hour, Alen? Everyone else is sleeping."

"Call in your team. I have two license plate numbers. That's where we start."

Allen answered his ringing phone, "Hey Allen, it's Kevin here. How's things!"

Kevin White was an old friend of Allen's from when he worked at the FBI. Kevin had a magnetic personality that attracted people. He and Allen spent time hunting and fishing occasionally and helped each other throughout their careers in the FBI. Before Kevin was requested to transfer to the CIA, they were partners as agents and worked very well together. They haven't gotten together much recently but often call each other up.

Allen did not want to let on about his situation, "Not bad, Kevin, and what about you?"

Kevin considered Allen's answer, "You have never answered that question. Not Bad, what's happening? Are you and Jen still together?

Allen answered him more upbeat, "Jeese Kevin, of course, we're still together. If I didn't know you better, I would think you were calling me to see if you could chase after her?" We are working on a challenging case right now, and I had my head buried in it when you called."

"Hey, I called to invite you on a fishing trip in Florida. They tell me the Grouper are biting these days."

"Love to Kevin, but I'm up to my ears for a while in this case."

Kevin ended the call with, "Hey, if you need help with that case, give me a call and give Jen a hug for me and send her my love, would you?"

"Ha, will do, Kevin. Take care."

17

His phone started ringing as it vibrated. Vlad reached for it on the armoire, "Anton, great to hear from you. How are things?"

Anton pauses for a second, unsure how to answer that question, "We have the two girls from the cabin."

"Very good, Anton, they are the wife and daughter of the FBI director, aren't they?"

Anton was careful in his wording, "Yes, they are, and he is dead. He had a vehicle accident."

Vlad smiled as he spoke, "Okay, I'll organize the boss's jet in the next couple of days. I need you to find out from them what they told the FBI after your incident at the Catskills. Also, check their phones for texts. The boss wants your mess cleaned up, no witnesses. The boss wants to fly them to Moscow to sell them for their limbs and organs or see if they will get a good price at the auction. He wanted to make sure they have been looked after permanently."

Anton replied, "Yes, I will do this."

Vlad was more serious now as he talked to Anton, "What about this program systems flash drive that our computer technician said went missing? That must be found. If it gets into the wrong hands, there is information on it that could bring down our business, and there is evidence of other business we do with several names, including yours."

Anton answered the only way he figured he could," the woman who took it died in the hospital yesterday."

Vlad was upset now, "That's good, Anton. Now you have a person and a location where it is. I give you forty-eight hours to get it. This is what the boss talks about when he says he wants everything neat and tidy, understand!"

Anton understood he was getting frustrated over the problems he had been faced with during the past few days. He needed to sleep; his team needed to sleep, yet the things that needed to be done became a longer list. He called up his team to tell everyone to go home and sleep.

He made some notes and jotted down a few notes about how to find that damn flash drive that was so important. Anton poured himself a generous glass of Vodka on ice and drank it down, then poured another, sipping it rather than drinking it. He went to bed while watching TV for a while, thinking, "Stupid American television," then turned the volume down to fall deep asleep.

When Anton woke, he heard the theme song to the Beverly Hillbillies show. Anton loved watching them because it was about stupid Americans, but he watched them because it made him laugh.

In the morning, he sent two of his men to the hospital to find Sharon's belongings. They were met by nurse Freson, who had spent a few years at the job. In her career, she had to put up with sisters, parents, girlfriends, and wives who came to her with every conceivable attitude most could imagine. She spoke perfect English; however, because her parents were of Russian descent, she spoke perfect Russian.

When Anton's men arrived and were directed to nurse Freson, they were a bit too arrogant with their inquiries.

"We don't have anything that belongs to Sharon Riley. Are you her family?" she asked.

"No, she doesn't have any family. Just give me her belongings."

Nurse Freson was getting angry, "Like hell, you two will get nothing of hers."

One of the Russians looked at the other and said in Russian, "stupid Bitch."

She told another nurse to call the police and said to the two Russians in their native language, "You are the stupid ones. If you think that by calling me a stupid bitch, I am just going to hand over all her stuff to you, you are both idiots."

The police arrived and got their statements of events of what had taken place, and they marched them in handcuffs into their patrol cars, taking them to the police station for questioning.

Jon went to the hospital the next day and talked to Nurse Freson once she arrived for her shift. "What were they after, just her belongings, or did they ask you and information about her?" Jon asked her.

"No, they were both adamant that I give them her belongings like they were entitled to them. They weren't family; there were no ties between them, yet they felt they deserved to have them, and they became upset that I wouldn't give them her belongings,"

Jon asked the nurse a few other questions, thanked her for her assistance, and gave her his card. Jon left the hospital and headed straight to where the two were detained to ask them a few questions. Jon wanted to know who the local leaders of the syndicate were. If they knew who they were, they would take them out and eventually cripple the organization.

Jon called Allen Fulton, the director, and brought him up to speed with the two Russians at the hospital, "It seems that all they were after was Sharon's belongings."

Allen cut in, "Sharon has either a story or a secret to tell us. Have someone go over to the hospital and press her for it. We need to get ahead of these guys."

"Great call, Allen. I have already dispatched agents Reg Hunter and Alisha Ketchell to interview her and provide security while she is in the hospital. I explained they needed to keep a low profile since she had been pronounced dead to keep her safe. What do you think about taking her to the same safe house as Jen and Becky?"

"Jon, I think that's a good idea for now. Of course, it depends on her interview."

18

Reg Hunter and Alisha Ketchell arrived at Room 238 at St Mary's hospital to provide security and to interview Sharon Riley after recovering from the stabbing she encountered. She was willing to talk and help the agents as she answered questions they asked, but she was assessing the two as if they were someone to trust in handing over the Russian flash drive she stole. She was still very sore, and occasionally, the agents would have to wait for answers until she resituated herself in a more comfortable position. The nurses would also delay some questioning as they would come in to check and record her vitals and to change out dressings.

Agent Ketchell established a connection with Sharon that Reg didn't, and he recognized this. Reg took a back seat in the interview process and would only ask questions that he had specifically to what was being talked about before Alisha changed the subject of questioning.

Sharon went through the whole story about the program, Joseph trying to sell the program, and that Standard Programing had nothing to do with the event. They asked about the security company's involvement, and she explained why they were there and the events leading to the first shot. She talked about her escape and how Jen and Becky fit into the escape. Before the agents left, Sharon asked about Jen and Becky. The agents informed her that they were not at liberty to discuss anything about the case.

"The mother, Jen, I believe, does her husband work for the FBI?"

Agent Ketchell answered her, "Yes, he is the director here."

Sharon looked at them closely, "I need to speak with him; could you arrange it?"

Agent Ketchell said to her, "Director Fulton has a full plate, Sharon, especially with his family's abduction. Anything you need to talk to him about, you can share with us."

Sharon replied, "I understand, but I must talk to Director Fulton, please."

The two agents returned to the office and reviewed the content of their interview with Sharon. The whole interview was recorded, and the notes that agent Hunter made while Alisha was taking the lead in the interview.

Agent Ketchell piped up, "At the end of the interview, she requested to talk with Director Fulton. She was adamant."

Jon spoke to both agents, "Allen talked about Sharon having a story or a secret that he wanted to get out of her. This may be the secret he was talking about. I will talk to him and have him go to the hospital and find out what she wants to tell him. Any idea when she will be discharged?"

Agent Hunter replied, "Within the next two or three days, they are running the last set of blood tests tomorrow, and we will see the outcome based on those results."

Jon thought about what the two agents told him, "That's fine, keep me well informed, and watch her room day and night. No one goes in without your supervision, Ok?"

The two agents agreed and left Jon's office; both felt the pressure that Jon was putting on them; however, it was most likely justified, considering the situation. When they returned to the hospital, they had a brief discussion with nurse Freson. They wanted to know where Sharon's belongings were located so they could also watch over them. She took them into a locked room with shelves of items from other patients that needed storage. She went over to an empty bin and was surprised there was nothing in it. She started looking around in the other bins with no success.

She stammered a bit, and finally, "It was right there. I put it in there myself!"

Ketchell started the questioning, "Is that door always locked? Who has a key?"

"It's a self-closing, self-locking door, you can't leave it open, and when it closes, it locks automatically." She stopped to think about the dilemma, "Maybe someone checked Sharon's stuff out. Let's check out the log."

As Agent Hunter left the storage room, he looked around the ceiling and spots two cameras, which were situated to cover every square inch of the room. As he leaves the room, he checks the self-closing operation and finds it closes as required. Before the door closed, he inspected the deadlatch assembly and found a tiny piece of wood wedged at the side. He opened his pocketknife, gently picked out the wood sliver, and placed it in a plastic bag for lab analysis.

By this time, he had the attention of both nurse Freson and agent Ketchell watch him as he worked with considerable detail and attention to the door lock. He then reached into his suit pocket and pulled out a toothpick. He turned the door handle to move the locking bolt inward to its fully open position and wedged his toothpick into the side of the bolt. Now Agent Hunter closed the door and then opened it without the key.

Hunter summarized, "Someone in this hospital did this so someone else could enter without a key. There are surveillance cameras mounted high on the corners of the walls. Where would we be able to view the video?" Agent Hunter then opened the door and picked out the toothpick he used; in doing so, he closed the door and demonstrated that it locks just fine.

Nurse Freson couldn't believe it, "Come with me, and let's go find this bastard!"

Agent Ketchell went to check on Sharon while Nurse Freson and agent Hunter looked at videos of the inside of the storage room. They ran the tape back to when Nurse Freson placed Sharon's belongings in the bin. They then ran the video ahead to find the person who put the toothpick in the door locking bolt. Then, the night after, the thieves who stole Sharon's belongings entered the room, and the other stayed outside as a lookout.

Nurse Freson was being very helpful, "The one who put the toothpick in the lock was out janitor, Wes Hewlett, but I don't know the other two who took her belongings."

Agent Hunter asked for Wes Hewlett's address, and after thanking her, he compiled a short report with pictures, identifying the need to get a search warrant for Wes's place, and sent it to Jon. Jon called him right back with a warrant and told him the SWAT team was on their way with four agents to arrest Wes and question him about the other two. Agent hunter stayed with Sharon while Agent Ketchell got some sleep on an extra cot they placed for the agents.

19

Director Allen Fulton entered Sharon Riley's room at St. Mary's hospital. She was bright-eyed and responsive to him entering her room.

"Hello, Miss Riley, my name is director Fulton of the FBI; I trust you are getting better?"

"Yes, the doctors say I will be out in two days. I'm looking forward to that."

Director Allen Fulton got to the point, "I understand you wanted to see me; here I am."

Sharon responded, "Your wife and daughter are Jen and Becky?"

Director Fulton answered, "Yes, they are; you met them when you escaped from the Catskills incident. Sharon, what do you need to talk to me about? I am busy with a pressing matter that we were hoping you could help us with. Our agents told me you had something that you wanted to talk to me about, that you felt you couldn't talk to them freely."

Sharon could tell he was a man of responsibility, "If you bring my purse over, I have something to give you."

Allen gets her purse and hands it over to her. She fumbles through all the contents of the purse and finally pulls out a strange-looking flash drive and hands it over to him.

"When Joseph and I were at the pond, the Russian computer tech had this to load the program into their system. When I retrieved my flash drive with the program on it, I had the opportunity to take it without anyone noticing it. Later, the computer tech was looking for it and accused me of taking it; that's when it hit the fan. I don't exactly know what it is, but I believe it might help your investigation."

Allen looks at the drive, "Thank you. I will have our computer people look at this in more detail."

"There is one other detail about me that you might need to know about."

She has Allen's total attention as she talks about being adopted, her research into finding her real parents after the hospital abduction of the two babies, and her discussion with the nurses and the DNA testing done. It was an intriguing story, but Allen was desperately trying to understand how this was pertinent to FBI business, particularly, this case.

Sharon read the confusion on his face and continued, "Everything led to Mikhail in Ruza just outside Moscow. I tried to get enough time off to see him, but of course, there was a language barrier. I don't speak Russian. So, after a month of researching, I found Mikhail's phone number and called him. I was grateful he spoke English, like many Europeans. I told him my story and, with some convincing, had him send hair and spittle samples so that I could have a DNA test performed. The test came back positive, and he is a family member, possibly an uncle or cousin. Considering his age, he would more likely be my uncle."

A flashback of despair hits Allen as he sinks into thoughts of Becky and Jen. He regains composure and starts to put this story all together. It wasn't working well for him. It seemed all over the place. He thought, is she a raving lunatic trying to bamboozle the FBI?

He decided to stop this whole thing, "Look, this was a great story, Sharon, but what the hell does this have to do with me and the FBI? Spell it out, please."

Sharon cuts to the chase, "I'm most likely the daughter of the sole person responsible for all this death and destruction. And the person who wants me killed! Since he has been trying to have me killed just like he killed my mother, I would do anything to help see the man die."

Allen was very surprised, not just about the story, but her honesty. It was full disclosure. He understood that Sharon needed protection and had her scheduled to go to a safe house immediately. Allen set up a sketch artist to get a visual on these guys they are dealing with and possibly facial recognition.

Now Allen had a much better understanding of what was happening here; there were still a few holes in the whole story, but still enough to work on.

Allen went back to the office once Sharon was in the safe house and the sketches were started. As he talked to Sharon, she talked about one Russian in particular, who was leading the gang. Allen also remembered the sheriff's people talking about one of the Russians who was giving orders. Sharon mentioned he was shot in the shoulder, and the sheriff's men said he was previously wounded because of blood on his shirt, and he was favoring it. He requested Sharon to have this Russians sketch completed first; when he left the safe house, they were well into it.

He arrived back at the office with Jon; he was going through the autopsy reports and the lab results of the evidence gathered. He gave a summary to Allen when he arrived. There was not much to go on other than some of the bodies were identified as Russian nationals who were in the US on vacation. The tox screen came back identifying two of the Russians were heavy users of Cocaine and had been intoxicated from Vodka. And they were able to track the Russians who died and identify those Russians still alive from the vast fingerprinting conducted at the sites, even though they do not know their names.

Allen was starting to pace. His family's well-being was being jeopardized every minute; they needed a break in the case. Jon spent hours interrogating the Russians arrested, but they were tight-lipped and not giving up a thing asking for a lawyer.

Allen walked through the war room towards his office. The analysts were madly following leads that they found from cell phone history and texts. One analyst was working on facial recognition of the sketches the artist submitted from her time spent with Sharon.

20

The analysts jumped up, "Got a hit off one of Sharon's sketches." He displays it on the big overhead monitor.

Allen yells out, "Let's go, everyone, Almar Rashid, 1492 Cedar Crescent SW. I want everyone on this: two SWAT teams, agents, and two ambulances on standby. Where's Jon?"

Jon comes in, "Let's go, everyone, have SWAT teams and an ambulance on their way, no sirens, silent approach."

Allen looks at Jon, "I should sit this one out, but if you find them, I want to know right away."

Jon runs through the war room, yelling back at Allen, "You can count on it, Allen."

When the FBI agents and the two teams of SWAT arrived at the little brownstone home on the quiet little cul-de-sac, everyone knew where they were to position themselves. One of the SWAT teams situated themselves at the front door with two agents ready to ram the door open. The second SWAT team was split up with two snipers covering both front and rear entrances as well as having exposure to the windows. Four agents were deployed, with two at the rear of the house working with the SWAT crew there. The home was surrounded, and the door was smashed in with the SWAT team charging through all three levels of the house, but no one was home. The agents and SWAT spent considerable time searching for some evidence indicating where Director Allen Fulton's wife and daughter may be located. There was nothing to link the abduction to the owner of the house. They left with nothing. This was not the big break they were looking for. Jon contacted Allen to give him the bad news. Allen was tired; he had been up for over twenty-four hours now, and his head was hurting bad. He took two pills and tried to rest on the sofa in his office. But the exhaustion and sleep deprivation were not the issue; it was the stress of his family constantly being under attack.

Jen and Becky were handcuffed and chained to a big pipe in a small room by themselves in a very uncomfortable position, so bad that sleep was almost impossible. Jen had been beaten up badly; there was dried blood from a wound in her mouth from when she got punched in the face. Becky was in relatively good physical condition, but she was scared. It was a lot for a fourteen-year-old girl to experience and to watch her mother so beat up.

One of the Russians came into the room.

"What is your passcode for your phone?!" He yelled at her.

Becky looked at her mother, "122435"

He picked up a phone and tried it, but it didn't work. He yelled at her, "I don't like being lied to!"

Becky screamed at him, "Mine is the other phone."

The Russian tried it, and Becky could see the display come on the phone. One of the other Russians opened the door to the room and wanted their abductor to see something in the adjacent room; he placed the phone down on the table before leaving. Once the door to the room closed and both Russians had left the room, Becky saw the opportunity and yelled out to the phone on the desk, "SIRI, call Dad."

Becky listened closely to hear the phone, "Calling Dad."

Allen was almost asleep. It felt so good to finally rejuvenate his deprived body with much-needed sleep, and he made a point to delegate some of his stressful responsibilities to Jon. It was soothing. He woke up immediately as the phone rang. His heart almost stopped when he looked at the display on his phone. It was Becky. He tried to listen, but he heard a distant voice he recognized.

He jumped up and ran out into the war room, yelling, "Track my phone call now!"

The Analyst's workstations blew up with activity as they tracked the call to an address and found the owner's name that was located approximately thirty minutes away. Jon flew into action as he dispatched SWAT, Helicopters, and all the agents available, including a few off-duty agents who volunteered should the need arise. Director Fulton was getting full support from his team on this case.

The army of SWAT Agents and helicopters converged upon the house and the occupants very fast, wasting no time in negotiation. There were SWAT officers who repelled the steady flow of helicopters, and agents penetrated the house's security guards swiftly and with one goal in mind: to get the director's family out.

Once everyone arrived, Captain Sam Gordon took over the deployment of the SWAT team. It was a huge house with a flat roof over most of the building, and the captain placed his men in key locations. The SWAT teams were in position controlling the roof and all four sides of the house. As standard practice, a SWAT team will be lead participants in the initial search. In this case, they had plenty of SWAT members on site, and Captain Gordon placed two groups, with one charging through the back door at the same time the charge was made through the front door.

There was little time wasted; with the SWAT and FBI coming through both doors, they initially ran into some heavy resistance, but as the Russians fell, so did the resistance. One of the Russians started a fire, which caused some issues as they had to put the fire out before it gained size; they had not found the director's family yet.

Jon ran through the carnage of debris and bodies, looking for Jen and Becky. He saw a door with a strange-looking lock on it and charged it, expecting to break it down, but was unsuccessful. Jon picked himself off the floor and signaled to one agent with a door ram. Once it was broken down, he was all smiles to see Jen and Becky. One agent grabbed the bolt cutters and cut the chains, and Jon removed the handcuffs, freeing them. They grabbed their phones from the desk, called Allen, and told them they were Okay. The ambulance was outside, and Jon took them to it for a check-over, especially Jen. In the privacy of his office, Allen started to cry.

21

It was a beautiful sunny spring day in the Comox Valley on Vancouver Island. Mike Stone was out feeding the cattle on his farm with his dog, Duke, and his pet cougar, Tigger. Mike had lived on the farm all his life. He truly considered himself fortunate to be able to live the life he wanted. He never dreamed of doing anything else or being somewhere else. He never considered traveling to a foreign country for a vacation. He was where he wanted to be. Mike was born in a little community just South of Courtenay on Vancouver Island and raised being an only child. He had great parents who gave Mike the freedom to explore his interests, supporting him when he wanted to go to college and later to university, and his passion for animals and guns.

He was a bit of a loner; he socialized with others and had lots of friends, but at 36, he never married, and he never found a woman whom he would be willing to spend the rest of his life on the farm. There was one that came very close though: his High School sweetheart, Jen. He fell in and out of love so many times with her that she got tired of waiting around and married his best friend, Allen. Allen knew that Mike really loved Jen, and when they were engaged, Allen had a talk with Mike about how guilty he felt, but he loved Jen and that he wanted Mike to be his best man. Mike explained that although he really loved Jen, he realized she would never be happy with him; she deserved to be married to him, and Mike accepted the role of best man at their wedding and wished the two of them a happy life together.

Allen Fulton was always destined to become something more than Courtenay could offer him, and he was accepted into the FBI academy in New York. When Allen and Jen came back home to visit family, they would always get together and have so much fun.

Jen was always making fun of Mike; he seemed like such good material for Jen to jeer him into humor; they were the best of friends. When Jen's parents passed, the visits seemed to end. Allen's career was skyrocketing. It was almost as though he was getting a promotion every time Mike called him. They were doing well, and Mike was genuinely happy for them.

Mike was saddling up his favorite horse he named "Festus," named after a TV character on a Western show called Gunsmoke. Like the character, Festus was a bit rough around the edges, but the smartest horse Mike ever trained, Mike thought Festus would be best described as sly as a fox, and Mike could always depend on Festus to do exactly what he wanted. The two of them would always volunteer to put on a good show for the crowd at the Annual Comox Valley Rodeo. The show was a humorous act that really showed everyone what a horse was capable of learning and doing, and where Festus was described in so many newspapers and TV shows across Canada as simply cunning.

Besides Allen, Jen, and Festus, Mike had two other best friends: his Rottweiler dog named "Duke" and a pet Cougar named "Tigger."

Tigger came to Mike's farm when two hunters in the high country found a baby cougar wandering down the road as they were driving up. The hunters had no idea what to do with it and brought the cub to Mike to see if he had any suggestions. Mike fell in love with the cub, brought it up on the farm, and kept it well-fed.

Mike mounted Festus and settled himself in the saddle; they left for the higher ridge. It was a beautiful scenic ride, especially when coming down into the meadows. Festus shook his head sideways several times as if to tell Mike he needed to lose some weight but finally decided to entertain the guy who fed him well and continued to take Mike where he wanted to go today. Close to the High Ridge, a stream flowed with the light noise of the water as it rolled over and fell off the smooth rocks that made up the creek. It was a creek that he would stop at ever since he was a kid to drink from on a hot summer day. Mike closed his eyes for a moment. It was so serene and so beautiful. The only noise was the wind in the trees and the occasional cow mooing for no apparent reason.

Mike opened his eyes and came to realize that chores must get done. And walked Festus to the hay barn and let Festus graze while he started up the old John Deere tractor and let the engine warm up a while. Mike used the loading fork on the tractor and selected a round bale to feed the cows with, and after pulling out the bailer twine, went back for another. As he watched Duke and Tigger attack one another as they played. Some of the mama cows showed a bit of concern when Tigger got too close to their calves, and Mike would call him back.

Mike recognized an old FORD pickup driving up to the gate at the entrance to the field. Ernie Ross had the farm adjoining his, and he and Mike got along well. Whenever Mike needed help, he would give Ernie a call and vice versa. Ernie was a character whose sole purpose in life was to make people around him laugh; that's why if you were looking for someone at a community function, you would most likely find them around Ernie.

Ernie gets out of his truck and looks at Mike, "Holy crap, would you take a look at the hood on that unit!"

Mike starts laughing, "So you noticed I got a haircut, did you?"

Ernie shakes his head, "Either that or ol' Festus mistook your hair for a mouthful of dead grass." Ernie changed the conversation to why he was there. "I noticed I had three extra cows in my herd this morning. I thought I'd come over and let you know since I didn't see you at the house, I figured I would check your fence back here."

"Thanks, Ernie. Once I finish feeding these cows, me and Festus will take a ride along the fence and check it out. I'll come over with the trailer and pick them up tomorrow if that's Okay."

Ernie smiled, "Sure, but it would be better for me if you came to pick them up late next week. We're planning on butchering this weekend."

Mike started to laugh as Ernie hopped in his truck to leave. He finished feeding the cows, put the tractor in the barn, and he and Festus started on their tour around the fence.

His cell phone started ringing. As he looked at the display, it was from Allen.

22

"Hello, father, how are you feeling today?"

The old man lying in the hospital bed looked frail and broken, barely able to breathe, let alone talk. He looked up at his son, very proud of the man he had become, a very powerful man who took the family business to a higher level than he dreamed possible; his son was an oligarch.

Once he was the man of power in his business, he gained respect, and people did what he told them to do. He taught his son well. The police and justice officials feared him, and he taught his son how to intimidate and take what he wanted. But now, the baton must be passed on to the next generation. His day had come and gone.

Andrei remembered the first time he took a man's life; his father was there, giving him encouragement and helping him through the emotional confusion he felt after. He felt proud that his father thought so highly of what he had done; they went out and celebrated with a nice dinner and a glass of wine. He later felt sick and threw up in the bathroom. His father knew and told him that the feeling you have now would fade the more you did it until finally, it became easy.

Andrei loved his father and would do anything for him. He spent millions of dollars on the development of the Mindsweeper program. This program, along with the American program, had the capability of reading and transferring the mind of one person into another body; it would give Andrei and his father immortality. Equally as important to Andrei, this program would enable him to program an army of master criminals. Time was of the essence for his father; the Mindsweeper program needed two things to run; the interface to connect with the mind, which was the program they got from Joseph McGee, and the other is the system program on the flash drive that Sharon stole, which allows all three to run simultaneously.

Andrei called Vlad to get an update on when he could send the jet to pick up the two girls and to find out if they had returned the systems flash drive that Sharon stole from them.

> Andrei was his usual miserable self, "So, you did not get the flash drive from that woman you killed, and you let the FBI director's family escape?"

> Vlad replied, "Well, the woman, Sharon, was killed, and the FBI found our safe house and overpowered us."

> Vlad could hear Andrei breathing heavily on the other end of the phone, "These are just excuses, Vlad. When they went to kill this Sharon, why did they not find the drive on her then? As for the FBI finding the safe house, you are not being careful enough; you are not being smart enough. Why can't you stay ahead of them? They are obviously staying ahead of you. You know I don't like potential witnesses; I like running a neat and tidy business. That's why I have been so successful; that is why I stay out of jail, understand?"

> Vlad knew he was right; he needed to take responsibility. "I will be leaving for New York this week and take a hands-on role to get all this straightened out."

> Andrei was short, "Good, tell me when it's all cleaned up! The return of the system flash drive is a time-sensitive priority."

Vlad did not want this; his leadership to run the business has been questioned, and he has failed Andrei. He needs to call Anton and inform him he is coming this week to help him get his business under control. He would have him complete the return of the flash drive from Sharon's personal items.

Vlad started to concentrate on what his organization needed to do to clean up these witnesses. He had his best man looking after things out there, but for some reason, it is becoming worse every day. The FBI is getting in the way of everything they plan. Maybe he should go out there and take care of this director, just kill him; that's all that needs to be done. Vlad thought he would delegate some responsibilities and leave himself.

He called Andrei to inform him of his plans, and Andrie shut him down,

> "Do you not have good people out there? Why do you need to go, let them manage this, if Anton can't do what we need him to do, then get rid of him and find someone else better that can complete the job. Have you forgotten what we are trying to accomplish here?"

> Vlad answered him, "No, I have not forgotten. We need more people."

Building up to the Russian Revolution, which started in 1917 under the rule of Nicholas II, Russia was being thrown into hard economic times, resulting in shortages of food and supplies for most people. The Russian army was steadily losing morale, and large-scale mutinies were present due to a shortage of food, clothing, supplies, and logistics issues, as well as the army had been defeated in numerous battles. Then Tsar Nicholas II entered World War One, creating an even greater economic pressure on the country and the people. Nicholas's high-ranking officials, along with the Bolsheviks convinced Nicholas II, that if he were to stand down as Russia's monarch, the unrest would subside. He agreed, and over time, the Bolshevik's established the government in Russia under Lenin. Trotsky, under Lenin was concerned about Russia's army and developed methods for the army to overcome their morale issue. Some of the methods were more experiential than anything. But the battlefield turned around, and Russia's army was winning, and morale improved tremendously.

Andrei studied what Trotsky had done and tried to simulate some of the trial experiments on his own people. He was very focused on developing an elite criminal force and taking control of countries by crippling their economic stability through criminal activity his organization committed, but they had to be the best. He also studied the Mindsweeper program the KGB developed, and he found Sergei to update and further develop to achieve his dream. He is so close; nothing will stand in his way, especially not this girl, Sharon, and not these witnesses. Andrei thought of his father; he wanted this program to work to transfer minds into younger bodies so he and his father could experience immortality. It will be beautiful; he is so close to his dream.

Andrei smiled as he fell asleep.

23

The training commander, Tig Armstrong, for special forces within the FBI, walked to the podium at the front and addressed the group of twenty-six agents selected for the advanced hands-on training,

> "Good morning, ladies and gentlemen; the next phase of your advanced training will include some of the most intense hand-to-hand combat you will encounter. Generally, for this kind of training, we would have an in-house instructor; however, I have found a contractor to perform this training instead because, quite frankly, I have not seen anyone who equals what Josie Santos is about to teach you. Josie"

She walked from the rear left side of the classroom and navigated her five-foot-seven-inch body up the middle between two rows of tables to the podium. She walked with confidence and purpose, and she caught the eyes and attention of all in attendance; she was in control. She was obviously fit, and her posture was perfectly straight as she walked, her long brown hair gently swayed with each step. She wasn't wearing make-up, she didn't need it, she wasn't there to make a fashion statement.

She had conducted many training sessions since Tig first brought her on board and she found most students come to the sessions to learn, but there were always those few that come to play the fool. It was her job to make sure they all left with the skills and knowledge, and enough hands-on experience for them to use what she taught them effectively in the field. As she walked up towards the podium, she heard one student as he whispered to the other,

" I wouldn't mind getting it on with her," and he started giggling like a little kid.

Josie took note of his name. She had everyone's attention as she introduced herself and gave herself as an example of what a smaller stature is capable of against a larger opponent.

> She got right into it, "The exercises will be hand to hand only; however, they will be in full contact. Does everyone understand full contact?"

> She paused to see if anyone needed clarification, then continued, " Great, so let's start off with an example of what I was just talking about. Mr. McEnroe, as I walked past you on my way to the podium, I heard you whisper to another student that you would really like to get it on with me. Well, McEnroe, today you get your wish; you are first up, but I must warn you, I like it rough. Now the objective of these exercises is that the first one to put the handcuffs on the other wins the bout, **ON THE MATS MCENROE, FRONT AND CENTER!"**

McEnroe stood up, and with a cocky smile, he started walking to the mats at the front of the classroom. He was six foot three inches tall and in good shape. He was being jeered by those in the class who knew him as a black belt in Jujitsu, and they were waiting to see how she was going to handle this. He had a smart-ass grin on his face as they faced off towards each other.

Tig stopped what he was doing to watch McEnroe get put in his place; he loved to see how she handled students who showed her the slightest disrespect. It's a hard lesson learned. He had watched her lead off the training many times and liked the way she got into the demonstrations right away, which gave her so much credibility with the students. With the class watching the time on the clock, it started as McEnroe grabbed her left arm with his right hand. In a split second, she responded by placing her right hand over his with her fingers peeling his hand off hers. As she did, she cupped his wrist and turned her body, giving her the opportunity to apply additional leverage. This twisted McEnroe's arm, causing his shoulder to start pulling out of joint. She then kicked him in the nose hard as he bent forward; she then kicked him again in the crotch. As he laid face down, yelling with pain, the class noted they heard the click of the handcuffs within fifteen seconds. She released the handcuffs and asked him if he wanted to see that move again for study purposes. He declined, and the rest of the students started laughing. McEnroe would be only one of the many showing up tomorrow with black eyes, but McEnroe would never make another inappropriate remark about Josie. Tig Armstrong tried to conceal his laughing, and finally left the training room.

Tig Armstrong walked up to Josie after the session.

He called her name to get her attention and asked her to her in a very formal manner, "Josie, you have been requested to be a part of a special assignment. I can't tell you what, and I can't tell you where, but because you are a contractor, you have the right to refuse since there is the potential of being killed."

Josie spouts up, "Not easy to decide based on that description, Tig. How long do I have to get back to you with my decision?"

Tig answers as he points to an executive jet outside the hanger, "In about thirty seconds, you will be boarding that executive jet."

Josie starts laughing, then gets serious when she realizes that Tig was not kidding, "But I need to pack and take a shower!"

Tig hands her flight documents and a fake passport, "You will be traveling under a different name; this assignment is of a high-security level, don't tell anyone or talk to anyone. You can buy what you need when you get there. Have a nice flight!"

Josie protested, "But I didn't say I would go."

Tig looked at her with a cracked smile and said, "You didn't tell me that you wouldn't, and your thirty seconds are up."

Josie shakes her head as she heads towards the plane and whispers to herself, "Oh, what the hell!" She considered that she had no idea who her contact would be and yelled out to Tig, "Hey Tig, who is my contact? How will I find him?"

Tig yelled back, "he will find you."

24

Allen heard the cell phone ring, and finally, a familiar voice answered, "Hello, Allen, you're quite a stranger in these parts. How the heck are you guys doing?"

Allen knew the politically correct answer would be "Great, couldn't be better," but this was his best friend in the world, and he needed his help.

Instead, Allen answered, "We've been better, Mike; where are you at right now?"

"Remember that old pine tree we used to climb when we were young, the one you fell out of and broke your arm? Well, I'm sitting down with my back against it, chucking rocks into that little stream we used to drink from."

"Is there anyone around you that could hear our conversation?" Allen asked.

Mike chuckled, "Yea, old Festus can probably hear you. He's close enough to trick me into giving him some sugar cubes."

There was no comeback, jeering, or laughing, he was very serious and not interested in humorous dialog. This was not the Allen that Mike knew. He let Allen ramble on until finally, Mike asked him point blank,

"Allen, what the hell is going on down there, are you okay, is Jen and Becky all right?"

Allen regains his composure, explaining the whole story to Mike in detail. The conversation lasted so long that Mike thought his cell phone would soon run out of battery. Allen finally finished the explanation with,

"And on this last abduction, they beat up Jen a bit."

Mike jumped all over it, "Hey, you want me down there, or do you want to send Jen and Becky up here? I'll look after them either way?"

Allen answered him, "What I need is for you to look after them until I can get this straightened out. Before you answer, I want you to have a clear understanding that these guys are ruthless, and they won't stop. They just keep coming. The total law enforcement deaths are up to fourteen, with another six in the hospital injured. Mike, if they follow the girls to Canada, your life would be in jeopardy. Also, there is a Sharon Riley who is also up to her ears in this mess. She would also need to come, and finally, I would be sending a bodyguard as well to help you."

Mike took it all in, " Sure, what about you, are you okay?

Allen was quite relieved that Mike would look after the girls, "Yes, thanks, I'm okay. I'm on my burner phone at my office in my office, so I feel I can speak freely knowing there is no one there at your end to listen in. I'll fly you to Calgary, where the girls will be entering Canada and you can pick up a rental there and drive back; hopefully, it would knock them off the trail for a while. Jen and Becky, Sharon and Josie will be leaving within the next day or two. I can't thank you enough, Mike."

"Hey no problem Allen, for you, Jen and Becky, anything, just ask."

Allen had fake identity documents made up for the four girls, as well as Mike. He made plane reservations in three different destinations and scheduled a corporate jet to fly to Calgary, Alberta, Canada. He also made reservations for Mike from Comox airport to Calgary for a one-way flight. Allen made a list of items, such as ear wicks, wildlife cameras, and 12 gauge shotgun shell brackets, that Mike may need. Jen and Becky were at another safe house for the time being, but he knew it was only a matter of time until they found them at this safe house and planned another abduction.

Allen picked up his burner phone and called his wife, "Jen, I want you to pack some things in a bag for you and Becky, just essential items. I want you to go to the Island. I talked to Mike, and he will look after you guys until I can get this resolved here. It may take a while because its source is from Russia and because of the political relations between the two countries."

Jen responded, surprised, "What about you, Allen? You are left in a dangerous situation without your family to help you. Send Becky, and I'll stay with you."

Allen thought about it for a short time, "No, I want someone I trust to look after you. I can't resolve this if I am constantly distracted by your safety. I want you to go; please don't make this more difficult than it already is. Buy what you need on the island if you forget something. There will be two others going on the same plane. Do not say anything to anyone. You will be leaving tomorrow at 2:15."

The FBI agents want to place the family in another safe house, rotating them through the twelve established safe houses in New York. Allen was under a great deal of pressure and decided to take his own family tomorrow afternoon to the executive jet hanger himself. No one was going to know where they were going to or that they even left the country, including his own men.

When Allen left the safe house in the morning for work, he took the bags with him, leaving them in the suburban. In the late afternoon, when it was time to pick up Jen and Becky, they just got in the suburban without bags. The FBI security agents saw them and started asking questions such as where are you going? When will you be back? Do you want us with you? Allen and his family left without obligation to answer any of the questions. The trip to the hangar was stress-free as there were no traffic jams from rush hour traffic at this time of day. Sharon was there when Allen and his family arrived, and Josie showed up just as they arrived at the hangar. Allen introduced everyone to Josie and helped them board the jet. As they were boarding, he took Josie aside, thanked her for coming along, and explained the situation a little more to her so she would understand the secrecy. And he gave her his card along with a credit card and told her to get whatever she needed. A huge weight came off Allen's shoulders as he watched the jet take his family to safety.

25

When Allen returned to the FBI office, he was bombarded by questions. Allen's boss, Sven Olsen, walked into his office and closed the door behind him; the frown on his face told Allen quite a bit; he was mad as hell.

"What the hell do you think you are doing, Allen? These guys are crawling all over your family, and you just send them off somewhere unknown, and you think these guys won't find them!"

He knew Allen well; Sven was responsible for most of Allen's promotions, he knew how Allen thought, and he knew how much he loved Jen and Becky. Whoever is looking after them at the other end, must be someone Allen knows well and is confident they have the capabilities to deal with an army of some of the most ruthless criminals, and his family will be looked after. He took everything into consideration.

"Of all the people, you are the one whose family is at risk, and you are the one who knows more about organized crime than anyone else. I guess with that in mind, you must think you acted appropriately; where did you send them?"

He paused for some time as Allen just looked at him. He was thinking if Allen broke any FBI policies and determined he had not. As long as he has his faculties in order, and it appeared he did. This must have been a traumatic experience for him, he was thinking, should he be pulled from this case? If so, it was too late now.

"Okay." He said, "But if you step out of line going forward, I will have to take you off the case, understand?" He looked at Allen again, "And I don't understand why you won't tell me where you sent them."

Allen was a little ticked, "It's best you don't know, sir."

Sven, the District Deputy Director of the FBI, had just returned to his office when William Townsend, the District Deputy Director for the CIA in New York, stormed into his office.

"What's going on with this Fulton family situation? Do you have them guarded in a safe house?

Sven thought hard on this, "And what business is it of yours or the CIA?"

William frowned, " it's all part of our investigation into Andrei Volkov. We need to make sure the family he is after is safe. If not, our investigation could trigger him to take adverse action against them, and then we are dealing with a situation worse than they are presently in. Sven, you have to agree with me. We don't want that, do we?"

"William, I have been told by the case director and the husband and father of the family that the family is safe and well looked after."

"That's good to hear, Sven; thank you."

After William left his office, he called Allen to tell him that he had just been contacted by the CIA, and they were concerned about the safety of his family. He called Allen more to confirm that he has his family well looked after rather than try to find out where they are. Allen confirmed that they were safe and they were well looked after, but Allen never alluded to where they were. Allen never divulged additional information, and Sven never pressed him.

Allen called his contact in the CIA to find information on the Russian crime syndicates to better understand what he should be focused on in dealing with this mess. He left a message for Kevin White to return his call. Allen thought the Russians might give up on chasing his family in Canada. There would be no reason for the chase unless, as Sven said, there is more to the story. He considered the Russians may have the perception that his family witnessed more than they did, in which case there would be more to the story. Allen decided to open his investigation to include more about what actually took place at the Catskills. He believed they got as much information from Sharon as she knew. He also believed she was being truthful and open about the incident, as well as the contributing facts leading up to it.

It was twelve-thirty, and Allen left the office for lunch. He needed the time away from the office. He was starting to have self-doubts. Should he have brought Mike in on his mess? Was it fair to him? Did he set him up for failure? Allen shook his head. He had a flashback of being pinned inside his vehicle and the Russians pouring gas on him with the intent of lighting him on fire. He could see Jen getting punched in the face and both Becky and Jen getting drug to a vehicle screaming.

Allen entered the restaurant, found a table to sit at, and waited for the waitress to bring him his usual Diet soft drink. She brought him his soft drinks while waiting for him to place his order. Ten minutes later, she brings him a Reuben sandwich on rye with Greek salad. He knew the waitress, and after some small talk, she asked him if there was anything else and gave him the bill for the meal, and she left.

Allen looked around the restaurant while he ate, noticing a few people he recognized, including Kevin White. Allen watched Kevin while he was talking to two men, explaining something to them and having difficulty with it. It appeared to Allen they were speaking a foreign language that Kevin wasn't picking up well. Allen continued to observe that there was always the chance of him being undercover, and he did not want to blow a possible cover.

As they walked past Allen on their way out of the restaurant, Kevin looked at him with a concerned look on his face as the other two talked to themselves in Russian. Once they left, Allen shoved the remaining piece of the Rueban in his mouth, and he followed them outside, keeping well out of sight.

Allen took out his notepad from his suit jacket pocket and his pen and, wrote the license plate numbers from all three vehicles and returned to the office.

Allen walked into the FBI office building and straight to Lee Magnason's office with the license plate numbers, " Lee, run these plate numbers for me, please. They are from some Russians who met up with Kevin White at a restaurant that I just ate at.

" I'll have it done right away and get back to you as soon as I have information."

26

Mike had precious little time to get ready. After talking to Allen, he realized he had to focus on details and worst-case scenarios and prepare for the battle he spent time preparing for when he was nineteen.

When Mike was nineteen, there was a great deal of concern over the Chinese and the Russians invading Western Canada. And at the time, he was young, and he got caught up in the conspiracy theories that Vancouver Island would be the first to get attacked. Over the following year, Mike did his research and consulted individuals with military training to understand strategies and preventable measures better. That's where he met Charlie Perkins.

Charlie Perkins was a sniper who was able to see how the attacks were affected by small things that could have changed the outcome of the battle. Charlie was retired and had nothing better to do than talk about his life's work and his passion with Mike. As a sniper, he taught Mike a lot about long-range accuracy and trajectories as well.

Mike asked Charlie to come to the farm to show him examples of the scenarios that Charlie talked about. It gave Mike a whole new way of visualizing battles and strategies on how to deal with them. As they spent time in each area of the farm, Mike took notes and developed fortifications and shelters to hide and attack from. Charlie also showed him other tricks he learned, but more importantly, Charlie taught him how to think. After a year, Mike concluded that the Russians and the Chinese were not going to invade Vancouver Island. He also wouldn't be saving the world. He took all his notes and diagrams that he made from his discussions with Charlie and put them all in a box under the spare bed; today, Mike was thankful he saved them.

As Mike reviewed the notes and diagrams he saved, he remembered the conversations and the examples that Charlie gave him. He recalled the point when Charlie tested him, and after he answered him, he would say to Mike, "Yep, you got it now!" It felt so good to hear his mentor say that to him, he had come a long way, to get to this point. Mike chuckled a bit when he remembered how disappointed he was when he realized he would never use any of the skills that Charlie taught him. It wasn't until Mike grew up that he realized that throughout life, we often deal with battles to some degree, and what Charlie taught him helped him deal with the many pitfalls in life.

He put the notes away and got started. The first thing was to call a moving company and load all his belongings from the house, except for the beds, placed into storage. He was preparing for an invasion.

He made a list of items he needed to buy, mostly ammunition and non-perishable food. He had four places to hold up and needed to stock each place with the same amount of ammunition, bows, arrows, food, and explosives. Should this escalate, the ten cases of dynamite he bought to blow up beaver dams will come in handy. He designed escape routes for each location should there be a need to move on. Mike spent enough time at each site to visualize the Russians coming for them, and he placed the dynamite in key areas with a cell phone detonation device, recording each phone number and location in his phone contacts.

Upon returning to the farm, Mike loaded his horses, except for Festus, and transported them to a friend's farm to look after them. He then made sure the cattle were in the back pasture, it had a creek running through one corner of it for them to get drinking water and far enough away from harm's way. He moved his new vehicles to a friend's place to keep them from getting damaged while leaving the old farm truck for their use.

Once the animals were looked after, he worked on the perimeter of the farmhouse. Mike set up trip wires hooked to dynamite mines along the South entrance and in the bushes surrounding the house. Mike remembered Charlie saying one of the things overlooked by either side of a battle was the lack of suitable escape.

He filled up the farm truck with fuel and checked the batteries in the drones, making sure everything was operational. He converted the root cellar in the basement into a safe room in case someone had to hide, and he shored up the outside entry so no one could gain access. Mike set up action-sensitive cameras around the house, primarily in the blind spots that were difficult to see from windows, and built a bulletproof cubical in the house out of quarter-inch steel in case they took on heavy fire. Mike grabbed his packsack and placed items he thought may come in handy if they were on the run—things like rope, tie-straps, batteries, additional knives that he had and his guiles suit.

Mike packed a bag for the trip to Calgary. In addition to clothes for the trip, he packed rope and tie straps to tie someone up and restrain them if necessary. Mike set up adequate escape plans for each hiding place. It took him all day and all night, and he almost missed his flight to Calgary the next afternoon. The only thing left was to make reservations for the rental truck in Calgary; he was ready now.

Mike boarded the plane, found his seat, stowed his carry on, and soon fell deep asleep after sitting in his seat. Throughout his dreams, he saw Jen as he remembered her in High School. He was picking her up to take her to the community dance. She was beautiful.

After an hour and a half of flying time, Mike was woken by an announcement over the PA system, notifying passengers the plane was starting its descent into Calgary airport. The flight attendants were scurrying up and down the aisle, picking up garbage from the passengers during the flight, and the person next to him was getting his briefcase below the seat in front. It appeared every passenger on the plane decided to get up at the same time to visit the bathroom during descent, making the attendants' job more difficult.

Mike could see the ground now and was looking to see what all the farmers were doing as the plane flew over. All the farms in their individual squares reminded him of a patchwork quilt his mother once made.

27

Mike went directly to rent the truck he reserved and drove over to the Executive hanger nearby and spotted the four girls. He hardly recognized Becky.

He came up behind them when no one was around the plane and "Hey everyone, great to see you again! How was the flight?"

He gave everyone a hug and introduced himself to Josie and Sharon.

Mike moved close to Jen, "I see you are sporting a fat lip and a black eye, you, okay?"

Jen replied, "Yep, but if I recognize the SOB that gave it to me, I want you to give him one back for me, Okay?

Mike smiled, "You got it, sister."

"My traveling name is Gary Taggart. It will take a while to get used to it, but Allen picked it out. Man! Is it ever great to see you again? I hardly recognized Becky."

Becky added, "You look the same as I remember you, Uncle Mike, I mean Uncle Gary!" Mike grabbed a luggage cart, "We can put the baggage on here. Just let me know when you see your baggage when it's unloaded; I rented a big assed pickup so we can all have some room." Jen piped up and said, "Big assed pickup, eh? You haven't changed a bit."

Becky added, "Ya, we all expected a fancy James Bond car with fancy gizmos that shoot things."

Laughing, Mike loaded the two small bags on the cart, reading the tags before he did, and commented to Jen, "I bet this is the least amount of clothes that you have ever packed on a trip. What about you, Josie? I don't see your bag?"

Josie replied, "I didn't get to pack or even take a shower."

Mike exclaimed, "That's terrible!"

Jen intervened and added, "Allen told us to buy whatever we wanted when we got to the Island."

Becky corrected her mother, "No, Dad told us to buy whatever we needed."

Everyone laughed at that and got seated in the truck's cab. As they left Calgary, they bought some take-out Chinese food and continued West. As they started through the Rocky Mountains past Canmore, both Sharon and Josie mentioned it was their first time seeing mountains of this magnitude and beauty.

Sharon asked, "How long a trip is it from Calgary to our destination, Mike?"

"About 12 hours to Vancouver, and then we take the ferry across to the Island and another hour and a half drive to the farmhouse where everyone will be staying."

Josie's eyebrow rose, "Are there no airports in Vancouver?"

Jen answered for Mike, "The idea was that if they were trying to follow us, they would have a difficult time tracking us from Calgary to the Island if we drove."

Josie nodded, and Mike wanted to know a bit about Josie, "So, since you are my best friend's bodyguard, tell me about yourself?"

Reflecting, Josie explained, "Well, I don't remember a lot of my childhood. I bounced around from foster home to foster home in Panama until I was placed with the Santos family, who were incredible people. They supported me throughout school and put me through martial arts training, and they came to all my school and martial arts functions and tournaments. I was told they both passed away in a terrible traffic accident when I was seventeen, and I worked as night security at a refinery while I stayed at the house and graduated and completed college. I was fortunate that I picked up martial arts very quickly, and I presently work for the FBI as well as Black Ops. as an advanced hand-to-hand combat instructor to the fourth-year and up-field agents."

Mike exclaimed," holy shit, that is very impressive Josie!"

Becky added, "Could you teach me?" Josie turned to her and said, "Absolutely".

"What about you, Sharon? I understand you have quite a story?"

Mike wanted to understand why she was there. Sharon told them the whole story, explaining that she was adopted, wanting to know who her paternal parents were, and the abduction she learned about in the Hamburg hospital. She went on to tell them about the DNA testing and her conversation with the retired nurse Helena. Then she told them about the conversation she had with Mikhail and the outcome of the DNA testing with him. Then she told everyone she planned to go to Ruza at some point to talk to Mikhail, to learn more about her mother, and to learn more about her father. Then she explained that she was a computer programmer and the events leading up to the attack at the pond where Jen and Becky found her injured, then finally being stabbed, and left for dead in the hospital.

Mike was blown away by Sharon's story, "it is totally unbelievable to what length these guys will go. Now I understand why Allen wanted me to hear your story."

Jen and Becky added their story to Sharon's and concluded that these guys wanted to kill them all, and they didn't really know why.

Josie realized there would be a lot of opportunities to get to know everyone on the trip and was especially interested in Mike's background and asked, "So Mike, tell me a bit about yourself. Since we are going to be working together, I would Like to know a bit about you."

Jen butted in to comment, "Oh, this should be fun, eh Mike."

Mike smiles and shakes his head a couple of times, "Behave yourself, Jenney!"

Josie starts it up again, "You guys obviously know each other. Where did you meet?"

Mike answers, "Grades 1 through 12 and a few more years after, I was the best man at Allen and Jen's wedding before they left for New York." He paused, then "I stayed on the farm after dad passed, and now, I'm doing what I like to do, farming and stuff."

Josie paused a moment and thought that there had to be more to this guy than just being a good ol' down-home farm boy.

Jen starts the conversation again, "What did you take in university, Mike?" "Animal behavior?"

Josie asks, "Why animal behavior, Mike?

He answered, "To better understand animals, I guess, to train them better, more of a hobby."

Josie wanted more, "So you train dogs for people?"

"Well," Mike said," Mrs. Calvert had a dog that wouldn't stop barking. I got that fixed for her."

Jen looked over at Josie, "Don't ask how he did it; I know Mrs. Calvert."

Both laughed while Becky Listened to her music.

Josie was determined to get more out of Mike, "So what was the most difficult animal that you have had to train Mike?"

"My cat," he answered.

Jen buts into the conversation, "Jeese Mike! Your cat was the most difficult to train?"

Mike started laughing, "But you haven't seen my cat!"

Josie and Sharon were envisioning a deaf and blind house cat with long claws.

Both said in unison, "Can hardly wait, Mike!" The laughter was keeping the trip enjoyable and making the miles go by quickly,

Mike had to keep it going, "Oh yeh, the cows aren't too quick to catch on either."

"You train your cows?" Sharon questioned.

Mike answered, "Yep, but don't go up to them expecting to shake a paw." This time, everyone, including Becky, was laughing.

Jen tried again to get Mike to talk about himself so Josie could get some idea of his value in the situation,

"Tell us all about what you took in college, Mike?"

He answered Jen, "Gunsmithing, bullet re-loading, and gun building. I can build a gun for most all calibers out of just about anything."

Josie intervened, "Is that why you took the course to build guns?"

Mike answered, "Kind of; it was Charlie Perkins, a sniper in the Canadian military base out of Comox, who taught me everything I know about long-range accuracy."

Jen added, "Mike has won long-range competitions and used to teach reloading and long-range shooting to the people interested in the sport. Do you still do that, Mike?"

"Yes, I do." Mike said, "And I helped a few young people who I knew were interested in skeet shooting as well, but not much lately. Tom Henderson, one of my students, has taken that over for me now. I got myself into bows and crossbows, won a few competitions, and helped a few kids interested in the sport. I still build custom rifles for people."

Jen added, "Mike has always been known in the area for his marksmanship and the quality of guns that he builds. He has probably built every rifle that has been used in competition on the Island. He's also handy with pipe bombs. Tell Josie and Sharon the story about the church roof, Mike."

Josie asks, "Pipe bombs?"

28

The conversation paused as they navigated through a small town, searching for a coffee shop. They finally came across a sign displaying CRABBY BOB's COFFEE with a neon OPEN light in the window, and the gang all decided to try it. It was originally a house that was renovated into a coffee shop and advertised rooms as well. The lady behind the counter greeted the group with a smile and suggested we choose any table we wanted. Once seated, she brought over a carafe of coffee and some cups for us to help ourselves to the coffee and asked them if they wanted anything else. Mike observed the activity of the other clients in the dining room. Some came in for tea or coffee, some for dessert, and one fellow who had a full meal, which Mike figured was the driver of the semi-truck parked outside. Everyone finished ordering, had their bathroom breaks, and were all seated at the table.

Jen waited for the waitress to come to their table with their order to resume the conversation they were having in the cab of the truck, " So, tell us about this pipe bomb Mike."

It obviously startled the waitress as she hit a glass of water with a coffee mug and almost dumped a cup of coffee on Mike's lap.

"It wasn't a pipe bomb, Jen; that was a different story. When I was 15, my dad and I were trying to help old man Hendricks take out a stump from a section of his field he was cleaning up. It was directly across the road from the Little United church. My dad looked at the stump and figured that because of its size and the fact it was well rooted in clay, it would take three sticks of dynamite to remove it instead of just one. Well, he was wrong because when the dynamite went off, it blew the stump clear out of the ground, up in the air, across the highway, and came down on the church roof. To his last day, my dad would never blow stumps on Sundays. I also learned quite a bit about repairing a roof as well."

Josie said, "I bet that was the last time you ever used dynamite."

"Hell no!" Mike blurted, "I have ten cases at home."

Josie exclaimed, "What on earth do you have ten cases for?"

Mike started laughing, "For a real big stump, a long way away from a church."

Jen asked Mike, "I love hearing that story about the tracker guy that you spanked really hard. Tell Josie and Sharon about your encounter with him."

Mike was feeling uncomfortable and said, "No, I don't want to talk about that, poor guy. I felt sorry for him."

Jen cuts in, "Okay, then I'll tell them. There was this TV show called Tracker, and it was about this hot shot tracker who would track people in the bush. The object of the show was for both the runner and the tracker to start at the same point, and the runner would try to get to a pre-determined spot before the tracker saw him. The tracker would give him a three-hour lead before chasing after him, and at 14, Mike took the challenge and was accepted. Mike knew the area well, and on that day, Mike led him into a huge marsh area where there were water channels throughout the whole area. Mike kept walking the area until he found a log that would carry his weight, and he hopped on it, polled his way through the marsh, and got off the log and out of the marsh, arriving at the destination in plenty of time to win the challenge."

Sharon asked, "What happened with the tracker?"

Jen answered, "He never did find a single track to follow. Then the tracker guy started with the excuses, not being happy being beaten by a 14-year-old kid, Mike offered to have a re-match, but the guy would not accept. The show ended shortly after that."

Josie thought it admirable that Mike wouldn't want to talk about the way he showed up that tracker. She thought he was very humble and modest about himself. Most guys she knew would jump at the opportunity to tell that story in a way that would make them sound like a superhero. Even though she still wanted to know more about Mike Stone, she was developing a very positive first impression of him.

The night was dark, and Josie, Sharon, and Becky were fast asleep. Jen was talking to Mike about where this person was and what that person was doing. She hadn't been back for so long, and it was good to catch up with the people she grew up with. She changed the conversation towards more of a heart-to-heart talk. She was curious to see if he still wanted the farm life and being alone if he ever thought about moving to a city and meeting someone.

Mike answered, "I love my life. I get to do the things I like to do. It's quiet, and I love the animals. When I have the desire to go to the city, I just pack my bag and go to one for a while, and when I come back, I feel grateful for my lifestyle."

Jen added, "Aren't you lonely?"

"Sometimes, but not often."

It was about 2:00 am when they arrived in Merit and pulled into a 24-hour gas station with a coffee shop. They ordered a coffee and a snack and sat down to rest from driving; Mike had driven from Calgary and needed a break.

Jen asked, "Mike, you want me to drive for a bit?"

Mike replied, "No, I will be OK. I just need to rest my eyes. It's only three more hours to the ferry."

At this time of the morning, there was no one in the coffee shop. Shortly after Mike and the girls arrived, two burly-looking guys came in and just ordered coffee. Mike recalled the clients in CRABBY BOB's. He remembered the customers were interacting with each other or at least drinking the coffee they ordered. As Mike watched these two guys, he noticed they were not talking to each other, nor were they drinking their coffee. Mike put two and two together, and since these two were not there to drink coffee or get together with their buddies for a good conversation, they must have been there for them.

29

Mike got up and went over to the waitress, who was on the opposite side of the coffee shop, to the two men.

He asked her, "Without looking at them, can you tell me if those two men by the entrance door were local residents?"

She answered him, "Never saw them before."

Mike thanked her and slipped her a twenty, then paid the bill for their table.

He went over to the two men and asked, "Hey guys, I noticed you are not talking to each other or drinking the coffee you ordered. Do you not like the coffee, or are you waiting for someone special, or are you two bored and like sitting around looking at women coming and going at 2:00 in the morning?"

One of the men became quite nasty and asked Mike in a heavy Eastern European accent, "What business is it of yours anyways? We are not bothering anyone?"

Mike smiled and went back to his table and the waitress became a bit alarmed but thought of the twenty dollars Mike gave her. The girls were wondering what Mike was up to as well. He came back over to the table and told the girls to watch out for those two.

After 15 minutes or so, Josie watched as the two men got up and walked over to their table.

Mike put on a big smile, "Hi guys, how's it going? Grab a chair and join us at the table."

The one man told them that would not be necessary, and they must come with them and showed them his Snub Nosed .38 in the holster on his chest. The other Russian had a much bigger weapon and gave the group a glance at it.

With both men with guns, Josie's reactions in this situation had to be much more intense, more widespread amongst both men before they drew their guns. The one Russian in front of her grabbed her right shoulder, and she spun him around with his twisted wrist, yelling in pain. The second Russian went for his gun, and Josie kicked him in the crotch. As he bent over in pain, she kicked him again in the face, with blood running from his nose. His gun came loose, and Mike picked it up, holding both men at bay.

By this time, Mike stood there in amazement; she put both assailants down before he could get his pistol out of the holster. She had it completely under control before he could respond.

> As Mike walked past the waitress, he smiled at her and asked, "Did you call the police?"

> "I hadn't had time, you want me to?"

> Mike answered, "Naw, they just need to sleep it off. We got it all under control," and he slipped her another twenty.

They went out to his truck, and he looked through his bags, grabbed four extra-large tie straps to tie them up, put the two men in the pickup box, and continued West towards Vancouver.

> "What are you going to do with them, Uncle Mike?" asked Becky.

Mike did not answer. About fifteen miles West of Merritt, they turned up a logging road, drove about ten miles, and turned right again onto a small secondary side road for another two miles to an open area where Mike turned the truck around and parked. He told the ladies to stay in the truck while he got out. Mike dropped the tailgate and pulled the two out and told them to take their clothes off. What clothes they couldn't take off because of the tie straps, he cut off, leaving them standing behind the truck in only their boxer shorts.

One man said, "Are you going to kill us?"

 Mike answered him in a tone that captured their attention, as well as the ladies in the cab of the truck, "Don't think it didn't cross my mind if you ever come after or threaten my family again, you won't be given the same courtesy that I am giving you now! Get over there by that mound of dirt!"

Mike was mad, "Who sent you?"

Mike directed his attention to one of the men, "Who sent you?"

"Fine then, if you won't cooperate, remove your boxers and throw them over here."

"But it's cold as hell up here." The man replied.

"I will give you all your clothes if you tell me who sent you," yelled Mike.

Neither man answered. Mike turned his attention to the other man and asked again." Who sent you!"

The man stood there considering his options and finally came out with a hard no!

Then Mike looked at him and told him to remove his boxers and throw them over.

Mike told them, "Fine, gentlemen, have it your way. Get over by that mound of dirt!"

The two turned away from Mike and walked slowly over to the mound. Mike threw the men's boxers in the box of the truck, jumped in the cab of the truck, and drove away. Mike couldn't figure out how they knew where they were, so they turned off their cell phones, but what about Becky's music that she was Listening to, and what about the GPS system on the truck? Mike did not know a lot about this kind of stuff.

"Hey Becky, do you have your iPod on airplane mode?"

She looked and said, "Yes, it's got nothing to do with my stuff."

Jen thought about a movie she recently watched, "Maybe they put a tracking device on the truck or something." Then she smiled and laughed.

30

It was a gorgeous day when they got off the ferry at Duke Point in Nanaimo on Vancouver Island. The water was Glassey smooth with barely a ripple and the sun shining without a cloud in the sky.

"That was my first ferry ride. I was concerned that I would get seasick, but I feel fine," Josie replied.

Sharon added, "My first boat trip as well; it was awesome, but the food was debatable!"

Mike intervened, "It's hard to imagine in the '60s and '70s, those kitchens could pump out great food back then. My father loved the clam chowder they made from scratch." But the problem back then was long lineups. If you were the last in the line-up, you would barely have just enough time to get a seat, have the waitress order and receive it, then eat, pay, and get to your car to disembark.

Mike told the ladies, "We will be stopping in Nanaimo to do their shopping list for clothes and various supplies." Make sure you have what's on the list, and, gloves that fit, and a good camo coat. I have supplied each of the sites with food and general supplies.

It took over three hours to get all four of the girls lined up with their new equipment, and they stowed away their purchases and grabbed an early dinner. Since the weather was clear and the water glassy calm, they chose a waterfront restaurant and sat outside. Jen and Mike had so many hilarious stories about the two of them growing up in the area, and everyone seemed to be laughing with them, but when Jen started snorting, it became so contagious that tears of laughter were streaming from everyone's eyes, even those at other tables, the waiters were unsure what was going on because they couldn't help but laugh as well, even though they had no idea what was so funny.

Upon arrival at the farmhouse, Everyone was getting ready for a stretch and a little walk while they all emptied the truck. Out of nowhere plodded Duke, Mikes Rottweiler, and everyone had to give Duke a good petting. Then everyone froze in horror as Becky came out of the farmhouse and saw a full-sized Cougar in front of her. Mike looked up. Josie grabbed for a pistol in a holster on her hip that wasn't there, and Sharon fainted.

"**TIGGER**!!" "Everyone, I would like to introduce you to the rest of my team."

Mike sat down on the ground, and he let the 130 lbs. cougar maul him a bit, "OK, that's enough, Tigger, get the hell off me."

She finally moved off Mike and lay beside him. "Hey, Becky, come over here, please?"

Jen said to Mike, "Anyone else but you, Mike!"

Becky sat down beside Mike and started petting and scratching Tigger's face and ears. Becky started to giggle.

"Mom! Tigger is purring!"

"Mike, what happened to all the furniture in your house?"

"After talking to Allen, I decided to send it to storage until it's over. There were too many irreplaceable items."

"It's been a while since I slept on a mattress on the floor."

Mike asked the group to freshen up, have a shower, and meet by the fire pit. He also called Jaydon, a young man who worked with him to train Duke and Tigger for a very special defensive maneuver; he wanted to give a presentation. Mike put coffee on and had a shower, then sat with his dog and cougar and the young man's family. He wasn't worried about Jen and Becky, Mike had known them for years, and they unconditionally trusted him. He had no time to spend on Josie and Sharon; the trust had to come quickly.

Jaydon and his parents came first. They loved watching how Jaydon and Mike had trained the two animals to work together to save someone from being abducted. When the girls came out by the fire pit, Mike introduced everyone and talked about why the Johnston's were there.

Mike got the demonstration underway.

> As Mike looked at the group, "It's always important to have a strong acquaintance with Duke and Tigger, I want you to always spend time with them, always.

> "We have trained Tigger and Duke to identify four different scenarios: single hostage taking, multiple hostage taking, single gunmen."

> "OK, Jaydon, take it away!"

> Sharon asked, "How old are you?"

> His mother answered, keeping Jaydon focused, "Sixteen."

Jaydon was one of the kids in the community that Mike spent time with. Jaydon loved watching and learning how to train animals from him, and because of Jaydon's patience, Mike told his parents that he was a natural. He was sixteen but looked twelve or thirteen and was a very confident handler. Jaydon had previously set up the presentation for Mike since he wanted everyone to have a clear understanding of what these animals can do. Mike also wanted them to know why they must build a strong relationship with them.

Jaydon took charge, using hand signals to bring the two animals forward. Josie noticed the sharpness of the hand signals: elbows down, palm up to come towards him, and palm down to back up. Jaydon kneeled to re-acquaint himself with both. Jaydon whispered to them, "Let's go."

"Follow me, everyone. These two would rarely travel with the main group as we are now."

Jaydon snapped his fingers and gave a hand signal, very crisp, palm down and towards the left for Duke to follow. Duke, the Rottweiler, left the group to the left, wagging its tail as it quietly went into the bush. Jaydon once again snaps his fingers and with a very crisp hand signal, palm down towards the right. The cougar immediately left the group and vanished into the bushes on the right side.

Mike took over from Jaydon since he left the group and ran up ahead. Shortly after, Mike could hear Jaydon playing the role. As they got closer, Jaydon was thrashing, and screaming, as though he was being abducted by some Madigan's by the hay, located in front of the calving barn.

Mike yells out, "Duke, hold."

Duke came out of the bush on the left and sat in front of Jaydon. The Madigan was suggesting there were no weapons, but Jaydon introduced a rubber knife to his act.

Mike loved this part, "Tigger, attack!"

They were both trained to work together, and both animals were in place. As Duke positioned himself in front of Jaydon, Tigger was waiting on the right side of the calving barn roof. When Mike gave her the command to attack, she was quick to respond and quickly there to attack the Madigan's. As Tigger left the roof with a thirty-six-foot lunge, she let out a blood-curdling scream. This took all attention away from Duke as he rushed in and grabbed the victim (Jayden) by the sleeve at about the same time as Tigger started the attack. Once Jaydon was safely away from danger, he went back in to help in the attack on the Madigan's. When Tigger landed on the Madigan, they exploded into pieces then Tigger thrashed around with parts of the arms, head, torso, and legs. It was a very impressive presentation. They continued the presentations for another hour, and for the last one, Mike sent Jayden to set up the next demonstration by the farmhouse.

Sharon, Josie, and Becky all sat down on some hay bales with their jaws opened in complete bewilderment to what they just witnessed. Josie now understood why the director sent his family here. She had a completely new appreciation for this backwoods farm boy.

Tigger came out from behind the bales of hay where she had just dismembered the Madigan, and she looked straight towards the farmhouse, ears straight back and growling. Duke also picked up on what was bothering Tigger and started growling as well.

31

Mike stopped the group and informed them that something else was taking place that he knew nothing about. The concern was that Jayden was not there, and Sharon and Josie both thought this would send the mother and father into hysterics, but instead, Mike asked them both to look after Jen, Becky, and Sharon. They agreed, and Mike and Josie started walking back.

Mike gave commands to the two animals, sending them to opposite sides of the path back to the farmhouse. As Mike and Josie turned back towards the house, and as they made the sweeping turn by the fire pit, A big Russian had a hold on Jaydon's shirt collar, with two other Russians coming up behind him.

> "So, Mr. Mike Stone, we finally meet. I want the girls, so hand them over, and we will not bother you further?" Anton snickered.

> "Okay, Igor, so you come on my farm, and then you show how pitiful you are by beating up a sixteen-year-old boy, who happens to be a friend of mine."

> "Hey, my name is not Igor, it's Anton."

> Mike was really getting ticked off, "Whatever, Igor, Anton, you all look butt ugly."

Mike wanted to provide adequate protection for Jayden before the action started. He walked with Josie just beside him on his right side and whispered to her if she was ready. Not quite sure what she was ready for, she agreed and stayed tight to his side.

> "Duke! Hold," Then right away, "Tigger, attack!"

Duke came in and grabbed Jayden from the Russian as Tigger let out a scream that scared the Russians and got their attention. The cougar attacked both Russians that were slightly behind Anton, aggressively attacking their face and throats. As Anton spun around with his pistol, Josie jumped in, knocking the pistol out of Anton's hand, and she was in full hand-to-hand with Anton. Duke took Jayden away to a safe distance from the Russians and returned to help. Tigger had the two Russians well in hand, and as Anton's pistol came to rest in front of Mike, Duke went after Anton. Mike picked up the gun and, as he picked it up, witnessed the one Russian left to deal with Tigger pull out a boot knife and stab Tigger in the left hind end. Mike quickly turned the gun to the Russian and made a killing shot.

Josie was fighting a formidable battle; for every strike to the face or kick that Josie made, Anton blocked and counter-punched or kicked her back. Duke came back to help Josie battle Anton, but before he could get there, Anton showed his superior strength over Josie. He picked her up with two hands, about to throw her into the rock fire pit that was currently ablaze. Mike was trying to get a shot off that wouldn't hit Josie. As Duke jumped on Anton and moved away, he was able to raise the pistol and fired once, causing Anton to crumble to the ground and Josie to fall directly on top of him.

Mike looked down at her blood-covered face and asked, "Are you alright!"

"Yep, all's good. Just need to get cleaned up a bit."

Once the attacks were over, Mike assessed Josie's injuries, finding nothing of major concern. He went to Tigger as she was limping on one side.

Mike got on his cell phone, "Got to get a vet out here for Tigger."

Mike took the track hoe and disposed of the three Russian bodies. The vet showed up and checked on Tigger. She needed stitches, so the vet put her to sleep for the process. The vet knew Mike and looked around at blood on the rocks where the two Russians died. He distracted her by asking if she thought Tigger's claws should be trimmed while she was out. She was very professional and left without answering him. She knew he knew the answer to that question.

"Do you want me to wake Tigger up?" the Vet asked.

"Absolutely. Thanks. Everything else good?" "Both healthy."

Mike could not help but think of how they knew where we were so fast. He went over to the vet, "I understand only the very basics of GPS, but you put chips in animals so they can be found, right?"

"No, the chip we place under the skin only gives identification, etc., not location."

"Could you find a GPS chip if you tried?"

She set herself up with the scanner and waited for Mike. Eventually, she brought out Sharon and Josie. First, they checked Sharon. It took quite a while, and finally, with a negative test. Next, Josie, the scanner was working normally as with Sharon; however, at her left ankle, everything started going off. Mike was in shock, and so was Josie.

Josie asked the vet, "Can you remove it out of my ankle?"

"Technically, yes, but I'm not supposed to."

The vet very carefully removed the chip and cleaned it off. Using her chip reading equipment, she could only determine it was Russian and unreadable by her.

"OK, clean it off and get ready for another leg of this call out," Mike explained to the vet. The vet offered Mike some information she felt relevant, "This chip was in Miss Josie's ankle for a long time, probably since her early teens. "

Mike considered this information and called a friend he had heard about who found an injured Eagle a while back with wings that became damaged down in Bowser.

"Hey Ron, have you released the Eagle yet?"

"Hi Mike, I think the eagle is ready. Do you know how to tell? Is there anyone you know who could assess it ready or not?"

"Yep, be there in twenty minutes."

As Mike drove to Ron's place, Clair, the vet, was starting to giggle as it all started falling into place for her. They arrived at Ron's place, and Clair checked the Eagle. She told Ron the Eagle was in good shape to release. And he was all game for that.

"Hey Ron, there is a bit of a catch here. I need to place a GPS chip in it, OK?"

Ron agreed, and the vet, feeling much more comfortable working on wildlife rather than a human body, had it done in no time.

Once done, they let the Eagle go as it flew away. Mike thought to himself, that should keep those Russians busy.

Josie took the whole thing in, stopping to reflect on what she had just witnessed. Josie sees Mike return to the farmhouse. He jumped out of the truck cab, saw Josie, and came over to see her.

"Mike, I knew nothing of the GPS chip in my ankle. I don't know what to say!"

"You don't need to say a thing. Your face said it all when the vet found it and she said it was there since you were a teenager."

"Thanks for understanding, Mike. This means so much to me!"

Mike nodded, "Okay, everyone, let's get some sleep, Josie. You sleep with Tigger and Sharon. You sleep with Duke."

Mike called Allen and informed him The Russians had arrived and sent pictures of those Russians who met their end.

32

After processing the evidence and the forensic information from the autopsies, the agents wrapped it all together in a presentation that made sense but didn't tell Allen and Jon anything worthwhile.

Allen started, "So after the hours of forensic science applied to truckloads of evidence and findings, all we know is that the people involved are Russians who have entered the US on visitor Visas for the purpose of holidays. Anyone else see holes in this story?" Allen paused for a moment, "What is the motive for all this?"

One of the senior agents stood up and calmly walked to the board, "According to the statements, it all started with Sharon and Joseph selling this program to the Russians, and during that transaction, everything went wrong for them. It appears the Russians decided not to pay the agreed-upon three million dollars. In Sharon's statement, she said that Joseph was concerned about the transaction being in a remote location and had a security company situated in the bush to watch out for their well-being. With Sharon being there as an unexpected and uninvited guest, in the minds of the Russians, they became agitated, and the lead Russian, Anton Ivanov, pointing his gun at Joseph, started the gunfight between the security and the Russians. Throughout all this, Sharon stole the program flash drive from them when she took her program drive, and the attention was swung to her as she tried to escape. It was shortly after that when Jen and Becky ran into Sharon trying to escape, and we believe since the Russians had injuries, they decided to leave. Still, they first went to the cabin with the intent to take Sharon there but discovered

Jen and Becky were there instead." The agent paused a bit for a drink of water, "We believe their motive for abducting the Director's family is simply to tidy up ends. We ran the fingerprints of the Russians from all the crime scenes through Interpol and discovered they all lead back to one man, Andrei Volkov."

Allen jumped in, "So it's all about this, Andrei Volkov, is it?"

Jon Marion becomes part of the summation, "Yes, it appears so. He can't be caught because he cleans up the witnesses; it's what he calls a clean organization." Jon paused for a second before he added, "That's why he is so tenacious in going after your family, Allen. That is what we believe the motive for all this is."

Lee Magnuson, the lab lead technician, added, "That flash drive that Sharon gave you, director, has an operating system we are working on. Also, we found several encrypted files that we cannot gain access to, and the lab crew is working hard to try and crack the code. The pictures you gave us, director, of the man killed trying to abduct your family once again, is one of Andrei's top men. We need to watch for Vlad or Vladimir Volkov. Its thought he may take Anton's place in the organization over here. Allen, I don't know who is looking after your family, but I suggest you warn them about Vlad and that in addition to him being a head man, he is also the snake's son."

After the meeting, Allen had security conduct a sweep of his office for any bugging devices and had three of his burner phones checked for tracing activity. Once he was satisfied that he could make a secure call, he made a call to Mike.

"Mike, how is everything going?" Allen paused to catch his breath, and Allen continued, "You have come in contact with a couple of the Russians, I understand?"

"All should be fine for now," Mike answered, "now we got that chip out of Josie's ankle, it should be a bit easier staying ahead of them."

"Did you ever find out what that was all about?" Allen asked.

"No, I'm a good judge of character. Somewhere in her past, their paths crossed, not sure when, the vet told me she must have been in her early teens when it was implanted. I am also not sure of the situation in which they met. It appears to me that Josie is truly concerned about how the chip was planted on her."

"I wanted to call you to keep you informed about our investigation, Mike. Maybe something we discover down here will help you with your efforts up there."

"Do you want to talk to Jen and Becky?"

Allen thought for a moment, "Normally, yes, I would, but not this call. I want to summarize what we have learned to date."

Allen went through the summary they had just completed with the senior agents on the case, along with Jon Marion and Lee Magnuson. He talked in detail about the Russian mob, which has infiltrated several military facilities and has stolen items such as grenades. Allen went on to talk about Anton Ivanov, the fella Mike apprehended at the farmhouse, explaining that he played a leadership role in Andrei Volkov's mob and that his son Vlad or Vladimir may be taking his place.

"If that's the case, there is no telling what may happen out there. Is there anything I can get you?"

Mike thought for a moment, "Is there any way you could get me night vision binoculars?"

Allen considered the request, "It will be dropped at your house by UPS in two days."

Mike asked how Jen and Becky got wrapped up in all this and the many questions and comments made about being in the wrong place at the wrong time. Their conversation was like they had done this all before, but more importantly, they were communicating as equals, understanding what each other is capable of and that of mutual respect. Allen did not have to tell Mike how much he appreciated what he was doing for him. It was a mutual respect and clear directive as to what needed to be done. Mike wouldn't have had it any other way. He loved Allen's family as though it was his own.

33

Catherine Marion had just finished putting a load of clothes in the washer and turned on the machine. As she went upstairs, she heard her "special " phone ring.

"Hello, who is this?"

In Russian, the voice answers, "Catherine, it's Vlad. Have you forgotten me so soon?"

In Russian, she converses, "Vlad, it's always good to hear from you. Where are you calling from?"

"I'm in New York. It would be wonderful to have dinner with you tonight."

"I would love to, but Jon is coming home from work soon. Maybe lunch tomorrow?"

Vlad thought for a bit, "Yes, that would be wonderful. I have something important to talk to you about."

Catherine Marion piped up, "Now you piqued my interest. What could be so important, Vlad? Are you and Anna starting a family?"

Vlad paused on the phone, "I wish that was it, you heard about Anton's death? Catherine, you are close to the director Fulton's family, are you not?"

"Yes, we are close, what do you need?

"I need you to help us take the young one. Can you come to Canada? That's where they are."

"I think I could get away. How's father?"

"As miserable as ever," Vlad laughed.

"What does he want with the girl?"

"This program he has developed is a big deal for him. He needs the program flash drive that a woman named Sharon stole, and now we are looking for it. Sharon died in the hospital, so she can't help us."

Katrina spoke out, "No, she is alive. She's in Canada with the others. I overheard Jon talk to Allen about it."

"OK, then we need to go to Canada right away, Katrina."

"No, if that flash drive is important, let me look for it here at the FBI office. If I can find it, then that's what father wants."

"What do we do with the director's family in Canada while we wait for you?"

"Go after them; we will always know where they are. If you have not got them by the time I get the flash drive, we can go after the girl and the mother together."

Vlad asked his sister, "Katrina, how long will this take?"

"Not sure. I'll keep you updated. Not sure who's got it or where it is? Probably in Allen's office; I'll let you know."

"Okay, and I will find everyone and go after the family, excellent plan. Great working with you, my sister," Vlad smiled and kissed her over the phone.

"You still owe me lunch tomorrow," Katrina said with a smile.

"You are on. Text me when and where and I will be there. I am going to get a plane ticket for Vancouver and pick up where Anton left off."

Catherine ended the call with, "Take care, my brother."

Regardless of what Andrei said, Vlad was determined to get things straightened out in Vancouver Island and bring the girls to

Moscow. He was looking forward to having lunch with his sister. He had not seen her in a long while. He remembered the two of them playing in the house. She was always better at games than he was, and sometimes he caught her cheating, but she would never admit to it. As kids growing up, they never knew their mother; they were told she died giving birth to Catherine, but they had nannies who watched out for them and taught them things that a mother would teach their children. Their father, Andrei, gave them discipline and was hard on them both as they grew up. Vlad remembered one time the nanny stood up to Andrei when he was scolding them about some little thing they did, and they never saw that nanny again. Both Catherine and Vlad knew what happened to her but never mentioned it. Neither Vlad nor Catherine had friends until they were fourteen years old. They were home-schooled and were never allowed to go to community functions with kids the same age. At eight years old, they were both taught how to fight as part of their homeschooling, and the teacher that Andrei selected to teach them was very good but very tough on them. Vlad could remember countless times they would come to the dinner table with bloody noses or battle scars, and their father would get mad at them for letting it happen to them. He remembered once, as they practiced fighting with each other, Catherine hit Vlad in the nose, making it bleed, and his father gave Catherine a big bowl of ice cream and would not allow him to have any.

When they became old enough to drive, everything seemed to change for Vlad and Catherine. For their first car, Andrei took them for a ride to each high-end car dealership and told them to choose any car they wanted. Driving away from the car lot in his new Porche was wonderful. He remembers the smell, he remembers the sound, and he spent the whole rest of the day driving around with Catherine; she was as excited as he was, and Catherine returned the experience when it was her turn to get a car.

Soon after getting the cars, their father started teaching them about the business, which opened their eyes wide, now they were understanding how money was made and what was needed to run the business.

Both Catherine and Vlad were told to move out of the house at nineteen, at which time Andrei bought them beautiful homes with maids and groundskeepers. Everything their father gave them was contingent on one thing: they had to stay on with the business. If they were to leave, they would lose everything, including their inheritance.

34

Mike was up early, tinkering in the machine shop and noticed Josie walking by; he caught her attention, and she came in.

"What on earth are you doing up so early?" Josie asked.

"Building some mini guns, let me show you what I mean."

Mike pulled out a penlight from his shirt pocket, he gave it to her to look at.

"Looks like a penlight to me, what is it?"

Mike takes it from her, unscrews it from the middle, and inserts a 22-caliber shell in one side of the two parts. He screws it back together and pulls the two parts away from each other and points the back end of the penlight towards a target stapled to the shed wall. He takes his thumb and rolls it sideways against a silver rectangular button. As the button moves to the side, it becomes disengaged from the latch, and the two halves of the penlight snap together firing the 22-caliber shell causing the bullet to shoot out the barrel and into the target.

"Oh my, that's tricky, but would that little bullet bring a fully grown man down?

"Absolutely! Mike intervened; it will bring down a 1400 lbs. steer."

Mike's phone started ringing, "Hello, who's this?"

" It's Allen, your night vision binoculars will be arriving at your house soon."

"Thanks, Allen, but got to go, sorry."

Mike and Josie returned to the farmhouse in time for Jen, Becky, and Sharon to just finish cooking everyone breakfast.

"Everyone sleep well last night?" Mike asked with a smile.

Sharon added, "I slept fine, Duke was a gentleman in bed!"

Josie butted in, "Tigger was fine as well, but she purrs loudly."

Jen asked, "So what's in store for us today, Mike?"

Mike spent some time thinking about how to answer that question. There were several issues that he needed to work on first.

" I don't think we are safe here in the farmhouse, I think we need to go to the first hide-out. Jen, do you remember that old trapper's cabin that Allen and I fixed up?"

" Oh man, that was a long time ago, I remember Allen trying to show it to me when we first started going out."

Everyone laughed and after everyone was done with breakfast and cleaned up, Mike started loading totes on the farm truck and before they left, he took Festus back with the cows on the high ridge.

There were two ways to get to the trapper's cabin; through a narrow path from the high ridge access; and by traveling about fifteen kilometers up the Island Highway to Buckley Bay and up the coal mine road where there was an abandoned rail track. Both were equally difficult to navigate through since alder and fir tree growth had taken over both routes over the years. Since they were already at the high ridge with Festus, Mike decided to travel that way, along the 7 kilometers of rugged road.

Jen asks with a smile on her face, " Jeese Mike, is this truck going to make it?"

"I know it looks rough on the outside, but this truck is a tank, I rebuilt most of it myself."

They finally made it to the cabin, and everyone unloaded the truck, the only thing that Mike wanted left on the truck was the quad.

Mike took the group around to show them the hiding spots and the escape zip line and explained about the boat at the end of the zip line that will be under camouflaged netting, in case they need to leave fast. The idea is to travel downriver to the ocean and off to another hideout like this one. Mike and Josie left the group in the truck and parked it about one hundred yards in from the edge of the high ridge field shutting off the path, spending time camouflaging the backend, so it wouldn't be seen. They unloaded the quad and took off back to the farmhouse.

"Why are we going back to the farmhouse, Mike?" Josie asked. "Let me show you."

Mike wasted no time, he started at the driveway from the road to the house and placed a big sign warning people to stay out. Then as he drove the quad just inside the gate, he got off and flipped a switch on a box, as he did the box emitted a laser-like light to the box on the other side. He then took the quad on the Southwest side of the farmhouse and raced around the bush setting trip wires for previously placed detonation devices with dynamite and shotgun shell receptacles. They finished by setting the motion detectors in the barns hooked up to pipe bombs encrusted with old nuts and bolts.

They needed to get going because it was starting to get dark. As they reached the High Ridge field, Mike heard something and shut off the quad. They could hear explosion after explosion in the vicinity of the farmhouse.

Mike looks at Josie, "That was timely, and should keep them busy for a while."

They reached the trapper's cabin and Jen came out, "What on earth was all that blasting going on, we were worried sick about you two!"

"We're fine, but I think there are a few Russians hurting a bit, we just set a few traps, and just in time, too. I thought they would wait until dusk."

Mike wanted to change the subject, "So, what's for supper, I'm starved."

Jen pipes up, "Well, based on your shopping skills for the occasion, it's beans, chili, or stew."

Mike puts on a hundred-watt smile, "sounds good to me!"

35

Jon Marion came into Allen's office and sat down in a fluster, "I've been working with INTERPOL trying to find the connection these Russians have in their homeland and one name keeps coming up, Andrei Volkov. He is heavily tied to the Kremlin and political ties to Russian politicians who the CIA has suspected as being involved with drug smuggling into the US as well as human trafficking." Jon paused a moment to collect his thoughts. " The CIA believes he is involved in developing an International CRIME ARMY, highly trained and highly skilled with weapons of all kinds. "

Allen sat up in his chair, " like a secret army the Russians can deploy to set up cells for criminal activity? It would create havoc in the US, but why, why don't they just stay in Europe, why come to North America?"

Jon looked at his friend, "It is believed that this can be a means of getting back at the US and possibly Canada for implementing sanctions against Russia over the war in the Ukraine."

Allen started with, "But that would mean this is politically supported by the Russians."

Jon nodded his head, "Yes, and because Andrei Volkov controls it, nobody can prove the Russian government has anything to do with it, and goes on without any resistance except for what we do in our own country."

"How long has this been going on for?"

Jon rubbed his face, "for about as long as the sanctions had been implemented, it's their way of getting back at us. I think the sanctions were just an excuse, one of my CIA contacts said they have been setting up cells in the US for the last thirty years. Allen, I'm afraid these cells are firmly integrated in our country."

"Shit," was about all that Allen could get out.

Lee Magnuson came directly into Allen's office. He had a pile of documents in his hands half organized in file folders with others falling out onto the floor as he came through the door.

"Sorry for the intrusion director, but we have come across some information from lab testing that I think you should be made aware of."

Lee tossed four pictures of the dead Russians whom the lab had processed, "the US ordinance used in these crimes bothered me, so I investigated further. Each one of these men has family members who are presently responsible for warehouse inventory at US Army warehouses located along the East Coast."

"Do you have their names?" Allen asked.

Lee anticipating their response handed them both a piece of paper with names and the addresses on it. Immediately, Allen called his military contact explaining the situation and the evidence discovered. Allen also told the commanding officer that he understood it was a military responsibility to investigate. However, he would appreciate having the FBI to work with them on this, and the commanding officer agreed and set up the operation.

Allen looked directly at Lee, "That was great work Lee, it was a piece of the puzzle that was still on the table, this will remove it and help us keep focused on solving the big picture."

Jon stayed behind as Lee left, " I don't want to know the particulars about where your family is and who is looking after them, but I wish them all well."

"Thanks, Jon, it's nice to know I have a friend on my side."

Jon's wife Catherine came into Allen's office, "Hello gentlemen."

Allen was a bit taken aback by the lack of consideration, "Hello Catherine, what brings you to my office, confession?"

"Very funny Allen, just making sure you guys are pulling your weight, after all, it's the taxpayer's money on the line here."

Allen wasn't letting her get away that easy, " did you at least bring cookies?"

All three started laughing while Catherine took the magnetic bug out of her pocket and placed it under Allen's desk without anyone seeing her. They chatted for a while then finally Catherine and Jon left Allen's office. It bothered Allen that Catherine came straight into his office without anything of significance to talk about. Ever since that bug in his pen, Allen had been extremely careful who came into his office, always closing or locking the door when he left it. But Allen, Jen, and Becky recognized Catherine and Jon as special people, they were family.

Allen picked up the phone on his desk and dialed agent Ron McKay, " Ron, where are you right now?"

"Good afternoon director, I am chasing down a lead I got from those license plate numbers you gave us, I'll let you know more after I interview a fella who may be connected with the abduction of your family."

"Excellent follow-up Ron, when do you think you might get back to the office?"

"In about an hour and a half, depending on traffic, what do you have director?"

"Just come straight to my office when you get back and don't let anyone know."

Ron paused for a second, "copy that director."

Ron McKay was a young and upcoming agent who was destined for promotion. He excelled in just about everything the Bureau tossed at him but had a deep understanding of behavioral analysis. Allen wanted him to lead the interrogation of one of the captured Russians who Allen believed had more to tell. In addition to Ron's acute behavioral analysis skill set, Ron also studied the Russian language.

36

In 1990, only a year before the KGB was eradicated in Russia, they began the development of what they called the Mindsweeper project. It was focused on controlling the minds of their military at the front line creating a fearless army of fighters, having no fear of dying, and courageously fighting battles that would normally be lost. The KGB searched for a person to take the lead role in this project and found the ideal candidate, Ivan Petrov, Sergei Petrov's father. Despite Sergei's age, he was interested in what his father was developing and spent countless hours with his father on the program copying and saving all his father's work. In the spring of 1992, the project was shut down and all documents created during the development of the Mindsweeper project were burned, except for what Sergei kept. In 2013 Sergei was trying to make some extra money and got into trouble with Andrei's business. Using what he learned from his father while developing the Mindsweeper program as a bargaining tool, Andrei spared his life and hired him on, earning a very meager salary.

Sergei Petrov walked into Andrei Volkov's office with reservations, the last time he visited the boss in his office he almost lost three fingers for something he didn't do. Sergei was the computer technician who developed the program flash drive that was missing and modified the American's program to enable mind transfer from one body to another. This was the program that would give the boss the chance for the immortality he was demanding from him.

Sergei was exhausted, he had worked on this flash drive non-stop since it went missing in the Catskills disaster. But Andrei never wasted time in telling Sergei that it was only an excuse, and he should have had backup copies, in the event of loss. Sergei was confident that Anton could recover the flash drive, that was until he was killed. So, he ventured to reinvent a program he had already developed, some from notes and some from memory, but he finally completed it.

Andrei came into the office, the first time Sergei saw him smile, "So, I understand you have completed the design of the Mind Sweeper program Sergei, tell me more about it."

Sergei was taking his time to answer Andrei politically correctly; he knew one poorly chosen word could turn this meeting into a catastrophic failure, "Yes sir, technically, the program should be able to transfer the mind from one body to another."

Andrei picked up on the emphasis with the word technically and challenged Sergei, "What do you mean technically?"

Sergei was feeling the stress of his challenge, "Well, it would need to be tested first before someone such as yourself would try it out."

"Then you try it out first to see if it works!"

Sergei jumped on the request, "If I do and something needs adjusting, we would be in a difficult situation if I was incapacitated."

"Fine, I will have two individuals ready for a trial mid-week. Can you copy a mind into several bodies?"

This question sent Sergei to left field searching for an answer, "Not presently, but I could probably have something in a week or two, why would you need that Andrei."

Andrei shot him a look, "I am going to build the ultimate crime army, and distribute them all over the world, I want to have my best people cloned to create a crime wave the world could never comprehend."

Sergei was caught off guard, "Okay, then I better get to work."

This scared Sergei, he wanted no part of a crazy man's plans to rule the world or whatever he was up to. But Sergei was caught, with no way out. If he ran and moved to another country, Andrei would definatly find him and kill him, Sergei would always be looking over his shoulder.

Andrei looked directly at Sergei, "Once you perfect the transferring of one mind to another body, I want you to think of the end goal. The next stage of development that I need, is for you to copy my mind and transfer it into ten people to start with, then a hundred, then a thousand, until I get my army, understand?" Andrei paused, he believed that Sergei could accomplish this, he was a brilliant technician, the best he had ever seen. Andrei considered it was time for him to start paying him accordingly.

While Andrei had Sergei's attention, "To show you how important this project is to me, I will sweeten the pot for you. I will double your salary after you successfully transfer a mind from one person to the next. I will double that salary again when you demonstrate you can copy a mind and transfer it into multiple bodies. I will then double that salary when I have my army of criminals, how does that sound?"

Sergei did some quick math in his head, "That sounds great Andrei, thank you."

Sergei left Andrei's office with a newfound hop in his step, he never expected that Andrei would ever offer him more money than he ever dreamt of making. He was so excited he walked into a side table in the foyer and knocked a vase over, and caught it before it hit the floor, placing it back on the table. He felt like working day and night on this project and muttered as he walked, "Sleep, why do we need sleep, what a waste of time, I could get this thing done so much faster if I didn't have to sleep." He finally reached his computer lab and started establishing a test sequence for mind transfer with the Mindsweeper program. He ran the sequence through the program and found there was an error somewhere in the program. Sergei worked tirelessly to find it but was unable to. He decided to finish up for the day and start back up tomorrow. On his way home, Sergei decided to celebrate and stopped at a nice restaurant on the way. He had a nice cut of pork tenderloin with root vegetables, which was his favorite, and a glass of house white wine. He started dreaming about all the money he would be making and what he could buy. For the first time in a very long time, Sergei was happy and thought of his father. He missed his father very much and wished he was joining him tonight for dinner.

37

After two days of staying at the trappers cabin, the girls were protesting having to eat beans, chili, and stew. In the early morning, Mike grabbed the pack sack, his bow, and a good supply of arrows, and left to find the ladies a more suitable menu to satisfy their culinary palate.

Leaving Duke behind, but taking Tigger, Mike sought after an old garden he planted years ago when he was preparing for the Russian and Chinese invasion. At the time, Mike didn't spend much time preparing the garden or planting, he depended on the plants re-seeding themselves, and whatever grew, grew. He was not surprised to find very little available, especially since it was mid spring and anything that grew hadn't time to mature yet, except for some early potatoes. With the potatoes in the pack, Mike ventured on, picking a common weed in the area, which is similar to beet greens or spinach, and early afternoon came upon a covey of grouse, which Mike got three with his bow. After he finished cleaning them, he placed them in his pack and headed back to the trapper's cabin to prepare dinner.

> As he approached the cabin, Sharon was outside relaxing by the creek and was startled with Tigger's approach, "Where have you been?"
>
> Mike answered, "Out shopping."
>
> Josie came out of the cabin, "You mean we won't be eating beans tonight?"

Mike laughed and started preparing the meal and eventually with everything cooking on the propane cook stoves, Mike took time to relax.

"So, what have you girls been doing to keep yourself busy while I was gone?"

All four girls stopped what they were doing and started laughing, Jen started up, "Well, we all went down to this new restaurant for lunch, but they ran out of beans, so we had their stew, mmmm, was it ever good, Mike."

Everyone started laughing and Mike took the ladle and stirred the grouse around in the frying pan. "Looks like it's already to eat, grab a plate."

Everyone ate their meal and Mike was complimented on his ability to put together a bush meal. After cleaning up, everyone was tired, and the four girls slept on the three bunks and Mike made up a makeshift hammock for himself and another for Becky.

Josie watched Mike working hard to make everyone's stay in the broken-down cabin as good an experience as possible. She thought he was a very thoughtful man, she enjoyed being around him and she particularly liked his smile--it was warm and inviting and she was drawn to his country charm. As she was drifting off to sleep, she giggled as she thought of what it would be like to live with a dog and a cougar the same way as Mike does, then finally sleep took over her mind and her body as she drifted off to sleep.

At first light, Mike woke to a robin chirping, it wasn't the robin chirping so much as it was the way it was chirping. When a Robin's nest is being encroached upon or threatened, they make a noise that is so unique, it cannot be misunderstood. As he heard the robin's warning cry, he looked down at Tigger. It wasn't long after Mike heard the robin that Tigger raised her head in the direction of the robin. The cougar started to growl at what was bothering the robin as it moved in the bush.

He hopped out of his hammock and woke the others, he wasn't positive there was a problem to deal with, but he wanted to be prepared with people awake rather than half asleep.

"What is it Mike?" Josie asked.

"Not sure, everyone pack up your bags for a hasty exit."

The wind had started to bello up strong from the Southwest, a typical wind in the area signifying a storm was approaching. There was a loud whirring noise that seemed to be getting louder, which was coming from that direction. Mike was thinking fast and determined the noise to be coming from remote controlled drones.

Jen said, "You can just shoot them down can't you Mike?"

"Yes, if it comes to that, but as soon as I do, I give away our location, if they see the cabin, they will know where we are."

Mike darted to some tote boxes that he previously put at the cabin. He tore the lid off one and pulled out a ghillies suit and put it on immediately. He grabbed two pouches and attached them to his belt and grabbed his shotgun and two boxes of shells and headed out the back door. Mike ran as fast as he could towards the sound of the drones until he found the perfect spot to sit and observe. There were four drones in the air, and they were searching in all directions. Mike removed one of the pouches from his belt and removed a half dozen ball bearings and secured the sling shot close to him with the bearings in the pouch. The drones were getting closer to him as they searched blindly through the dense forest and underbrush. The wind was creating problems for the drones as they would sometimes get blown into a tree and the operator would have to get it back in service again.

A drone was coming straight for him, staying perfectly still, fully camouflaged in his suit, he watched it come. Mike grabbed the sling shot and the bearings waiting for it to just pass over his head, he raised the slingshot, let the pouch go and knocked two blades off the drone. It came down about twenty yards from where he was, and Mike looked over towards the Russians and one of them was making his way to the crash site. Careful not to be seen, Mike went over to the crashed drone and smashed it with a nearby rock.

The trappers cabin was not in sight of the crash site however, the Russian lost sight of where the drone went down and had the presence of mind to venture too far North, placing the cabin in full view. He talked on the radio and Mike noticed the others were walking in his direction.

The cabin was built on the top of the hill and was a straight climb up from where he was located, and realized he had little time to get there before he ran out of cover. Mike took off staying behind trees and underbrush as he raced up the hill to the cabin. By the time he was fifty yards from the cabin, he felt his legs burning from fatigue and every breath he took, it was like a knife cutting into his lungs, just a little way further.

> Mike exploded through the back door of the cabin, "stay away from the windows or out of sight and put on your Zipline harness."

Mike rummaged through another tote, this one longer and pulled out a rifle, he grabbed some shells, loading it and yanked out the chimney pipe that went through the wall. He then set himself for long range shooting. Through his scope, Mike could see one of the Russians laying on the ground for a bench rest position. He recognized this from his many years on the rifle range, using the very same technique.

A bullet came whizzing through the window, followed by a thunderous roar of the rifle blast. Mike took aim on the sniper with the rifle doing the shooting, it was more technical due to wind gusts. Mike squeezed the trigger of his rifle and it let out a roar that deafened everyone in the cabin. Mike missed his shot, re-loaded and decided to send a message. He took aim at two, who were close together side by side, this shot did not miss it's target. Mike re-loaded again and hit the sniper in the chest, the other three Russians ran back to their vehicles and waited there.

Mike was watching through his scope and saw another vehicle arrive with the remaining three Russians who ran back. By looking at his mannerisms and the way he carried himself within the group, Mike could tell easily that one of the newly arrived Russians was a boss of some kind.

A tanker truck drove towards the cabin along a narrow path on the left side, keeping well hidden. As it approached the location where the sniper fired at them, it moved directly in line of sight. Mike looked through his scope and was unable to see the driver, then suddenly it started pumping fluid out of a pipe located at the top of the unit. The tanker made its way to the right side, pumping fluid from it and spraying the trees and brush. The wind picked up the smell as it entered the cabin, and it was easily identified by Mike as gasoline.

Mike's mind was racing, with the wind and the amount of gasoline sprayed out, maybe two minutes before they would be engulfed in flames.

> "Everyone, listen up we all need to leave now, grab your packs and meet me over by the Zipline!"

Everyone scrambled and ran over to where Mike showed them to go, Becky happened to be first at the line and Mike hooked her up and pushed her off the makeshift landing. By the time Jen, Sharon, and Josie left, Mike had the harness on Duke and Tigger, and all three went at the same time. Both animals were having a rough time with it, but Mike was confident they would live through it. The line was almost a straight drop down to the river, but it leveled out providing time for each one to slow down. By the time Mike, Tigger, and Duke got to the endpoint, the girls had released themselves, allowing Mike and the animals time to land. Everything went well except Mike did not account for his weight being more than the animals and he ended up too close to Tigger, and consequently, got clawed. They were about to go to the boat when Mike noticed the Zipline wiggling. Realizing the Russians were about to use the Zipline, he disconnected it from the tree.

The Airboat was Mike's pride. From when he was a kid watching television, he loved the concept of the Everglades airboats. They removed the camouflaging that Mike had carefully covered it with and under Mike's direction, started navigating the boat down the river current using poles.

"We just need to pole up to that point that comes out, then I'll fire up the engines, after that."

They came up to the point and Mike jumped in the operator's chair and started the engine.

"Grab a seat and buckle up, if you don't have a chair, sit low and hold on!"

As Mike throttled the engine up and spun the boat down the river, it felt like the boat was flying as it was traveling with the current of the river. The river was quite narrow at this point and until it widened, Mike was holding back on the throttle, he didn't want to lose control at this point. He could see ahead where the two rivers joined, that was where he could open it up. There it was, the river was getting deeper, and it was safe to take off, just at this point, a rifle shot came from upriver on top of the high ridge on the South side of the riverbank. Mike opened the engine up and started dodging back and forth, avoiding getting hit. Another rifle shot from the same vicinity, this time they hit the boat.

"Mike, we are taking on water!" Becky cried.

"We're OK," Mike said confidently.

They picked up speed fast, and Mike knew they would be in open water soon; with that, they were safe from those behind them. Mike also knew the Russians would be tied up at the trappers cabin for a while and decided to do something they wouldn't expect. Mike made a call for someone to pick them up and he tied the boat up at the wharf. Jayden Johnston borrowed his dads pickup to pick them up and took them back to the farmhouse. Mike had everyone except for Josie hide out in the hay mow of the calving shed, while Josie left with Mike on Festus. Mike grabbed some quarter inch cable and some dynamite, and both left on Festus. They stopped short of The Russians; it was easy to find since the fire was still burning up the hill. Mike wasn't sure what he wanted to do with them so decided to prepare for both scenarios. Taking the dynamite and the cable, Mike went towards the Russian's vehicles by himself. He was very careful not to be seen, and crawled under the rear one, attaching the cable around the steering tie rods back to a tree. This took him a while, so Mike elected to place dynamite and cell detonator above the fuel tanks of each unit, then took some additional cable to connect the steering tie rods of the other two vehicles back to the other vehicles, by doing this he was able to save time. Mike left back to where Josie was and being careful not to be seen.

About thirty minutes after Mike returned to Josie and Festus; the Russians started returning to their vehicles. Mike identified the boss figure he had seen earlier at the trapper's cabin. He and a driver got in one of the vehicles and started to leave, when the cable tightened, the steering tie rods bent causing the vehicles steering mechanism to completely fail. With the vehicle unable to steer, the boss figure investigated and changed vehicles. They removed the cable on the second vehicle and started off down the path. The other three got in the last car and took off to find them coming to the end of the cable and shortly coming to a grinding halt. Mike pulled out his cell phone and shortly after making his call, the car blew up. He looked at the car that had left with the boss, and Mike made another call.

38

Andrei Volkov made a call to Catherine as soon as he got the news that Vlad had been killed. It was hard for Andrei to make the call, but he was madder than he was sad.

"Catherine, I need you to look after a few things that Vlad was working on for me. Since Sharon is still alive, I need you to terminate her or bring her to Moskow. She witnessed the shooting. I also need the director's family. They all witnessed the shooting screw-up with Anton, and they are responsible for Vlad's death, I want them to pay."

"What about the program flash drive you needed?" Katrina asked.

"Forget the flash drive; I have a new one developed. Those stupid American FBI investigators will never figure out the encryption to my organization's secrets anyway. I want those witnesses dealt with!"

"Alright, I have one thing left to do, and then I will travel out to Vancouver and get her for you, father."

The phone went dead. She knew he was upset. She knew how determined he was to have Vlad take over the organization and take his place as an oligarch. This Catskills disaster cost the organization a lot of good people. Although she would never tell her father, she questioned the necessity of it. But she needed to prepare, and first thing, she needed to retrieve that bug that she had planted under Allen's desktop.

It was eleven-thirty, and she knew that Allen often eats lunch out, especially since Jen and Becky weren't there. She threw on a sweater and headed to the FBI office parking building. Once inside with her visitor's pass, she went straight to Jon's desk to find him absent. She saw the opportunity to get into Allen's office since he would most likely be out over lunch. The door was closed, and when she went to open it, she found it was locked.

She could not understand. Allen had never locked his office door before. She would have to wait until he returned. She grabbed a coffee from the lunchroom and waited in Jon's office. After two hours, she decided to leave and just go to Vancouver to deal with the daughter, then just go back to Moscow with the girl in Andrei's jet. She had accomplished about all she could with the FBI. She made the airline reservations to fly to Vancouver in the morning and prepared herself never to return.

FBI investigations were going too slow for Allen. He wanted closure to this mess and to have his family safely back into their home, living a normal life. He was also tired of expecting Mike to turn his life into an upheaval of hell. Allen knew that Mike would volunteer a hundred times, but this was asking too much of him, yet there was no one else who could do what Mike was doing. The whole FBI, under his direction, couldn't keep his family safe. What really bothered Allen was, with the key player in Russia while he was alive there would be no end to this nightmare in sight.

After the interrogation with the captured Russian, Allen, Jon, and Ron McKay sat in his office to analyze the conversation they had. Allen found it interesting how Ron was able to get as much out of the Russian as he did.

> Jon started to talk, and then Allen put up his hand to stop the conversation, " just a moment, please."

Allen picked up his phone, leaving his office while making a call. He hung up and returned to his office. Jon and Ron were both unsure what the director had up his sleeve, but he put his forefinger to his lips to keep quiet. Shortly after, Lee Magnuson's lead cyber technician, William, walked into Allen's office and took out an electronic device from his pocket, turning it on and moving it around the room. He brought the device down towards the director's desktop, and as he moved it to the front of the desk, it started to sound off, along with the visual display of lights flashing. He looked under the desktop to find a small device attached to the underside of the top. Before removing, William put on a pair of medical gloves, carefully detached it, and examined them, eventually turning it off.

"It's safe to talk now. "He said, "looks like we got a good fingerprint here."

William took the device to the lab for processing. Jon and Ron were bewildered.

"How did you know? They asked.

"I didn't, but I had a burning feeling that something was not right, like when you have that feeling someone is staring at you, and you turn around to find someone looking directly at you. I can't explain it past that." Allen regained his composure, "Let's get back to the interrogation, Ron. I thought you did an excellent job. Can you tell me more?"

Ron commented on an observation he made, " Thank you, director. I believe he's scared; he wants out, but he can't. They will kill his family." Ron went on, "but I don't believe we can offer him adequate protection since his family is in Russia."

A silence fell over the group in the office. They concluded it wouldn't matter what information they got. They couldn't do anything about it anyways since it was an international issue.

"I'll call my contact in the CIA. Maybe he could brighten this up a bit."

Lee Magnuson came by Allen's office and tapped on the door to seek admission. Allen waved him in.

"Allen, a few things I wanted to talk to you about. We could not get a match on those fingerprints off that bug, so we sourced Interpol and are waiting for them to contact us with the results. We found chips like the one found on Josie on four of the six Russian bodies in the morgue. Last but not least, we have traced these bodies back to Andrei Volkov's organization. Now, we know that's not new news, but what is new is he is not with the Russian mob. He is an oligarch tied heavily to the Kremlin."

Lee paused for a moment to take a sip of coffee, "The oligarchs are a powerful group who are not only rich but have incredible ties to the Russian politicians. In order to be in this class, they must have a wealth of over a billion US dollars, they must run an organization that can create economic volatility, and they must have strong ties to politicians. To give you an idea of their growth, in 1997, An American magazine identified only four oligarchs; today, there are over one hundred and twenty, and Andrei Volkov is one of them. Within the last fifteen years, he has brought his organization to the international level, and he is well regarded amongst the group as well as the political theater as someone who is making an impact in Russia."

It was quiet in the office, then Allen asked, "Any comments, gentlemen?

Ron said with confidence, " his demise will be his ego, find a way to cripple his ego, and his organization will crumble."

That wouldn't have been the first thing that Allen would have thought of, but after thinking about it, it made sense. Considering the great work Ron did in the interrogation, it certainly was worth trying.

"Lee, if you don't mind, I would like Ron to work with Jon on this for a while to head us down the right track."

Lee agreed, "I think that's a fantastic idea." He stopped abruptly, then remembered something else, "remember the security company who assisted Sharon and Joseph in the Catskills? Well, the story, as Sharon told it, one had survived. We have been trying to get in touch with him for a long time now but unable to. Well, NYPD just received a body that resembles him in the morgue and is presently working on confirming identification. He was shot with a twelve-gauge shotgun. Other than Sharon, Jen, and Becky, there are no other witnesses to that incident."

Allen solemnly looked at Lee, " and that's the motive for all this pandemonium. They won't stop until all the witnesses are dead."

With this, everyone cleared Allen's office. He sat in his chair, put his hands over his face, and wept enough to help but not enough to fix the problem. Fixing the problem at this point would take an act of God, something he could not do or have anyone do, especially in his capacity as director.

39

Catherine Marion was at home sitting in front of her computer, monitoring the bug she planted under the desktop of FBI director Allen Fulton's office. She was listening when Allen discovered it and knew she left a fingerprint on the device. She was thinking of her options and decided to make a run for it because it wouldn't take long before they found that she planted the device and was part of the Russian effort to kidnap the director's family. She considered Jon her husband for a while, but the whole marriage thing was for convenience's sake to get into the FBI operations. She reflected that he was a good husband, but he was American, and it was time to move on. And now that Vlad was gone, she could be the father's number one in the organization and be accepted as an oligarch. She transferred all money from their bank, investment, and insurance accounts to her personal credit card, taking only eight thousand dollars in cash. This would be below the maximum to travel with as she entered Canada. She bought her ticket to Vancouver and started packing. She had six hours before the plane left.

She considered writing Jon a note but then thought she might need that time to escape or that it might signal them to take action to foul her plan to take Becky and Jen out. She took her bags to the sidewalk and waited for the taxi.

Her cell phone rang, " Hi Jon, what's happening in your world today?"

"I'm just calling to let you know that I made reservations at your favorite restaurant for seven pm."

She thought for a moment, " Oh, wonderful! Should I put on that sexy dress that you like so much"?

Jon responded immediately, " Yes, that would be fantastic. You look irresistible in it."

Catherine finished the call, saying, " I'll see you then, don't be late."

She arrived at JFK International Airport in good time to get checked in, clear customs, and find the gate. She was famished since the preparation for the trip took her mind off lunch, and across the Concourse from her was a restaurant offering a meal that looked appetizing. She had the time and moved over to eat before her flight left. After ordering, she considered what she might have ordered with Jon that evening. She also thought of how mad he would be once he put it all together. She changed her focus to Allen's family; it was unfortunate they happened to be in the wrong place at the wrong time. But what is important is to eliminate the witnesses from ever testifying in a court, whether domestic or international. Her father ran a tight ship when it came to witnesses. He raised them with the understanding at an early age that witnesses would weaken an organization, especially one tied to politicians and oligarchs.

In Vancouver, Catherine looked at her watch and noted the time. With the difference in time zones, it would be around seven o'clock in New York, and Jon would be at the restaurant waiting for her. She took out her cell phone, pulled out the SIM card, and threw both the phone and card in a trash container. She then took out her burner phone and called Boris Berezovsky, one of Vlad's senior leaders, to make sure there was someone to pick her up at the Comox airport.

Catherine Marion, or Katrina as she is called by her Russian people, felt comfortable working with her Russian comrades once again and closer to her father's organization. This should not take too long; all she needs to do is get them on father's plane, and his men will look after the rest. This farmer is not to be underestimated. He has killed some very skilled gunmen up to now. She will need to make sure she keeps that in mind.

The flight from Vancouver to Comox was forty-five minutes, and the small shuttle aircraft found turbulence once it started its descent into Comox airport. The small aircraft flew in the clouds for most of the trip, making it impossible to see it was raining heavily in the area, and once below the clouds, Katrina could see the grayish, dismal downpour. She exited the plane and met up with Boris, both smiling and grateful to see each other.

> In Russian, Boris offered, "My condolences to you and your family on your brother's death."
>
> "Thank you, Boris. We must remember to stay attentive. I understand this farmer is tricky."
>
> "Yes." Boris answered, "he will do things unexpected."
>
> "I want a good night's sleep and a shower first, then let's get the leadership group at my hotel tomorrow morning and come up with a plan. We need to do something unexpected, something he would not expect us to do. I have some ideas that I want to run by your people tomorrow."

Katrina checked into her hotel room in Courtney and had a shower and a change of clothes. She went downstairs to have something light to eat before going to bed for the night. She chose a n artichoke and salmon salad and a glass of Pinot Gris from a Penticton winery. After her dinner, she decided to spend some time having a nightcap in the hotel lounge with a singer playing his guitar, singing Willie Nelson songs into the night.

The storm that blew in from over the Pacific dissipated, leaving the dusk-lit night somewhat tropical, with the bright green lawns and the vivid red flowers on the rhododendron bushes. Katrina sat on a bench that was cut from a huge log with carvings along its entire length. As she sat there, she closed her eyes and focused on her plan. She went over each step in detail. It was so clear to her.

As she walked into the lobby area to go to her room, the girl behind the desk called Katrina over to the desk.

"There is a message for you, Mrs. Marion."

"Thank you," Katrina replied.

As she opened the message, her face dropped to the floor. It was from Mike Stone.

40

Jon made it home in complete confusion. The only good part of the whole situation was that he had a good dinner, but on the other hand, he had difficulties paying for it. Jon's mind was racing, "Was she abducted, was she lying in a ditch somewhere, was she in a hospital?" Jon Marion phoned every hospital and 911 office in the area, but nothing came through. It wasn't intended. If so, she would leave a note, wouldn't she? Jon had lots of questions, and he was afraid The Russians were after her as well, but why?

He called Allen, thinking maybe there was something that he didn't consider. Allen would see it right away. He's like that, like that bug he sensed that was in his office today. He called Allen and explained the whole thing to him.

"Jon, I want you to bring in four or five items that only she would have touched."

"What are you saying, Allen?"

"You know that fingerprints and all means of identification, such as DNA, are the first course of establishing identification. Jon, you are emotionally wrapped up in this case."

"You are right, Allen. I will bring the items in. Sorry about my behavior."

"Jon, meanwhile, I would suggest you freeze your financial accounts."

Allen didn't know a lot about Catherine's background. He remembered her for always being good to Jen and Becky and, once introduced, spent a lot of effort in developing a relationship with them.

Maybe too much effort, tomorrow may tell a story or a secret. Allen called Mike to update them and to just see how Mike was enduring the situation. He also sent Mike a picture of Catherine just to keep him informed the best way he could. He wasn't sure she was involved, but everything Jon told him pointed to her being involved in some way, but he was not sure how.

Mike considered everything that Allen told him. There were four high-end hotels in Courtney. He knew receptionists who worked at two of them. He called them. At first, he got nowhere with the name Catherine Marion. The second had Catherine Marion registered in their hotel.

"Hey Mike, don't tell anyone I gave you this information, eh!"

"Don't worry, Judy; I won't tell a soul; one more favor if I could, just leave a paper message to her, "Welcome to Courtney, have a great stay." Then just print my name on it."

"Will do, Mike."

"Thanks, Judy, take care."

Mike called Allen back to inform him that he had found Catherine Marion and gave him the name of the hotel in Courtney. Allen, in turn, contacted the local RCMP to have her arrested. The local RCMP responded in good time, catching her checking out of the hotel. Katrina was held in a jail cell without a cell phone or anything else to communicate with. The RCMP contacted Allen with deportation details, and she would be headed back down to New York to face the various charges the authorities had to deal with there.

It was eleven thirty at night, and now he had to inform Jon about all the details of his wife's performance over the past twenty hours.

"Jon, sorry for waking you this late, but I have some information on your wife that I think you should know about right away."

Allen had Jon's undivided attention and was listening to every detail.

Allen continued, "We found her in Canada, and the RCMP have her in custody in preparation for deportation back to New York."

Jon had two questions that came out without thinking, " Allen, what the hell was she doing in Canada, and how did you find her there?"

"I can't help you much there, Jon. I am holding both answers as security risks; you don't need to know. I am just calling you as a curtesy call to let you know that she is fine and she will be returning home soon."

"You said she was in custody; has she been arrested, and what for?"

Allen was surprised at the last question; it didn't sound like Jon, " Because she took your money and ran, Jon."

"Did you gather those items that I asked you to?

"Yes, they are right here in a plastic bag., I'll bring them in the morning."

After Jon hung up the phone from Allen's call, he went downstairs to his office and turned on his computer. He hadn't checked e-mails in a while and was curious to see if Ruby responded to his request for information on his wife's cell number. He had several new e-mails but opened the one from Ruby. As usual, she was very thorough. Her report identified several calls to and from the Moscow area as well as some lately from and to the Courteney, Canada area. Jon checked her texts and found several identifying intel from the abduction, specifically giving information that she gained from Jon. There was the evidence he needed to confirm his wife Catherine was a spy working for the Russian mob to gain intel and instrumental in the planning to abduct Jen and Becky. He sat in silence for some time to digest what he had just learned.

Jon thought for a while and sent the whole report to Allen. If nothing else, it may help Allen understand that he was on his side. Jon decided to go to Courteney and help Allen bring her back. Because she was his wife, he understood Allen wouldn't think well of him taking on the task of bringing her back, but at least he could help Allen. Jon then gathered up hairbrushes, tooth brush, her coffee mug from this morning, and a few other items that she may have left DNA or finger prints off. Since he decided to leave, he took them to Allen's office before he left.

He packed his bags after he sent a text explaining that he was going to Courteney to help somehow. Jon also had a feeling as Allen did when he found the bug in his office. That deep gut feeling told Jon that it wasn't going to be an easy task, and it most likely could use Jon's help, but they weren't prepared for what was coming their way.

41

Agent Sievers arrived in Courtney from New York in the mid-afternoon and was scheduled to return with the prisoner in about six hours. He knew very little about her, but understood she was tied to an international crime syndicate somehow and married to Jon Marion, a FBI lead. On the trip, Agent Sievers considered several times what it would be like if a spouse turned out to be a Russian spy. He couldn't comprehend the concept. But today he was bringing back a spouse who did just that.

His return flight back was in six hours and the RCMP arranged a patrol car to pick him up at the airport and give him a ride to a hotel room so he could change clothes, have a shower, or sleep until it was time to go. He had little time to prepare for the flight and took his "GO" bag, which was a small bag with the necessities for a two-day trip anywhere. As he went through it searching for his toothpaste and shaving gear, he reflected on his instructor in the academy making such a big deal about these bags and what needs to go in them. He always took notes when he rambled on about how this was important and how that was important to take, and why some things were not needed. In his five years with the FBI, he never went without anything that was considered a necessity.

He slept well on the flight from New York to Comox. He enjoyed flying on the FBI's Dassault Falcon 8X executive jet. It was fast and allowed a person to stretch out, relax and sleep comfortably. The room was well appointed with all the items a tired traveler could ask for, but there was nothing he needed more than a good meal.

It was four-thirty local time, but almost seven in New York and after his shower, felt refreshed to go down to the restaurant downstairs. He just put on his coat when he heard a knock on the door, identifying they were room service. Agent Sievers went to the door and looked through the peephole in the door. He couldn't see much through the fisheye aperture, but noticed a soiled napkin on the cart which made him wary.

"I didn't order room service; you have the wrong room."

The voice on the other side of the door yelled out, "here are our hotel ID's to prove we work for the hotel."

Agent Sievers thought for a moment, is this the oldest trick in the book being used on him?

He yelled out to them as he removed his pistol, "Ok, put your badges up by the peep hole so I can see them."

Instead of moving his face by the peep hole, Agent Sievers removed his side arm to witness two quick shots in succession, one directly below the peep hole about an inch and the other one directly above the peephole about an inch.

Sievers was shocked and tripped over his shoes as he backed up from the shots that came through the door. It had good sound effects since both assailants thought they had hit the agent and he had fallen to the floor from his wounds. The two Russian assailants started beating on the door, eventually opening it to find Sievers in perfect condition with a nine-millimeter Glock pointed directly towards them. The first Russian through the door didn't see Sievers at first, Sievers told him to drop firearm, instead he pointed his gun at Sievers, and he shot him. The second Russian made a move for his pistol lying beside him on the floor, while the other missed the agent with his first shot and wasn't given the chance to get the second shot off.

Agent Sievers quickly kicked the guns away from the two corpses and checked for a pulse on the two assailants. Once determining they were both deceased, he called the incident in and waited for the RCMP to attend the scene. He took pictures of the two Russians, sending them off to Allen Fulton with a summary of what happened. After he gave his witness statement, he finally got to eat and was picked up by the RCMP at the hotel to take the prisoner, Katrina Marion, to the FBI plane and back to New York.

Corporal Morley D. Hahn and Constable Jordan H. Blackburn came in the RCMP suburban around eight-fifteen to pick up Agent Sievers. He threw his GO bag in the back of the unit and took the scenic route to the Courtney RCMP detachment. Constable Blackburn was driving, taking us directly down into the underground parking lot, where they waited a few minutes for the prisoner to be escorted to the suburban. She was dressed in a florescent orange "prisoner" uniform with handcuffs and shackles to limit her movement as she walked in short steps across the parking lot.

Sievers observed her closely as she walked towards the suburban. He had seen many prisoners take this walk and she clearly did not exhibit any of the mannerisms or behaviors of a person who is about to be sentenced to life in prison. Corporal Hahn talked to the officers who brought her out as she got into the back passenger seat beside Sievers.

As they were about to leave, Sievers asked to stop the vehicle. Constable Blackburn obliged, and Sievers and Hahn had a discussion out of hearing range.

> Hahn started, "What's up?"
>
> Sievers responded the best way he could, "There is something wrong here, by the way she is conducting herself. Corporal, I have seen many people walk out to the transport vehicle and she is too confident, and too sure of herself and she has a smile on her face?" As I remember on my way here, this Comox airport is relatively remote, isn't it? I remember driving on a two-lane road?"
>
> Corporal Hahn answered, "Well, I guess as compared to an international airport, you could say it's remote, but where are you going with this?"

Agent Sievers had never worked with the RCMP before, asking for things are easier when you're at home. "How easy would it be to have a helicopter take this prisoner to the airport from here?"

Corporal Hahn was set back with this request, "It's not likely, I need more evidence than the fact she's not behaving like most prisoners. Sievers, it's only a ten-minute drive."

Sievers gave it his last-ditch effort to change the Corporals mind, "The FBI will pay for it."

Corporal Hahn looked at agent Sievers, "Would it make you feel better if I drove?"

Sievers shook his head, "Send a suburban to the airport ten minutes ahead of us as a dummy, then I'll consider a compromise. I have been educated by the FBI to spot behavior and mannerism of people and I've seen how accurate it is, that's all the evidence I need."

Corporal Hahn considered what agent Sievers said, "OK, we take an extra patrol car with us, how's that?"

"Two extra patrol cars, each with two men." This was Sievers final compromise.

Corporal Hahn finally agreed and took the time to get the other cars and men lined up. They left the underground parking lot of the RCMP station in convoy, with one patrol car ahead and one behind. Sievers noticed that Katrina Marion was a bit fidgety, he felt with the other police backup. It knocked her confidence down a bit. He found this interesting.

As they turned onto Knight Road, they noticed some construction signs ahead of them, along with equipment.

Agent Sievers said to the Corporal, "Have your men tighten up the distance between vehicles, please."

As they did, they came upon the construction activity, a tractor with a high-boy trailer backed up across the road blocking off all traffic. The Corporal, identifying a potential situation, put the suburban in reverse and tried to maneuver away from the area and head back the way they came. As he worked his way out of the situation, he was facing three large trucks taking the width of the road. He spun the suburban around and was able to drive forwards, with more control and traveled along the ditch to bypass them. At this time, shots could be heard with the patrol cars and the assailants. Sievers could see out the back window that it didn't look good for the men in the patrol cars since they were being shot at from all sides. They were almost where they felt they were safe, and a vehicle stopped ahead of them and got out and placed a bullet into Corporal Hahn's bullet proof vest. He was writhing in pain from the bullet and dealing with the windshield that blew up in his face as the bullet went through it.

Regardless of it being a good or bad decision, Corporal Hahn decided to speed up and drive past them. There was a great deal of luck involved with this decision, but he knew they would avoid killing Katrina. With most of the bullets trying to take out the driver, Sievers moved right over close to Katrina, however, he did not know she was highly trained in hand-to-hand combat.

Katrina waited for the perfect time when he turned his back towards her. She placed her handcuff chains around his throat and strangled him until there was no chance of life. She then grabbed his service pistol and shot the RCMP constable twice in the head. Katrina then pointed the gun at Corporal Hahn and told him to stop the vehicle. When the vehicle stopped, she shot him several times, making sure he was dead. She exited the RCMP suburban and walked calmly over to three men on the road, "Good to see you gentlemen, now let's pay this Mr. Stone a visit."

42

Jen was restless as she tried to get to sleep. It wasn't the bed or Becky; it was just too much stuff running through her head. She was concerned for Becky more than she was concerned for her own safety and well-being, but when is this marathon of attacks going to end?

Jen carefully got out of bed without waking Becky. She needed a glass of water and decided to take some aspirins to try and help her sleep. As she went to the kitchen, she passed Mike's bedroom. The moonlight shone bright through the windows, allowing her to navigate through the house without additional lighting.

As Mike laid there, she recalled all the fun times they had when they were in their late teens and early twenties; it seemed like a lifetime, but actually, it was only a decade long. Seeing Mike lay there in bed brought all the memories back, from when they first went out, to when she told him she needed more. A tear rolled down the side of her cheek, not in regret but realizing that was the end of all the fun from her early life. She loved Allen deeply and told herself over and over that she would marry him again. Somehow, Mike was different. He made her feel excited every day she was with him. Now being around him every day, brought back that same excitement and she couldn't help herself. She tried to rationalize her thoughts but couldn't, she loved Allen and was married to him, and she loved her life in New York. And then Mike came back into the picture, and everything was changing again.

She put her emptied glass on the counter and entered Mike's bedroom. She could hear his gentle snoring, a sound that she remembered often that would put her to sleep. She straddled his sleeping body with her legs as she kissed him on the lips.

Mike woke up startled, "What the heck is this about, what are you doing?"

"I got up for a glass of water and noticed you in bed all by yourself, it got me thinking about when we were going out," Jen answered.

Josie woke from a voice in the house and decided to find out where it was coming from. As she walked quietly into the kitchen, she saw Jen on top of Mike. After realizing what was going on, she left to return to her bedroom and leave them to their privacy.

As she turned to walk back, she overheard Mike talking to Jen, "we can't do this, Jen. We had our time together and now, that's behind us. I was my best friend's best man at your wedding, and I will not dis-honor him."

Jen was disappointed, "Mike, it's not like it's a forever thing, it's just a tonight thing."

Mike was trying to leave this situation as friends, "that won't make it any easier for either one of us. We both know we will feel like hell in the morning." Mike paused for a while then said, "I understand the stress this ordeal is placing on you is unimaginable, don't compound that stress with more, it will cripple you and ruin you and your family. You must agree with me that it's not worth it, right?"

As Jen got off him, she agreed with him and kissed him on the cheek this time and left his room. She sat on the porch for a while, wondering about her own sanity throughout all this chaos, and started crying hard. Mike heard her sobbing and got up to comfort her, as they sat together on the outdoor sofa, they talked as Mike talked to her to relax her from her emotional state.

"Mike, life isn't fun anymore, we used to have so much fun without even trying."

He answered, "Yes, it is still fun, we must keep it fun, and you have so much to be happy about, especially with Becky and Allen." Mike smiled, "If you want, you could pick another fight with Gail Williams, she still lives in the same old place."

Jen started laughing, "Oh no, only you would remember that! I really decked her, she deserved it."

Mike laughed, "About the only time I ever saw you mad, except for when Miss Cox tried to have you expelled from Library."

Jen smiled, "Yea, I remember that I would have gotten away with it if Judy Brandreth didn't snitch on me, but I got her back good."

Mike was curious, "I didn't hear about that, what did you do?"

"Really, I thought everyone heard about that. One day I took that shortcut down by the Tsable River to get to our house and caught her and Gord McNab skinny dipping in the river. I grabbed their clothes without them knowing and hid them."

Both Jen and Mike started laughing as quietly as they could. Jen looked at Mike with a smile on her face, "Thanks Mike, I feel much better now. You can always make me feel so happy."

Josie carefully walked back to her room so no one could hear her. She was very surprised that Mike would turn Jen down, she was a beautiful woman, they knew each other well, and she wanted him, she was vulnerable, and Mike was not taking advantage of her.

As Josie lay in her bed, she began to understand the depth of Mike's integrity and compassion, the same integrity that has gained him the respect he has amongst his friends and within the community. She had met so many men during her training classes with the FBI, and before that as she learned her trade in martial arts. Her last relationship ended with her boyfriend, at the time, cheating on her, which she never got over. It was the act of being cheated on that bothered her. She got over him quickly, but it was so unexpected or unpredicted.

It was Mike's calm way of dealing with stressful situations, and his kindness in helping others without expecting anything in return. She had feelings for a man that she barely knows for three days, but the more she thought of him, the deeper her feelings became. She felt she could trust him at her most vulnerable moment. He made her laugh, and the way he made her feel, there were so many things about this man.

Finally, as she closed her eyes, she drifted off into the oblivion that she woke from. She dreamed of having pets and feeding cattle and riding horses and being with Mike Stone.

43

When Allen Fulton reviewed the RCMP report of the massacre at the Comox airport, he was ready to send the entire US military. Agent Sievers was a good friend of the directors and was deeply upset over his passing. He contacted Mike to inform him, but he had already known about the shooting since it was being broadcasted over the media every half hour.

Thirty minutes from Allen's call, Mike's neighboring farmer, Lars Erickson called Mike, "Hey Mike, are you doing some work with your excavator down by the pull out just west of your house?"

Mike replied, "No, I'm a bit busy here right now with some unwanted guests."

Lars added, "Yea, I gather that, I just drove by there, and noticed three rental vehicles parked in the pull out by your excavator and thought I'd give you a shout."

"Glad you did. Could you check if there is anyone there now, and if the cars are still parked there, could you fire up the hoe and dig a ditch across the access to the highway?"

Lars replied, "But they wouldn't be able to leave the pull-out if I dig the ditch."

Mike answered his friends concern, "Exactly, dig it fast and get out. That pull out is on my land and they didn't ask permission to park their cars there."

Lars parked his truck on the side of the road and got up on the excavator. He turned on the main switch that isolates the battery from the rest of the machine. He started the engine on the excavator and turned the unit around to start digging the ditch. It was fine soil and sand mixture so the time it took to dig the four-foot ditch was minimized. Once completed, Lars took the excavator down the road to Mike's place where Mike gave him a ride back to his truck.

As Mike returned to the Island Highway, he looked down towards his place and observed several people on the road by the pull-out where Lars dug the ditch. Despite it taking longer, Mike returned home another way avoiding the group at the pull-out. The road was very rough and Mike's cell phone bounced off the passenger seat and under the rear seat, and with about five minutes left before getting home, the cell phone started to ring and wouldn't stop.

As Mike came within view of the farmhouse, he got out of his truck to find the cell phone. Not recognizing the number on his display, he put the phone in his shirt pocket and drove up his driveway to the house.

> As he turned in to park, he saw Becky running out the door, "Mike! They have mom and they said they were going to kill her!"
>
> "Where's Josie and Sharon?" Mike demanded.
>
> "Sharon hid in the basement and about four guys ganged up on Josie, she's hurting." Becky came up for air, "Mike, where are they taking mom?"

Mike grabbed his long rifle from the truck along with his pack and ran with Becky in the house. He assessed Josie's wounds, she looked worse than she was and helped her wash the blood off her face. Mike told Becky to go downstairs with Sharon and for Josie to follow him up into the attic. Mike went to the south side of the attic and smashed the window out. From this vantage point, he could see the Russians trying to figure out how to get their vehicles over the ditch and not having much success. He could see everyone well, but it was a mile and a bit away, a long shot, not impossible just technically very challenging.

He looked through his scope and was able to see Jen; she appeared to be beaten up pretty bad. The gun he had with him was a rifle he had shot many times at long range competitions, it was very convenient, but this was much different. This was no competition, this was Jen's life. Sweat was forming around his eyes, and he felt perspiration run down his armpits.

He loaded a shell into the breach and pushed the bolt forward to lock the cartridge firmly for the shot. He was watching as the Russian abductor grabbed Jen by the hair and threw her to the ground. He then pulled out his pistol and aimed it at Jen, just as Mike squeezed off a perfectly placed shot. The Russian dropped his pistol and folded like a wet rag as he hit the ground. Mike realized he had to finish what he started and killed the other three.

As Mike looked through his scope, he could see Jen was alright but crying. Mike and Josie jumped in the truck and headed down to where Jen was. Mike picked her up and placed her in the back seat of the farm truck and took her back to the farmhouse. She held on to Mike around the neck tightly and didn't want him to leave her. They sat around the fire pit as Mike tried to calm Jen down. Sharon came out from her hiding spot in the basement and joined in the re-telling of the shooting incident once again.

Jen looked around and couldn't find Becky, "Where's Becky?"

Mike knew he told her to go downstairs, he looked at Sharon, "where is she, Sharon?"

Sharon looking nervous with everyone staring at her, "Well, that lady took her, I thought you knew all about it. When she came to us, she said that Director Allen Fulton asked her to come and help Mike, Becky knew her."

"Where the hell did she take her?" came from everyone in the group.

Jen exclaimed, crying, "Yes, where is Becky, and who was this woman?"

Sharon muttered, "I have no idea. Becky called her Mrs. Marion."

Jen couldn't believe it, "Catherine Marion! That bitch, when I see her next I'll……"

Mike stopped her, "Jen, lets focus on saving our energy on getting Becky back."

Mike took Jen and Josie to the hospital to have them checked out, then proceeded to call Allen to report Becky being abducted. Allen suggested to look around the airport hangers while Jen and Josie were being checked out and Allen was checking flights being booked. Mike didn't think about the airport, if this is where they were taking her, he didn't have time to waste.

44

Catherine was sitting beside Becky in the back seat of the SUV as the driver sped off from the farmhouse.

Becky was not feeling safe. She felt something was wrong, "so where are you taking me, Mrs. Marion?"

"We are going to meet up with your mother and Mike," Katrina answered her.

Becky was thinking how she could confirm Catherine's true intentions, "I'm going to need my medication soon, will Linda and Rachelle be there as well?"

Katrina knew nothing of a Linda or a Rachele, or for that matter medication, " They will be there, and your mother had us get addition medication for you, you are well looked after."

Becky now knew she was in trouble, being abducted by her family's closest friend, and the wife of her father's closest colleague at work. She looked around for opportunities to get out of this situation. She saw they were headed for the airport, then pretended to be sick and started puking up towards Catherine. Avoiding being hit by a nasty heave, Catherine moved over against the left-hand door as Becky curled up in her act of abdominal cramps. As Katrina moved, her purse fell over, and a syringe fell out and rolled under Catherine's seat. Catherine noticed Becky reaching for it, and the last thing she wanted was to have her use it against her as a weapon. As Catherine pushed Becky's head and torso downwards, she couldn't push her down far enough to avoid getting an injection in the ankle. She fought Katrina hard and now Becky was under Katrina, wedged between the front and rear seats as she applied all her weight on top of her. Becky couldn't move.

She knew she didn't inject her with the full needle volume, but hoped it was enough. Finally, Becky relaxed as the drug was showing its effect which eventually put her to sleep. She got her hands under her and pushed as hard as she could, pushing Katrina over on the seat.

Now Becky had to deal with the driver of the car she was riding in. With a very clear understanding that either victim or abductor would die, she rammed the needle into the top of the driver's right-hand shoulder and squeezed the last amount out of the needle. The driver writhed and squirmed with pain as the needle was moved around throughout the injection. The driver stopped the vehicle to go after Becky and tie her up, but just before the vehicle stopped, Becky jumped out and ran. She watched the mad man run after her, gaining distance, then finally, the drug kicked in and he fell to the ground.

She waved down a passing motorist and got a ride to the Courtney detachment of the RCMP, giving her story and account of the incident. She called her mother and Mike to explain that she needed a ride back to the farmhouse. The RCMP dispatched six patrol cars out to the scene, but they were too late, the car and passengers were gone.

After getting Becky, Jen and Mike called Allen to give him an account of the abduction incident.

Becky spoke up, "Dad, it was Mrs. Marion, and she was giving orders to the others!"

"Very interesting, I guess I have a few things to discuss with Jon Marion, the case lead." Allen paused while he took some time to let it all resonate, "I wonder what part if any he is playing in all this."

Jen interjected, "Well, why don't you go down to his office and ask him?"

"That's the problem, I can't. He hasn't showed up for work or answered his phone since Catherine ran away on him."

Allen decided to text Jon with the latest developments of his wife. He was shocked that she would be a major part of his daughters abduction. He remembered all the time that Jon and Catherine were part of his family's outings, and now this. Allen gave up waiting for an immediate response from Jon, he had no idea where he was or what his plans were. He tossed his cell phone on his desk in frustration and continued with his other work. He was on his way to the kitchen area to make himself a coffee, his comfort during this chaos. The cell phone chirped out a noise that indicated a message had been received. He walked over to his desk and picked up the phone to see the display reading a returned message from Jon. It said:

> *I am very sorry for what my wife has done, I do not want you to think I had anything to do with her actions, but I will accept full responsibility, I should have seen it. I searched our home and found additional information on your family that she must have sent them, I have left it on the kitchen table for you to review.*
>
> *Based on the documents I found, discovered she left for Courtney, and I am on my way to deal with her myself.*
>
> *Jon*

Allen immediately tried calling him, but only received a text message back,

> *I will call you once I have completed my objective.*

Allen had no idea just what his objective was, but only assumed that based on the text message, Jon was on his side. Allen immediately called Mike to update him on Jon's communication by text. Allen contacted Lee Magnuson from the forensic lab,

"Lee, have you gotten anything from that bug you guys found in my office?"

"No." Lee said, "Europol had nothing either."

"Do you have a data base of all fingerprints of FBI spouses?"

Lee didn't particularly care for that question but answered, "yes we do."

"Run it and let me know if you find anything there."

Lee said "Sure, hold the line and I'll do it right now, it won't take long."

The computer monitor flashed a few times until the match was found. Lee continued,   "Oh my god! I got a positive match for Catherine Marion, but you already knew that, didn't you?"

Allen answered him, "Yes, I did."

Lee added, "We also found an additional fingerprint behind the back plate of the bug when it was put together. It's becoming more difficult to find a match on it; we are running it through international sources as well."

Allen piped up, "Let me know immediately when you find a match on it, thanks, Lee."

45

Andrei had Sergei Petrov give a presentation of the developments of the Mindsweeper program. This project would catapult the family business even higher, and Andrei was getting impatient for its completion.

"So where are you at with the Mindsweeper project?" Andrei demanded.

Sergei was nervous but had finally completed, "We are completed with the implementation of the American's software program and ready to test on humans."

Sergei noticed a smile on Andrei's face, a very rare occurrence over the past several months. Sergei knew how important it was for Andrei to have the Mindsweeper program running for several reasons. One of those reasons was that in his older age his body was deteriorating, and Andrei wanted to transplant his mind into a younger body before it completely collapsed like his father's, his dream was immortality. The second reason was to be able to develop an elite group or army of criminals that could be programed to conduct various criminal acts such as hand-to-hand fighting, long range shooting, high speed driving, etc. His goal was to cripple international economics through this highly efficient army of criminals and eventually take over countries as they weaken from the financial stress his men place on them. Sergei was getting excited during the development of the Mindsweeper program because he could see that it was possible, and he wanted to become a part of it. Imagine, to have immortality, who wouldn't be excited?

Andrei replied, "Very good Sergei, I will have two participants ready for initial testing this week, to prove to me it works. With these participants, you will transfer the minds in each other's bodies. Will you be ready?"

Sergei answered his boss, "Yes, I will be ready, when would you want to test the programing segment to the project?"

Andrei snapped back, "It's not when I want to do it, it's when you want to do it. You should have a clear understanding by now just how important this project is to me, as well as the time sensitive nature it has."

Sergei was quick to respond, "The end of next week would work well for me."

Sergei went back to his computer lab and over the next three days, his team validated calculations, program specifics and theory. He delegated sections of the program to individuals to triple check. Sergei was under specific time restraints now and wanted everything to go as planned. Andrei volunteered to find the participants for the tests, what if they put up a ruckus at the last minute, that would create difficulties to the process? He needed to do some research on putting them out to sleep prior to the actual transfer. Sergei reflected for a few minutes on his first creation, and the outcome of the mind-transferring they did that day. Although not completely successful, it gave Andrei's father some more time.

Twelve years prior, Andrei's father was terminally ill, and when Andrei heard the news that he had six months left, he took it very hard. He was very close to his father, the man taught him so much about the business and life, Andrei could not imagine a day without his father. He searched for a solution and even with all the influence Andrei could offer, there seemed to be no solution for his father's depleted health. He read an article about a brilliant computer programing expert who was studying mind scanning for police interrogations.

Andrei confronted him and hired him to develop a program to transfer his father's mind to a healthy younger body. With the limited time available, Sergei developed a program that was not yet tested. One day, the hospital called Andrei to inform him that he should expect his father to pass within the next few days and with this, had Sergei test the program on his father. Initially, the test was a success, however, over a period of six months, his father's health went from that of a twenty-year-old to someone closer to a hundred.

Sergei expected to be shot, but instead, Andrei had him work on the program to find out what needed to be done to enable the program to be reliable. He still felt that he could save his father. That is when Sergei discovered that a missing component was required to enable the mind to accept the brain of the recipient body, which is where the program that the American, Joe McGee developed, came into play. Joe had developed the program to attain acceptance of the program each time it was used in order to record accurate medical data for the technologists to analyze.

Sergei was excited about the new revisions to the Mindsweeper program. Once this program is made known to the international theater, he will be famous. He needed to ground himself. He knew there were a few steps to go before his picture got placed on the front cover of magazines and media. He spent the next two days being the devil's advocate, coming up with things that could go wrong, and troubleshooting the solution. With the two issues that he went through, he came up with a solution, and after two days, he sat in front of his computer, satisfied with the outcome of his work. He was now ready and confident the program would work.

> At ten o'clock the following morning, he got a call from Andrei, "Are you ready to complete a mind transfer on my father?"
>
> Sergei answered, "I was hoping to test it out on a common person first, Andrei!"
>
> "There's no time, you said you would be ready, now it's time for you to produce."

"OK, there's really nothing else I can do at this point anyways, let's do it."

Andrei commanded, "Good, I'll see you in your lab in an hour."

"Andrei, what about tomorrow?"

"What about in an hour?" Andrei challenged him.

Sergei answered, "OK, in an hour."

Sergei got his team together and had everything set up, making sure all the hardware was connected correctly; one loose connection could send someone's mind flying around the room. Besides, once he turns the system on, the outcome will offer him either a raise or death.

46

Jon Marion was sitting at gate 37 in Vancouver airport, waiting to board his flight to Comox. Jon was lacking all comprehension of why Catherine did what she said to Allen's family, when he discovered it. He couldn't believe it, no more than he could understand why she did this to him and to their best friends. He couldn't believe that she was a spy while being married to him, sucking information from him and sending it to God only knows who. He was reflecting on their relationship and their marriage; did she ever love him?

As the voice over the PA system called out to inform the passengers that the Comox flight was boarding, Jon gathered his carry-on baggage and entered the plane. It was a smaller commuter plane suitably designed for the thirty-minute flight, but inside, Jon was challenged navigating through the isle passenger seating and stowing baggage in the over-head bins.

After finding his seat and getting buckled in, the plane was backed out of the gate and taxied on its way to the flight's runway. The sudden lurch forward started the plane on its way down the runway, and Jon felt that familiar lift-off as the plane ascended into the clouded sky.

Jon looked downward. He could see the rugged coastline and the sailing craft lazily anchored in the bays and docking areas. Jon closed his eyes and pictured himself on the deck of one of those boats anchored outside of a sandy beach, forgetting all about life's stressful moments without care.

Jon's attention was turned to reality as the flight attendant came over the load speaker to announce the plane's descent into Comox airport. Jon waited for those ahead of him to leave the plane and took his items out of the overhead bins. A lady was having problems removing her baggage, and Jon helped her before getting his own. She smiled at him with a beautiful smile that caught and held his attention for just a bit too long. Another passenger asked him to hurry up, and he pulled away from her luring gaze. He stopped for a minute and checked all his pockets for wallets and passports.

After picking up his baggage on the carousel, he went over to the car rental booth, completing his paperwork. The attendant asked if he wanted full insurance coverage for the vehicle. He paused as this was an option he had never considered in the past, but today, he said, " Yes."

He loaded all his baggage from the cart into the vehicle. Since he was with the FBI, he was able to bring his pistol with him, provided he completed a stack of documentation the Canadian Customs required, and this was approved when he entered Canada at the Vancouver airport. He removed the pistols from their case and donned his holster, placing one of the pistols in the holster. He took the clip-on holster, attached it under his seat, and placed the second pistol in it. He set his GPS on the dash of the SUV and turned it on to let it re-set itself to its current location. After entering his hotel address, he drove off along Knight Road towards Courtney. As Jon drove to the hotel, he couldn't help but notice how green the Comox / Courtney area was. Lawns, trees, and flowers all displayed a beautiful backdrop for the town. It had just rained, giving the streets and sidewalks a clean appearance.

Jon checked in to the hotel, took his baggage up to the room, and had a quick shower to freshen up from the ten-hour trip. He decided to have an early dinner and plan his day for tomorrow. Jon looked at the menu, which offered many of the local delicacies, and chose a Steak Neptune, which was an eight once steak smothered with crab meat, and a glass of Chateau Neuf-de Pape wine. The dining room overlooked Discovery Passage as he was entertained by the numerous boats traveling back and forth. One ship that came very close to the shore in front of the dining room was a cruise ship with all its splendor navigating its way safely on its Northern route.

As Jon was losing himself in the scenery, a tall, slender man in a Western hat sat down at his table across from him.

He did not introduce himself, " welcome to Courtney Jon. I take it your trip was pleasant."

Jon was surprised, " sorry, you have me at a bit of a disadvantage. I just landed in a place I have never been to. You recognize me and know my name. I didn't catch your name?"

Mike gave Jon one of his warm country smiles, " correct, I didn't offer it."

Jon was a bit confused, " why are you sitting at my table?"

" Excuse me for being blunt; I want to know why you are here. I want to know if you are working with me or if you are my enemy." Mike paused to organize his thoughts, " and I want to know now."

"Well, whoever the hell you are, it's simply none of your business now. Please leave."

Mike responded, " I understand Catherine bailed on you, and you followed her here. Why are you and Catherine trying to abduct Jen and Becky?"

Jon was trying to figure this guy out. He asked himself, was this the guy who was looking after Allen's family? He decided to take the chance. " I'm not! I'm best friends with Allen and Jen. I'm here to right the wrong my wife has done to his family."

Mike was trying to figure out if this guy was telling him the honest truth or just stringing him a line of what he thought Mike wanted to hear, but he wasn't sure about him.

Mike got up to walk away, "Have a great stay here in Courtney, but if we meet again, it better be on friendly terms."

Surprised, Jon said, "that sure sounded like a threat to me."

Mike turned looking at him face to face. "You can take it any way you want to." Mike retorted, "I see you have a nine-millimeter side arm strapped to your right side. I asked myself, who takes a pistol to dinner in a restaurant when they are the only ones at the table in a place they have never been before? For your well-being and information, I am packing as well. I have two three-fifty-seven magnums strapped on my right and left sides, and I know how to use them."

Mike started to leave Jon's dining table," you need to call Allen."

"What's your name, and how can I contact you?" Jon asked.

"My name is Mike."

Jon asked, "Mike, who? What's your contact number?"

"Get it from Allen," Mike said as he left the dining room.

Jon figured that this must be the one looking after Allen's family. "Do you want my number; how will you contact me?"

Mike Stone walked out of the dining room without acknowledgment. He already got it from Allen. Jon considered what Mike had told him, went back to his room, and made a call he didn't want to make. Allen later texted Mike to let him know that Jon had contacted him and that he gave him Mike's last name and cell number.

47

Andrei was looking at his organization, and now, with Vlad gone, he needed someone with solid leadership capabilities to lead his organization into the international theater. He analyzed everyone in his organization, and with the exception of an informant he had deep inside the CIA, he couldn't come up with a heavy-hitting leader. Vlad was the only one capable of taking on that role. In order to mentor someone within his group, he would have to spend almost five years, and he did not have that much time considering his goals. His daughter Katrina was a potential leader, but he was not pleased by the way she was taking over from Vlad.

The director's daughter should have been in Moscow by now, and all he got back from Katrina was excuses and a long story about a farmer. There was only one person that he knew who could fill this void and get the results he needed other than himself, and that was his father. In his present state, he was unable, but in a young body, his father could work with him to develop the business and create the economic havoc that he needed to take control of countries.

After consulting Sergei, Andrei considered the risks, and with his father's present condition, should something go wrong, death wouldn't be a bad thing. He had a young man whose health and fitness were ideal for the transfer and was locked up in a holding cell until they developed the Minesweeper for the mind transfer process. Andrei spent a great deal of effort and time going over each detail and had their lawyer review the last will and testament of his father. Andrei wanted to make sure everything was in place in case his father died in the process to ensure that everything would legally be his.

Andrei had his father taken to the computer lab for the transfer, and the young man Andrei selected was also moved to an area where he could be held in restraints. Ivan Rabinovitch was twenty-six years old and came from a family who imported goods from North America. As a young man, he made the mistake of chasing the money and quitting his father's business to make twice the money with Andrei. Ivan was asked to terminate a family who was caught sending information against Andrei's company to the international media.

Ivan was told to terminate the family, which included some young members, and Ivan refused. He was placed in a holding cell for two years. Ivan was not told what he was about to participate in but knew he wanted nothing to do with it. During the two years he spent confined, he had to keep fit and comply with a demanding supervised work out and was fed a very strict diet. He couldn't understand why Andrei was looking out for his health with such detail. He was told that he would be doing his time and then coming back to be part of Andrei's crime team.

From his cell, he could see Sergei preparing helmets and equipment and attaching a helmet to an old man who was barely able to speak. Once Sergei was satisfied with the old man, three security guards came to his cell, wrestled him to the floor, and put on a restraining suit on him. As he lay on the bench in the computer lab, he wrestled with them as they tried to attach the helmet to his head, eventually placing straps over his head and the rest of his torso to hold him still. Ivan heard Sergei tell Andrei the process would take about forty-five minutes. Ivan tried to find out what the process was, but no one answered him.

As Ivan lay there, unable to move, he looked at all the computer equipment and wires he was hooked up to. Andrei was there himself, and Ivan found that in itself disturbing since Andrei was only ever in attendance for any activities that were extremely important to him, regardless of importance to anyone else. Ivan thought of his mother and father, and as he felt a tear pool up and run down his cheek, he wished he had the opportunity to take back that decision he had made in haste. He didn't feel the money was worth it now.

Then Ivan felt a low-pitched humming that pulsated with his heartbeat. Even though he wanted no part of it, it became soothing and pleasant. It felt as though he was floating, and he became aware that his arms and legs stopped fighting the restraints until all muscle tension was relaxed. He was starting to drift in and out of consciousness and unable to hear voices in the room. Ivan drifted unconsciously into black oblivion without recollection of things happening around him or voices.

When Ivan regained consciousness, he became aware of the activity around him. There was something wrong with the way he felt; he was extremely tired, and he hurt everywhere. There were people asking him silly questions: what's your name? What day is it? Where was he? What bothered him was, as simple as the questions were and as hard as he tried, he couldn't remember. He looked to see there were no restraints on him and, in his attempt to escape, fell off the bench and lay on the floor. He looked around and saw Sergei and the security try to help him back on the bench and, in the process, saw himself on the other bench.

This other version of Ivan was as he remembered himself, and he had everyone checking him out and helping him walk, obviously from past skills obtained in a lifetime many years ago. He watched Andrei approach the other and started to give him a hug, calling him father. At that time, Ivan figured out what the process entailed, but at the same time, it was too late. He realized his life, for as long as it may be, was destined to be held captive in a dying man's body. The staff rolled him and the treatment bench into the cell where he had been held captive for the past two years and told him he would be looked after tomorrow. Calmly, he understood exactly what that meant and accepted his fate.

Dominik, on the other hand, awoke from the process feeling invigorated and strong. Dominik felt better than he had ever felt in his life. He was getting used to this new body, eye-hand coordination needed some work, and he found some issues with walking. His mind felt sharp with improved reflexes as the doctors checked him out, and his ability to answer the same basic questions as was asked of Ivan was found to be simple and answered with instant responses.

After hours of checking Dominik's medical condition, the doctors ended up recommending physiotherapy to help him regain balance and eye-hand coordination to enable him to return to walking faster. They moved Dominik to a room in the Palace, which he would find more comfortable and closer to Andrei.

Despite the time of day, Dominik could not sleep. He was excited with his new body and understood what he could now accomplish with his son. He smiled as he danced around the room. He fell over twice but picked himself back up quickly and continued dancing.

48

After his conversation with Jon Marion, Mike was unclear as to what needed to be done at this point. He quietly asked Josie to meet him by the calving barn, at which time he summarized his conversation with Jon Marion to Josie, then called Allen on his cell phone and placed the phone on speaker. He summarized his conversation with Jon and asked Allen for some information on Jon to get an understanding of which side of the fence he was standing on. Was Jon truthful when he said he was trying to hold his wife's actions accountable, or was he plotting against them in trying to abduct them again?

"Allen, you have gone through the training, and you have the resources. I need to better understand this guy. You know him better than either Josie or me," Mike said.

"I have my immediate thoughts, but let me run this by our senior behavioral analysts, and I'll give you a callback. Until then, watch out for the both of them."

Mike and Josie both gave the "copy that" acknowledgment as the director hung up the phone at his end. Mike was in deep thought, and Josie did not want to disturb him. She enjoyed Mike including her in these discussions; it made her feel appreciated as part of the team making decisions and plans. She also enjoyed being with Mike by themselves. She could feel herself being drawn closer to him every time they were together.

As they walked toward the farmhouse from the calving shed, they heard three SUVs drive up to the front door of the house, and six people got out and rushed inside. They heard screaming from Becky and Jen. Mike realized they needed to work fast. Mike and Josie ran into the workshop and grabbed a bow that he was finishing and as many arrows as they could carry. They ran out of the workshop and hid behind an old tractor that was close to the ATVs. Mike wasted no time running to their vehicles, slashed the front tires, deflating them completely, and returned to where Josie was. He whistled loudly to beckon Tigger and Duke, but they didn't come and didn't answer.

> From the house, Mike heard a familiar female voice, "Well, Mr. Stone, I see we are meeting again to answer your question from two days ago. Yes, I am enjoying my stay in Courtney. If you are looking for your dog and cat, they are in the basement sleeping. I understand you think highly of your pets, probably more than the three women. I have no intentions of hurting either one unless you show any resistance in allowing us to leave the house and drive away."

Mike did not answer; he had no plan, and they had the upper hand in the situation, but he vowed they would not leave his property with Jen and Becky. He spotted a very subtle movement on the other side of the house; it appeared to be proceeding to the farmhouse with a gun drawn and staying behind cover.

A moment later, Catherine came out with Jen. She grabbed a handful of her hair and led her through the back door. She looked mean and shook Jen's head with a scowl on her face, like a vengeful brat. In her other hand, she held a forty-five ACP handgun. Mike could tell she had held one before. The others started to come out of the farmhouse; they were tied, and the Russians threw them down on the porch while Katrina held Jen up like a trophy for Mike to look at. Catherine was far enough away from Jen he could make the shot with his bow but not with the pistol.

Mike noticed that the silhouette of the person on the other side of the house was no longer there. He whispered to Josie to watch for Jon to come around the west side of the house to see if Jen would run and give her some cover with the pistol if needed. He laid out four arrows on the tractor tire, and as Catherine bashed Jen's head into the post, he stepped out from behind the tractor tire and placed two fatal arrows in each of the abductors who were on the porch, the first into Zani and the second into Lokai. Then, yelling for everyone to run, he laid out another four arrows.

Becky and Sharon ran to the east, behind the cars, and Jen broke free from Katrina's grip and ran west toward one of the outbuildings. As three Russians came running out of the house, Katrina yelled at them to go after them, and two Russians ran after Sharon and Becky. Mike fired two arrows, one missing and one hitting the Russian in the chest. He grabbed another arrow and sent it off quickly, finding the fatal spot in the other Russian. The last Russian abductor threw his gun down and put his hands indicating that he had enough.

Katrina Marion fired three shots in Mike's direction and immediately ran after Jen.

Josie fired off a series of three shots in Katrina's direction, and Mike yelled out to her,   "It's over, Catherine. You are the only one alive. Drop your gun and walk towards me."

She retorted back, " it's never going to be over."

"Well, let me re-phrase that then, it's over for you."

Katrina dropped her gun and continued chasing Jen. She knew he would never shoot her unarmed. Josie could see what she needed to do, and she left the pistol with Mike and took off after Katrina, catching up to her just before she grabbed Jen. Katrina leaned over to her left ankle and grabbed her second pistol attached to a holster on the calf of her leg. Katrina swung the pistol around, and Josie grabbed it from the side, twisting it out of her grip. As Josie swung the pistol towards Katrina, she kicked the pistol out of Josie's hand, and the gun landed on the ground amongst the ferns.

Josie and Katrina were now fighting hand to hand in a fight that appeared to be equally matched. Katrina was able to get behind her with a choking grip around her throat when Josie found the opportunity to roll out of the strangle hold and hit Katrina in the nose so hard, you could hear the cartilage crack as it broke. Katrina grabbed Josie's arm and, twisting it, threw her to the ground. Josie got up and drop-kicked Katrina in the collar bone, breaking it, leaving Katrina writhing in pain as she got up and kicked Josie in the stomach, knocking the wind out of her. Katrina did not give up and used her weight to fall on Josie's chest.

Mike was on his way to help Josie, but it was taking him a while to get there. Josie twisted her body to get behind her and put Katrina in a choke hold that Katrina could not get out of. Katrina pulled her left boot up to her hand, and she grabbed a knife from inside of it. She was about to stab Josie when Jon came out from behind a huge spruce stump with his gun in hand, pointing it at Katrina and yelling at his wife to stop. She raised the knife to thrust it towards Josie's thigh when Jon shot into the air. Katrina stared at him with hatred and thrust the knife toward Josie's thigh, barely missing as it hit the ground.

Josie just had enough time to move away. She grabbed Catherine's knife hand with both of hers and twisted sharply as Catherine winched with pain. Josie freed up her right arm and punched her as hard as she could in Catherine's broken collar bone. The pain Catherine experienced was so intense she had to let go of the knife as it dropped away, and Jon took out his handcuffs, placing his wife under arrest.

Mike, Jon, and Josie called Allen to summarize what took place. Allen told them he would be coming himself to take Catherine back to New York and question her. Allen told Mike and Josie that they did a great job and thanked Jon for being there when he was needed.

> "Catherine or Katrina, which I guess is her Russian name, will be interrogated by every law enforcement association in the United States to find all affiliations to Andrei. This

is the first time we had a prisoner who knows all the players in the game."

Allen added, "Do you have sufficient security resources to hold her as a prisoner until I get there tomorrow morning?"

Mike and Josie started to laugh as they watched Duke place his nose six inches from Katrina's as he was staring her down, " I'm sending you a picture of my security team looking after the prisoner."

Allen looked at the picture, "Hey Catherine, I'll see you tomorrow morning. Meanwhile, you make sure Mike treats you good, eh!"

After hanging up the phone, Josie asked Mike, "Hey, is there a bar or something we could all go to and have some fun? It would be good to get our minds off this for a while?"

Mike looks at her with one of his big country smiles, "There sure is, and I think I could get Becky in as well."

Jon said to Mike and Josie, " you guys go ahead and have a good time. You deserve it. I'm going to watch over the prisoner for the night. She's not going to escape this time."

Mike considered it and went into his shop. He picked up two Apple air tag tracking devices and, without Jon or Katrina knowing, planted one on Katrina and another on Jon.

49

They changed into the cleanest clothes they had loaded themselves up in the big truck Mike rented in Calgary and headed off for the evening at the Pub in Fanny Bay for some food and fun. Fanny Bay is a small coastal community that has a very well-known pub that offers its guests great times in a quaint, friendly environment. The pub was built in 1938 by a very talented French carpenter whose attention to detail made the pub an island attraction for tourists and locals. Mike and the girls stopped before entering as they read a sign over the door that said, GENTLEMEN.

Josie said to Mike, does that mean we can't go in this entrance?"

Mike explained as he showed them the other entrance, which had a sign on top of its door saying, LADIES AND ESCORTS.

"I guess that was important back when it was built, but now it makes no difference."

They all walked into the pub, and it was busy. An old high school friend of Jen's grabbed her and sat her down at their table to talk to her and catch up since they had not seen each other in a while, and an older gentleman shouted at Mike, asking about all the blasting they heard on his farm,

Mike just answered, " Beaver dams!"

"They are pesky critters. " The old man added, then turned to go back to his table.

"Wow, Mike, this is a great place. You know most of the people in here? "Asked Sharon

"Most, but there's quite a few moving in from the big cities to relax in the country that I haven't met yet."

The waitress came over to take the drink order. She looked at Mike, "hi Mike!"

Mike smiled and answered her, " Hi Linda, good to see you again. Bring us some glasses and a pitcher of draft beer, please."

She turned her attention towards Becky, to the point of staring. "You got I.D. on you?" she asked Becky.

Before Becky could say a word, Mike butted in, " No, she didn't bring ID because she didn't think she needed it."

The waitress answered Mike quickly, "Yes, she does. She doesn't look nineteen to me."

Mike answered her back just as quickly, " She's my twin sister, and I got my ID. That will work."

"Mike, you are so full of BS, you forget that I know you don't have a twin sister!"

The waitress looked at Becky again, " You got someone to vouch for you? "

" Ask Ernie. He knows me." As one of the clients in the pub walked by their table, " Hey Ernie, can you vouch that I am Mike Stone?"

Ernie figured out what Mike was up to. It has happened before, "Sure is. Make sure he tips you well, though."

Mike gave the waitress a hundred-watt smile, and she forgot who or what she was checking, "Okay, what's your pleasure? Oysters are our special of the day."

They asked the waitress for a menu. The beer arrived about the time Jen finished her conversation at the other table and ordered.

Jen asked Becky, " Any problems? Did they ask for ID?"

Josie and Sharon started laughing, " Mike had the waitress under control. He told her she was his twin sister, but the waitress knew him and called his bluff. After that, we have no idea what happened."

Jen starts with a big smile, "Oh, that must have been Linda then. She's been after Mike for some time. She can't refuse him."

Mike smiled, " I celebrated my nineteenth birthday here three times."

Jen and the girls were laughing so hard that Sharon had to go to the bathroom. The regulars playing darts were getting louder as one of their team members fouled up a shot and lost the game for them. Another regular, Martin Bjornson, and his brother were singing their rendition of Achy Breaky Heart with their heavy Norwegian accents. Les Kenedy came in after spending the day out fishing. He was talking about a fish that came unhooked, and the fish got bigger after each beer he drank.

The pub was finished in a Tudor style with dark wooden beams crisscrossing the ceiling and striped wallpaper that was tasteful to the décor of the pub's theme. Drink glasses were hung upside down on a rack above the bartender's workstation as he was busy with someone wanting pickled eggs. Mike caught the bartender's eye as he looked around the room and ordered another pitcher of beer before their meal came to the table.

The meals were served by an old girlfriend of Mike's, which made for an uncomfortable situation for Mike but a great opportunity for Jen, who knew all about it and teased him, making Mike's face get a bit red. They all dug in with hunger.

" I Never thought I'd see you blush, Mike, but Jen's doing a great job," Sharon said.

Jen saw the chance for a dig, " Yeah, he has a regular harem in this place. Right, Mike?"

Mike laughed it off and smiled. After dinner, Mike and the girls left for the farmhouse. It was nice to have some fun and put a smile on their face, considering what they had been through over the past 10 days. On their way across the parking lot to their truck, they didn't notice the two SUVs parked watching them, and they didn't notice one follow them home.

50

Mike left the farmhouse with Jon and Cathrine while Josie, Jen, and Becky drove to the airport in a separate car so Jen and Becky could see Allen. Allen did not want to waste time in getting Catherine back to New York. While being tied up to the point where she could barely breathe, Catherine was complaining that her restraints were too tight and trying to negotiate being let loose. All her rantings fell on deaf ears as Mike drove the truck around to the executive jet hanger. Josie, Jen, and Becky drove up behind Mike, and they got out of their car to give Allen a big hug and a kiss. Allen came with his most trusted agent, Mark Cunningham, and he stood behind Allen with his handgun out and ready.

Allen did not waste any time, " Okay, let's get Catherine aboard. They are going to fuel up the plane, and then we are scheduled to fly back immediately."

Allen and Mike transferred Catherine from the truck to the plane while Mark watched with his handgun out and ready.

"Take these restraints off me. They are too tight!" Catherine ordered.

Jon glared at her, "Not a chance, Catherine, not until you are at thirty thousand feet!"

Mike and Allen had to wrestle with her a bit as they went up the stairs, onto the plane, and seated. She was becoming a bit unruly until Jon slapped her with the palm of his hand. She stopped, realizing she shouldn't expect much from either Jon or Allen.

Jon took Allen aside and told him he wanted to spend a little extra time up here, help Mike out if need be, and come home once this all gets straightened out a bit. Allen agreed with him and thanked him for that.

Catherine was being hauled off to the plane and protesting," I have rights, and this is brutality."

Allen laughed, " so you have stooped so low as to try all the feeble lines that Jon and I have heard throughout our career. You are fucking pitiful, Catherine or Katrina, whatever your name is. I don't think you understand your position here, and I would suggest that you start telling us about all your hidden comrades!"

Catherine looked at Allen, " I won't tell you a dammed thing. I want a lawyer."

Allen looked at Jon and then at Catherine, "Catherine, you misunderstand your position as a terrorist. Miranda rights don't apply with terrorism, and when the security of the country is at stake, if you can't give us what we want, then we'll just turn you over to the CIA. If we can't persuade you to talk, they certainly will."

Catherine's face went white as a ghost. She remembered several situations in Jon's career when he had told her about sending prisoners who wouldn't talk to the CIA to interrogate. She remembered him telling her it always ended where they got the information they were after. She also remembered him telling her of a couple of occasions the prisoners died from their treatment while being interrogated.

The plane lifted off from the runway and ascended to flight altitude. Mark and Allen changed Catherine's restraints to leg hobbles and hand cuffs. Allen moved into a seat directly across from Catherine and placed a camera and recorder in front of her.

Allen started as Mark recorded visual and audio. "This is director Allen Fulton. I am with FBI agent Mark Cunningham; it is June 12, 2023, at 16:29 hours. We are interviewing Catherine Marion regarding her involvement in connection to several abductions and attempted abductions of the family of director Allen Fulton."

Allen's voice was steady and a bit monotone from all the times he has been required to use this script to introduce himself and others in a formal interrogation. He was playing by the book on this one; he did not want to lose this case due to non-compliance with FBI procedures. He has seen it before, where they brought in a suspect who was guilty and ended up having to let him go on a technicality.

Jon Marion was aware of the attention to detail that Allen was giving on this interview, which was un-nerving and caused Catherine to become very nervous. This made Allen confident that she had a lot to tell and that her lack of confidence would make it easier to get the information out of her. The only problem that Allen thought could be a problem was that Catherine might understand some of the tactics that Allen was using throughout the interview. Allen decided to play it out and see what came from it. Allen was a very experienced interviewer and had cracked a lot of suspects; he would simply adapt as he needed to.

> "Would you like to start at the beginning? How did you get into this situation with the Russian mob?"

> She tried to divert, " Allen, we were the best of friends; you know I would never do anything to compromise that."

Allen felt himself getting agitated and seeing right through what she was trying to do, especially since the interview was being recorded. If he said or reacted out of emotion, he could compromise the whole interview. Allen spent a great deal of time on the way to Comox, going over the events of the case with Mark, and right now, he is glad he did. Allen had to remove himself from the interview since it was getting personal for him, and he could feel emotions starting to affect how he wanted to deliver his questions. It was also a great opportunity to coach Mark.

For recording purposes, Allen made the following note. "For the records, I am handing over this interview to FBI agent Mark Cunningham."

Catherine figured out exactly what Allen was doing. She realized she could not get away from implicating the others.

Mark wasted no time, "I want a complete and detailed organizational graph identifying everyone in this Russian mob presently located in Canada and the United States, including you and your position!"

Catherine tried sidestepping the question, and Mark came back harder and slammed his open palm down on the table. "Catherine, you are not picking up on what I'm laying down here. If you can't give me the information I need, you will be handed over to the CIA or NSA, and you will lose fingers and toes. You will be waterboarded and strung up for days on end with your arms dislocated. If you still decide to keep silent after that, you may die when they hang you upside down with your head under water, understand!"

Catherine remained silent but noticed that Allen was seated forward in the plane, reading a newspaper. She came to the conclusion that Allen was not going to help her in any way and thought if the shoe was on the other foot, she would do the same. Catherine picked up the pencil and started drafting out the chart of Andrei's organization, which is presently in North America. She was very detailed, including address and phone numbers, and included everyone except for one. Allen continued reading the newspaper with a smile on his face.

51

Andrei was in a very good frame of mind, the Mindsweeper project exceeded his expectations with the mind transfer of his father. Andrei could hardly believe how young he was, younger than he had ever remembered his father being. Given some time to prove his father's mind transfer worked without side effects to his father over time, he will undergo the process himself. Andrei smiled as he thought about immortality and taking over countries, as they fall apart and while he creates economic crises. This thought brought him to his next priority in the development of the Mindsweeper program, which was to develop Mindsweeper to enable him to program his army of criminals. Andrei studied the documents that Sergei kept of his father's research back when the Mindsweeper was first conceived by the KGB. With Sergei's help in translating the technical sections, Andrei researched the documents to better understand what it was originally being developed for.

Andrei requested Sergei to meet with him to discuss the path forward in the Mindsweeper development. Sergei didn't mind meeting with Andrei to discuss the development these days, after the success with his father, Andrei has been exceptional to work with.

> Andrei started the conversation immediately as Sergei entered his office, "You exceeded my expectations with my father's mind transfer, you have done well Sergei, thank you."

> Sergei felt very special, in the time he had worked with Andrei, this was the first time he had ever given Sergei praise, it meant a lot to Sergei. "You are welcome, Andrei."

Andrei kept the conversation on point, " With this success, we need to work on the development for the next phase of the program, which is programing our workforce. Correct me if I am wrong but when the program was first developed by the KGB, the programing of the soldier's minds was what it was intended?"

Sergei answered him, "Yes, you are correct, there are two parts to the mind programing. The first part is programing the hardware such as the computer and helmets themselves, which we have completed at this time, the proof being the transfer of your father. The second part is developing the software to program them with, which we only have the old files that I copied from my father's work. I have looked closely at this program development, but it is very old and out of date, focused on frame of mind only, it needs work. I understand that you want to be able to program your workforce to be able to complete specific competencies, such as picking a lock on a safe or rappel the side of a building or cliff."

Andrei answered him, " that is correct, there are many more things that I want them to be able to do very well, things that I know very well."

Sergei intervened, " these will take the time to develop, I will also need to work with you on a complete list of what you need them programmed to do, meanwhile, I will work on updating the mind frame parts to the old program. I will create the program to make your army the most fearless and effective criminals the world has ever encountered, but this will take time to develop!"

Andrei shouted at Sergei, " how long will this take?

Sergei answered him, "It's a lot to put together, it could take up to two years."

Andrei snapped back, "not acceptable Sergei, I need it sooner, way sooner. You need to figure out how to do it."

Sergei considered what Andrei said, " so these are all things that you can do well?"

Andrei looked at Sergei, "Of course, I can do them well, what's your point?"

Sergei looked at Andrei with a smile on his face, "then we will clone you, this way you can have your army soonest."

Andrei smiled, "yes, an army of me."

Dominik was focused on the work out sessions in physiotherapy, the doctors were pleased with Dominik's progress with the therapy. He worked very hard, sometimes too hard and they had to add non-physical activities such as shooting pistols and rifles. They spent considerable time on his computer skills and basic computer technologies and applications. There were several times in the day when this technology overwhelmed him, but everyone was amazed at how quickly he overcame his shortcomings and mastered what he was being taught.

Dominik worked a twelve-hour day in physio and computer technology, and with this new body found it easy, without being tired. He felt young again and powerful, he had a young body with the experience of someone eighty years old, and he was young enough to pursue his dreams. As he talked to Andrei, he realized that the family business was lacking the leadership and experience it needed to expand to his son's desire. He found from his discussions with Andrei that he had big goals, and believed deeply that they were achievable. At first, he considered Andrei's vision of world dominance as a goal unachievable, and as he learned more from him, found that in fact, it was simply well thought out.

Dominik thought of Ana, she was beautiful and so warm, he loved her very much, and right now he missed her. They had a wonderful life together with their baby, he often wondered why Andrei would kill her. Who cared that she was a prostitute, they were in love.

52

Allen left his office for lunch, today he decided to treat himself to his favorite food truck, he was a regular customer there, and with that, Allen had a regular order. Allen was first introduced to the owners of the truck when he was in the vicinity and a young wannabe thief decided to rob them just after lunch. As they talked about it after the incident, they considered it a perfect situation where Allen was just coming towards the truck, and the thief ran directly towards Allen as he bolted away. Allen reacted with speed and experience, as he assessed what was happening, pulled his gun and arrested him almost immediately, and the money was returned to the vendor within minutes. The owner of the truck was so grateful, he offered to make Allen one of his signature specials at no charge. Allen could not believe the flavor of the meat and the side orders, and it became his regular lunch at the truck.

Allen stood in line and was recognized by the vendor, Harvey Keagan, " Allen, good to see you, want a regular?

"Thanks, Harvey, yes that would be great thanks."

Harvey was busy, there was a long lineup of customers, and he was keeping up with his client's orders, his truck was well known for great food, and people were willing to wait as they stood in line.

Allen's order was up and after he paid, he sat down at a table to enjoy the succulent flavors and textures of the meal that made this his favorite. As he sat there alone eating lunch, his mind ventured off to his family, he missed them so much, that he was reminded of Jen and Becky almost constantly. He was grateful for having Mike as a friend and included him as he had concerns for his family's safety.

Allen had just got back from lunch and arrived at his office when the phone rang. " Allen, it's Kevin White here returning your call."

When Allen first became a field agent for the FBI, he tried to recruit Mike several times. He thought it would be fantastic to be partnered up with a good friend, someone smart, someone he could trust no matter what. Mike's love for the small town farm life put an end to his efforts. Kevin White became his partner for several years, and they gained the respect and camaraderie necessary to become partners. When Kevin transferred to the CIA, they didn't get together nearly as much as they wanted, but each had their own lives and after Kevin's divorce from his first marriage, they remained friends but became distant. He recently remarried to Karen, but neither Allen or Jen liked her and their visits became awkward. Every once in a while they would call each other and sometimes get together. They both had lives that became more demanding. Allen was starting a family as Becky was born and his promotions within the FBI required an increased demand on his free time. Kevin with his transfer to the CIA sent him all over the world and the divorces ruined him financially.

"Kevin, thanks for getting back to me so quickly, I have a situation that I could really use some help with."

Kevin answered in his flamboyant and confident manner, "Lay it on me, man, I'd love to help an old friend out."

Allen summarized the situation that Jen and Becky were in and explained the Russians were not stopping. Allen explained the need to take action to end this, otherwise it will go on and on forever. Allen explained to Kevin they had traced all activity back to Andrei Volkov. Since he was familiar with Andrei, Allen asked him what the CIA could do to help.

Kevin commented, "Yes, Andrei Volkov. He has been in our sights for quite some time now. Because he is a very powerful person with strong ties to politicians and the underground, he has been evasive, we can't get the evidence we need to convince the authorities to arrest him. Honestly, Allen, I think even if we did, they wouldn't do anything anyway, the police are bought off and the criminal system over there is in a shambles. I'm sorry Allen, but we can't do anything to help you, I would suggest that you talk to them and reach a compromise that you both can live with."

Allen was quietly trying to digest what Kevin just told him, "Well Kevin, since they want to kill my wife and daughter, I doubt a compromise could be made."

Kevin makes a sour face, "Yep, you're in it rough Allen, I would really like to help but my hands are tied, wish you the best of luck though."

Allen was getting madder by the minute, was that a slap in the face or what? Allen pauses, " Well Kevin, I don't imagine your hands are tied very tight."

Allen hung up, mad that his good friend wouldn't help him and his family in a time of crisis, but more that he was shrugged off by him. Allen needed to work on something mindless to occupy him until he got over Kevin's response to his plea for help. He decided to clean off his desk and file the mounds of documentation he acquired from the crime scene. He noticed a brown manila envelope on his desk that had been placed by someone, right on top of the mess of paper. Allen removed the letter that was inside the envelope. His mouth dropped as he read the letter.

STOP INVESTIGATING ANDREI VOLKOV OR YOUR FAMILY WILL DIE.

Allen called Lee to take the letter and check for prints. Lee came to Allen's office immediately and inspected the document with acute detail, then took the letter to the lab for testing.

Allen called Mark Cunningham and Ron McKay to come into his office for a summary of what they have found out to this point. He assigned them both to work together and further investigate the Volkov's family business. The other part of their assignment was to determine just why they were so focused on abducting his family, he couldn't quite figure out if an additional motive could be present, there must be another reason other than to get rid of potential witnesses.

Allen decided to conduct an interview with Catherine to see if additional information could be pulled from her. This time he was going to have Ron McKay in on the interview and after, have him do a behavioral analysis to try to unveil something new that would shed more light on this investigation. Allen wanted a clear direction about where or how to find what he was looking for.

53

Allen Fulton spent several hours reviewing the organizational chart that Catherine Marion drafted, outlining the various people involved with Andrei Volkov's Russian mob. There was a total of thirty-six people of interest, and he gave his analysts the job of hunting them down. It was a huge manhunt that extended across the US as well as several in Canada, primarily in the Vancouver / Courtney areas, and the FBI agents along with the local law enforcement were bringing them in. There were two things that Allen needed to do, get fingerprints from his boss and Kevin White. In preparation, Allen had sprayed the glasses, enabling them to pick up fingerprints easily.

Allen's boss, Sven Olsen came into Allen's office without knocking, "So Allen, where are you going with all this, what is your end game?"

Allen was surprised at the question, "What do you think my end game should be Sven?"

Sven looked around Allen's office noticing pictures of Jen and Becky, " I would think it would be to protect your family and put an end to all this fighting with the Russians."

"And what do you think I am doing?" Allen paused, "There is only one way to end all this and that is to get rid of the source, and because it is international, I can't do that without the CIA, and they are somewhat non-comital and told me they need more evidence tying all this to Andrei Volkov."

"Bloody CIA." Sven said in frustration, "The FBI has a group of agents, headed up by a senior agent that I know very well, I have been pushing to have them work exclusively in Europe for situations just like this, let me get back to you."

Allen poured them both a drink and asked, "What about jurisdiction rights?"

"Thanks for the drink, they will be working alongside EUROPOL, which gives them full jurisdiction, however, they must develop long-term relationships with the local authorities. We don't want a bunch of agents going into the various countries demanding and trying to take over the situation, and we want to be welcome back should the need arise."

Allen considered his situation, " that would help me out considerably, can our agents make arrests?

Sven looked at Allen, he could tell he welcomed the help, " yes, providing they do it with EUROPOL's approval, which won't be a problem since they welcomed the help from us. Also, between terrorism and cyber-crimes affecting the US, we have been keeping them quite busy and with the added group working internationally, we can drastically reduce their case load."

Allen considered his time frame, "When can we utilize this group, it would be better sooner than later?"

" I'm not sure Allen, it's a new development, let me find out and get back to you." Sven gazed off in thought, "Maybe this could be their first case, I know they are anxious to get started. Allen, since this is brand new, let's keep a lid on it for now."

Allen listened to his boss with a great deal of attention and agreed to keep the information about the development of the international division of the FBI and its association with EUROPOL quiet. This was new hope for Allen to end this chaos and get life back on track, he missed his family so much, that he was becoming mentally exhausted.

Sven knew Allen was getting tired, " I see you in your office late at night and early in the morning, what are you working on so feverishly Allen?"

" For the most part, all the evidence from the crime scenes, I have Mark Cunningham and Ron McKay helping, I have put Mark in a case lead position, and the two have been working out very well."

Sven asked, "How's your man making out with your family Allen?"

Allen looked directly at his boss searching for the hint of a snide smile, there was none, " they are doing well."

"Where are they and who is it that is looking after them?" Sven asked.

Allen did not answer him which indicated to his boss it was either not going well or he had overstepped his bounds.

"Sven, it's best you don't know."

Sven shook his head, put the empty glass on Allen's desk and walked out the door. After he left, he called Lee and asked him to meet him in his office right away. When Lee came in, Allen told him he wanted the lab to take the fingerprint off the glass and file it as Allan – FBI. Lee wasn't sure what Allen was up to but did as he was asked. He then called Kevin White and asked him to come to his office, he needed to find out more about Andrei Volkov. Kevin happened to be in the FBI office at the time and told Allen he would swing by his office before leaving.

When Kevin arrived, Allen was prepared with pertinent questions that would give Allen a chance to see his facial response, as well as body language. When Kevin arrived at his office and after a few minutes of small talk, Allen calmly walked over to his bar and poured Kevin and himself a glass of Scotch. Allen asked the questions he had prepared and then finished the meeting by finishing his drink. Kevin also finished his drink, put the glass on Allen's desk and left through the office door.

Allen picked up the phone, "Lee, sorry to bother a busy man, but I need to see you again in my office."

When Lee entered Allen's office he said, " Allen, you're becoming a regular, how can I help you this time?"

Allen pointed to the empty glass on his desk, "Same with this glass only file this one as Allen – CIA."

Lee Magnusen looked at Allen for a while and said, "Is there something else I should know about these fingerprints? You seem to be keeping a tight lid on them."

Allen agreed that he needed an explanation, " I can't right now, but I promise you I will after you check these prints against the prints of the letter and the internal parts of the bug you found on my desk."

With that, Lee took the glass to lift the fingerprints off it at his lab, he was a bit unsure of what Allen was up to, but he had never had issues with Allen's request in the past.

Allen had a whiteboard brought into his office and closed his window drapes before he started to put the information together on the board. They had nineteen in jail from Catherine's organization chart, and Allen started with that. He then filled in the ones who had been killed.

He noticed there were not enough leaders in Catherine's chart to accomplish the chaos they had created to this point and came to the conclusion that her information was not complete. He decided to interrogate Catherine again tomorrow for the rest of the names. He turned his whiteboard around so none could see what he had written, opened the drapes, and left for home for the day.

54

Sharon came running out of the house crying and yelling as Mike drove up the driveway, he drove over to see what was going on.

"Mike! They took them, they are going to kill Jen, and they said they are going to kill you and me too!"

Mike was trying to get more information, " who took her, which way, where's Josie?"

Sharon was barely able to get it out of her mouth, "It was a group of about seventeen, led by a young guy, maybe mid-thirties, he and three others took Jen and Becky and left about a half hour ago. About twelve others took Josie and left past the barn, Josie couldn't stop them, they beat Jen and Josie up bad Mike." She paused for a moment, "They killed Duke and Tigger, Mike!"

"I had enough of this bull shit, go in the bush and hide, don't come out till you hear my voice."

Mike was mad; he went to the stable and saddled up Festus then loaded up some dynamite and other items including his long rifle, Crossbow, arrows, and a couple of boxes of shells and the night vision binoculars that Allen had sent him.

Mike took off on Festus, since he did not know where anyone was, he took the back trails instead of the main roadway to avoid running into them. It was getting dusk and the clouds from the overcast hid the light of the moon. He was just able to see objects, but he was not able to see details. Since he was the one looking for them, they were using the poor visibility to their advantage, Mike needed to turn this around and use it to his advantage. He found a spot that was safe to scan with the night vision binoculars while moving them from side to side in hopes of picking up movement. Mike found the main group was located about mid-point in a narrowing, where two fields met at an open gate, he estimated about ten to twelve. Mike listened carefully and picked up on a faint moaning sound of a female in pain, he assumed that it was most likely Josie. He set his compass for the direction of the female moaning, and took his crossbow and arrows, leaving Festus untied. As Mike crawled along the top of the grass, he rushed without making any noise to reveal his location. As he got closer to where the noise was coming from, he saw Josie with her arms tangled around the bottom strand of the barbed wire fence. He could see they had her hooked up to a taser gun that was locked on, he had to turn the gun off.

He could not see anyone in the field close to them, but noticed two bushes, where he cultivated the field a month ago, and knew there should not be any bushes in this field. Mike took a chance that they were the Russians hiding in camouflage suits, and without raising his crossbow to reveal it, he bent down until his eye met the sights and squeezed the trigger, sending the arrow into the bush. It fell over and the other bush beside it said something to it in Russian. Mike loaded his crossbow for a second shot, this time he revealed himself. Before the Russian could raise his gun and shoot at him, he got up on one knee and placed an arrow, killing the remaining Russians guarding Josie. Assuming there were no others in the immediate area, he crawled back under the fence and took their guns. He then rushed over to the taser gun lying on the ground and snapped the lock off.

Once the Taser was dealt with, he untied Josie from the barbed wire fencing as she began to relax from the release of the electrical charge. Mike went over to her to hold her while she regained her strength. He noticed the beating that showed and the blood running down her face from the extent of her wounds.

"Mike, they have Becky and Jen, I did the best that I could, but there were too many of them and they knocked me unconscious from behind."

Mike tried to calm her down, but Josie cut in, "This was all just a diversion, to give them time to escape, I don't know where Sharon is. I was here with these two thugs to lure you out in the open, they wanted to kill you as well, but I am thankful you are safe, but they killed Duke and Tigger Mike!"

Mike knew the main group of Russians needed to be dealt with or they would return to the farmhouse when he, Josie and Sharon were asleep and kill them all. There were too many of them to deal with by himself, he needed help and there was only one ace that he had up his sleeve.

Mike whispered to Josie "How are you feeling now, can you go for a ride with me, there is one more thing we need to finish up before we leave for the farmhouse tonight?"

The clouds started breaking away from each other, opening the beam of light that Mike needed to finish this evening off. Mike helped Josie on the saddle, then mounted the horse himself while sitting directly behind the saddle that Josie was on. As though Festus knew what was going on, he leapt forward with such strength, knocking the back of Josie's head into Mike's face as her weak body reacted to the thrust of the horse. Mike held on to Josie as he placed both his arms around her while he held tightly to the horn of the saddle and dug his heels into the horse's flank to let Festus know he needed to move fast. Josie had never ridden a horse much, but never at this speed, Mike sensed this and told her to lean all the way forward, and as she did, she felt his body also lean forward touching hers. Josie felt weak from the taser treatment and felt herself swaying back and forth between Mike's arms as they rode. She could hear Festus breathe hard as he was working as hard as he ever worked for Mike and with every stride the horse made, she could hear the leather sinches and straps creak as they tightened under the tremendous strain of the ride.

They rode hard along the dirt roadway and across the first pasture, Mike dismounted Festus and opened the gate to the second pasture, the field where the cattle were in. He attached a rope around a fence post and tied the other end onto the horn of the saddle. Being very careful, he had Festus pull out the gate posts on both sides to give the herd more room to get through. Mike took Festus down by the creek to get some water to drink while he took out his night vision binoculars to find where the herd was. Mike pulled out two sticks of dynamite holding them in one hand, while he dug his heels into the horse, and they were off again. Mike took a long sweeping arc around the backside of the herd, in doing so, he whistled and yelled, bringing the whole herd of two hundred and forty to their feet. Mike took Festus a long way past where the herd was located, and as he turned towards the cattle to send them on their way, he threw one stick of dynamite behind them and shortly after a second. As the dynamite exploded the herd started running away from the blast with Mike yelling at them to keep up their momentum.

Since Festus could run faster than the cattle, Mike slowed the pace slightly, but he was pushing the herd to move quickly. Once the herd was past the first gate where they pulled the gate posts, he started to speed them up and threw out another stick of dynamite at a safe distance behind. The moonlight was just enough to enable the herd to run at this point and now the herd would stay on course along the road, directly to the field where the Russians were hiding.

Josie was feeling stronger and able to sit straight on the saddle, she could hold on now with enough strength and she was learning fast. This was all so foreign to her; she was depending on Mike to know what he was doing and quickly found out that he did when the herd started to veer off the path to the right. Josie was well past fearing the unknown, everything she experienced with Mike was an unknown experience. It wasn't so much concern with his decisions, it was getting used to his solutions, there was no book to learn this from, there has never been anyone who taught this solution for the situation they were in.

They were coming up to the final field where the Russians were, and Mike started to press the herd one last time. Festus stumbled on a large piece of sod, which was pushed out into the road by the herd. It threw Mike sideways on the horse's hind end and knocked the saddlebags and the long rifle off the saddle, Mike moved back up on the horse and situated himself straight behind the saddle once again. He had lost all his equipment and supplies.

55

By the time the herd passed through the open gate to the field the Russians were hiding in, the herd was in a full-fledged stampede. Josie could hear the thunder of the stampeding cattle's hoofs as they beat the ground, it was the most incredible experience she had ever witnessed. Mike was able to ride Festus up to the side of the herd just after they cleared the gate and because he lost all the dynamite in the saddle bags, he took out his pistol and started shooting in the air to help steer the herd to the left, right into where he figured the other Russians were hiding. The herd swung to the left, as calculated and Mike and Josie could hear the Russians yelling and screaming as the herd took them out trampling them into the dirt.

The last of the two hundred and forty head of cattle cleared the area and Mike figured that it would be over for this bunch, but he thought he needed to be sure, he had to make sure there were no other threats and stopped Festus. He got off the horse, he didn't want Festus getting killed over this as well, so he told Josie to remain on Festus.

> "Josie, I got something that needs finishing, there's no point in you getting wrapped up in it, Festus will know when it's time to come and get me. If Festus doesn't come for me after the last shot is fired, then get the hell out of here!"

Josie realized there was no point in talking him out of it, she stayed on the horse praying for Mike's safety. He checked that both pistols were loaded as he turned, she watched him walk off, disappearing into the darkness of the night.

Mike could hear the cattle, they were a bit noisy after their run, and he headed straight towards them. As he walked slowly, listening for moaning from injured Russians, he could see the destruction the cattle made of the blind the Russians hid behind. The Russians built the blinds of poles and branches, but they were feeble against the herds' stampeding hooves which destroyed everything in their path, including artillery, supplies, and the Russians themselves. Mike picked up a box of long-range ammunition that he had seen on the ground, the long-range rifle didn't make sense since visibility was minimized from the dusk of the night. He continued along the path of destruction with both pistols in his hands, and then Mike started seeing the dead bodies trampled to death and the rifle that went along with the cartridges. He looked through the scope to find it was a night vision scope. He loaded the rifle with a cartridge and scanned the area with nothing was found. He waited a while and heard the high-pitched squeak of barbed wire being pulled through fencing staples, like someone stretching it, trying to get through the fence. He picked up the rifle scanning the fence-line.

He saw the Russian was caught in the middle strand of the wire and Mike gave him the opportunity to give himself up, but he shot at Mike missing him, Mike thought of Becky and Jen and, he was not interested in giving him a second chance. Mike leveled the rifle and squeezed off a shot killing the escaping Russian at the fence. It was finally over for this bunch, he knew Josie would be worried so gave two whistles to signal Festus to come to him.

Mike picked up driver's licenses from all the Russians and waited as Festus and Josie made it through the darkness to where he was. When Josie saw Mike, she jumped off the horse and ran to him throwing her arms around him, and kissing him on the lips, the moment seemed to take its time, not hesitant, and definitely not rushed.

With a big smile on his face, Mike offered, "Well, do you always welcome your men home after a day's work like that?"

Josie smiled, "thank god you are safe."

Mike helped Josie back on the saddle, and then he mounted the horse himself, sitting behind Josie as they rode back to the farmhouse. Even though Josie was strong enough now to sit straight in the saddle herself, Mike had his arms around Josie, and she was okay with that. They were both quiet as Festus found his way down a path that was very familiar to him, they knew Jen and Becky were gone, and both Duke and Tigger were dead.

They finally made it to the farmhouse; Mike had never felt so sad with his best friend and her daughter gone, and he had no idea what condition they were in or where they were. Mike was also grieving for Duke and Tigger, his memories of training Duke from a pup and the day his friend the hunter brought Tigger to him. He became overwhelmed, emotions flowed, and he began to tear up. He shook his head trying to regain his focus. He needed to find Sharon, and Josie needed some medical attention.

He called an old friend who was a paramedic with his own ambulance business. It was lucky he was available to come over right away. While he was looking after Josie, Mike took Festus out to look for Sharon. After about thirty minutes, he found her, and they both left on Festus to go back to the farmhouse.

On the way back Sharon said to Mike, " I'm not sure how to say this to you Mike, but as I mentioned, I have learned quite a bit of Russian. I overheard them talking in the house they were organizing an executive jet for Moscow and taking Jen and Becky on it."

Mike was shocked as Sharon summarized the conversation she heard, as close to word for word as she could translate. They came up to the farmhouse as the paramedic was putting all his equipment away.

"For someone who took a beating like that, she's in very good condition, some wounds to heal, some bandages to replace now and again, but she is in good medical condition."

Mike was grateful, " thanks for your help, Paul, I owe you big time for this. Send me the bill and I will see you get paid."

Josie looked in a lot better condition once the blood got cleaned off her face. The three of them sat at the kitchen table and summarized the incident over speaker phone with Allen.

Mike felt bad about the situation. " I'm very sorry about this Allen, and I take full responsibility."

"No sir." Allen paused, " it's not your fault, its simply not your fault."

Mike was mad, " Allen, we both know what needs to be done, before calling you, Josie, Sharon and I, came up with a general plan. We need to terminate this Andrei."

Allen stopped Mike, "Mike, I know you are an incredibly resourceful man, but you don't know anyone in Moscow, and don't try to BS me. How are you going to execute any plan over there?"

Mike challenged Allen, " but you forgot about Sharon's story, her uncle lives there." Mike took a moment to organize his thoughts, but it didn't work, there was just too much to process. "Allen, just get me a fucken plane!"

Allen knew Mike all his life, right now he was mad and irrational, or was he? Both Mike and Allen deep down knew they needed to go to Russia to save his family and to kill Andrei, in order to end this mess. Allen already talked to the CIA, and they wanted nothing to do with it, especially with the war in Ukraine. Everyone is on pins and needles with Russia threatening to pull the nuclear trigger if the United States gets involved in that war, and close political ties to the government have been established. If they went over, the States would hold no associations or responsibilities with the group, and they would be left to fend for themselves, even if that meant jail. He wished he never got Mike and Josie involved in it. As for Sharon, she got into it herself.

> Allen was very solemn as he spoke with the group on the phone, " I would never ask any of you to do this for me or my family, your risk level is extremely high, I recommend that you become aware of the risk throughout each aspect of your trip. The United States of America and Canada will neither acknowledge this assignment nor offer you any support if you are caught. I am truly sorry about that. All I can do is come over myself and help you somehow if you get caught."

> Mike wanted to cut a long speech short, " I'm in." Josie and Sharon thought for a couple of seconds then both in unison, " I'm in."

> Allen said, " thank you from the bottom of my heart." Then immediately after, " You are all crazy, Mike, I will personally transfer you $ 50,000 for the executive flight and hotel rooms, you can pay from your own account keeping the money trail away from being tracked to the two countries."

Mike lined up the plane out of Vancouver in the next two days. They had little time to waste, Jen and Becky's life expectancy was completely unknown. The only thing Mike knew, was the Russians wanted someone to follow, or they would have simply killed them both and left without them.

Josie and Sharon had a shower while Mike buried Duke and Tigger, and then he took the track hoe out to the field to dig a hole for the Russians and picked up his saddle bag and rifle. Mike came back into the house exhausted; he could only think of showering and sleep. He turned on his outside motion sensors, with Duke and

Tigger, there was never a need but with the two of them gone, there definitely was a need. Mike showered and crawled into bed, it felt so good to be clean for once and the sheets felt so good on his freshly washed skin. Mike just closed his eyes when he faintly heard footsteps entering his room as they got closer. He opened his eyes to see Josie lifting the covers and getting into bed beside him. Mike thought about how beautiful she was as she slid into the bed, there was no need to talk, everything was clear and understood, they wanted to be with each other. As tired as they were, sleep would have to wait.

56

Josie and Mike were enjoying a quick breakfast of toast with Mike's favorite coffee when Sharon came into the kitchen.

"Good morning, Sharon, we can whip you up some bacon and eggs if you like.

"Good morning, toast looks good to me."

Mike looked at Sharon, " Josie needs to get some more clothes from town, need anything?"

" No, unlike Josie, I had some time to pack for a longer stay, I'm just going to catch up on laundry, thanks anyway."

After breakfast, Mike and Josie hopped in the truck and headed for Courtney. It was overcast in the morning with a touch of humidity and drizzle, which was common weather for the coastal town. The trip took less than thirty minutes on the old Island Highway, but it seemed like five minutes to Mike and Josie, as they laughed at some of the stories of Mike getting into trouble when he was a kid. They were pre-occupied with each other and did not notice the car following them into town.

Mike parked the truck in front of the clothing store and they both went in, Josie went over to the women's undergarments making him feel uncomfortable. Mike told her to take her time, he had to go across the street to get an electrical outlet adapter for the European electrical outlets and left. A man came into the store, and because Josie was aware he was watching her, she was watching him out of the corner of her eye. He came over slowly, but she could tell he was only in that store for one reason, and that was for her. Finally, he was about ten feet from her pretending to look through the items on the rack behind her. She took out her camera and without him noticing, she took a picture of his face.

She was reminded of one of her martial arts instructors who explained because she was picking up what she was taught so quickly, he wanted to teach her the art of speeding up her reaction timing. It was very specific to situations such as this, she closed her eyes and focused all her energy on slowing down time, or to be more realistic, speeding her awareness timing.

She opened her eyes and watched his every move, his every change of movement and his every shift in balance. She noticed short erratic shifts and movements without purpose, she now knew he was serving a purpose in the store other than shopping. She waited ever so patiently, and with discipline and experience of over a hundred simulations and fights with her instructor. At the time she never believed she would ever use this skill, but here it is.

The man was careful, he too appeared to be skilled with some form of hand-to-hand fighting, but not hers. She noticed he was right-handed, very important to watch for his extended right leg behind him for balance and power. He came across her blind side and there it was, the extended rear right leg moved behind him, then almost simultaneously the shift of weight to keep him balanced as he attacked.

Josie also shifted, only she shifted towards him with her right leg behind her from the forward trust. This caught her opponent off guard as he tried to protect himself by blocking her right arm, but she came at him with her elbow and he missed the block, resulting in him getting a broken nose. She stepped back one step to set herself in her defensive stance, He showed her his gun, and she spun around with a torpedo kick that sent him flying, knocking over the sock and toque display stand. She ran towards him, grabbed his hand, twisting his wrist before he could unholster his pistol, and slammed his face into an old-fashioned butter churn the store displayed for the store's theme. She was ready for him to come at her again when Mike came through the store's entrance, he immediately tried to figure out what was going on. Mike told the cashier to call the police. The man saw Mike come in and he attempted to escape past Mike, but Mike ran towards him and gave the man fleeing, a knee in the gut which laid him out, curled up on the floor. Mike noticed he was trying to grab something under the left side of his coat and Mike removed the Colt 9 mm handgun from its holster.

When the RCMP arrived, they put handcuffs on the man and searched his pockets for any other weapons or other paraphernalia he might have. Lieutenant Morris came over to Mike, asking for his statement as well as Josie's and the clerk's and reading them to find they all said the same thing in different words and different ways, but they all said the same thing.

Lieutenant Morris was a good friend of Mike's, they worked together as Mike would often make repairs on their service revolvers free of charge and they both volunteered for gun safety education in the various communities.

> "Mike, there is something wrong with this story that everyone is telling us that happened here. Can you shed some light on it for me, please? He paused, " without giving me any bullshit, do you think that I am going to believe that she defeated him in a fight?"

> Mike answered with a smile on his face, " yes sir she did, she works in New York as an advanced hand-to-hand fighting instructor for the FBI."

> Lieutenant Morris was astounded, " really, well, I truly wish that I could have seen that fight then. After we cuffed him, we checked his pockets and found his badge in his pocket, he is a special agent for the CIA. Mike, how well do you know this, Josie Santos?"

> Mike answered honestly but didn't want to spill the beans on what he was up to on the farm, " for only a week or so,

but she came to me from a friend who is well affiliated with the director of the FBI in New York."

"Mike, if I didn't know you better, your story would sound so fishy, I would open up an investigation on you."

"Okay, thank you very much Lieutenant Morris, have a good day."

"And Miss Santos, behave yourself please, I wouldn't want you getting mad at anyone else."

57

Mike called Allen to update him on Josie's run-in with the CIA agent. Allen couldn't think of a single reason for the CIA to be after Josie and had them send him the picture of the agent's face.

Allen started asking questions trying to make sense of it all, " where is he now?"

Mike summarized what he found out from the lieutenant, "The RCMP have him in a cell, they have different concealed weapons laws up here and since he threatened Josie by showing her his gun, they won't be letting him out. They are checking out the authenticity of his credentials, but the lieutenant said because the CIA agent was apparently working in Canada without previous notification of intent, he was working out of jurisdiction. Canadian RCMP are taking this very seriously."

Allen had to have someone there to look after the CIA attack on Josie and to find out what was going on, " Mike, I need you and Josie to call Jon and talk to him about this and hand it over to him since you are only there for a short time, you're leaving tomorrow evening right?"

"Yea, that makes sense Allen, we will give him a call once we're done."

"I'm going to talk to my boss again, he said he was going to chat up his CIA's contact. Maybe I can now get Kevin to say something worthwhile when he opens his mouth."

Mike was getting tired of all the talk, " Okay, we all have a lot to do so let's get on it, talk later Allen."

Allen called his boss and left a message to call him back then called Kevin White to arrange lunch tomorrow and he agreed. He spent some time going over questions and conversations he wanted with them both. Allen was not confident either one was putting in the effort into this chaos as they could, he expected commitment and he expected them to actively participate, it may be happening to his family, but it was not a personal matter, it was their responsibility in their respective roles.

Allen answered his ringing phone, " hello, Fulton here."

" Allen, it's Lee here, we have a positive match to the fingerprints on the bug and the letter. It took a while since the match was interdepartmental, 100% positive match to Allen – CIA. Who is this Allen, we need to record the fingerprint properly. I need a name."

Allen answered Lee, " those prints were from Kevin White, the CIA lead for Russia.

The others were from Sven.

Lee exclaimed, "Mike, what are you up to?"

Allen answered Lee, " I just need to remove key people from being potential threats that's all."

Fifteen minutes after completing his call with Lee, his boss Sven came into his office, " what's up Allen?

"I just received confirmation from Lee that the prints from the threatening letter and the inside of the bug were the same and belonged to Kevin White with the CIA."

Sven shook his head and took what Allen had just told him into what seemed like deep consideration before he responded to Allen. "This is not surprising me, I just had a heart-to-heart with my equal in the CIA, he was not at liberty to answer the many questions I had regarding Kevin White, and they are very frustrated. Best I can tell, they knew Kevin was becoming a problem for a while now. All he told me was to leave Kevin White alone and he was no longer to be investigated by the FBI, he added the CIA is looking into the matter and will resolve it permanently."

Allen took over the conversation, " Sven, guess what, I'm getting frustrated and quite honestly I don't care about these guys, I just want my family back."

" Allen, just give it a little patience, let's see how this shakes out over the next week."

Allen was going to tell Sven that Mike Josie and Sharon were going to Russia tomorrow but decided against it. They finished their farewells and Sven left Allen's office. Allen wasn't sure, he didn't trust the CIA for any help, but maybe he could beckon Kevin's friendship at lunch to get better clarification on this mess.

Allen decided it was time to interrogate Catherine, she would be a key to putting all this in order. He had a deputy bring her to the room for questioning. He gave her the usual thirty to forty-five minutes to sit and think about it all. In most cases, that works well, and leaving his file open on the desk for her to review indicates she has been approved to go to Guantanamo Bay. Allen previously set up the illusion and asked Ron McKay to attend with his better-than-average analytical skills that proved their merit in a previous interview with these Russian terrorists.

Allen met Ron outside the interrogation room prior to entering, "good to see you again Ron, with the success you had with the last interrogation with these guys. I wanted you here for this one to analyze Catherine, she is a key in this mess we are in."

Ron asked Allen, " what exactly do you expect from this interrogation and exactly what information do you want?"

"She missed a few people from the organizational chart she gave me, I want the rest of the names. What I expect from this interrogation is to have her open up about this mob she is obviously so heavily involved in and tell us how the CIA is involved."

Ron suggested to Allen, " assuming you have the questions you want her to answer, you take the lead with them, and I will add to the questioning as I see fit to get her to correctly answer. Are you OK with that?

58

Mike called Jon and scheduled a meeting at the farmhouse later that evening. When Jon arrived at the farmhouse, he was very friendly and opened a comfortable dialog to break the ice. Mike made coffee and set out mugs for each one at the table. While the coffee was brewing Jon asked about the farm and Mike told him the history of the farm and about his parents. Mike did not want to go into details, since the meeting was about something much more important.

Mike and Josie summarized the attempted abduction at the clothing store to Jon, " I received a copy of the picture of the agent's face you sent Allen, very helpful by the way, and we confirmed he is a CIA agent working under Kevin White. It's interesting that Kevin is involved because we have been getting some information that Kevin is becoming a rogue agent. With this, Allen asked me to head up investigations into him. The CIA want to look after it themselves but since this is supposedly causing so many problems for them and they have been dragging their feet, Allen suggested that I work on it while I'm here. Kevin is a family friend of Allen's, and he is working on this from his side as well. Josie was there anything else about this guy that you can tell me about?"

Josie looked at Jon making direct eye contact, " Knowing that he was a highly trained CIA agent, I thought he lacked tact. He followed me into the women's under garment section of the store and pretended to be looking for something. I made my selections and moved to where the lady's tops were, and he followed me over." Josie started laughing, " when Mike came into the store with me and saw where I was headed, he turned around immediately and left to go across the street to the hardware store."

All three laughed, and Josie continued, " He wore a European cut suit, not high-end end but what you would expect on an agent's budget. He had some martial arts training, but not the level that I would expect for a CIA operative. When I asked him a question, he answered in perfect English, so he was not a direct member of the Russian syndicate that we have been dealing with up to now."

Jon thanked Josie for her observation and detail of the man who tried to attack her. Jon made some notes and asked Mike if he had seen anything else of value in the investigation.

Mike answered Jon, " there has been more not said than said here, when are you going to tell us the rest of the story Jon? You have been here for three days, and this is all you have? We are going to Russia risking our lives to rescue Allen's family. Damn it, Jon, we need it all, and we need it all now!"

Jon thought for a while and agreed with Mike, that they needed to know the whole story,   " Kevin White has reportedly been working for Andrei, keeping him clear of our investigations from the Russian oligarch. The problem is, there is no evidence of it and until someone finds proof, the CIA will not act upon it. Maybe this is the proof everyone has been looking for."

Mike started getting a bit sharp with Jon, " so, not only do we have a Russian dictator on our ass, now we also have the CIA chasing us as well!" Jon was recalling conversations he had with Allen, "so why didn't Allen tell us all this morning on our call."

"He found all this out from his boss when they met two hours ago."

Mike thought about this for a minute, " why are they after Josie now?

"It's a bit of a mystery, neither Allen or his boss Sven, nor myself understand why."

"Well Jon, Allen said he was getting in touch with Kevin himself tomorrow for lunch, I'm assuming he will get it straightened out with him then."

"Hopefully so Mike, I'll be on my way now Mike, good to see you again Josie. Good luck over there you guys."

Mike was mad at the whole thing but was more determined than ever to bring Jen and Becky back, but also to kill Andrei and now Kevin has become a new target. Mike went to his room and got his good western cowboy boots and took them out the door to the shop. Josie followed him into the workshop and watched him place the heel of his boot on the bench vise securing it. He then removed the heels of both boots and using the drill press, drilled ten quarter-inch holes, stopping a quarter inch from the bottom. Mike then placed two 22 caliber Long Rifle cartridges in each hole before securing back on his boots. Finally, he nailed on heel Blakey's so he could show the security at the airport why the metal detector showed metal on his boots. He gathered up the eight 22 caliber pen rifles he made previously and gave two to Josie. He brought out Sharon and they set up targets on the fence behind the shop and showed them how these guns work, and explained they were for short range only. Mike had them load the pen guns and prepare them for shooting. They each had four shots and got used to rolling the trigger toggle to fire the pen. Mike then placed two folding knives that he modified to fit into a camera case, explaining they shoot the blade out of the handle, again for short range, and demonstrating to both Sharon and Josie how they operate. He also placed a high-strength composite gauntlet, he designed just for him.

Mike was thinking about arriving in Moscow, " Sharon have you contacted your uncle yet to tell him we are coming?"

"Yes, I have Mike, and he is very excited to see us, and he wants us to stay with him, he will look after us."

It was dinner time, and everyone was hungry, Mike had everyone get in the pickup and they went to a restaurant by the Denman Island Ferry wharf in Buckley Bay. Everyone ordered fish and chips with lots of Tartar sauce on the side. It was a welcome treat and all three said they ate too much as they waddled out to the truck. Ernie was fueling up his truck and waved to Mike as he walked by, and Mike walked over to him to chat.

"Hey Ernie, I'm going to be travelling out of the country to put an end to this chaos I inherited, could you look after the farm while I'm gone, the horses are at Ted's place. I don't know for how long, should take no longer than two weeks but may end up for quite a while. If so, do what you got to do, I will accept any decisions you have to make on my behalf."

Ernie was willing to help Mike anytime, but he was a bit concerned with the last part of what Mike said. " Sure, no problem, Mike, you're in it a bit rough with these guys eh."

" Yea a bit, got to cut the head off two snakes."

Ernie extended his hand," best of luck and may God bless you Mike, stay safe. When you come back bring me some of that cheap Russian Vodka eh."

"Thanks, Ernie, will do."

Mike hopped in the truck and Sharon commented, " he seems like a great fella, he sounded so sincere when he said God bless you, is he religious Mike?"

Mike answered solemnly, "He was definitely sincere, but he's never been to church a day in his life."

The three read between the lines and realized what was meant throughout this conversation. It was a dangerous mission and the possibility of not returning was very evident.

The three spent the next two hours finishing packing for their trip, they all were seasoned travelers, but as they went through the process, they were plagued by the doubt of missing something important. Mike made tea for the girls and perked up a bold coffee for himself. They all went through what they packed in an attempt to remember something they may have missed. Sharon thought of taking extra clothes for Beckey and Jen in case they needed a change, they all agreed, and she went through the closets and packed a couple of outfits for both.

After they finished the evening off with lighthearted conversation and laughter, they were all nervous about the unknown, and even more nervous about what was known. Mike lit the fire pit and brought out the cookies he bought at the restaurant, and they sat quietly watching the flames as they somehow soothed their minds. They watched as the flames danced in the fire pit, like a primal ritual of good travel and safe return from their mission. The beating of the drum could only be heard in their imaginations as they sat there taking in the sacred sendoff of their forefathers.

After finishing their coffee, tea, and cookies, they cleaned up a bit and headed off to an early night's sleep. Sharon noticed that Josie was now sleeping with Mike. It's not something that bothered her, but it did surprise her. She got ready for bed and read a few chapters of a book she had just started, it helped slow down her mind. She heard her phone indicate she received a message from Mikhail, "I will pick you guys up at the airport. Please let me know the flight and hanger number." Sharon did not know the answer to either and answered, " I don't know, I will let you know in the morning." Mikhail texted back, "they know you are coming and preparing for your arrival, be careful." She decided that Mike should see this. Mike read the text and calmly said to the girls, "well, we will be ready for them, bring it on."

59

Andrei was in a good state of mind since he heard the FBI director's wife and daughter had been captured and on their way to Russia. This had gone on far too long and now finally it's over, they are on their way, and he will have them here alive until someone needs a heart or kidney transplant. Neither one was anything special, he could have gotten organs from a local resident, but this was an FBI agent's family who were witnesses, and now he could get back at them after all these years. Andrei searched for the opportunity, but it seemed the opportunity never came about. When Anton's men searched the cabin after the Catskills incident, they found the family that was staying in it at the time, was an FBI family and this was immediately relayed to Andrei.

Dominik was very proficient in demolition, he became an explosives expert in the Russian Red army when he was in his mid-thirties, and it became his trade. About eight years ago, Dominik came to New York to demolish the Stock Exchange building, he believed it would be fitting for the US to lose what they hold dearly.

Eight years ago, Dominik and his crew set explosive material on key structural members under the trade center. As they completed the placement of the explosives and set the detonation devices, they were exiting the area when they were caught by the FBI who were following up with a lead they received from an informant. The arrest resulted in four of the Russians being shot and killed and the detainment of Dominik. Dominik was not cooperating with the FBI, and since this was considered an act of terrorism, even though the explosives were not detonated. The FBI was not letting Dominik off the hook, and they handed him off to the CIA for additional questioning. The CIA had special skills at interrogation that got results, and Dominik was sent to Guantanamo Bay and exposed to the most brutal interrogation techniques unimaginable to most. After six months, Dominik suffered neurological injuries from the exposure he was subjected to during his stay in the Guantanamo facilities. After two years the CIA did not get anything out of him, they loaded his beaten and useless body on a plane and sent it home on a plane to decay. Since then, Andrei vowed to get back at the United States Federal Authorities, and now he has the family of one of their directors, and he may ruin their heads and give them back to this director on a plane, just like they did to his father.

Dominik entered his son's office, "we have the family, and they are detained in the cell downstairs, the mother is beaten up a little, but the young one is fine."

Andrei smiled, "you can do it better than anyone I know, you still got it, Father. What's up with this farmer? What's his story, did you kill him?

Dominik looked at his son," I left twelve good men back to kill him and tied up his girlfriend as bait. They should have finished them both off, but I can't contact anyone. There is no way he could have killed them all, that would be impossible."

"That's alright father, it's all over now, we don't have to worry anymore."

Dominik looked straight at his son, " I hope you are right, but I believe he will follow."

Andrei looked at his father, "who will follow?"

Dominik answered his son, "the farmer, he has special skills even though he has never spent time in the military, I don't quite know how to explain it, but he is someone to watch out for, if he is alive, he will come."

"Father, he would be crazy to come after the girls over here, he doesn't know anyone."

Dominik stared at the ground with concern," Still."

Sergei barged into Andrei's office, he was smiling and acted so excited, "Andrei, I've got it, the program is ready, I can't believe it, I can now clone to multiple minds. I can build your army of criminals, we can start right away!"

Andrei smiled, " wonderful news Sergei, we will start the day after tomorrow, first thing in the morning. I will have ten candidates and try it out before proceeding further."

Sergei glowed as he was praised by Andrei, "Thank you, Andrei, I will be ready in the lab."

Dominik had mixed feelings about this army concept his son was so passionate about and wanted Andrei to think about how this would impact the authorities. Dominik was concerned that if the rise in criminal activity from Andrei's army places pressure on the authorities, they may push back with combined forces from multiple authorities in multiple countries. They would not survive that, they are making good money now, and they should be happy with that.

He owed Andrei his life, only Andrei could have the vision to develop a computer program that transfers minds from one person to the other. He can't put him down to accomplish that, but sometimes he goes too far. Dominik's mind ventured off to a woman he loved dearly and a daughter they had together, he was sure Andrei had her killed because he did not approve of her. Dominik had a chip placed under her skin so he would know where she could be found later, but he got sick. He sent his daughter away to a foster home in South America to keep safe from Andrei, he often wonders how she is today, or what she looks like. The last time he had seen her was when she was four years old, it seemed like a lifetime away, and in many ways it was.

Andrei looked at his father, "what country do you think we should target first Father?"

Dominik considered, " I think we should start in a smaller country in Europe or the Eastern bloc. What about Denmark?"

Andrei thought about his father's recommendations, " I would like to stay away from the Eastern Bloc for now, Denmark is worth looking at, great idea."

Dominik took charge of the conversation, " Andrei, I want you to really consider this army strategy and taking over countries vision you have well engrained in your head, I strongly disagree with it. The international theater will not accept it, sooner or later they will combine forces and overpower us."

Andrei said to his father, "the time is right, I need to put pressure on our high-priced help. We are paying these guys in positions of authority to keep us from this activity."

60

After Allen reported that Kevin White's fingerprints were confirmed on both the death threat letter he found and the listening device on his desk, the CIA opened an investigation on him. The CIA confirmed Kevin's dealings when they found his secret bank account in the Cayman Islands, but until now, neither the CIA nor the FBI were ever able to find actual evidence of his illicit activities. The problem was most of the evidence was circumstantial and a good lawyer could have it dismissed in a court. Frustration grew within the CIA, and they decided Kevin needed to be taken out permanently, but it had to be done to ensure no ties to them.

Tamasvi Levy was serving year two of six consecutive life sentences for multiple murders she committed over eight years. She agreed during the bargaining between the district attorney and her lawyer. If she didn't take the deal, the DA would prosecute her in a state with supports the death sentence, and she would have been executed by now. The execution would have been a fitting death for Tamasvi since she was a professional assassin who killed over thirty-six people in ten years, some were high-profile politicians and drug lords. She didn't really care but she had a line, she respected children, and she respected the elderly. For all others, she charged top dollar for her services, and she got it because she was good, very good. One of the main reasons she was that good, she was discreet, she left no trace back to her or the client, and she was in high demand.

Tamasvi was a stunningly gorgeous Israeli woman who kept herself in perfect condition. She kept her long hair neat and trimmed. Her body was flawless, perfectly proportioned as she worked out daily. Her legs were long and slender, and her face was striking, even without makeup she was beautiful and unforgettable to the eye. But there was more to this luring beauty, even her name meant the one with darkness inside. She was highly trained to fight and kill by the Israeli Mossad, spending seven years at their training camps, she became their top agent, then left to become an assassin for hire.

She was escorted by two prison guards, one on each side of her. They knew her well as she placed a few prisoners in line over the two years she was there, they both knew she could take them both out if she wanted to. They opened the door and entered a pitch-black room with a single light directed in her face, it was so bright she could not see the man sitting directly behind the light.

> She took one step forward, " that's far enough, do not come any closer! Guards, you can wait outside please."

> Tamasvi stopped, " what's going on here guys, this is not a typical friends and family kind of get-together."

> The voice from behind the light talked, " Tamasvi, I am here to make you a deal you will not be able to refuse, so I suggest you listen carefully. We could use a person with your skills and talent, we would like you to eliminate someone for us, and in return, you will be set free to roam around as you, please. There are rules and if the rules are not complied with you will be killed, no discussion.

> You will eliminate this person without resulting in any trace back to any authority in the United States.

> You will never assassinate anyone in North America or associated lands such as Hawaii or Alaska.

> You will never talk about this meeting or anything discussed during this meeting.

> Is everything understood?"

> She spent a minute to process, "yes sir I understand completely."

The man spoke again, "perfect, then these two guards will escort you to a holding cell and you will stay in that cell for about forty-five minutes while the paperwork is being processed. Then there will be two men in suits who come to escort you from the holding cell to their vehicle and they will have a change of clothes for you. As you are transported, the two men will give you keys to the safe house and a car. At the safe house, there will be a brown envelope on the table with all the information you need to take this man out. Also in the envelope, you will find a credit card that we will top up to two ten thousand dollars, your passport, driver's license, and documents with several pictures of the target. You will also find a burner phone in there with only one number programed if you have questions or need something. Again, is everything understood?"

She answered the mystery man, "yes, very clear sir."

The guards opened the door and escorted her to the holding cell. As the mystery man had said, two other men gave her a change of clothes to change into and escorted her outside the prison walls, and they gave her the keys to the house and the car. Tamasvi walked up the sidewalk to the house and opened the door, noticing the envelope on the table. She then emptied the contents of the envelope onto the top of the table and found everything the mystery man said would be inside.

The first thing that needed to be done was new clothes, she couldn't think of a more relaxing pastime on her first day of freedom than going shopping for a new wardrobe. She reviewed the contents of the envelope and read that Kevin was seen last week at the Royal Turk Hotel in Cockburn, on the Turks and Caicos Island, she used the phone to reserve a flight to the Grand Turks capital in two days.

Tamasvi was very pleased with her selections of clothes, she bought formal dresses stylish enough for a ballroom Chasse. She bought some swimwear, and couldn't think of anything else but spending time on the beach after being cooped up for two years in prison. She was grateful she looked after her figure, it would have been easy to give up with six consecutive life sentences. When she tried the barely there bikinis, she admitted to herself, that she's still got it all in the right places. She shopped for her casual suits and after getting some luggage to put it all in, she decided to have lunch at a small deli-bakery eatery, choosing a salmon croissant with capers and cream cheese and a glass of Pinot Gris. She marveled at how wonderful freedom felt today as she sat in the outside dining area, being able to feel beautiful again and especially buying clothes with someone else's money.

She noticed a man in a suit jacket who had been following her while she shopped, and now, pretending to read the paper as he sat there with a coffee. She went inside the main area to use the washroom and when she came out to return to her table, she came up behind him and whispered in his ear,

> "You are quite obviously following me, I have noticed you for some time now. You are one of three people; a creep, in which case I can kill you in your sleep; an agent with the federal authorities, in which case you are pitiful at your job; or someone trying to gather the courage to ask me out on a date, the later would be a fatal mistake."

She caught the man off guard, and he was left speechless. He tried to come up with an excuse but nothing of any sense came out of his mouth.

> She guessed, "so, you are a federal agent, why are you following me?" She grabbed his ear and twisted, "who sent you?"

The man broke away from her grip on his ear and left without answering her. She hopped in the car and left for the house, she wanted to spend some time researching this Kevin White before she left. Of the many skills the Mossad trained her on, she found behavioral analysis, was a skill that helped her considerably to understand the man she was hunting down.

 Once at the safe house, she unpacked the car, bringing all her prized purchases in and laid them on the bed, removing all the store's tags and stickers. She carefully folded the clothes so as not to wrinkle and packed them in the suitcase for the trip. She picked one casual suit for traveling and placed it on the dresser. She had one small suitcase left to pack that was for toiletries and make-up, she would shop for these tomorrow.

Tamasvi arrived at the Cockburn airport just after lunch and scurried around as she passed immigration and customs, found a luggage cart and now was waiting for her three bags. She heard the horn indicating the conveyors were starting up and watched several parents coaxing their kids off the carousel. As she watched at a distance, she noticed all three bags coming down the conveyor to the carousel and waited until she was close enough to lift them off onto her cart. With her cart full, she proceeded to leave the terminal and find a taxi.

Traffic was heavy with motorists blasting their horns frequently at intersections, as they navigated through the city to her hotel on the beach. After checking in, she asked the attendants at the check-in if they had Kevin White registered as a guest. While they would not give her that information, they offered to put her through to his room phone and directed her to the public phone on the wall. She heard the phone ring with no answer, so she left a message for him to meet her at the Ocean Side bar when he got the message. From her room window, she looked at the outside lounge through her binoculars to confirm he was there. Within an hour, he arrived at the lounge, looking around for a woman who ghosted him.

61

Allen and Ron McKay entered interrogation room three, that's what the sign on the door indicated, but since the building was built, policy changed to call them interview rooms. Everything else about the room remained the same, other than the table in the room was permanently secured to the floor, and policy was re-written to include the person being interviewed must be handcuffed to the restraining bar secured to the table. The reason for this change was, one male being interviewed stood up in anger and threw the table through the one-way mirror, cutting several spectators and it took the three interviewers piling on top of him, to stop him, he was a big man.

> "Good morning, Catherine, I hope you are finding our facilities to your liking, did you have a good sleep last night?"

> Catherine looked at him and said sarcastically, " very nice, yes I slept well thank you."

Allen looked at her with disgust. He recalled six months prior at Christmas, Jon and Catherine came over to the house and spent Christmas with them. He remembered Jon volunteering to carve the turkey and Catherine helped Jen in the kitchen with cooking and cleaning after dinner. He remembered Catherine with Becky, helping her with a Christmas craft she was painting. He would have never believed she could turn into this. But he needs to be professional, he must leave his emotions at the door when he enters.

> "Catherine, you know who I am, probably better than anyone in this office building, so I need not introduce myself. Before we get started, I would like to introduce you

to Ron McKay, he will be participating in this interview with me.

Allen placed a pile of documents on the table and picked out the organizational chart that she gave him on the plane, and then he started, "Catherine, there have been several others who have been identified and arrested, who are not on your chart. On the plane we made a deal where you give me the names of the organization, and I will keep you away from Guantanamo, do you recall that deal?"

Catherine looked at Allen, " I vaguely remember it."

Allen challenged her, " vaguely remember, I thought it would be on the forefront of your mind, at least, that's what I would expect." I don't think you understand what happens to people who go to Guantanamo! Those who go there give the information we are looking for, or they return wishing they did, the lucky ones die.

Catherine looks at Allen with a sour look on her face, " you idiot, I know more about Guantanamo than you obviously do. I've seen what happens to people who don't talk, and you are not going to intimidate me, or scare me into talking about our business because it's our business, not yours!"

Allen looks over at Ron and gives him the head nod and he took over the interview,   " Catherine, you mentioned that you know more about Guantanamo than we do, tell me about it?"

" It's a disgusting place, it takes a normal healthy person, and turns them into vegetables. They come back ruined and broken, and no hope of returning to normal."

Ron waited fifteen seconds then, " who do you know that came back from Guantanamo like that?"

Catherine realized she let a small cat out of the bag, " no one, its just what I heard, leave me alone."

Ron continued, " it is a disgusting place Catherine, you are right, I don't believe anyone should be sent there, I couldn't imagine a family member, like a parent or a sibling going through that and coming home broken." Ron looked at Catherine, she was deep in thought. He continued, " tell me how you felt when they were returned to you ruined, unable to function properly, and with no hope of getting better?"

Catherine started to cry, " it was horrible, he couldn't eat by himself, and he needed constant care, you ruined him, you Basterds."

"Who was he Catherine, a brother, a father? Who Catherine?"

Catherine realized she said too much, " I'll never tell you, send me to Guantanamo if you want, they can mess me up as well and send me back to Russia ruined the same way they ruined him!" She sobbed and Allen gave her the box of tissues.

Allen started back in on her, " Tell me about Kevin White with the CIA, where does he fit in Catherine?"

" That egotistical idiot doesn't fit in anywhere, where did you come up with his name in all this?"

Allen smiled, " well, we pulled both yours and his fingerprints off that bug you planted under my desktop, we also pulled his fingerprints off of a threatening letter someone placed on my desk. That's where I came up with his name, now where does he fit in your organization?"

Andrei hired him on to keep the Feds from investigating our business, what an jerk!"

Allen looked over at Ron and he gestured to end this interview. Allen considered they got quite a bit of info for the time spent and had the guards take her back to her cell. Ron and Allen finished their notes and took a few moments to reflect on their conversation with Catherine.

Allen looked at Ron, " that was very good Ron, I think she is protecting a family member as you alluded to in your questioning. I believe that person is a very close relative."

Ron as he was reviewing notes, " yes, I agree Allen, I think we should hand this over to the crime analysist's to find out her full family. Did her and Jon have children?"

" No, they didn't, but they often talked about wanting children and raising a family."

" Allen, I don't think we should conduct a follow up interview until we get answers from this one. I believe she will open up to us, but she seems to hold us responsible for this person tour at Guantanamo, she called us both nasty names."

 Allen laughed out loud, " I don't know about you Ron, but I've been called a lot worse."

Ron started smiling at Allen, he recognized him as a very experienced and knowledgeable man with over four times the time in the field as he does. Ron had the greatest amount of respect for Allen, and it showed.

62

Sven Olsen came into Allen's office unannounced with a man who appeared to have been sleeping on the streets for most of his life. As a man who lived all his life in the cold climates of Canada, he could never understand why some New York slum residents wore their balaclava in the summer, other than possibly partake in criminal activities. Allen was thinking this man had the ugliest, dirtiest balaclava that he had ever seen, the man wore on his head like a toque, and the man was not only filthy, but he smelled.

> In Sven's most boisterous way, " Allen, I would like you to meet the FBI International's lead for Europe, Pat McLear."

> Allen said to himself, I didn't see that coming, and extended his hand to the man" good to meet you, I heard a lot about your operation Pat."

> He looked at Allen with a solid steel eye to eye connection, " likewise, I was told you have a situation that you needed some help with, how can I help you?"

Allen and his boss Sven took Pat through the two-hour summation of the incidents leaving nothing out.

> Allen finished and, " so, can you help me?

> Pat looking at Allen, " you're in it rough Allen, where is your family?

> Allen winced, "Andrei has kidnapped them and taken them to Russia, and my only hope is that you and your team would help me bring them back safely."

> Pat played with a piece of paper he found on Allen's desk, "we can try, we are done with our undercover project here in New York that we have been working on for the past six

months. Our team was to start up the international district with five other agents, so we are pretty much ready to go. This may very well be the first case for the team, which also includes agents from Europol.

Allen was satisfied, " I also have a group of civilians that are working on the rescue of my family, Mike Stone is a personal friend of mine."

Pat became a bit animated, " No, I'm not working with a bunch of amateurs Allen. They run the risk of jeopardizing my team."

"Well Pat, I don't know you, but I know Mike Stone and you will work with him, or we will get someone else who can."

Sven was floored by Allen's response, " Allen these guys are a group of professional FBI agents trained to bring positive resolution to situations like this. You need to listen to him, he can bring your family back alive."

Pat was surprised at the directors response, "director Fulton, you need to remove your emotions from this and let me look after this with our group.

Allen looked at Pat, " you have everything you need to get started on this, get it done."

Allen ushered both Pat and Sven out of his office, " I have a lunch appointment for noon."

Allen showed up on time at the restaurant that him and Kevin agreed to meet at. It was a cooler day with a slight wind from the North. He smiled whenever the cold weather came out of the North, the New Yorkers would blame Canada for it. He selected a seat by the window inside the restaurant, keeping well clear of that darn Canadian cold. The waitress came by to take his drink order, and he explained he was waiting for another person and ordered for a Diet soft drink with ice.

Allen looked around the restaurant looking at the massive beams the building was built from. It was originally a warehouse built in the early eighteen hundreds and converted into office space and this restaurant. He looked at his watch and noticed Kevin was already ten minutes late. Allen was always punctual, and he did not want this appointment to cause him to be late for the rest of the day and got the waitresses attention to order.

Since Jen has been away, Allen has been delinquent in eating a proper breakfast, so lunch is important to him. Allen ordered a Salmon power bowl with quinoa and spinach. When the meal came, Allen looked at his watch determined he was thirty-five minutes late and he was not coming. He tried calling him and the call went directly to the message service, and he left a brief message. Allen finished his meal, giving the waitress a sizable tip and left for the office.

Allen was five minutes from the office on his way back from lunch and his phone started ringing.

> " Allen, it's Ron here, Catherine just tried to commit suicide in her cell. She's in the prison Hospital, the doctors have her stable now."

> " Thanks Ron, I'll be right there."

Allen walked directly to the parkade and sat behind the wheel of his BMW i8, leaving for the prison hospital. Allen parked and walked briskly to the prison entrance, down the hall to the infirmary. He met Ron outside the door, and they talked.

> Ron looked shocked, " she beat her head against the cement wall, trying to kill herself, she ended up knocking herself unconscious." Ron regrouped his thoughts, " I don't think she wanted to go to Guantanamo."

> Allen gave it all some thought, "she is protecting someone very close to her, we need to find out who that person is."

"The analysts are working on it, apparently she is related to Andrei, they are looking for her mother and father."

Allen told Ron, "Maybe they could find Andrei's mother and father, it may be easier to use Volkov for a last name, you never know what hides under different rocks."

Allen looked at Ron, " I can't do anything here, can you stay here and keep me notified if anything changes, I have to go back to the office, I had a great lunch, but Kevin didn't show up for our appointment."

63

Mike, Josie, and Sharon woke up to sit out on the veranda of the farmhouse. It was a beautiful morning, one well worth worshiping with coffee and friends. Since the three were introduced, they became more than just friends in a very short time. They all knew what they were getting into but had no idea what to expect. On the veranda that morning, they talked and laughed, and often there were times of silence where each one had their own thoughts, their own fears, and their own desire to get Jen and Becky back. They went through what they packed several times as a group, and many more times by themselves, until finally the time had come to go.

Mike put all the baggage in the box of the rental truck and left the farmhouse, hoping to see it again soon. They arrived early at the hanger to drop off the bags and allow Mike time to take the rental truck back, he wouldn't need it after today. After the ground crew loaded the baggage on the plane, Sharon, Josie, and Mike boarded the plane for a sixteen-hour trip to Moscow plus a quick stop in London to fuel up.

The plane was very spacious for the long trip allowing them to fully lay down and get a comfortable rest, and due to the time change, they would sleep during the last half of the trip. During the first half of the trip Sharon read a novel she was reading and brushing up on her Russian language. Josie and Mike played Super Mario that came with the plane, intended for kids during the flight.

After getting some sleep, they landed in Moscow and waited for Mikhail to pick them up. Sharon told him which hanger it was, but Mikhail was not sure which one it was, Sharon was nervous he wouldn't show up. After waiting an hour, Mikhail drove up with a big smile on his face.

Mikhail got out of his vehicle and immediately wanted to know who his niece was, except for a few pictures Sharon sent him, he had never seen her since birth. After the hugs were done, they all piled in Mikhails jeep, and they headed off to Ruza. He drove for about an hour and a half as Sharon and Mikhail talked, sometimes in English and sometimes in Russian. As they entered Ruza, they passed over cobblestone sections of the streets, and small houses that gave it a very quaint and historical appeal.

Then finally, they arrived at Mikhail's house. It was an older house that showed work done to keep it maintained, and thoughtfully landscaped with lawn, shrubs, and flower gardens. As the girls entered the house, they noticed it was decorated in a way a bachelor would, not necessarily color coordinated and definatly missing a woman's touch. Mike on the other hand felt right at home. Mikhail showed his guests their rooms, it was convenient that Mike and Josie slept together since he only had two spare rooms in his house, and they unpacked their belongings.

It was eight O'clock in the morning and despite the sleep they got on the plane, the group was jet lagged and weren't sure whether to go to sleep or stay awake. Mikhail offered coffee and they sat around the table, getting to know each other better.

Mikhail's English was better than everyone expected since Sharon spent so much effort polishing up her Russian on the plane. Mike was quite relieved since he was a key person in this whole mission and a breakdown in communications between them would be challenging.

> Mikhail was very interested in Mike, " tell me why you are here, Sharon explained the basics, you are looking for someone?"

Mike gave Mikhail a short version of what happened, explaining they are here to rescue Jen and Becky. Mikhail was not surprised Andrei would do something like this, and explained that Andrei is a powerful man, and to accomplish this would be difficult. He went on to explain Andrei's organization, that he has people everywhere including police, they probably already know you're here. The thought of the latter was a bit unnerving to them, but Mikhail confirmed that it was possible.

Mikhail told them the story of the mob setting up a prostitution ring in Ruza, and the abduction of Kyela. Mikhail also told them about the decimation of the sex house, and the murders of many of those who burned the house down, including his parents.

"But that was back when Andrei was only apprenticing under his father, Dominik, in the business. Dominik was a ruthless man, I swear Dominik and Andrei were responsible for my parents murder. But there is one thing I know for sure, that Andrei was directly responsible for the murder of my sister, Kyela."

Mike asked Mikhail, " did you report to the police?"

Mikhail started waving his hands and shaking his head, "The authorities are all paid off to protect him and his business."

Mike thought about what Mikhail just said and understood it was going to be more difficult than Mike first expected, " so Mikhail, where does this leave you, can we count on your support?"

Mikhail smiled at Mike and picked up his phone. Someone answered and they spoke in Russian for a while, then hung up. " Mr. Mike, for over thirty years now, I have been waiting for someone to come to my house to help put an end to Andrei and his business, and here you are. Andrei murdered my sister who I loved more than you could ever imagine. I am not the only one who feels this way, and I have called those in the community who are willing to commit to getting rid of Andrei to meet."

While this news excited Mike, he became concerned that Andrei would find out about the meeting and send someone. Mike asked

Mikhail to watch for unfamiliar people who may be Andrei's men. Mikhail did not think about that and agreed with Mike. He also asked about a gun, Mike was feeling the necessity to have some form of protection other than Josie. Mikhail left for a storage room and came back with something that surprised Mike, a Colt 45 caliber automatic pistol, with two boxes of shells.

As they left for the meeting with Mikhail, Mike considered if Andrei's presence would be noticed, but he realized there would only be about twenty people or so there, and they would be manageable. When they arrived, Mikhail was challenged to find a place to park, and Mike had a new appreciation for how much Andrei was hated.

They entered the hall with just over two hundred people talking to each other, none with smiles on their faces. Mikhail convinced Mike these people were willing to fight Andrei and burn his palace down, they all hated him with vengeance, and they all had their own story why.

Mike was not prepared for this turnout, and explained to Mikhail there were a few things he wanted to know about, so took a few minutes to write a few questions that came to mind that he wanted answers to. He gave the list of questions to Sharon so between her and Mikhail they could get the answers to. He went up to Mikhail and asked him to get their attention and introduce them to the group, then ask these questions. He turned to Sharon to write the answers down as they gave them.

Mikhail hollered out asking for everyone's attention and introducing them as people who have family that has been abducted from North America and brought here for whatever reason by Andrei Volkov. Once that was said the room roared with dissention and hatred. Mikhail regained their attention and started asking the questions, after the questions were answered Mike found out what he wanted to know at this point. They were all willing to fight Andrei and help them get Jen and Becky back, they all had firearms and ammo hidden away, and they knew where they could get explosives to blow up the palace. Mike grabbed Sharron's hand and pulled her over towards Mikhail and thanked the crowd for their support in English and Russian. He asked Mikhail to explain they would be working on a plan then notifying the group when it's time to go. The crowd started cheering as they raised their hands. Mike figured they would be ready today if asked to, he was grateful for the group and grateful for Sharon and Mikhail.

64

Tamasvi dried herself off after her shower and wrapped a towel around her as she dried her hair. She smiled as the sun felt so good on the little Caribbean Island. She reflected on her term in the prison, and how glad she was to be given this chance for freedom, to bask in the sun on a beautiful beach. The weather forecast for the day was clear and sunny, Tamasvi decided to spend the day relaxing on the beach and worship the sun god. After brushing her hair, Tamasvi carefully put on her make-up and watched out her window for Kevin. By the time she finished her make-up and nails, Kevin showed up at the restaurant.

Kevin White walked into the lounge that doubled as a breakfast bar for those travelers staying at the hotel and wanting breakfast after a night's sleep. He selected a table with a view of the ocean, to sit, he had no idea he was being watched through binoculars by one of the most dangerous assassins in the world. He sat down and started reading the newspaper he had brought in, the waitress came by, and he ordered a coffee, drinking it as he read.

She saw him enter the breakfast bar and decided to make herself noticed by him for the first time. She left her room wearing her barely there bikini and a see-through top, that extended just low enough to cover her bottom. As she walked into the breakfast bar, she selected a seat that would be in his direct view when he put his paper down from reading. She felt every man's stare as she sat waiting for the waitress, and smiled to herself thinking how predictable men are, and so easy to kill. The waitress brought her coffee, juice and a plate for the breakfast buffet and went over to the display to look what was offered. The buffet was complimented with scrambled egg, bacon, sausage, ham and roasted hashbrowns as well as every fruit imaginable. She was hungry and decided to dig in deep, but she would do it with a second visit, it's not lady like to have a plate overflowing with food.

Kevin had no intentions of having breakfast this morning until he put the newspaper he was reading down on the table and seen Tamasvi. He was stunned by her beauty and decided he had to meet her. He immediately took a plate from the waitress and made his way to the buffet and started a casual conversation that progressed to an invite to his table for breakfast.

Kevin decided introductions were in order, " hi, I'm Kevin White."

Tamasvi decided to use one of her practiced aliases, " it's good to meet you Kevin, I'm Adrianna Rodrigues."

The two had travelled extensively and had a great deal to talk about, and towards the end of breakfast, he asked her if she wanted to have dinner at a local restaurant that serves incredible seafood. She was playing hard to get, telling him she wants to think about it first and for him to call her before he goes to dinner. He agreed and she left him her number to call.

Tamasvi was satisfied with the first introduction, she felt he was a bit self-serving, and his ego would become the death of him, with that she smiled and continued to the beach to allow her body to absorb the rays of sun it has been lacking for the past two years. She adjusted the umbrella to shade only her face, then laid down to relax as she listened to the surf pound the shores of the sandy beach. As she thought of how she would kill him, by injection or by strangulation, maybe throw him overboard in shark infested waters. At that, she fell asleep, living her dream of lying on a white sandy beach, basking in the sun.

Tamasvi was in her room thinking about how she wanted tonight's dinner to unfold. She had already selected the skirt and top she wanted to wear, nothing too casual but a bit revealing to keep his interest.

The phone rang at precisely five-forty-seven, and she accepted his invitation to dinner, and met him in the lobby at seven O'clock. They sped away in his rental convertible BMW that had the new car smell even with the top down and Kevin drove through the local traffic with confidence. Kevin was a good conversationalist with a keen sense of humor that made the trip to BuBu's Crab Shack entertaining. Once there, he held Tamasvi's door for her as she got out, allowing the valet attendant to park it while he flipped him a twenty-dollar bill. The restaurant was decorated with rough boards and fishing nets on the walls with humorous signs attached to the walls amongst the variety of local pictures. The floor was rough boards, worn smooth from years of customers walking in and out, and the band was playing a mixture of Calypso and reggae music, giving atmosphere to the dining experience. She searched the dining area for camera's, but she was unable to find any, and she avoided being seen by staff when possible.

Tamasvi started out, "tell me a bit about yourself Kevin, where were you born, what do you do? Are you married?"

"Wow, well, I was born in Pheonix, Arizona, and travelled with my family around the states, living in Atlanta, Dallas, Seatle, and New Orleans. My father was with the FBI at the time, and we moved around a lot. Presently I am a free agent working for large corporations and governments helping them with cybercrimes. And no, I am not married, I am presently divorced."

Tamasvi noticed a white ring around his finger indicating he was just recently divorced, or he took his ring off for dinner and was lying. The waiter came by to order drinks and appetizers as they talked and gave them a menu with a long list of specials for the evening. The evening floated by as the conversation went back and forth between them, she told him she was born in Panama City, she was not married, and she is an entrepreneur, looking for international opportunities. She often swung the conversation around to him so she could feed his ego a bit.

Kevin was in love with her, he didn't care if she was a gold digger or not, he was willing to be her sugar daddy, and let her know he was wealthy. He felt as though she was responding well to him talking about things he owned and his plans for future financial growth. Kevin talked with Andrei a week ago about the Mindsweeper program. Without telling her about it, told her that he was working on a project called the Mindsweeper program in Moscow that was huge, bigger than anything he had ever tackled before. He watched her respond and she told him how wonderful he was to land something that enormous. He enjoyed listening to her tell him how wonderful he was.

They finished the evening and drove back to the hotel with the wind in their hair laughing and joking as they drove. As Kevin said good night, he came close for a kiss, and she stopped him, thanking him for dinner and told him, "As for this, perhaps some time, but not tonight."

65

Anastasia Orlov relaxed with a cup of her favorite tea in her home office, she loved her home, and had it decorated exactly the way she dreamed. After twenty years her business had given her the lifestyle she always wanted, except she was lacking a family. She had few people she could have a pleasurable conversation with, and she never had the opportunity to raise her family, that was taken away from her. She watches her son at a distance, disgusted at what his father raised him to become, but Dominik got what he deserved.

She recalled the day Andrei was born, they were both so happy and so in love, they were about to have something very special. She watched Andrei grow up to his thirteenth year, then seen Dominik start turning Andrei into a heartless criminal like himself. Anastasia rebelled against Dominik's desire to mold Andrei into the criminal he wanted him to be. Dominik became tired of her constant rantings and found her very distracting. He had many authorities paid off and had Anastasia arrested and put in prison. After a year, she begged him to let her leave, and promised to never bother the two of them again. Against Dominik's better judgement, He agreed, and Anastasia returned to a life of freedom.

She had no money when she returned to the city, living off the streets begging for food and almost froze to death during the cold months of winter. She begged Dominik and Andrei for money to help her get set up for winter with good warm clothes and sleeping bag, but they denied her. She begged for the table scraps from the kitchen, she knew how much food was thrown out, but again she was denied.

She had a friend who showed her where to find food and helped her survive winter, she was forever in his debt. Pavel built her a nice shelter with plastic tarps he found for her and made her a floor using shipping pallets and used Styrofoam he stole at the dock yards. Finally, she was comfortable from the wind and the snow, she would survive the winter.

She was not satisfied that just surviving was going to be how she would live for the rest of her life. She wanted a nice bed, with satin sheets and she wanted beautiful things again, and she wanted to eat good food and wear nice clothes. Pavel gained Anestasia's trust, and they became close, she needed him to start her own business of crime and he was willing to help her do it. They found two girls who were looking to make extra money at night, and money started to come in, then they doubled their business. The business grew to the point where they rented a nice warm apartment for the following winter.

After saving as much money as possible, they started dealing in light street drugs, which again doubled their business income. Anastasia was well known as the fairest business owner in Moscow, which attracted more girls and drug suppliers because of the trust she instilled. She was starting to get some muscle from the competition in the third year and was able to hire her own muscle to push back. At this point she decided her business was big enough for her to live a comfortable life without the stress of having to pay off authorities. Pavel was also very comfortable and within five years of when they first met, they were married.

Despite Anastasias promise to Dominik to never bother the two of them again, she vowed to destroy Dominik and Andrei for what they did to her. The opportunity never came, and Anastasia was always grateful for what she and Pavel had, so never went looking.

She became a very powerful women, because of her leadership style, she never needed to intimidate to get someone to do something. She was truly loved by all the people she met and had deep friends that would do anything for her. Often, she helped some of the shop owners as thugs would try to blackmail them for protection. Anastasia found out and put an end to it with her security team, and the shop owners were so grateful. News of what Dominik and Andrei did to her spread through the streets like a hurricane, and she had everyone's respect. Everyone was on her side, and Anastasia knew that should the opportunity present itself, they would all fight for her to destroy Dominik and Andrei.

When she heard what happened to Dominik when he was sent to Guantanamo Bay, she did a happy dance in the street. The pedestrians walking by asked her why she was dancing, and that got back to Andrei. He had murdered four of her key people, after, she cooled her heels for a while since she was concerned about Pavel getting hurt. After this, Andrei had a lady who got along well with his mother, to find information about her and to keep him informed of what she was up to. As it turned out, she liked Anastasia and brought her more information than she brought back to Andrei. She would have some insignificant details about what his mother was doing, just to satisfy him.

She told Anastasia about the family of the FBI director's that was kidnapped and brought to the palace, with no knowledge of what will become of them. She also informed Anastasia of the Mindsweeper program that Andrei and Sergei had developed, and that Dominik had been transferred into a twenty-six-year-old man's body. This horrified Anastatia as she thought of the young man and his family. She started searching for what she could do but decided to think about it for a bit, she didn't want to react out of haste.

The old feelings of hate she once had and subsided, returned this time with determination to end these vile men. She became more focused on destroying them than ever before. She had a meeting with her key people and discussed the situation to make a plan to take him out, but nothing worthwhile became of it and like before, her rage subsided in the following days.

Anastasia's business was prospering and her relationship with Pavel growing by the day. They often talked about how wonderful it would have been if they first married young and could have had children of their own. It was their dream to leave their fortune to their children, develop a legacy for people to talk about and their children to aspire by.

They decided to adopt a boy and a girl, maybe a bit older, maybe becoming foster parents would be better. Anastasia remembered how she hated changing Andrei's diapers, a child old enough not to wear diapers. Yes, they both agreed, and she will follow-up with the foster child placement tomorrow. They were both excited and looking forward to meeting likely candidates. They both celebrated being parents with a glass of wine and a toast.

66

Mike woke from a sleep after the meeting with the enraged townspeople, he recalled his surprise with the turnout. He got out of bed slowly, trying not to wake Josie, and walked out into the kitchen-living room area where Mikhail was deep in thought over a cup of coffee.

"Help yourself to the coffee, I won't guarantee it will be the best coffee you have drank, but it's coffee, it says so on the can."

Mike appreciated a good sense of humor, " it's just fine Mikhail, thank you."

Mikhail was trying to get a read on Mike, " I will show you pictures I have of the palace where Andrei lives."

Mike looked at the pictures and started with the questions he needed answers for in order to come up with a plan, " how many of Andrei's people are inside the palace?"

Mikhail had his hand over his mouth as he looked at the ceiling, as though he was watching a fly, " about twenty at the outside, but it varies. I sat at the front gate for days monitoring the traffic flow in and out, there were about six to ten cars an hour traveling in and out. But it's the police that you need to worry about, they will come immediately, if he calls."

Mike asked Mikhail, "how can we stop that communication to the police?"

"Of course, communication would be made by either land line or cellular. We could cut the lines at the road stopping the land lines, but shutting down cell phones would be something that I don't know anything about."

Mike thought for a moment, "do you know of someone within the community who is smart with computers and cell phones, someone really smart?"

Mikhail looked at Mike, " what are you thinking?"

"We really need a cell signal blocker, one strong enough to cover the whole palace and grounds, do you know someone with one?"

"One moment," he dialed a number and talked to the man at the other end in Russian. Alexi knows a man who can build one."

"Perfect, have him build us one and bring it to us to try out, this will be key to our attack efforts on the palace."

Mike talked to Mikhail about the plan that he was thinking about, they would cut the phone wires from the house, this would look after the land lines. At the same time, the cell signal blocker will knock out the cell communication. The towns people split into two groups, stopping all traffic coming in and going out of the palace, then Josie, Sharon and me go into the palace to rescue Jen and Becky.

"Mike, he said, you are going in too light, let me go in with you."

" I need you to coordinate the towns people, on the outside because when we are coming out with Jen and Becky, I don't want to have to be looking over my back. I want someone who has my back and watching it for me."

Mikhail nodded his head, " I understand Mr. Mike, we will cover your back."

"Perfect! Then the last thing we need to do is place some dynamite, you said you can get some."

Mikhail thought for a minute, " not exactly, we only have C-4, it is actually better, it packs a much bigger punch when it goes off."

Mike smiled at Mikhail, " sounds good to me, do you have anyone experienced in using it? Because I don't."

" Oh yes, we use it all the time."

" So, you will have people to plant this in the palace to blow it up, great, keep in mind nothing blows up until we are on the plane, OK?"

"Yes, understood Mr. Mike."

Mike thought of one other thing that may give them an edge, "could you get me a crossbow and a pile of arrows?"

Mikhail considered Mike's request, "unlikely, but let me try, it may cost you."

"That's fine, I'll pay what it's worth, also every townsman must have a gun and extra ammunition."

Mike was pleased with what they accomplished at this meeting with Mikhail. He had concerns, however, his plans for breaching into the palace and rescuing Jen and Becky were not particularly clear in his head. He got Josie and Sharon together and summarized what he and Mikhail discussed.

After a lunch of leftover pork roast made into a sandwich and some kind of soup that tasted somewhere between cream of broccoli and seafood chowder, they left to see the palace.

As they drove by, Josie commented, "I see why they call it the palace."

Mike was looking at the wrought iron fence around the perimeter and noted the security cameras attached at the top. Mike looked at the palace itself, he counted four security guards patrolling the outside of the building, all within range with a good cross bow. Also, something he didn't consider, there were four Doberman

Pincher security dogs. He would have to put them asleep, prior to breaching the gates of the palace.

Mike spent a lot of time searching for camerasand motion detection devices such as lights in the trees and the gardens that surrounded the palace. He was satisfied there were no other surprises for them. Everything looked fine, they would be ready it two days. They left for Ruza.

67

After Sharon and Josie got up and had breakfast, they were all sitting around the table asking Mikhail questions about the area and the people in the community. Mikhail explained to them the people have hard lives, but they make the best of it. It was why they are so open to help us make it better, they are very defensive when forced to go backwards.

Mikhail talked about Kyela, and told Sharon what a wonderful person she was, he always had a warm smile when he talked of her. He told Sharon that he would like her to meet Natasha, Sharon's paternal aunt, on her father's side. After Kyela's death, Mikhail stayed in touch with her and often went to see her when he went to the city. Mikhail talked to her about Sharon and wanted to meet her. Sharon was elated and agreed to see her, and decided the afternoon would be the best time. Mike agreed and wanted Josie and him to accompany Sharon and Mikhail to visit her and left after lunch.

Natasha Gusev was in her sixties, a very slender woman with a warm smile and a welcoming heart, she made everyone feel at home. She brought out some baking and coffee for her guests, Mike noted her coffee was much better than Mikhail's, but didn't say anything. Natasha talked about the relationship between Kyela and Lev and explained how much in love they were, and why Kyela was drawn away from Andrei.

Natasha talked to Sharon about her paternal father Lev Gusev and explained all about the relationship with her mother (Kayla Kuznetsov). She told them that Andrei was not the one that killed her father, and that it was the CIA. They were surprised.

Lev was a double agent, initially working for Russia, obtaining information from US informants working deep within the embassy and supplying to the Russian military. The CIA was investigating him, and Lev encountered a CIA agent by the name of Alysha Harm, who convinced him to defect and provide key information to the US. Alysha was investigating Dominik and Andrei for several years, at the time, Dominik was the head of the family syndicate and had Alysha killed. She was replaced by CIA agent Lawrence Thomas who wanted in on Dominik's business to provide protection from and keep them out of the CIA's crosshairs.

Lev Gusev found out about this and threatened to report Lawrence to the agency if he didn't stop working for and taking money from Dominik. Lawrence was making good money and had no intentions of ending it and had Sharon's father killed. Her guests noticed a tear run down her cheek when she spoke of Lev, it was understood she loved him dearly.

Natasha found it difficult at times to speak of her past, " it was a hard life by myself, and I never married, with Lev gone I couldn't afford to eat. I started working for Andrei's mother to put food on my table, surprisingly she is a wonderful person, both her and Pavel. There is quite a story of how Dominik had her sent to prison because she tried to stop Dominik from corrupting Andrei. When she was finally successful in talking him into freeing her from prison, he would not allow her back to the palace. She was left out on the street to find food in dumpsters and live in a cardboard shelter, she told me she would have died if it wasn't for the help of Pavel, who was also homeless.

Her guests were shocked that a man could be that heartless, Mike commented, "where is she now?

Natasha answered Mike, " in Moscow, she and Pavel started a business from nothing and built it to what it is today, and they both live a comfortable life in their retirement. She vowed that someday she would take

Dominik and Andrei out, but as she explained, the opportunity never presented itself. Maybe you should talk to her, she has the deepest hatred for them, and she might be able to help you."

Mike jumped all over it, " how can I meet her, talk to her, can she be trusted?"

" If you like, I can arrange it, she will not talk to anyone she doesn't know, and yes, she is the most trustworthy person in Moscow. She is a woman of deep integrity."

Mike explains, " Natasha, because our friend and her daughter are held captive by Andrei, we have little time to waste, can you get us to see her right away?"

Natasha considered her guest's situation, " please, one moment."

She picked up her phone and searched through her contact list and selected Anastasia's phone number and pressed on it. Her guests could hear the phone ringing on the other end. After several rings, Anastasia answered and the two women talked in Russian, then hung up.

Natasha told the group, "She wants to see you at her place for dinner, she invited me as well so I can show you how to get there. A warning, when you talk to her, you must speak from your heart, she knows the difference."

They arrived at the address that Natasha showed them and walked up the path to a modest but well-appointed and maintained home. An elderly lady answered the door, and after she and Natasha exchanged hugs, the group was introduced to Anastasia Orlov. The group was escorted into the sitting room by Petrov and started the small talk to cut the ice by asking where they were all from and how they happened to be together that evening at her home. Each person spoke for themselves, and Mike summarized the situation they were in and why they came to see her.

Anastasia started in on the group, " you want my help, I'm assuming that Natasha has filled you in on my story, and you must have figured out that if I help you, I would be taking on some risk. Why do you think I would risk this to go back to the streets and eat food out of dumpsters again, especially at my age?"

Mike looked at her and he could not visualize her doing that, " that would be the last thing I would want to see happen. Based on what Natasha explained to us, you have been looking for the opportunity to crush Dominik and Andrei, but the opportunity has never presented itself. I couldn't agree more about your risk, however with the four of us here and the two-hundred-armed towns people of Ruza, the risk to you will never be lower.

Anastasia looked directly at Mike, " and what do you need from me?"

Mike looked directly at her and not breaking eye contact, " I need four to six good people well-armed who know how to fight."

She looked at him again, " what is your general plan?"

Mike looks at her, " I am risking a lot by sitting with my enemies mother, explaining my plan, however I have been told you are the most trustworthy person in Moscow, so I will trust you. We will cut off all communications to and from the palace and disable the security cameras and internet. I am a marksman with a crossbow, and I will silently take out the four or five guards located on the outside, then myself and my group will enter the confines of the palace gates and enter through the front. Where your people will come in is they will come in as part of my group to assist me in the rescue. The two-hundred-armed townspeople will monitor the entrances, stopping people from coming in and going out. They will also cover my back when I come out with Becky and Jen."

"What about Dominik and Andrei?" Anastasia asked.

Mike explained, " well Dominik won't be an issue since he was sent back from Guantanamo an invalid."

Anastasia exclaimed, " he's not an invalid now."

Anastasia explained to Mike that she gets reliable inside information about what's going on at the palace, and about what Dominik and Andrei are up to. She explained to the group about the Mindsweeper program and Dominik undergoing a mind transfer into a young body. She also explained that he was the one who kidnapped the FBI director's family. She explained further that Dominik is a very dangerous man, he has fifty years of criminal experience in a body of a twenty-six-year-old.

Mike was stunned, " boy, am I glad we had this little chat."

Anastasia made the group a deal, " here is what I will do, I will give you six of my best security people to go in to make your rescue with you. I will also give you my IT expert to shut down the sophisticated alarm system at the palace that you don't know about. Here is what I want you to do for me in return. I want you to take Dominik back to Guantanamo for the rest of his miserable life."

Mike answered, " I will take him back with me, I am not sure about Guantanamo for the rest of his life, but the director is more likely to entertain your offer than not. At the very least, he will be thrown in jail for the rest of his life, and as a bonus, we give you the palace. how's that work for you?"

She smiled and looked at him, " Mike you seem to be an honest and trustworthy person, that will work for me. By the way, they will probably hold them in the basement, the door to gain access is on the right of the kitchen, you can't miss it. Okay, that's settled, let's eat."

Anastasia looked at Sharon. "How do you fit into all this Sharon?"

Sharon told her story from the research at the hospitals to the retired nurse and the other parents of the second abducted baby, and the DNA testing proving she was not their child. She told the group how she determined that Mikhail was her uncle and discovered instead of Andrei being her father, that Natasha's brother Lev was.

Anastasia became serious as she asked Sharon, "Did you ever find who the other baby was?" Sharon answered her. "No, I've been preoccupied with my own ancestry."

Anastasia became very quiet as she was thinking. "How old are you?"

"I'm thirty-six." Sharon was concerned she said something to offend her. "What is it?"

Anastasia shook her head. "The other one is Katrina."

 Mike, Josie, and Sharon were all shocked with this news, Mike comments, "So Catherine Marion was raised as Andrei's daughter, but she was actually born to a German couple? I wonder how that played out."

Sharon added. "Yes, I would like to know that too."

Anastasia concluded. "Oh my, I guess every family has its twists, Desert anyone?"

68

Mike was up early, too many thoughts running around his mind, It was a lot of information learned last night and a lot to process. He wished he had a pill that would wash it all out and let him sleep in like he did when he was a teenager, and that of course led him back to think of Jen and Becky. The more Mike learned of how ruthless Andrei was, and now with the news that Dominik was living in a healthy body, there seemed to be a greater sense of urgency. They had to work fast and be prepared.

Mike was pleased with the dinner engagement with Anastasia, he didn't expect a woman of that grandness to be associated with one of the most ruthless criminals in Europe. Despite the fact she was a criminal herself, Mike had a sense of respect for her. She brought herself from living off the streets, to a life of richness, not so much in a monetary sense, but she had values and compassion, and a woman of her word.

With Anastasias help, the mission of rescuing Jen and Becky was looking better, instead of four people charging into the palace, there would be ten. Mike thought Anastasia gave them a very useful tip by telling them where Becky and Jen would most likely be. It will give them a direct focus on where to go first, he could have Anastasias men stay guard at the doorway as him, Josie, Sharon, and one other would go to the basement, and rescue the girls.

Mikhail was not up yet, so Mike challenged himself in making a pot of coffee. It was not something he had to have or was addicted to, but he was looking for the comfort or soothing associated with drinking a cup of coffee that was most important to him. As he heard the coffee percolator chug and circulate the coffee, his mind went elsewhere. Mike was thinking of Festus and the little creek that ran through the pasture by the high ridge on his farm. He was thinking about everything that led him to this place to rescue Jen and Becky, and then he thought of Josie. He felt different about her than he had ever felt for any other girl he had been with. Even with Jen, it wasn't the same, it was very different, yet he could not find the words to explain to himself how it was different.

The coffee had finished percolating in the old glass percolator that he made coffee in, and with consideration for the coffee Mikhail made yesterday, he gathered up enough courage to try a cup. Mike was thinking to himself, it looks like coffee, and it even smells like coffee. With what Mikhail said yesterday, it even says it's coffee, then it's got to be coffee. He took a slurp and tasted it, by gosh it even tasted like coffee. Mike heard someone stirring, and out came Mikhail with a big smile on his face, Mike poured him a cup and put it in front of him on the table. Mikhail was excited that he had a cup of coffee waiting for him and with a "thank you," he took a big gulp. He just got out of bed and his hair was not combed yet, looking as though he got hit by a tornado last night. His two-day stubble and deep crevices on his face made him look like an old, weathered fisherman that Mike remembered talking to at the government wharf as a kid.

After taking another drink of coffee, Mikhail asked, "Mike what did you think of our visit's yesterday?" With his eyes poised at Mike, he took another gulp.

" First off, I learned a lot about what a person can accomplish if they set their mind to it, secondly, we both learned some valuable information about the palace security system and where Jen and Becky may be held captive, what about you?"

Mikhail rubbed his face, " when Dominik was the head of the family business, he was ruthless, I think you have gathered that by now. If he is in a young healthy body as Anastasia mentioned, we need to have one eye always looking behind us."

Mike took the burner phone that Allen sent and made a call to update him on their status. Mike summarized the trip, the community meeting, and the visit with Natasha and with Anastasia. Mike told Allen they were going to hit the palace for the rescue tomorrow morning early at four O'clock. Mike asked Allen to arrange a plane to pick them up at noon, and Mike requested a nurse and first aid supplies in case they got into trouble.

Jen and Becky were held captive in an eight-by-eight-foot cell with two bunks to allow them to sleep. Becky was concerned with her mother's health, the food they gave them was terrible and neither one could eat enough for a decent meal. Becky helped her mother clean the blood off her face from a cut she received from the butt end of a rifle, when she kicked one of the guards in the knee cap. They talked about if anyone will rescue them and when that might be, Jen was confident that Mike would come. They spent their time with each other talking about what they could do to help in the rescue, but day five was coming up and they faded to only talk about they hoped they would come.

Jen thought about her house in New York and family life with Becky and Allen, she hoped that they could all get back together again. She knew how worried Allen was and how it must be bothering him. She also was worried about Mike, he sacrificed so much to protect them and if he comes over, he would be risking everything he holds dear to him.

69

Tamasvi was feeling good about herself as she hung up the phone, Kevin called wanting a second date. On their first date, he talked big about a computer program that was going to make him millions, she fed his ego, and he loved it. Tonight, she would learn more about it, she was curious, was this computer program such a big deal? If it was, she could make something from it, if not, then she would just kill him and move on to the next hit. She was meeting Kevin for dinner at the hotel at seven O'clock, she made a hair appointment for four-thirty to spruce it up a little. She learned throughout her career that presentation is important when you work a mark, and even small details make a difference.

Kevin was an easy mark for her, he played along with her game even though he didn't know it was her game. She laughed a little bit as she thought how easy he was to manipulate, he was like putty in her hands. She figured out how she would kill him, not tonight, not until she determined the value of this computer program. She must be careful though, she must stay away from his room, and he must stay away from hers, there cannot be any forensic ties.

It was mid-morning and Tamasvi decided to catch some sunrays on the beach, she put on another barely there bikini and headed to the beach. She sat down on the lounging chair applying sunscreen to her legs, she noticed how the sun's rays had started to do its work on her prison white flesh. A young man came over to where she was sitting and offered to spread the tanning lotion on her back for her. She gave him the bottle and he proceeded to spread the lotion, while she held her long hair away for him. He came too close to her breast, and she asked him to stop, ignoring her warning. With lightning speed, she grabbed his hand while twisting his wrist and spun him around. He dropped to his knees in pain as he yelled at her to let him go. She brought her mouth to his ear whispering a threat that she would kill him if she heard him trying that on any other women on the beach. As the young man could feel his shoulder dislocate, she let him go and he ran away rubbing his shoulder. Tamasvi laughed at him as she watched him run away as fast as he could.

Tamasvi loved how her skin felt after spending the morning in the sun. She looked at herself in the mirror, quite pleased with the touch up on her hair. It was six O'clock and she slid into a different dress that she bought in a local shop yesterday. It was a solid white dress with a stretch that accented her curves, a perfect dress for the second date. After she checked herself over in the full-length mirror, she started on her way to the dining room.

She arrived in the dining room ten minutes late on purpose, Kevin was already there trying to find something to keep himself busy while he waited. When she entered the dining room, he stood up and smiled then pulled out a chair for her to sit. Kevin was absolutely stunned with her beauty and grace as she walked across the room. He wasn't sure, but he felt he was in love with this princess, who so recently came into his life. The waiter came to take their drink orders, then dashed off as though the size of his tip depended on how long it took him to serve the drinks. They were playing some old romantic Tony Bennett and Harry Belafonte music. The small talk went over what they were doing today, then Tamasvi wanted to know about the Mindsweeper.

"Last time we talked, you mentioned something big that you were working on called Mindsweeper. How is that going?"

"I am going to Moscow tomorrow and pick it up, I'm so excited, this is the big chance I have been waiting for."

Tamasvi quizzed Kevin, "that's fantastic, sounds like you're going to fall into some money."

Kevin was very up front in telling her, "Beyond your wildest dreams!"

She asked casually, "good for you Kevin, you are so ingenious, exactly what does it do?"

"It can transfer one mind to another, copy one mind to several, like cloning, and it programs minds, pretty wild stuff." He figured he could show her the vision so she could understand the money side. " I can copy and sell this thing and sell it."

She wanted more, " and you know how to do this?

"No, but Sergei knows how, and we will work together."

Tamasvi was curious, "would you let me know when you bring it back, I would like to take a look at it."

Kevin walked her to her room and at her door, he moved in to kiss her, this time she let him. He wanted to come into her room for a night cap, but she told him perhaps next time. Kevin was fit to be tied, he wanted her so bad. He will get together with her when he gets back from getting the Mindsweeper program and show it to her. His flight leaves at eight thirty-five in the morning, but he couldn't sleep. He was thinking about Andrea, how smart she is and how beautiful she was. He got back to the task at hand, to steal the Mindsweeper, he needed a plan. He decided to create a diversion, to take everyone's attention away from the computer lab area, so he could sneak in and get the computer and program.

The next day, he arrived in Moscow as he did before, but this time, because his return flight was scheduled within hours of the arrival flight, Moscow Immigration sent him to interrogation and grilled him for three hours, they finally let him go, forcing him to work twice as fast to create a diversion, steal the Mind sweeper, and catch the plane back.

Kevin took a taxi to the palace and gained access past the guards at the front. He went inside as the taxi waited for him by the entrance. He walked along the hall to the right and straight into the kitchen and downstairs into the computer lab in the basement. As he went in, he seen Jen and Becky contained in the holding cell, without stopping for them, he went on to get the computer and program from the desk. As he went by, Jen yelled at him, "Aren't you going to let us out?" Kevin didn't even acknowledge them and ran off up the stairs, he heard some voices above in the hall, and hit the fire alarm as he went by. Two guys looked at him as he entered the hall and he said to them in Russian, the fire is in the kitchen, they need help to put it out. The men ran towards the kitchen as Kevin entered the taxi and off, they went. About the time they discovered the Mindsweeper was missing, Kevin was flying over the North Sea, thinking about his date tonight with Tamasvi. Jen was very upset when she seen Kevin leave and started to cry. Becky tried to soothe her mother, when suddenly, Jen yelled out "now I remember where I recognized that guy at the cabin packing the rifle, that was KEVIN WHITE!!"

70

Mike was relaxing in Mikhail's home and had just come out of a mid-morning snooze in his reclining chair. Not that having a little sleep was customary with Mike, but jet lag was getting the best of him, and the sleep made him feel much better. They needed to get together with Anastasia's people tonight to go over the plans and that would take place at seven O'clock. Mike just about went back to sleep again as he listened to an old-fashioned clock with a pendulum that made a gentle tick, tick, tick, as it swung back and forth.

Mikes cell phone started ringing, " hello, Mike here."

The voice on the other end talked to Mike in English, " this is special agent Pat McLear with the International division of the FBI. My sources indicate that you are in Moscow attempting to rescue Director Allen Fulton's family from the residence of Andrei Volkov, is that correct?"

Mike recalled a situation a long time ago that he watched his father get out of a situation by pleading ignorance. " Does Director Fulton's family need rescuing?"

There was a pause on the other end, eventually, "where are you right now."

Mike replied," I'm in the recliner, I just come out of a sleep, could you give me a while to wake up?"

Pat replied, " Okay I'll give you awhile."

Mike hung up and called Allen to find out what this guy was up to.

"Hey Allen, I just got a call from a Pat McLear, he asked a bunch of questions about me rescuing your family from Andrei Volkov, What's that about."

"He's the lead for their international division. My boss set me up with them to help rescue Jen and Becky. I gave him your number as a contact when they come over, but he's been hanging out in the office here. I don't know when he is going to leave."

Mike was shaking his head, " if his team doesn't leave within the next couple hours, he will be too late."

Allen answered him, " sounds like he's going to be too late for the rescue but perfect timing for taking the credit. I'll have a talk to my boss and see what he thinks, meanwhile don't go in until I give you the go ahead."

Mike was pissed, " Christ Allen, is there someone with you with a loaded gun pointed at your head."

"Mike, its chaos here, I got Deputy Directors from the FBI, CIA, ATF and the NAS breathing fire at me. We got to wait until everyone is on the same page. Now, Mike that is a directive I have given you on the record. Now, off the record, do as you see fit.

 I am going on vacation for two weeks and won't be available, I am chartering an executive jet so I can have some leg room. See you tomorrow, understood. Oh, and by the way, that Pat is an idiot.!"

Mike laughed, "see you tomorrow, Allan."

Mike was thinking it seems to be getting better as we go, with the addition of Allen going in for Jen and Becky, it will take a huge load off his shoulders.

Josie walked in the room, " what are you laughing about?"

Mike smiled, " I just got off the phone with Allen, he's up to his butt in political BS, and is going on vacation for two weeks."

"That doesn't make sense, where's he going on vacation?"

Mike looked at Josie, "he's chartering a private jet to Moscow, we will have a plane on the ground waiting for us to leave when we rescue Jen and Becky."

Mike's phone rang again, he put it on speaker so Josie could hear, " Hi, Pierre."

Pat responds, " My name is Pat, not Pierre."

Mike apologizes, " Oh, sorry, eh."

Pat wasn't sure if he was sarcastic or not, " where are you?"

Mike answered, " I told you I was in the recliner."

Pat wasn't letting up on him, " so, you're not in Moscow?"

Mike was smiling, " that's right, you need to straighten out your informants."

Pat came back, " do you know it's a criminal offence to lie to a federal agent?"

Mike had enough, " Aren't you done fluffin your feathers yet?, Don't bother calling me unless you have something worthwhile to talk about."

Mike hung up, he didn't have time for distractions, and he had no time to talk to someone who wasn't interested in solving a problem. It sounded to Mike as though he was more interested in creating more problems. Josie went to the kitchen and made a pot of tea for them, and Mike sat in the recliner satisfied they had a solid plan of attack.

Mikhail returned to the house from somewhere, " Mike, I found you a crossbow, and some arrows, will this work?"

Mike got out of the recliner and examined the crossbow and arrows Mikhail brought in, " I think they will work Mikhail, is there a place that I can practice with a few shots, the sighting may need adjustment?"

After tea, they all went out to a small farm outside Ruza and set up targets at the estimated distance Mike would be shooting to. At first, Mike was disappointed since he wasn't hitting the target at all and was concerned the arrows were faulty. Mike inspected the arrows again to find a third of them slightly bent. After removing the bent arrows and adjusting of the sights, his shooting drastically improved. Mike was now hitting the center of the targets five out of five shots, he was satisfied, he's ready for tomorrow.

71

Anastasia's men showed up right on time. Sharon and Josie served them coffee and they got down to discuss the plan. Since Mikhail was very familiar with the palace and surroundings, he had drawn a diagram. He identified where security cameras were placed around the yard and where the outside security guards usually are stationed. He then drew the rooms themselves inside the palace, showing the group where Anastasia thought Jen and Becky may be held.

Matvey, the surveillance specialist took the floor and informed everyone where the hidden motion sensors are located and the estimated area they cover. He showed them the cell signal blocker he had and went to discuss the process for shutting down their security systems. He proceeded to inform them, each of the three systems were independent from each other and will require individual attention. Matvey explained each one in detail, then discussed the process of the phone landline in the palace.

Mike thanked Anastasia's men for their presentation. Mike continued and went over the second phase of the mission after all cameras, sensors and communications shut down.

> Mike started as he pointed to areas on Mikhail's diagram, " I have ear wick's that we will use to communicate. Once Matvey tells me he has completed shutting everything down, he will tell me. Then I will start shooting the outside guards with the crossbow, there should not be any more than six stationed around the palace itself. The crossbow is silent and will not attract attention, so we should be able to maintain the element of surprise. I'm not sure what will be needed to breach the palace itself, but we have C-4 explosive and an expert to blow the doors of the front

entrance if needed. Mikhail will organize the towns people to take over the front and rear gate entrances. They will keep everyone from entering and leaving, we want a clean job here, when we leave, no one will be left to fight. Once breached, Sharon, Josie, Mikhail, Allen, Anastasia's men and I will all go inside. Our primary objective is to Rescue the girls. Once the girls are in the van, we go after key individuals. Allen will be with his family, Sharon and Mikhail will take two of Anastasia's men and clear all the rooms down this wing to Andrei's room. Josie and me will take two of Anastasia's men and go down clearing each room along this wing to find Dominik. Once all key people have been looked after, then Sharon will take two of Anastasia's men to find the computer and the Mind sweeper program. After it's all over, Anastasia's men will guard the house and hand it over to her. The townspeople return to Ruza, and we will leave to catch a plane. Is that clear to everyone?" Everyone agreed they understood. "Great, see you all at four O'clock.

Mike made a clear plan that everyone understood, he distributed the ear wick's to Anastasia's men, and everyone left to their respective homes.

Mikhail was quiet, " Mike, I am forever in your debt, I have been waiting for the moment that I could do damage to Andrei, and here it is, thank you."

Mike left the kitchen to go to the living room, " Come with me please."

Making sure they were out of hearing distance from the others, " What's between you and Andrei, I want you to lay it all out on the table when we are in the palace. I don't want you to come back out of the palace, until you are spent, done, and finished with him. Whatever you need to do, I don't care what that is, but get it done while we are in there. After you do, you will then be able to rid your life from continuously grieving your sister's death. You must let go Mikhail, this is your big chance, I want you to have a good life my friend."

Mikhail had tears in his eyes, " thank you Mike."

Mike asked Mikhail for some common tools, and he came from a closet with everything he asked for. Mikhail watched Mike as he removed the heel from his boot, removed the small rifle cartridges in them and replaced both heels back on the boots. Mike loaded all the penlight guns that he made in preparation for tomorrow morning.

He showed Mikhail how they worked and how they shot, explaining they are very lethal, despite their size. He placed them in secret holsters he made, that lie at belt level.

" Pat me down and see if you feel them?

Mikhail did a very thorough job of trying to detect the guns but was unable to feel anything. Mike took out something that looked like a penlight, he showed Mikhail, " what does this look like?"

Mikhail looked at it, "it's a pen light."

Mike un-screwed the two halves apart and took one of the 22 caliber cartridges that he removed from his boot heel and placed it in one end of the penlight. He then screwed the two halves of the penlight together and pulled the two opposing halves apart until it clicked.

Mikhail looked at it, " What is it-Oh, I see now!"

Mike looked at Mikail, " it is a miniature gun, in case you are in trouble, you can ward off or kill your attacker." He gave it to Michail as Mike shows his knife off, " this is my special knife, ironically, I built it from one I saw built by a Russian rifle enthusiast, you just swing this little lever to disengage the safety, and push this silver button in."

72

Kevin was excited when he got off the plane at JAGS McCartney International airport in Turks and Caicos Island. He carried Sergei's computer by hand, he did not want it leaving his sight. He selected a luggage cart from the wall by the carousel, he made sure the computer was in the top rack where it was always in sight. Kevin scurried out to the rental car and headed off to the hotel, he could hardly wait to show Tamasvi. He called ahead and made a date with her for a drink in the lounge at the hotel. He put his baggage away in the closet and hid the computer between the top and bottom mattress of his bed. He took a quick shower and put on fresh unwrinkled clothes before meeting with Tamasvi.

They were playing Calypso music in the lounge and as he strode up to her table, he reached over and gave her a quick kiss on the lips, she smiled at him and welcomed him back to the Caribbean. Kevin was like a little kid, barely able to slow himself down to tell her all about the program. Tamasvi was intrigued as Kevin talked about the mind transferring and cloning process that Kevin was explaining to her. She was interested in how he could make money off this program, and he went on and on about all the opportunities the program opens.

"Well make sure you put that computer in a safe place."

" Tamasvi, I have it well hid, it's between the top and bottom mattress of my bed."

" Kevin you are so smart, no one would ever find it there."

Kevin laughed, "you're looking casual this afternoon, what have you been up to?"

Tamasvi made direct eye contact with him, " well, if you must know, I have been organizing a special night with you."

Kevin just about broke his jaw when it hit the table, "that sounds very exciting, where are we going for dinner, or do you need me to make reservations?"

"No," she smiled, "I have everything looked after, I have to go now, but meet me back here at six and dress casual, we are going to have a picnic on the beach, I hope you like picnic's." and Kevin agreed.

Tamasvi gained a complete understanding of what the program could do, and how she could make money off it. She had no idea how it operated, but even by itself, it had to be worth something to someone. Since Kevin told her where he hid it in his room, she didn't need him anymore, so she can fulfill her obligations to the mystery man and get on with her freedom. She very carefully removed two small dermal patches, laying them upside down on the table in her room. She put on a pair of surgical gloves, and removed a tiny vial from her bag, placing it on the table. After drawing up a small amount of the liquid in the vial with a hypodermic needle, she proceeded to place two drops of the liquid on each patch then put everything away, letting the patches dry. She had used this poison before finding it very effective in causing a heart attack, and it quickly dissipates leaving no trace to be found in the autopsy.

Kevin showed up on time and Tamasvi went into the dining room to pick up her picnic basket she had previously arranged. Kevin saw the basket and smiled thinking he hadn't been on a picnic for years.

Kevin was impressed, " you really did come up with a special evening, thank you for being so thoughtful."

She turned to him with a wide smile, " the picnic is only part of the evening."

Kevin was like a puppy dog on a leash as they carried the basket and her bag down the beach toward the fishing dock. When they arrived by small open boat, and Tamasvi started placing the bag and the basket in the boat, Kevin was curious.

Kevin smiled at her," where on earth are you taking me?"

Tamasvi laughed, " hasn't a girl ever taken you on a boat ride before Kevin?" She thought his reaction was hilarious. " Yesterday, I asked the locals where I could find a nice private beach, and they told me where one was." She got in the boat and started the outboard engine. " I made a deal with a fisherman to borrow his boat, and here we are." She could see the bewilderment in Kevin's face as she handled the boat like a pro. " I lived by the ocean when I grew up and my father was a fisherman, he took me out every day and taught me everything I need to know."

Kevin sat down as Tamasvi navigated the small boat out into the channel and off to the beach. As she sat sideways on the bench seat in the boat, Kevin looked at her with her long hair blowing in the wind, he was thinking she was a goddess.

As they came in towards a beach, Kevin was taken back by both her beauty and her knowledge of operating the boat. Once landed on the sandy beach, they removed the picnic basket, blanket and small travel bag. They emptied the basket contents on the blanket as they sat beside each other with their backs against a log that had drifted in years ago. Tamasvi placed her bag directly behind Kevin and made a plate of food up for them. They sat on the blanket eating and drinking her favorite red wine and taking in the beauty of the secluded beach.

When they were done with their food, Tamasvi leaned over Kevin and kissed him passionately. Kevin responded as she carefully reached into her bag and placed the two dermal patches on his back without him knowing. Dusk was setting in for the evening and

Tamasvi wanted to get Kevin in the water so she wouldn't have to drag him.

Tamasvi looked at him, " Kevin, Lets go for a swim, then we can make love on the beach."

Kevin was flustered, " I didn't bring my bathing suit."

Tamasvi smiled at him, " Either did I." as she proceeded to dis-robe and walk down the beach into the water.

Kevin was thinking to himself that there was a whole other side to this woman that he is about to explore as he walked into the water with her. Tamasvi had it timed perfectly, by the time he was waist high in the water, he turned to embrace her, his chest started feeling heavy and was unable to breathe. She made out she was concerned and told him to get into the boat to lay down on the middle bench seat. By the time she got everything they brought in the boat, he was dead.

Tamasvi placed a cinder block brick in his lap and strapped the brick to his torso. She scrubbed any possible D&A remanences off his body and carefully removed the dermal patches on his back. There was nothing left to tie her to Kevin's dead body. She moved the boat to the middle of the channel and dumped him overboard, watching him sink into the abyss.

After docking the boat and walking back to the hotel, she took Kevin's room key from his pants and let herself into his room as she wore latex gloves. She checked between the mattresses, finding the computer and taking it to her room. She left Kevin's clothes and wallet in his room on the night table. She was done, now she needed to find Sergei.

Tamasvi sends a text to the Mystery man she talked to about the hit on Kevin informing him he was dead. Text read – the mark is looked after. She received a text back, Good to hear, I need you to go to Moscow. She thought to herself "that was convenient."

After inspection of the computer, Tamasvi found a tag glued on the bottom of the computer with Sergei's name on it and phone number to call if found. She called the number and she explained that she had the computer, and she could bring it to him if he cut her in on any business generated from it.

Sergei was agitated," why would I want to do that, it belongs to Andrei Volkov?"

Tamasvi laughed, " because I am a professional assassin, I'm not someone to mess with. Where are you?"

Sergei's eyebrows raised, "point taken. I am in Moscow right now."

"Perfect, I will see you there in a day, text me an address to meet at before I go to Andrei's place, I will be staying there for a couple nights."

Tamasvi made her flight arrangements and checked out of the hotel, as she left for Moscow. She would miss the sun, sand and warm beaches.

73

District Deputy Director William Townsend, with the New York district CIA just returned into his office. He was glad Kevin was looked after, his mouth was getting to be a problem. Their investigations into Andrei was getting close to tying him to Kevin. The CIA could not have scandal in their ranks, or at least nothing traceable. He could handle the FBI International division, But Sven and this Allen are presenting a problem. This Mike Stone is screwing up his plans, Andrei has communicated his displeasure and was asking him what he is doing about it.

He decided to pay Sven and Allen a visit at their office today, if they were not going to do anything about it then he would fix it permanently. He left his office, picking up a taxi to the FBI main office, he paid the driver and headed up the street towards the office. Since it was almost lunch and he forgot breakfast this morning, he picked up a hot dog at a street vendor. It was eleven-thirty and entered the building to get to Sven's office before he left for lunch.

"Sven, what is the progress with your directors family, I heard this farmer is over there attempting a rescue, is that correct?"

Sven was less willing to cooperate with the CIA than he once was, " why would he be over there, he doesn't know anyone?"

William was agitated, " Look, if I find out you have anyone attempting a rescue over there, I'll…….."

" You will do nothing! Quite frankly I'm about sick and tired of you coming into my office and trying to tell me what I should and shouldn't do. Now, I don't have time for this, you found your way into my office, you can find your way out."

William left Sven's office and headed straight for Allen's office. When he arrived, he found out that Allen was not there and asked his secretary where he was. The secretary told him that he was on vacation for two weeks and that Sven would be taking all his calls. William was upset with her answer and asked where he went, and she replied that she did not know. William rushed out of the office and left the office building to return to his office. Since it was noon by now, William got another hot dog, this time smearing mustard on his white shirt, which made him more upset.

He arrived at his office a little after one O'clock and changed his shirt. He picked up a burner phone out of his desk and texted I need you to look after Mike Stone in Moscow, see picture, regular fee.

He didn't know what Allen was doing taking vacation when his family is held captive, if William was a betting man, he would say that he took the time off to go to Moscow to rescue his family.

He called his agents in Russia to make sure that they follow Allen once he arrives at the Moscow airport and to keep him updated on his movements. He then called Pat McLear to tell him the same thing. Then he called Andrei to inform him about Tamasvi coming for Mike Stone.

74

Tamasvi left the airport carrying the computer and program in her right hand and placed it in the rental car from the airport Kiosk. She had the address for the palace but planned to first meet Sergei at a pre-determined coffee shop close by. She arrived fifteen minutes early, spending the time to mentally prepare for her meeting with him. She didn't much like Sergei, at least to talk to over the phone, he sounded weak and frail, he was easy to intimidate. She wanted a fifty / fifty split of the profits from the sale of copies they will make and sell. This should be a profitable business arrangement, she thought it through many times. She had an offshore account in the Canary Islands where he can transfer money straight into. She won't have to do a thing, she smiled and thought it was almost too easy, but it really was that easy.

Sergei came over to her table, " Are you Tamasvi Levy?"

Tamasvi looked at him showing him no excitement, " So, you must be Sergi, how are you today?"

Sergei wasn't much for small talk, " do you have the computer and program?"

Tamasvi looked at him, her training told her he was scared of her, " Yes, I do have the computer with the program." She looked at him, " we are going to go into business together."

Sergei lived in a world of mistrust, he was skeptical, it seemed more of a question than a statement, " You and me going into business together? "I don't think so."

Tamasvi looked him straight in the eye, " you will copy the program and we will sell it on the internet for three million apiece."

Sergei was getting concerned, " Andrei won't like that."

Tamasvi was thinking how stupid can a man get, " look you idiot! Don't tell him, got it?"

Sergei thought for a moment, " and if I don't proceed with your plan?"

Tamasvi looked at him with a smile, " I'll sneak into your bedroom tonight and slit your throat, and there will be nothing you can do about it."

Sergei was mad, " hey, was that a threat?" "No, she told him, it was a promise."

Sergei considered his options, and they added up to slim and none, " Okay, I'm in."

She gave the computer and flash drives to him, and he locked them in a storage box in the computer lab. He thought Andrei wouldn't find out anyways as long as he developed the program to do what Andrei wanted it to do, he will be OK. Besides, Andrei promised to double his wage when he was able to transfer his fathers mind, and he refused to pay up. This would give him all the money he wanted, in order to leave Andrei, he was tired of him.

75

Mike, Sharon, Josie and Mikhail were the first ones there, he had to look after the dogs. He mixed in a natural sleeping drug he found at the drug store with some hamburger meat and fed the dogs. At three-forty-five am everyone met at the park bordering the palace West boundary. Mike let out a sigh of relief after he went through the group to find the head count was as planned. Mike found a pistol for Allen and contacted Anastasia's security expert to shut everything down. Once Mike received confirmation, he started identifying targets outside the palace. Mike was being careful to take them out in order, avoiding the other guards from seeing them fall once killed.

The palace had a flat roof on the main section of the building, Mike noticed two security guards stationed at both ends. He decided, since they have the best view, to take them out first. Mike could tell they were bored from looking at nothing all night and were not really paying attention. The guard on the right was just staring down on the roof top half asleep. Patiently, Mike watched the guard on the left as he walked back and forth along the roof. When they were Far enough away from each other, he took out the one on the left. He then reloaded his crossbow and took out the guard on the right, this gave the group a better opportunity to move in without being spotted.

With the security system down and the security guards taken out on the roof, Mike and Allen breached the perimeter gate and hid behind a group of brushes. As he sat and waited, another guard came along the right side of the palace and started looking up at the roof. It appeared to Mike that he was looking as if something was wrong, he could hear him talking. Mike had no choice but to take him out right away as he raised his crossbow making a perfect shot. Patiently, Mike waited and a second came around from the left side of the palace dressed in camouflage. Mike leveled out his crossbow and made a clear shot as he seen him fall, they waited for additional activity. After waiting a while, Mike, and Allen both ran up to the two fallen guards dragging them out of site behind some trees.

Based on previous surveillance of the palace, Mike was convinced there should be two more. Using his ear wick to communicate, Mike informed the group he had killed four of the guards and asked the group if they can see the others. The towns people covering the back entrance came back informing Mike of one at the rear of the building. Mike had to be careful since the back of the palace was open, with few places to hide. As both him and Allen worked their way carefully to the back of the house, one of Anastasia's men informed the group of someone sneaking around behind them.

Mike estimated that the guard in the back should be in view very soon and told Allen to cover his back. Allen rolled into a dried-up creek bed while Mike crawled quickly to the outside dining table on the sundeck. Mike saw the guard and squeezed off a perfect shot, but he fell against the deck furniture making a noise. He loaded his cross bow and turned to see the sixth guard sneaking up behind Allen. Mike didn't have time to warn Allen on the ear wick and raised the cross bow up and fired his arrow into the guards chest. While initially confused, Allen turned around seeing the guard fall behind him. Mike then whispered in his ear wick that all six outside guards were dead.

He called Anastasia's security men, Josie and Sharon to meet at the front door. Anastasia's security technician analyzed the lock and tried several ways to open the lock but was unsuccessful. He noticed an electrical box to the right of the door, smashing it open to expose several wires that he seemed to understand. After cutting two key wires, he tried another code as the group heard a click, the door unlocked, and they were in the palace.

The plan was well understood by all and like clockwork, the group knew their job and positions. Using flashlights, the rescue team scurried through the hallway to the kitchen and found the door to the basement. Four men stayed back to guard from anyone entering the kitchen and going down the stairs after them.

Allen and Mike quietly walked down the stairs, entering a large room, searching as their eyes strained to find where the girls were. They walked through what appeared to be some kind of laboratory, then they heard Becky crying. They followed the noise until they found the girls caged in a steel cell. The group looked around trying to figure out how to open the cage door without keys. Finally, Allen spots a bar and with everyone pushing , breaks the lock and opens the door.

Sharon identified they were in a computer lab and took a quick look around. The girls were very emotional when they saw Mike and Allen, they spent time quieting them down then they got the girls up the stairs and out the front door. Mike told Allen to get them in a car and to the plane immediately, while he looked after the second half of this mission. Allen's thoughts were racing a hundred miles an hour trying to come up with a better plan. He wanted to help his friend, but with the time available Allen couldn't come up with anything better, leaving with Jen and Becky

The group went back In and split up into two groups. Mike and Josie on one with Mikhail and Sharon on the other. Both groups had Anastasia's men with them as they searched room to room. They started on the ground floor, clearing everything there, then they went upstairs with a full understanding there would be people there.

Mikhail explained to the two groups, there were two main wings of rooms upstairs in the palace. As they proceeded, each team took a wing to clear by entering each room confirming it cleared before continuing. Mike and Josie's group entered three rooms that were empty, then in the fourth, they found Tamasvi. No one knew who she was and was treated like an enemy, with Anastasias men binding her hands tight to a heating register with tie straps.

Mikhail's group opened the door to the last room on this wing. As they entered, Andrei woke from a sleep and yelled at the top of his lungs for the security guards. They were in their security room and fell asleep watching television, waking to Andrei's yelling. They grabbed their guns running out the door, where they were both shot down as Anastasia's men were there. Andrei was told to lay on the ground with hands spread wide until Mike finished. Andrei was snarling like a wild animal in captivity, yelling death threats to them all. Anastasia's men restrained Andrei's hands and feet.

<h1 style="text-align:center">76</h1>

Mike's team opened the last door and upon entering found a young man putting his clothes on. Dominik was awake from Andrei's yelling and the shooting, and sat on the bed, yelling at them. Mike was trying to figure out who this was and remembered that Anastasia told them that he transferred his mind to a young man's body.

Mike walked up to him, "good morning, Dominik, how's your day going so far?"

He looked at Mike closely, " So, you are that farmer they call Mike Stone, you came to Moscow to rescue the girl and her mother."

"Well, Dominik, you are a smart man, do you really think you would get away with kidnapping my best friends and killing my dog and cougar? I've got a good mind to put a bullet in your head right now."

Mike looked at one of Anastasia's men," tie him up." He then looked at Josie, "Josie, watch this guy and shoot him if he even looks at you the wrong way."

Dominik looks at Josie and asks her, " is your name Josie Santos?"

Josie was confused, " yes, why."

Dominik looks at Josie, " because, I am your father."

He had everyone's attention now, especially Josie's, " I met Ana, your mother about 34 years ago when she was a prostitute. She was so beautiful, so warm and caring, we met several times and after a year we fell in love. I loved your mother more than any woman I had ever met. We never married, Andrei would not accept Ana as part of the family despite my many attempts to convince him. About two years after we met, we had you. When you were born, your mother and I were so happy to have a daughter, and we spoiled you.

But Andrei showed his hate for you both. Although I can't prove it, I believe he killed your mother, and I was concerned with your safety. I had a GPS chip in your ankle and gave you to a foster group in Panama so I could always find you. I wanted to be with you and be your mother someday, but I got sent to Guantanamo, got sick and that was the end of that. I since found out that Andrei found the GPS tracking code and had you followed recently, but I could not do anything while I was sick.

While Josie stared at Dominik, Anatasia's men tied him up so he could not move, but just stared at Josie. There were so many thoughts both warm and cold with this news, everyone in the room fell silent. They didn't know what this meant, they were concerned that she may be the enemy, or that she let them down a path, everyone except for Mike.

Mike said loudly, "Okay everyone, let's get our heads back to the mission."

They all walked out of Dominik's room, leaving a man to guard him at gun point.

Mike had no idea who Tamasvi was, he asked one of Anastasia's men to guard her, telling him to shoot her if she tries anything.

They walked down the wing to Andrei's room, " Well, well, if it isn't the head of the snake himself, you look a little tied up at the moment Andrei. I sure do thank you for your time."

Andrei was hissing and snarling at them, " I'm going to kill you all."

Mike looked at him, " not in this lifetime." Mike pulled out his Colt revolver and shot him in the knee, " that's for kidnapping my friends.

Andrei was screaming in pain, "you can't do this to me."

Mike raised his pistol again, shooting Andrei in the other knee, " that's for killing my dog and cougar."

Andrei was writhing in pain, Sharon grabbed the pistol from Mike and shot him in the left shoulder, " and that's for killing my mother."

Andrei was still alive and crazy with the pain he was dealing with, " I'll see you all in hell."

Josie came forward, " did you kill my mother?"

Andrei looked at her, " So, you're Josie Santos, yes, I killed that whore." Josie leveled out her gun and before she shot, Mike whispered something in her ear. She nodded her head and shot Andrei in the other shoulder.

Mike handed Mikhail his pistol, he looked at Andrei and yelled at him, " you killed my sister!"

Andrei looked at him with what life he had left, " She was nothing but a whore too."

For over thirty year's Mikhail dreamed of this day, this moment and was standing in front of the man he has hated and wanted to kill all that time. He recalled that day at the hospital when his beautiful sister was taken away from him. She was so special, and he loved her so much, they often talked about what they would do together as they got older and with their families. That was all taken away from them, because of this man, this monster who could not comprehend what it was like to love.

Mikhail raised his pistol and shot Andrei, finishing off a legacy of evil and torment. As excited as Mikhail was to end Andrei's life, all the emotions of that day in the hospital when Andrei's men murdered Kyela, flowed inside him. He fell to the floor crying and calling her name over and over "Kyela, Kyela." Mike helped him up and comforted him while he regained himself. Mike helped Mikhail down the stairs and had Sharon help him to his vehicle, then returned to the palace. She noticed the townspeople at the front entrance had captured a frail young man trying to enter the palace. She talked to Mike using the ear wick, Mike suggested the townspeople hold him in captivity until he gets out there. He wanted her to find out as much as she could about why he was trying to enter the palace.

77

While Anastasia's men grabbed Dominik and escorted him to the car to be transported to the executive jet. Mike and Josie went to find out more about who Tamasvi was and why she was there. When they opened the door to the room, they were surprised to see that she freed herself by cutting the tie straps with something. The guard that was watching her, lay dead at the side of the room. Mike and Josie were very alert as they searched the room, and contents of closets for the missing woman.

They did not think to check the large air vent located beside the bookcase. She watched as Josie and Mike separated just enough for her to get out from behind the vent screen. She only had the guards knife with her, then Josie came back in the room and went to check the on-suite washroom.

Tamasvi saw Mike and she walked to him quickly, she was on a mission with only one thing in mind. Mike turned to her, and she thrust her knife in his shoulder. She came after him again, jabbing, swiping, her knife at him as he tried to avoid her attack. The pain of his wound was too intense for Mike to protect himself from her viciousness as she came after him. Josie saw Tamasvi's focused attack on Mike and came after her, catching her wrist as she swung and twisting until Tamasvi dropped the knife out of her hand. From Tamasvi's left side Josie kicked her in the face and blocked a series of right and left jabs. Josie saw the opportunity and quickly moved forward as she raised her arm, driving her right elbow into Tamasvi's nose, as blood started down her face. Tamasvi grabbed a fire poker that was lying at the nearby fireplace and hit Josie hard, knocking her on the floor. She got up and Tamasvi hit her again, knocking her on a table, breaking it as she hit the floor. Josie got up and landed a perfectly placed punch to the throat, followed by a hard kick to her stomach, knocking the wind out of Tamasvi, without the ability to catch her breath. Josie followed up with two fast hurricane kicks to the stomach and Tamasvi lay on the ground gasping for breath.

Josie recalled the day in her training when she met the Grand Master Yu. He was a very wise man who was very knowledgeable in advanced techniques and visited the training schools about twice a year. During his visits, he would give special advanced training for those students who excelled. Her teacher took a special interest in Josie because she picked up on moves and techniques quickly and thrived to learn more. She remembered his visit on one occasion, when she was the student picked for special training. The Grand Master was teaching the art of the Fly, it's purpose was to increase the students' reaction time, he called it Kuaisu yundong. It was very hard to achieve, and the Grand Master was only there for a week, so practice was required after he left. It takes intense focus and requires a deep meditative state. She achieved that state several times during practice after, but never for very long, she had never used it in a fight.

Tamasvi now back up on her feet, came after Josie again, this time knocking her down a short set of stairs. When Josie got up, she felt an intense pain in her side, wincing as she touched it. Tamasvi seen she was hurting in her left side and started to focus her attack there. The more Tamasvi hit her there, the weaker Josie became. Tamasvi made a very hard and perfectly placed kick to Josie's side and Josie was almost done, her side hurt so bad tears were flowing from her eyes and she was finding it difficult to see as she continued to block back the fleury of punches and kicks Tamasvi was sending her way. She saw she was winning and said to Josie, "I'm going to take great pleasure in finishing you off for good!"

As she fought in this battle like she had never done so before, she thought of the Grandmaster's special training. She said to herself "Grand Master take me to Kuaisu yundong." she heard herself answer," you know the way." She said to herself once more.

"Grand Master but it is so difficult to get there, help me." She heard herself answer again, "you have been there before, you can find it again." Despite the pain and the constant waves of punches and kicks, she calmed herself down and focused.

Eventually, she felt calmer, there was no fear, she became an angel dancing like a ballerina as she fought, her opponent was moving as though she was in slow motion. Josie was no longer challenged by Tamasvi, she couldn't touch her, and Josie found it very easy to avoid getting hit by her. She blocked her kicks and weaved and ducked avoiding her punches. In the heat of her most formidable battle, she was enjoying the experience of Kuaisu yundong, but she knew that Mike was injured and needed to end this fight quickly and for good.

Mike watched as there was nothing he could do, the knife cut a muscle that was giving him a lot of pain. He watched as Josie was getting beaten badly and when he seen her get hit in the left side, he knew she was hurt bad. Then when Tamasvi picked on her left side, each time Josie would flinch and wince with pain. He was worried she was going to lose this and afraid of the consequences. Then he saw something happen to Josie as she gained speed and agility, moving around taking control, she was playing with Tamasvi.

The table quickly turned as Mike watched Josie attack Tamasvi's face with a barrage of quick punches and well-placed kicks. The blood was flowing from Tamasvi's nose now and Josie was not letting up. She hit her with four direct hits to the throat causing her to collapse on the floor. Josie wasn't letting her get up, she positioned herself behind Tamasvi with a chokehold. Tamasvi was thrashing around to try to get a hold of something she could grab but Josie had a good grasp on her throat and didn't let go until she finally lay still.

> Josie still furious from the fight, and with adrenalin still surging through her body, let go of her and yelled at the dead Tamasvi, "Not this time, Bitch!"

Josie collapsed on the floor exhausted catching her breath, every bit of energy she had was spent. She slowly rolled over to her side, looking at Mike sitting on the floor in a blood-stained shirt watching her in amazement. It was over now, and she slowly got up to help him outside.

78

Sharon was with the townspeople as Josie was helping Mike out at the front entrance and along the sidewalk. She came over to Mike, and she could see Josie was beaten up bad, and saw Mike was bleeding from his shoulder.

Sharon was concerned, " what happened to you two?"

Despite being in pain, Mike still wanted to clean this up before he left, "who is this guy?"

Sharon turned towards Mike, " I can't get much out of him, he won't talk. He was the Russian computer tech. at the Catskills mess, he was trying to have me killed."

Mike looked at Sharon, "Have these people tie him up and throw him in a car, we are taking him to New York, he'll talk there."

"My name is Sergei, I don't want to go to the United States with you guys."

Mike looked at him, "Start talking Sergei, or you will travel back to New York tied to the tail of the plane."

Mike scared Sergei, " Okay, Okay, I am Andrei's computer technician, I developed the Mindsweeper program."

Mike thought for a few minutes, "Okay, tie him up and let's take him with us anyway." Sharon, can you find this Mindsweeper program thing and bring that as well."

Sharon scurried off to the computer lab and searched for the computer or the program itself. She searched everywhere and finally found a locked cabinet. She took a bar that was close by, sticking it through the locking bail and twisted the lock until it broke the latch. She quickly found the computer, grabbed it and rushed out to Mike.

Mike looked at what Sharon held in her hands, "Is that the computer and program that's been causing all this chaos?"

Sharon shrugged her shoulders, "I think so Mike, it's the only one down there."

"Okay, I'm calling Allen to get that jet fired up and ready for us to leave this place. Mikhaila, thank you and make sure you thank the townspeople for us, we couldn't have done it without them."

Mikhaila turned to the group and said something in Russian and they all cheered. He came over and shook Mike's hand, "Thank you, Mike, thank you for what you have done for each and every one of us."

Mike looked at Mikhaila, "are you ready to take us to the airport?"

Mikhaila hopped in his car and drove with a smile on his face as they talked about what had happened over the past three days. Mike and Josie explained to everyone in the car what happened after Tamasvi stabbed Mike in the shoulder. There were several questions asked but what was she doing there, and who was she, were unanswered.

They arrived at the executive jet, loading people and baggage from Mikhail's car to the plane's baggage compartment, and as they were ready to board,

Mike went over to Mikhail to shake his hand, as he looked at him gave him a big country smile, "Anytime you are on Vancouver Island, give me a call, and I'll make you some camp coffee, that will give you a whole new appreciation for your own."

Sharon ran over to her uncle giving him a hug, "Let's keep in touch."

Mikhail gave her a hug back as everyone boarded the plane, finally, she followed in turn, waving as she looked back. Mikhail walked back to his car as he thought about Keyla and her beautiful daughter.

As Mike got on the plane, he removed his coat, revealing a blood-soaked shirt. Allen thought ahead and when Mike requested first aid supplies, he brought a nurse as well. With Josie assisting the nurse, they patched up Mik"'s shoulder. The wound was deeper than they first thought, requiring stitches and dressing. Jen watched how Josie cared for Mike, how she was careful not to make the pain with the stitches worse as she helped the nurse. Once Mike was patched up the nurse turned her attention towards Josie as she checked out her cuts and bruises from the fight. Josie sat beside Mike the whole way back helping him open the wrapper on his sandwiches and removing the top off his drink bottles. They fell asleep with their heads together, Jen remembered what that felt like.

Allen was sitting beside Jen and couldn't help but notice Jen staring at Mike and Josie, he knew how much Mike meant to Jen. Allen didn't believe anything took place between them, especially watching Mike with Josie now. As Allen got up to watch over the prisoners for a bit, Josie got up to use the washroom. On her way back to her seat, she sat down beside Jen.

> Jen looked at Josie, " thank you for all you did in in our rescue, I will never be able to repay you, you risked a lot."
>
> "I was glad it all worked out, how are you?" Josie asked.
>
> " Been better but right now I feel grateful for all of you."
>
> Josie explained, " Mike orchestrated the whole rescue, I can't believe he came all the way here and found an army to fight with him. He is a very special man, but you already know that and so does the director, that's why he sent you to him." Josie stopped for a minute, then, " Jen I know

Mike means a lot to you, I just wanted to let you know we are falling in love, I don't want you to be mad at me."

Jen stopped and was still, " no, I'm not mad at you, I'm mad at myself for not being the woman Mike wanted. I had to be the woman who needed the bright lights of New York. I was never cut out to be a farmers wife, where riding horses in the meadow and drinking coffee on the front porch was something special. I have to be honest, it's not going to be easy, but I'm happy for you. Look after him." She gave Josie a hug, then Josie got up to return to sit beside Mike. She realized that Jen was hurting inside badly.

79

Anastasia was informed by her men the palace was cleared, with no remaining threats. She was curious, she wanted to see her new house, it had been a long time. Her men drove her and Pavel to the front gate, as they opened, she had memories of the palace, it was beautiful. They walked into the grand entrance area where she had met with so many visitors. Some were politicians, some were businesspeople, and of course family. But her memories locked on the day she left for good and hadn't been back since.

Anastasia and Pavel walked around the bottom floor, stopping at the kitchen. It was a huge kitchen with the dining area off to the left side. She remembered purchasing the table, Dominik wanted one big enough for six sittings down on each side, it was huge.

They went upstairs and saw the mess made from the fighting. Tamasvi's lifeless body lay on the side of the hallway. She could see the bullet holes made in the plaster and the blood on the walls and floor. Then they went into Andrei's room. Andrei sat there, riddled with bullet holes in his legs, chest, and head. Anastasia thought she should be crying for her son's death, instead she was rejoicing. As he sat there hunched over, she thought of how pitiful he looked now and remembered him as a tyrant. A man who helped his father throw his mother out into the street in winter, denying her table scraps to live on.

Anastasia talked to her people to remove the bodies and have them taken somewhere, she didn't care where. She organized some people to clean up the mess and some trades people to make necessary repairs from the takeover. She also thought some new colors would be in order, she liked her new home, she always did. Mike Stone was a man of his word, she decided she would do something special for him.

Anastasia and Pavel walked out on the back sundeck area sitting at the table she remembered so well. She remembered them as a family, eating meals out here, it seemed like a lifetime away. The rhododendrons were in full bloom set in a backdrop of vivid green grass that snaked through the many flower gardens. She and Pavel were very happy here, he could see himself with a coffee in the morning out here reading his favorite book.

Her phone sounded, it was a text from Mike Stone, " Dominik was in FBI custody in New York awaiting approval to be sent to Guantanamo." Anastasia smiled and replied to his text, " Thank you."

80

The plane arrived at the New York hanger, despite the passengers sleeping on the trip, they were all exhausted. Mike had his dressings freshly changed prior to landing with the nurse giving him orders to see his doctor once he got home. Allen arranged for hotel rooms close to the FBI office for everyone and told them to come to his office at 10:00 am sharp. There were four FBI agents waiting to take Sergei and Dominik to their holding cells. Allen told Jen and Becky they would be staying at the hotel for a while since their home was in ruin.

> Jen looked at the group with a smile, " That's fantastic, now I get to do all that remodeling I was bugging you about."

Mike laughed, it was good to see Jen with her sense of humor back, he felt she was starting to get back to normal.

> Mike and Josie got in a cab, heading to the hotel, " we have to get you some new clothes Mike, you don't have anything clean for the office tomorrow. I'll take you shopping."

> "Okay, but I'm not giving up my boots and hat."

> Josie looked at him, " I'm fine with the boots but Mike, have you seen the condition of your hat?"

> Mike took his favorite Western Hat off to inspect it, " Yeah, there's a bit of everything on it, but it should wash off with a little water."

Josie looked at him with a gentle smile as she shook her head. Mike inspected his hat again and agreed to lose the hat for the office. Mike felt a bit uncomfortable as Josie had him try on this and that, but when they were done, they both liked the new clothes.

After checking in to their hotel, they went for a walk to Central Park. It was a new experience for Josie to have a man to be with, a special man that she felt deeply for. They ate dinner at a little Italian restaurant that she would come to by herself, it was different with Mike. Josie helped Mike with the all-Italian menu and she ordered them a bottle of her favorite red wine. As they waited for their meal, Mike held her hand as they talked.

Mike asked Josie, " so, what's on your agenda now that you have returned to North America?"

Josie smiled, " Well, I thought I might take a trip to Canada, they say it's beautiful this time of year."

Mike smiled, " well, I can't speak for the whole country, but I know of this little place on Vancouver Island that is particularly beautiful that I think you should see."

Josie was feeling a little playful, " well Mike it sounds intriguing, how long would you recommend a person plan to stay in order to see all of its splendor."

Mike looked at her, smiling, " it may take some time, let's see where it goes."

81

It took everyone a bit of time to find Allen's office within the FBI office building, but everyone showed up on time. As soon as Mike and Josie walked in, they all had to comment on his new clothes and without a hat.

Josie laughed, " it was a small compromise, I agreed he could keep his boots on."

Allen addressed the group explaining the purpose of the meeting and the importance of the statements they will be giving.

" These statements will be considered legal and truthful, they must be written factful without opinions or emotions." He then introduced eight people sitting at the back as statement coaches. "They are coaching you to complete your statements properly, but in no way are they to tell you what to say." Everyone pick a coach into a spare office and lets complete these thoroughly, thank you everyone."

The groups went with their coaches into an office by themselves and completed the statements about the ordeal that they had to deal with. Some had less to write in their statement and others such as Mike had a great deal, and the coaches were very active with him.

Once they were completed to the coac"s satisfaction, they left. Josie stayed behind while Mike and Allen could spend private time together.

Allen looked at Mike, " I can't express my gratitude Mike, I have no idea where this would have ended up if you were not there to help me." Allen shook Mike's hand. " If there is ever a time when I could help, please let me know and I will handle it."

Mike looked at Allen, " well, now that you mention it, there is one thing that you might be able to do for me. How are you at getting Josie immigrant status in Canada?"

Allen looked at Mike, " really my friend, you're that serious? Congratulations, I'm really happy for you."

" Thanks, man, if you can do something to help, we are even."

" So, that would mean that you need two tickets back home?"

Mike answered Allen, "yes, first class would be nice."

Allen grinned, "I can do better, why don't you take that executive jet directly to Comox."

" When does it leave?"

Allen told Mike, " I'll let you know within the hour."

Lee Magnason came barging into Allen's office, "I need to talk with you and Sven right away."

Mike and Josie started down the elevator, as the doors opened, Pat McLear was standing by the entrance and came over to Mike and Josie.

Pat looked surprised to see Mike, " what the hell happened to you?"

Mike wasn't about to answer to him, " just a little domestic dispute with the miss's."

Pat wasn't sure what to think of that but decided he didn't want to get into the middle of it. " So, you were telling me the truth, you weren't in Moscow, what are you doing here?"

Mike considered this another stupid question, " me and the misses came to watch the Yankee / Blue Jays game."

Pat didn't follow baseball, "Yeah, that should be a good game, I was going to go but we are scheduled to go to Moscow and rescue the directo"s family. By the way, do you have any information that could be valuable?"

Mike was holding back, "No, as soon as you told me to leave the director's family alone, I just watched baseball."

Pat wasn't sure about that, " perfect, well, we have it well in hand anyways, we'll have them home before they know it."

82

Mike's phone rang, it was Allen and Mike smiled telling Josie that it was Allen, probably with our flight time. Allen explained there were some interesting developments to the investigation. He asked if they both could meet right away before they left. Mike explained they were down at the entrance to the building talking to Pat McLear.

Allen was a bit excited, " Where is that little rodent anyways."

"He just got on the elevator." Mike looked at the floor number the elevator stopped at. " Looks like he got off on the seventeenth floor Allen."

" What the hell is he doing on the seventeenth floor, that's where we keep all the evidence locked up."

Mike had a plan, " I'll go up to that floor and if you travel down, we should be able to catch him."

Mike and Josie hopped into the next available elevator to the seventeenth floor and stood there waiting. Soon after, Allen, fully armed with three additional agents, met them. Allen had an extra pistol he handed to Mike.

"Stay here in case we miss him, and don't shoot unless absolutely necessary."

Allan and the three agents left, returning with Pat McLear in handcuffs, Mike handed Allen his gun back. Allen stayed back while the agents took Pat to the cell for later questioning.

Mike was curious, " what's going on Allen?"

"Lee Magnuson and his computer analysts finally cracked the code on an encrypted file. It was located on the systems flash drive that Sharon stole from the Russians at the Catskills crime scene. She gave it to me at the hospital and they have been working on it ever since. As the analysts worked on it, they found agents in the CIA and FBI that were working for Andrei. Pat McLear was one and another was the District Deputy Director for the CIA. We are getting a search warrant to search his office and his house. We also have his picture and the associated arrest warrant for him. There were others on the file, and we are gathering them up now."

"Send me a picture of them and their names, just in case I run into them."

" Okay Mike, sending them through now, I haven't received word on the plane schedule but shouldn't be long now."

It was one thirty and neither one had lunch. Mike and Josie walked down to a quaint little bistro bar where they served soup and sandwiches out on the street. They sat down at a table, ordering a lunch special and enjoying a warm New York afternoon.

As they got up to leave, Mike spotted a subtle movement behind a structural pillar out of the corner of his eye. He looked to see William Townsend looking right at him, he appeared to be talking to someone. Mike got on his phone and immediately called Allen, informing him the District Deputy Director for the CIA was watching them.

"I'm not far away Mike, find a store to hide in if you need to."

Mike turned to Josie to tell her to go into the store when he was hit on the back of the head with the butt end of a gun, and he was unconscious.

Josie started fighting two men as they came after her hard. She was getting sick of this chaos and decided she was going to put an end to it.

The CIA agents were unaware of her skills, underestimating her. They soon found themselves opening a hornet's nest of problems for themselves. Josie had one yelling in pain as she grabbed his gun from his holster, shooting the other as he pulled his gun on her. She pointed the gun at the one she had on the ground, threatening to shoot him.

From behind her, she heard " I'm District Deputy Director William Townsend. Put down the gun, you are under arrest." Josie looked around to see him with his gun pointed at her."

> Josie didn't understand, "these guys attacked me, ask the thirty people who witnessed it."

The people from the group watching all agreed with Josie and backed up her story.

> " These men you attacked are CIA agents. They were apprehending you and Mike for the multiple murders of foreign nationals."

> Allen and Sven came running up to the scene with their guns out and badges displayed, " no, it is you that is under arrest, put your gun down and give yourself up."

> William Townsend turned to see Allen and Sven standing there with their guns drawn.

> William yelled at Mike as he was gaining consciousness, "You bastard, you wrecked everything, I had a perfect situation with Andrei and you wrecked everything, DIE!"

Before William could pull the trigger on Mike, both Sven and Allen shot him dead. Other FBI agents arrived and placed the man that Josie grappled to the ground in handcuffs, taking him away.

Josie and Allen rushed to Mike's side " are you okay Mike?"

Mike looked at Allen, " you sure know how to show a guy a good time Allen, but I've had enough fun, just get me a plane home."

Allen got the executive Jet ready and had the medical team check Mike out before he left. On the plane Mike could relax now, it was all over. He fell asleep several times, but woke up beside Josie, smiling.

83

Mikhail was sitting in his reclining chair recalling the events of the past week. He would never have believed the justice day would come when he would end Andrei's life. He felt sad, but after hearing the pain he put everyone who came in contact with him, he realized it needed to be done.

He got to know his niece a lot better. He remembered that little girl that him and Kyela played with in the Hamberg hospital. He felt he had family again, someone to visit him and maybe someone he could visit. He would be there if she had a baby, that would be something very special to him, the thought excited him.

He thought of Natasha, he felt she was a wonderful person. He got to know her again, she had aged but so did he. Maybe he should take her for dinner or coffee sometime. The past week had been the most intense time in his life since Kyela was murdered. Now it's over he felt better, more confident, maybe he should call her some time, yes, he told himself, he should call her sometime.

Mikhail got up and cleaned the house and made some lunch for himself. After Lunch, he washed the dishes and cleaned up some more, then sat in his chair and stared at the wall. He realized that his life was boring, he wanted more. He got out of his chair, walked to the phone, and called Natasha.

84

Sharon went straight to her home in New York, it felt good to be home finally. She started a load of laundry as she unpacked her bag, taking time to boil the kettle for tea. She hadn't realized just how quiet her life had been, the past three weeks had been a whirlwind of activity. She sat recalling everything that took place as she drank her tea, she decided that she was going to spice up her life.

She watched Mike and Josie's relationship develop, they comforted each other, supported each other, and made each other laugh. She wanted what they had, she wanted to have someone here right now to hold her. She recalled something one of her high school teachers told her, that if you find the need for change, never procrastinate. Sharon thought of her uncle having never married at his age, she didn't want that life. She got out her computer and signed up on an online dating site she had been researching for a while. Today was the day that she would make that change for herself, for her life, she submitted her profile and smiled. The dating site platform makes suggestions and sends them by e-mail, and she was excited to see the suggestions it chose.

Sharon looked in the fridge, to find food she left that had gone bad, she made out a detailed shopping list and left. After grabbing a little something at her favorite coffee shop to eat, she completed her shopping list and returned home. It was quiet in her apartment and since she was battling jetlag, she quickly fell asleep on the couch.

Sharon awoke to a "Ding" on her phone indicating an email had been received in her email account. It was an automated e-mail from the dating site informing her a well-suited date was selected and accepted them informing her. She scrambled to find who this person was, giggling once she discovered that Jon Marion would like to take her for a coffee.

She remembered the first time she met him at the Catskills crime scene. She thought he was very nice to her and handled the questioning and statements very professionally. Looking back, she never considered going out with him, but she was willing to give it a try. She returned the request accepting the date and waited for him to return with a time and day.

She was impressed at how quickly the site worked as she briefly scrolled through the potential men who had signed up. There were a few but she thought she should just let the platform do its job. She didn't want to spend the day on a computer, so she put it away in the bag. As she opened the bag up, she spotted the three flash drives she downloaded the complete Mindsweeper program on. Sharon took the flash drives from her bag, and opened her room safe, placing them inside and locking the door. She said to herself, " just for a rainy day."

<h1 style="text-align:center">85</h1>

Allen called Jon to meet him in his office. Allen thought long and hard about the decision he made and even ran it by Sven to make sure it made sense. It was a tough call, but Sven understood and backed him. Accountability at some level was needed after all Allen's family was placed in unbelievable risk of being killed. Then there were the others, Mike and Josie were placed in a terrible situation, risking their lives. Allen decided he would never place a friend in that situation again.

Jon came into Allen's office, not sure why he was asked to meet with him. Jon was a bit nervous, he was sure he wasn't getting a raise or promotion and was hoping he wasn't getting fired. Allen showed him a chair for him to sit down on, Jon noticed he wasn't his usual cheery self. It seemed that it was all business today with Allen as he spoke to him in a very formal way.

> Allen started, " I'm not sure if you were aware that Lee's cyber group unlocked an encrypted file that was on that flash drive that Sharon gave me. That file contained a complete list of names in Andrei's organization. Included in the list were the names of CIA, ATF, and FBI that had their hands in Andrei's cookie jar. These federal agents have been all rounded up, including Catherine, and several have died in the process. This crisis that my family and friends have endured over the past month is finally over."

> Jon added a few words, " thank god for that."

> Allen had more and continued, " I am sure you can imagine the stress this put me and my family through. I only hope that Becky will come out of this normal with professional help. Jen isn't the same woman she was, and she also needs

a psychiatrist helping her to get through this. As for me, I'm just trying to hold it all together, its been very difficult."

Sympathetically, Jon said, " I'm very sorry to hear that, Allen."

Allen got down to what the meeting was about, " Jon, you and I have a long history in the FBI, and it has been a rewarding relationship, up until Catherine became involved. I don't blame you for anything she did, however, she gained a great deal of information from you that she passed on to the enemy. For this reason, I can no longer trust you to keep your professional and your personal lives separated. I no longer want you on my team.

Jon was floored, " so, does this mean I'm fired?"

"No Jon, I talked with Sven about this, and he has a new posting for you that has just become available. We want you to be the lead on the international FBI division. It will be a lateral move, and since you have no family, it would most likely work out for you."

Jon was relieved, " I have a few questions about the assignment."

Mike ended the meeting, " then you need to schedule a meeting with Sven."

Mike showed Jon out and shook his hand. He had a meeting in a half hour with his new lead.

86

Allen helped Jen and Becky into the hotel with their bags, while Becky had a shower immediately.

Jen said, " I need to do some washing or buy some new clothes since we can't get into our house. Allen, I don't have anything to wear, and neither does Becky. I got to say Allen, shopping right now is the last thing I want to do right now.

Allen thought a while then picked up his phone and called his assistant, " Lisa, I need you to take the rest of the day off and come over to my hotel to help my wife out for the afternoon."

Lisa agreed to go shopping for the girls, returning with everything they asked. There was a specific reason why Allen asked Lisa, she had an extensive background in crisis psychology, and she was good. When Lisa came into the hotel Jen and Becky were so grateful, all Jen wanted to do was burn the clothes she had spent the last week in.

Lisa looked at Allen, he knew it was his signal to leave, " hey, I'm going to do some shopping for a few things we need."

Allen left while Lisa worked her magic, talking to both Becky and Jen about the horrible experience they had been through. Ideally, she would talk to each one individually, but Lisa had the experience of conducting her assessment with them both together.

She first asked them to recall the abduction and they talked about how they were treated by their captors. Becky started crying when she thought about the food they gave them. "They treated us worse than anyone would ever treat an animal."

Lisa asked questions about how they felt throughout the abduction. Becky and Jen were quite strong, they both felt confident Mike would find them and they would be rescued but were fearful of what could happen in the meantime.

Then Lisa talked about the present, how they felt and if they could sleep through the night. They talked about their feelings for each other and if that changed at all throughout the horrific experience they had gone through. Finally, they talked about their relationship with Allen as Jen's Husband, and Allen as Becky's father. Lisa noticed through the talk, Jen would bring up Mike's name several times, more than she expected.

Lisa then had them talk about Mike, she noticed both Jen and Becky spoke well of him, telling her about some of the things he did. Lisa also noticed a distinct smile cross Jen's face that was so subtle, but she could see it. Becky started talking about Josie and her fighting skills, Lisa noticed the distinct smile go away on Jen's face. They talked for a while longer, enough to let Lisa know there were no actions of aggression done against each other. Jen even told Lisa about Josie's conversation with her on the plane when she gave her a hug. Lisa smiled and excused herself as she left the hotel room.

Lisa met Allen at their predetermined coffee shop about five miles away. Allen was anxious to know how they weathered the experience.

> Lisa started, " Your daughter Becky is fine, she indicated to me that she is a strong and healthy girl. She may have things that will come up from time to time, but with a hug and support she will get over what is bothering her at the time."

> Allen was concerned, " what about Jen?"

"What is your relationship to Mike Stone? How long have you known him?"

Allen answered, "I have known Mike Stone all my life, he was the best man at my wedding, I trust him with my life, and I trust him with my family's life."

Lisa kept digging, "how long has Jen known Mike? What is Jen's relationship with Mike? Were they ever romantically engaged?"

Allen nodded his head, " yes, they sure were, everyone in the community was shocked when Jen and I were married. Everyone expected Mike and Jen to be getting married."

"Before this incident, when was the last time she seen or talked to Mike."

Allen thought for a while, " probably six or seven years ago."

Lisa considered, " who is Josie?"

"She was sent to assist Mike in protecting and to rescue my family. Mike and Josie have become an item, sounds like they are in love."

Lisa gave Allen her assessment, " both Becky and Jen are fine. They will have bad days and they will have good days. It is my expectation that over time, the good days will overcome the bad days, but keep watch on that Allen. Should things go the other way they will need professional help, but for now they are fine. Jen is hurting bad Allen, she has spent a great deal of time with Mike throughout this, and it has brought back a lot of memories of that High school sweetheart. Now that Josie has entered Mike's life, it's quite possible, some of those early memories won't be the same."

Allen thanked Lisa and left for the hotel room to be with his family that he missed so much over the past two weeks. He decided to talk to Jen and Becky about taking a holiday, maybe on a cruise ship somewhere, anywhere but Russia.

He got to the room, the two of them looked so beautiful, and he was so grateful for their safety and being with them right now. Jen was feeling better, he could see it in her eyes, and in her smile. "So, let's get some dinner, I got something I want to talk to you about."

Becky was curious, " What do you want to talk to us about dad?"

Let's go on a holiday, what about a cruise in the Caribbean."

87

Mike and Josie left the executive hanger, very thankful to be back home. The green lawn and trees looked magnificent to Mike despite the fact he had seen them all his life.

Josie was curious, "What's the first thing you're doing when you get back to the farm Mike?"

Mike smiled, "well, I'm going out to the pasture and give Festus a big hug."

Josie laughed, "so, it's all about the relationship with your horse, is it?"

The taxi pulled up the driveway, and Mike noticed a few things blown up from the activity. The repairs could be made, he would call on a local contractor to look after that. Mike really missed being greeted by Duke and Tigger, he grieved for them both and Josie could tell.

Mike assessed the damage in the house, then called the moving company to move his belongings back. Today he wanted to go for a ride on Festus with Josie, so he scheduled a time to haul the other horses back. When the horses showed up on the farm, he brought over a beautiful buckskin mare for Josie.

" Here Josie, you can have this horse, she is very gentle to ride and perfect for you to learn on."

Josie asked, " what's her name?"

Mike thought for a bit, " I never named her, I'll leave that to you."

After a while Josie said, " I want to name her after my mother, Ana."

Mike agreed it was fitting under the circumstances, it might help Josie heal from the news of her mother. Josie wanted to be close to her mother, and as far away from her father as she could get. Josie loved her horse and wanted to be with her often.

Once the house contents arrived and everything put in its place, Josie felt at home. She learned the stories about pictures hung on the wall, and trophies that Mike was awarded for his various skills competitions. Mike and Josie finished the afternoon with a bar-be-que steak, Caesar salad and baked potato. After they cleaned up the dinner mess and Mike sat down to a coffee, with Josie drinking a lemonade as they sat in silence.

Josie broke the quiet, " Mike, can we take Festus and Ana for a ride, I really want to see more of your farm."

Mike and Josie saddled up Festus and Ana and left the stable walking the horses gently to get Josie used to riding. They stopped for a while when they reached the high ridge and as they looked South-East, they could see the ocean and Denman Island. With the exception of the horses chomping on the green pasture grass, it was silent, so different from New York. On the way back to the farmhouse, Josie seen the holes in the pasture where the dynamite exploded when they started the cattle to stampede the Russians.

Mike got a call on his cell, " Allen how are things in New York?"

Allen sounded like his old self once again, " A lot less stressful now. I just wanted to call you and let you know, Dominik was just sent back to Guantanamo, I must go Mike, I just wanted to let you know."

After looking after the horses, Mike and Josie decided to have an early evening.

Josie looked at Mike, " well this is quite a novelty not to be sleeping on the floor."

In the morning, Mike was showing Josie how to do the chores and look after the animals. A delivery van pulled up into the driveway, and the driver got out of the cab and went to the door on the farmhouse and proceeded to knock loudly. When no one answered, he started yelling for "Mike Stone", and Mike proceeded very carefully towards him.

As the driver of the van saw Mike, he said to him, " are you Mike Stone?"

Mike looked at him suspiciously, " yes I am, how can I help you?"

The man offered to shake Mikes hand, " good day Mike, you are a hard man to find. Do you know an Anastasia Orlov who lives in Moscow?"

Mike smiled, "yes we do."

Tom started a rehearsed script that Mike could tell was told many times before, " My name is Tom Jesperson, I represent a company which raises rare animals for domestic pets. The animals have not been harvested from the wild, they have been bred and available to clients who are looking for domestic pets that are non-typical. Anastasia researched our company. After a lengthy discussion over the phone, she bought you a very rare Snow Leopard cub."

Mike was excited, " wow a snow leopard, let me take a look."

As they walked towards the van, Tom was informing them of how to care for the animal. Tom went on and on about the importance of this and that, Mike wasn't listening, he knew how to look after a big cat. In the van was a large pen, and as Tom removed the cub out of the pen, giving it to Mike. Mike took the cub and held it as he sat down on the lawn and played with it.

Mike yelped as the cub grabbed his finger, " Man, is his claws sharp, Be careful Josie."

Tom left all the information with Josie and Mike signed the waybill, " anything before I go?" No one said anything, Tom could tell they weren't listening, he has seen it before."

Josie was curious, "What do you teach it first Mike?"

"Nothing special right away, it needs to understand its new environment first, and it needs to become comfortable with us. In about two weeks, we will house train it."

Josie questioned Mike, " Have you picked a name?'

" Not yet, one will come. I'm going to call Anastasia and personally thank her."

Mike found the number on his phone, " Anastasia, how are you today, It's Mike here?"

"Mike, it's so good to hear from you, all is good in Moscow, did you receive your gift?"

" That's why I'm calling you, to personally thank you from the bottom of my heart. That was a very thoughtful of you, thank you." Mike paused " Also, just for your information, I just received a call from Director Fulton that Dominik was on his way to Guantanamo."

"That's wonderful, you are a man of your word. Send me a video when you teach the cub new tricks, I would like to see the results of your skills. While I have you on the phone, I need to talk to Josie, I don't have her number."

Mike said with a big smile, " well she's sitting right here, I'll give her the phone."

Mike passed her his phone, " hello."

"Josie, it's so good talking to you again, put the phone on speaker so I can deliver this message to Mike as well."

Josie said curiously, " you are on speaker with the both of us."

Anastasia continued, " I have been given the duty by the courts in Russia to go through the process of probating the will of Dominik and Andrei. It will take a while because Andrei was the sole beneficiary of Dominik's estate. With him dead, then it follows Andrei's beneficiary, Vlad, who is also dead. I have worked with a lawyer here and we have come to an agreement with the courts. It basically states that Dominik's estate will be divided up amongst his immediate family. The only family Dominik has that's still alive is me, his wife. When my men helped you guys out in the rescue, they heard Dominik tell Josie that she was his daughter. Josie, I have worked on the numbers, and considering all things you are entitled to over thirty-five million dollars."

Josie was speechless, " Oh that's unbelievable, but he's still actually alive."

Anastasia answered, "No one would believe an eighty-two-year-old man in Russia is a twenty-six-year-old man living in the States. As far as Russia is concerned, he is dead, they even found his dead body. If he does survive Guantanamo"

Josie thanked her very much and wished her well, Josie was very excited now, she didn't need to go back to work. Josie was happy right here on Mikes farm, she would immigrate to Canada.

"Mike, what do you do when you are not farming, what are your pass times."

Mike thought, " I help others out and spend time showing the kids of the community stuff."

Josie smiled, " I could teach them martial arts, it would be fun."

Mike smiled at her, taking her into his arms, they kissed as Mike picked her up in his arms and carried her into the farmhouse.

Watch for the next Mike Stone novel by Jim Rawlins

HIGH ARCTIC SECRETS

Chapter 1

1

September 2023

Emma Hennessey was in a frantic hurry, she had to find him quickly, the situation had gotten out of hand, she was afraid for her life and on the run to stay ahead of them.

Emma was thirty-two years old, born in Rhode Island. Her shoulder length brown hair lay against a flowered blazer jacket and pant suit, but today, fashion wasn't important, she could just as well have been in denim. She obtained her degree in journalism at Columbia after two years at Queen's college. Her first job was at the local newspaper while being coached by Ashley Thomson, one of their top reporters. She thought she learned a lot from college and university. She quickly learned it was nothing compared to what she learned on the streets of New York, with Ashley. They became good friends, she had so much respect for her, as a reporter, but more importantly as a person.

Emma was brought up in a strict Catholic family, her father was an iron worker who worked on Union projects in the area. He was of Scottish decent and was born in Philadelphia, later to move to New York. His father's thick Scottish brogue influenced her father to carry a noticeable Scottish accent. Her mother was a French dressmaker, a trade that was handed down by her mother before her, and she worked at home. Emma remembers her mother sewing beautiful wedding gowns for brides to be, some with long trailing lace. She would often dream about how it would feel to be in a beautiful gown like that. But Emma preffered blue jeans casual, it was unlikely that she would ever put on a dress, let alone a gown, but still, she would dream.

Even though both her parents supported her, and paid for her education, her father tried to steer her to something else other than journalism. Her father always complained the reporters would always report negative information and never talk about the good things people do. Her mother thought being a journalist would be exciting, and she could eventually work internationally.

After two years it felt as though reporting for the newspaper was too controlled. Between the government and corporate funding, the newspaper regulated what was said, and about who. Emma decided she would choose a role more suited to her values and why she delved into the journalist career. She chose an independent journalist opportunity, giving her freedom and choice. She enjoyed this since it allowed her to follow up on stories that she found important to write about and to inform others of. She was described as tenacious, she never let her stature get in the way of getting the story, several tried to intimidate her, all unsuccessful until now. She truly knew now what it was like to be frightened, they were coming for her, and she knew it.

She met a lot of people and made solid relationships with her contacts, with always one ear open for a story. Despite her displeasure with social events, she often attended them to meet new friends and be in the know. Her mentor with the newspaper, Ashley, once told her she needed to develop her social skills. It was something she took to heart and signed up for workshops on social marketing to enable her to make new contacts quickly. Ashley told her it was part of her job skills, and her success going forward will depend on it.

Emma was not presently in a relationship, the last one recently ended in a difficult situation that she took control of and dealt with. She was strong-willed, and Luke Morton tried to control her most of the time. Luke lived a fortunate life, as the stepson of a politician who made a fortune from investments in the oil industry. She met Luke on-line, at first, she liked him, he was so spontaneous, he was exciting. After about six months, he started trying to control her, where she went, why she was going, telling her that she had a stupid job and should get a new career. When Emma returned from Denver after being away for two weeks, she caught him in her bed with another woman. After kicking them out, she had her locks changed, and never wanted to see him again. At two in the morning he returned, banging on the door waking her up. She threatened to call the police, and he left soon after. Shortly after that, the crisis that she was in today began, the story she was investigating became a lot larger scale than she expected.

She was going public with a two-part story she had been researching for the past two weeks that incriminated some very powerful and influential people. She had just finished the second part and had it on the press for distribution in the morning. That evening, Emma attended an evening function the LA Times Journalist Guild was hosting and at eight O'clock she decided to leave. Two men with masks came out of nowhere and strong armed her to the side where no one could see them. They told her to stop any additional reporting or investigating of the story. They told her if additional information about the story is made public, she will die. She explained the story was already out with morning distribution. They told her "If it's in tomorrow's paper, you will suffer the consequences." and they left.

She told Brad, who was her best friend, and he suggested that he stick around her, like a bodyguard. Brad came to visit at her at Emma's home the next morning then needed to get back to the office. When he went to his car, he noticed his front tire was flat, and Emma lent him her car. She saw him open the driver's side door thinking what a wonderful person he was and how thoughtful he was in her time of need. He sat down in the seat and the next thing she remembered was her car, with Brad inside, blowing up in a ball of flames. After calling 911 the police and fire were on their way, Emma sat on her front porch, drained of the strength she once had, powerless to help Brad. When she saw them removing his body from her car she started crying and went inside her house.

Emma was completely lost, her best friend was gone forever. She answered what she thought was well over a hundred questions from the police, giving them her witness statement. After calling her boss, who had little to offer, she called Ashley, in New York. She was hoping Ashley could give her some advice or directions about what she needed to do next. Ashley told her she had investigated a story a while back about a man who protected a family from the Russian mob. It was a hell of a story, and she told Emma that she needed to see him. Ashley mentioned she no longer had his phone number or address. She proceeded to explain how to get to Fanny Bay, but she told Emma that she had to find him herself from there.

After the Fire Department and police left, Emma packed her clothes and caught a cab, arriving at the airport at three-twenty. She had little time to waste, her flight to Vancouver left at five-thirty-five. On the plane, she just wanted to sleep and ended up sitting in the window seat, beside a woman. Emma's first impression was that she was safe, she seemed friendly enough. About thirty minutes into a two-hour flight, her imagination was getting the better of her. Maybe this woman was following her, maybe she was the one who planted the bomb in her car. She closed her eyes and fell asleep before she started thinking of Brad and began crying again.

The plane's landing gear touched the runway at Vancouver Airport. She looked out the window, noticing the weather had changed and in addition to it being dark out, it was raining hard. She rented a small car, leaving for the ferry terminal at Horseshoe Bay, just catching the last of the boarding cars. On the ferry across to Vancouver Island, she was sure she recognized one of them. While not sure she stayed out of sight, staying low in her car to avoid his eye contact. She had no idea what they would do if they caught her. Brad, her best friend, met his demise and now lies on a stainless-steel tray in the Los Angeles hospital morgue. It's unlikely the autopsy will uncover anything. She knew they were professionals avoiding any tracking back to them, or the syndicate who hired them. She was in a mess, one that she wanted to wake up from a deep sleep and call a nightmare, but no such luck.

She disembarked from the ferry and traveled North from Nanaimo along the old Island Highway. Using her GPS, she didn't want to drive by it, Ashley mentioned Fanny Bay was very small. Emma called directory assistance attempting to get his phone number and talk to him, but no such name was listed for a landline. She started to panic, "What if he moved and he no longer lives here? what would she do?" She drove past a restaurant and a store on the highway, both were closed at this time of night. It was very dark out and raining hard as huge rain droplets splattered against the car's windshield, the wipers barely keeping up. As she continued driving through the tiny hamlet, she came upon a local Pub that was open, located on the Ocean side of the highway and she stopped. She was scatterbrained from sleep deprivation, the trauma of watching Brad die, and her concerns and fear of them finding her.

She was scared, she had never been inside the Fanny Bay Pub before, fact is, she never knew about Fanny Bay until she was told about it by Ashley. She parked her car around the back and walked in the main entrance to the pub from the front. It was pitch black out and typical of the area, raining hard with the south-west wind blowing the storm inland from the Pacific.

She entered through the front entrance of the Pub. It was a beautifully handcrafted building. The post and beams construction and heavy wooden moldings on the ceilings accented the room with a welcoming appearance, not what she expected for such a small town. She opened the door, it seemed like everyone was staring at her, she was almost expecting someone in the crowd to jump out and attack her. But she came to realize she was just a new face in town and the locals were simply noticing someone walk in. She stopped for a while and considered that he might be in there and her query may make it uncomfortable for him and her. She didn't like feeling uncomfortable, but this was what she travelled all the way from Los Angeles for. She needed to accept uncomfortable as the new norm. She was a journalist after all, she dealt with situations like this before. The only difference was it was her life was on the line.

She walked slowly to the barkeeper's station, she was nervous, he wasn't looking at her, he was busy mixing a round of drinks for a boisterous group at a table. What should she say to get his attention? She remembered what Ashley told her and finally told herself, "Emma, for gosh sake get yourself together, this is your only chance to get through this mess alive. She recalled that vision of her car blowing up, " you don't want to end up like Brad, do you?" The barkeeper finally turned around and he appeared friendly, asking her "Can I help you?" Emma was a strong woman, you had to be a journalist, but she started to cry, and couldn't stop the tears from pouring down her face. The stress of what she had been going through over the past month and the sleep deprivation was affecting her. Besides that, she was depending so much on a man she never met, she was scared.

Mark the bartender had never felt comfortable being in the presence of a woman crying. He called Sue, the waitress to come over and help the young lady out, and they found a vacant table and sat down. When Emma said someone was after her, Sue made an extra effort to assess her mental state. Once Sue determined she was truly running from someone, she wanted to call the police. Emma was quite animated explaining she did not want the police involved.

Sue was confused, " how can we help you?"

Emma said to her, "I desperately need you to help me find Mike Stone."